A Justified Death

Paula Harmon

January Press

Dedication

This book is dedicated to Josephine Butler (1828-1906). who campaigned fearlessly for women's rights and also for the raising of the age of consent, the abolition of child prostitution and an end to human trafficking.

It is also dedicated to my lovely late father, Richard Downes. who is very much the inspiration for Roderick Demeray. Dad had the same superlative skills at exasperating his daughters, imagination beyond bounds, eccentricity, more books than shelf space and the longing to travel. If only he'd had Roderick's money to fulfil all his dreams!

One

London, Saturday 8th November 1913

There is never anything good about fog.

In the middle of her party, Margaret stepped into the hall to cool down after a lively if restricted polka and felt her happy mood fade as she spotted opaque yellow-grey fingers slithering under the front door and across the tiles.

The cheerful chatter of friends and happy squeals of children filtered through the sitting-room door behind her, and for a few moments, Margaret imagined herself as a gatekeeper – the only thing between their cocooned safety and an outside world where streetlights had been smothered, sound was distorted and evil might be lurking.

'A cup of tea for your thoughts,' said Dr Gil Trewellan, walking up bearing a tray.

'I'm resisting an urge to kill the fog by stamping on it.'

'That's not very scientific.'

'It always seems alive and malicious,' said Margaret. 'I want to know who it's misdirecting and what it's hiding.'

'No one and nothing, I'm sure,' said Gil. 'And it's not as if you haven't grown up with London fogs. This isn't even a pea-souper. It'll be gone by morning.'

'I know. Sorry. It was just a feeling.'

'Well, don't let it spoil your lovely party. I'm so glad I could come.'

Margaret pulled herself together. 'So am I. And I know our house isn't really big enough for all these people, but it's lovely to have it so full and noisy. It's usually so boringly quiet.'

'A party's all the better when it's a bit squashed and informal.'

Margaret properly registered the tray in his hands. 'Why are you carrying that? Freda's supposed to be serving the tea.'

'Really? Dinah was preparing it when I went to the kitchen for some water. She seemed concerned that your friends would clodhopper on her bunions when she brought the tea in. What could I do but offer to help?'

'Hmm. Clever Dinah.'

Gil chuckled. 'I always liked her when she charred at your flat, even if she told me off for being untidy.' He straightened his tie, making it more lopsided. 'But given how important Fox is, I thought you'd have someone more refined as a housemaid.'

'I do,' said Margaret. 'Dinah only comes when I need extra help. She was delighted that she'd see you again. I think she was secretly a little disappointed when you went to Switzerland and I married Fox.'

'I love you very much, but if I'd ever proposed it would have been for the sake of appearances on my part, and I wouldn't be cruel enough to ask. You need a proper husband like Fox, even if he's bad at protecting you.' Gil put his head on one side. 'Maude says you were injured a few months ago.'

'It wasn't Fox's fault and I'm fine.' Margaret touched the neckline of her dress to check it hid the scar on her shoulder.

'You need a nice quiet life.'

'Do I?'

'Yes. But for now, where's the music? You owe me a dance.'

The sitting room door opened before Margaret could touch the handle, noisy chatter blasting out along with Maude's sons and Alec, who collided with Nellie as she walked up from the kitchen.

Gil ushered Margaret into the sitting room, put the tray on a low table, ruffled his dishevelled curls into more chaos, then turned his attention to the room.

In an armchair nearest the fire, Margaret's father was reading a picture book to Edie. She sat on his lap, leaning against him, thumb in mouth. With her other hand, she held his silk cravat against her cheek. It was still a little pale from a recent cold, and her eyelids were drooping. Margaret sighed.

'What is it?' said Gil, squeezing her hand, 'Is something other than the fog bothering you?'

'Yes. Dr Naylor wants me to work more days in the hospital. But when Edie became so ill…' Margaret took a breath and steadied her voice. 'It's been an awful few weeks. I dread to think how inattentive I've been at Dorcas Free. But Dr Gesner was kind and Dr Naylor eased the pressure, so I must have got away with it. I thought she might stop me going to Weymouth next weekend.'

Gil smiled. 'Weymouth will do Edie the world of good, even for a few days. She's very much on the mend, and well enough for her second birthday party.'

'It's not precisely a birthday party,' said Margaret. 'The twins were so fragile when they were born that every year they survive feels like something to celebrate. I suppose the party is really for me and Fox.'

'Ah,' said Gil. 'Then I wouldn't have missed it for the world.'

'Ungill! Ungill!' Alec squeezed through the guests and pulled at Gil's hand. 'Play trains on stairs with SamajohnnyaNellie!'

Suddenly fully awake, Edie scrambled off her grandfather's lap and hurried over to pull on Gil's other arm.

'Come on then, young people, show me what to do.' He winked at Margaret as he left the room. 'Fragile? They're nearly pulling my arms out.'

Fox put another record onto the gramophone, side-stepped Katherine, who'd been trying to teach him new dance steps all afternoon, and joined Margaret. He nodded towards her father. 'Your sister thinks it's too noisy for him, but he seems happy enough.'

Margaret's father had neatened his cravat and was casting around for someone he could continue reading to. His gaze settled hopefully on Maude's twelve-year-old daughter Becca, who stood near the window with Margaret's cousin Lucy and nephew Ed. It seemed unlikely Becca would admit to being interested in any children's story. She was currently attempting to look grown up by standing in the fashionable sloping-shoul-dered way of mannequins and moving-picture stars, periodical-ly pulling on her skirt as if that would help it appear longer.

'If Becca gets any more languid she'll fall over,' said Fox.

'The papers call it the slinker slouch,' whispered Margaret. 'Maude despises it. She keeps asking me to explain to Becca how it'll ruin her digestion.'

'Will you?'

'Why waste breath? What girl of that age really believes an adult unless it's a very young one like Lucy? Ah, now she's copying Lucy's pose instead. That's better.'

'Becca's much shorter. She won't be able to hear if she doesn't stand up straight.'

Lucy, pretty in a blue velvet dress, was smiling. She gave the younger girl as much attention as she would someone of her own age. On the other hand, Ed looked sulky. Having come directly from an army event, he was still in uniform. But if he'd hoped to make an impression, he'd only managed to make a brief one on Maude's oldest son.

'I think Ed's hoping that Becca will go up in smoke if he glares at her enough,' said Margaret. 'He really has it bad. I've never been sure whether Lucy's noticed, though. She's just generally nice to everyone.'

'Ed and Lucy are cousins,' said Fox. 'I was never attracted to mine. Were you attracted to any of the million you have?'

Margaret lowered her voice. 'Goodness, no. As for Lucy and Ed... They're not really cousins. Aunt Alice and Uncle Donald adopted Lucy as a tiny orphan. Didn't I ever tell you?'

'You didn't.'

'I suppose I never think about it.' Margaret frowned. From the moment Aunt Alice had clasped the feeble baby in her arms, Lucy had been part of the family. Now the sickly infant was a healthy young woman surrounded by love, with a bright future ahead of her.

'Do Lucy and Ed know about the adoption?'

'I've no idea.'

Fox put his arm round her waist. 'Incidentally, Katherine says James will drive your father home shortly if you don't mind their leaving early. She thinks he's getting tired.'

'James?'

'Ha ha. Your father. James has an early start tomorrow and he has things to prepare before he goes. Maude or Phoebe can take Katherine and Ed home.'

'I'll do it,' said Margaret. 'I need to learn to be confident of driving in fog.'

'I'm not sure whether to be more worried about you or the car,' said Fox. 'Come and dance, in case it's the last chance we have.'

By six, the party was over and all the guests bar Katherine and Ed had gone. Margaret let Fox start the car and light the lamps while she and her passengers settled inside.

The thickening fog made the air feel greasy and cloying. The pavement and road were slick with a combination of coal-oil and moisture.

'Are you sure you don't want me to drive?' said Fox.

'Stay behind with the children: I can manage perfectly well,' said Margaret, then wished she hadn't. The lamps didn't seem equal to the gloom and she didn't feel equal to the drive, even if it was less than four miles there and back.

'Perhaps we should walk,' said Katherine.

'You'll be sodden and filthy if you do,' said Margaret. 'I'll drive at walking pace. Anyone behind us can lump it.'

She steered the car into a road that might as well have been a tunnel for all she could see. Katherine and Ed huddled under a blanket. Margaret frowned as they crept forward, aware the wheels weren't gripping the road as they should.

'Lucy's starting a job,' said Ed gloomily.

'That's good, isn't it?' said Katherine. 'She can't start her nursing training till next summer. She may as well do something now. First-aid classes, isn't it?'

'More than that. She'll be teaching the three R's to a bunch of rough, uneducated women in some dreadful class in Archbold Street.'

'We didn't bring you up to be a snob,' snapped Katherine.

'I didn't mean it like that.' Ed's voice was sulky. 'I just meant what the papers keep saying about white slavery and girls getting snatched. Lucy's so innocent: she thinks everyone's as nice as she is. I'm not happy about her going into nursing, either. She should do something more refined. Or better still, wait to get married.'

'Honestly, Ed,' said Katherine, 'I despair. What has happened to you? It's up to Lucy what she does. And if, God forbid, you ever have to fight for your country, you'll be fighting for *everyone*, not just the refined and genteel.'

'Can I just get out and walk from here? It'll probably be quicker.'

'*No*,' said Katherine.

There was a brief, uncomfortable silence. A few other cars appeared out of the gloom, crawled past, then disappeared.

Now and again, the headlights picked out barely visible wraiths slinking along the pavement or crossing the road. How stupid of people to wear black in the winter.

Margaret attempted to change the subject. 'Where's James going so early tomorrow?'

'Wales,' said Katherine. 'He'll report on the mine disaster at Senghenydd. Perhaps Ed doesn't think he should bother. Why do rough men and uneducated women matter?'

'I didn't say that,' said Ed, his voice low. 'And I don't think it. I didn't know Dad was going there. It'll be—'

'Awful,' snapped Katherine. 'Two weeks, hundreds still missing and no hope of any of them being alive. I imagine the ones who survived are glad of the nurses who are treating them. Especially the nice ones.'

'That's not what I meant. I'm sorry, Mother. I'm just worried about Lucy.'

'If it helps,' said Margaret, sighing inwardly, 'I'll offer to give a talk at one of her classes. Then I can reassure you about her pupils and confirm that she's being treated with respect.'

'Thanks, Aunt Maggot.'

'Hmm.'

Another silence as a wraith drifted across the road. Margaret slowed, unsure if it was a person or a strand of fog. It looked too portly to be the latter and reminded her of her father, ambling about lost in his imagination.

'Father hasn't taken to wandering since he moved in with you, Kitty?' she said. 'You know, getting confused and trying to go back to Fulham.'

'He's not a cat, Meg,' said Katherine. 'I needn't butter his paws.' From her voice, she was still irritated. 'And no, he hasn't.'

"I hope— I wish... I'm sorry.' Margaret grimaced. 'I don't know what I can do to help, apart from have him stay now and again.'

'Don't worry,' said Katherine, more gently. 'You have small children and work fixed hours. Ed's away most of the time, and while my job is quite unpredictable, it allows me some freedom. I can keep Father company if necessary, but he's making a new group of friends in Marylebone to replace the ones he left in Fulham. Besides, you've invited him for lunch tomorrow, even though you have Gil coming too. You've nothing to apologise for.'

They were nearing Marylebone Road. Margaret slowed before she crossed it. The streetlights, struggling to penetrate the fog, turned it into a squirming, dirty-yellow monster, swallowing and vomiting whatever passed through.

Something with headlights was coming down the road, faster than seemed wise. Margaret decided to wait till it passed. In the corner of her eye, she saw another wraith and turned towards it. This time it was definitely a person, dashing into the road. The other motor car swerved, but the fog had made the road slick and greasy. The car slid sideways, spun, then crashed into the figure. Even the fog couldn't deaden a thump and a scream.

Two

Margaret unfroze, steered her car to the pavement, then got out with Katherine and Ed and joined a small group of people who had emerged from the fog to see what had happened.

The light of a lantern blinded Margaret. Then the person holding it lowered their arm to reveal a man in a driving coat, crouched beside a young girl huddled by the nearside front wheel of a motorcar. For a dreadful moment, as she knelt, Margaret thought it was Becca, then saw light hair instead of dark and a gauntness in the cheeks that Becca didn't possess.

The girl was still, her eyes closed.

'I didn't see her in time,' said the motorist. 'It's not my fault. It all happened so fast. The car just slid. Is she dead?'

'No,' said Margaret. 'Merely knocked out, and she's coming round. Hopefully you didn't hit her hard enough to do much damage, but we'll see.'

'Are you a nurse?'

'I'm a doctor.'

'Dorcas Free's just there,' said Ed. 'What do you need? I can move fast.'

'A stretcher at least,' said Margaret. 'Thank you.' She watched Ed disappear, then peered up at the shadowed faces around her. 'I need something to put under her head. Sir, please hold that lantern so I can see.'

'Less mere align,' slurred the girl. Her eyes opened and she stared about her. 'Let me alone! Let me alone!' She started to move, then cried out.

'Where does it hurt?' asked Margaret.

'Arm. Ribs. Ankle. Head.' She frowned at Margaret. 'Are we by St J's?'

'St Julia's is some distance away. We're near Dorcas Free. We'll get you there as soon as possible.'

'Isn't that... Am I still...? I gotta go.' She lifted her head a little and her eyes started to roll back.

'Here.' Katherine tucked the blanket from Margaret's car under the girl's head as she came out of her faint again.

'I didn't mean to hurt her,' said the motorist. 'She was moving faster than I was. If she hadn't run out—'

'We'll establish facts later, sir.' A policeman had arrived with a torch. 'We need a doctor.'

'I'm a doctor,' said Margaret. 'And help's coming from Dorcas Free.' She touched the girl's limbs gently.

'What's happened?' A male colleague from the hospital crouched beside Margaret. Two orderlies lowered a stretcher to the ground.

'It's good to see you, Dr Perch. This girl was struck by a car—'

'I didn't mean—' bleated the motorist.

'The car was travelling at no great speed. Her right forearm seems to be broken and I suspect bruised or broken ribs. Her ankle and head hurt, but hopefully one is merely sprained and the other merely bumped. The light's too poor to be sure of anything. Shall we get her to the hospital and—'

Dr Perch turned to the orderlies. 'Gently does it, chaps. You heard Dr Demeray.'

'Don't wanna go to 'orspital,' said the girl. Her voice was quiet but determined.

'I'm afraid you have to,' said Margaret. 'What's your name?'

But as the orderlies lifted her carefully onto the stretcher, the girl fainted again.

Margaret stood up. 'I'll come with you.'

'I'll need to take your statement first,' said the policeman.

'Stand down, Dr Demeray,' said Dr Perch. 'You're on leave today and we have plenty of staff at Dorcas Free. Thank you for what you've done so far. I'll telephone later to say what's what, but I'm sure she'll be fine.'

⁂

'I thought you'd have had enough of guests,' said Gil, as they settled to lunch the following day. 'But thanks for inviting me before I travel to Weymouth. Hotel food is never as nice as home cooked.'

'You wouldn't say that if you'd visited while Vera worked here,' said Fox, with a grimace.

Gil laughed. 'Margaret wrote that you spent more time eating out than at home.'

'It was an expensive year, what with one thing and another.'

'I never knew what you meant about Vera's cooking,' said Margaret's father. 'One has eaten a good deal worse when travelling.'

'I've only ever had delicious food abroad,' said Margaret.

'That's because you've never been further afield than unimaginative places in Western Europe. You might feel differently if I'd taken you on my travels and you'd been faced with eyeballs on a platter.'

'Yes,' said Margaret, 'I might.' She scowled into her plate. Her father had spent most of her childhood travelling, coming home occasionally to publish books and give magic-lantern talks on his trips. She recalled the rapt audiences, the enthusiastic applause. She and Katherine had joined in as if they didn't mind that he was away for months at a time. But they had minded. However, her father was as oblivious now as he had been thirty years before.

Fox squeezed her hand gently. 'I'm not sure Vera didn't serve up eyeballs once or twice.'

Margaret giggled.

From outside the dining room came a clatter and a hissed exchange.

'Is everything all right?' said Gil.

'Freda and Nellie seem to be at loggerheads,' said Fox. 'Isn't that something that falls under your jurisdiction, Margaret?'

'I've other things to think about.'

'That girl?' said Fox. 'The hospital's confirmed she's recovering well. You can see for yourself tomorrow.'

'What girl?' said Gil.

Margaret explained. 'She's very thin and keeps passing out. Dr Perch says she switches between English and what they think might be Yiddish when confused. She says she can't recall her name or where she's from. She must have hit her head harder than I thought.'

'She's in the right place,' said Fox. 'Maybe *our* young women need—'

The door opened and Freda walked in bearing the soup tureen. With a face like thunder, she filled their bowls, then topped up their glasses with sherry before withdrawing.

'A quiet word,' Fox continued. 'Or we might have to revert to eating out again.'

'It's troubles of the heart, I think,' said Margaret. 'I suspect at least one of them has a boy, wants to have one, or is being pursued by one. But why that's making them argue, unless they like the same boy, I don't know. It seems a long time since I had to unravel that sort of thing.'

'Did you have any troubles of the heart, Meg?' said Margaret's father. 'Apart from the regrettable Owen and perhaps missing another opportunity.' He glanced at Gil. 'I thought you were busy with work until you met Fox.'

'Maude was forever breaking hearts, Father,' said Margaret. 'Phoebe and I always had to help.'

'One day it'll be Edie and Alec,' said Gil.

Fox choked on his soup. 'Dear God, don't say that. I'd like to think they'll both turn out more sensible.'

Gil laughed. 'I doubt it. But they're so adorable. I've been called some things in my time, but my favourite is Ungill. Far better than Uncle Gil. Don't ever make them pronounce it correctly. What is it Ed calls you, Margaret? That was always charming.'

'Maggot,' said Margaret.

'I'd hardly call "Maggot" charming,' said her father.

Margaret shrugged. 'He went through at least two years of using my proper name, which was both sad and irritating. Now he's reverted to Aunt Maggot, which is somehow reassuring.'

'Is he enjoying the army as much as he thought he would?'

'Very much,' said Margaret. 'He'd like to get into the Flying Corps but competition is stiff and he's still very young, so he may not succeed.'

'Who wouldn't want to fly?' said her father. 'And the younger you are, the easier it is to learn.'

'Dangerous, though,' said Gil.

'Very.' Margaret glanced at Fox but his face was impassive. He was still sure that war threatened and it was a moot point whether Ed would be safer on the ground or in the air. 'Let's change the subject. Won't you be lonely in Weymouth until we join you next weekend, Gil?'

'No. A Swiss friend is staying in the town too: Raoul Favre. I imagine we'll travel about a good deal. I'll show him the wilds of Dorset, as he's shown me the wilds of Switzerland. I look forward to introducing you: I know you'll like him.' Gil stared into the middle distance, a soft smile on his face, then cleared his throat. 'My offer of a job at the sanatorium is still open, Margaret, and I'd love to work with you again. Won't you consider it? The air would be so much better for Edie. If not, perhaps consider a position in the countryside. South Devon or Dorset, maybe. Anything's better than this foul London air.' He nodded towards the window.

'I'm needed at Dorcas Free,' said Margaret. 'One of the doctors had to leave in the summer and hasn't been replaced yet. And horrid as smoky fog is, we live some way from the centre of London and the worst of it. Edie will improve as she grows and I know what to look for.'

'At the sanatorium you could work the days or hours you like, however you like. We need you there.'

'Maybe one day.'

'Switzerland's a lovely place to live. You're in the midst of mountains but they still seem distant. It seems unreal sometimes. It feels secure and safe.'

'I imagine it does,' said Fox. 'A perfect place to bring up a family.'

Margaret ignored him. 'Don't you miss London?'

Gil shrugged. Perhaps the time when he and Margaret had worked together at St Julia's seemed as distant and unreal as Swiss mountains, along with his wretched rooms in Tottenham, relative poverty and the risk of imprisonment for breaking laws about whom he should love. He couldn't be prosecuted in the Swiss canton where he lived if anyone suspected his relationship with Raoul was more than a friendship, but that wasn't to say the locals would approve. And it was a long way from the avant-garde theatre that Gil had once loved.

'Sometimes,' he said. 'But I have a job I adore. London doesn't feel like home any more. The only thing I'm sorry about is that I can't go to Phoebe's dinner with you and Maude on Wednesday. I sense she has something brewing. Do you know what?'

'I hope you're not spending all your leave wondering what we're all thinking,' said Margaret. 'I hadn't spotted Phoebe looking less than serene. But don't worry too much about missing it. Etta and Percival will be there too, and you never could abide Etta. I imagine it's the thought of her and Maude sparring that's worrying Phoebe, if anything.'

After lunch, Margaret went to the nursery to see the twins and try to establish what was bothering the maids, even if she had no idea what to do about it.

Nellie was jiggling Alec on her hip in a pause from putting away clean laundry. Margaret took the next item and folded it.

'It's rather foggy again, ma'am,' said Nellie. 'I'm not sure about taking the twins for a walk.'

'I agree,' said Margaret. 'They'll have to play in here. The master and I will be seeing Dr Trewellan off shortly, but we'd like you to know that we're giving you an extra half a crown to say thank you for helping with service yesterday, and also for dealing with the twins when they were overtired after the party. You can spend it when we're in Weymouth.'

'Ooh, doctor! Thank you! So kind!'

'Not at all,' said Margaret. 'Freda will have the same. Perhaps you could go shopping together.'

'We *could*.' Nellie's expression closed down. 'But I daresay she won't.'

'Why—'

'Freda's being foolish and putting herself in danger. Here, doctor, let me, else I'll have to iron them all again when you've gone.' She handed Alec to Margaret and shook out the vest

Margaret had put away, then refolded it in precisely the same way.

'What do you mean, "in danger"?'

'I'm not telling tales.'

'You just did.'

Nellie folded another vest, biting her lip. 'I think she's meeting a fellow, ma'am. I saw her talking to someone who didn't look quite the ticket.'

'What makes you say so?'

'Because she's judging him on what he looks like,' said Freda, entering the nursery.

'That doesn't sound like you, Nellie,' said Margaret.

'I didn't mean that and I don't care,' snapped Nellie. '"Man looketh on the outward appearance but God looketh on the heart." I know that.'

Freda grunted.

'But he scowls so, Freda,' said Nellie, with concern in her voice. 'I don't think you should be walking out with someone you don't know nothing about and maybe eloping and ending up in a strange country all alone.'

Freda rolled her eyes and turned to Margaret. 'It's not like that at all, doctor. I've better things to do in life than get married just now and you can't judge someone just cos they scowl a lot. It's not like people who scowl a lot can't be perfectly nice.'

She glanced at Margaret, then Nellie, and for a second the two maids shared a conspiratorial grin. But Nellie's soon vanished. 'You can't be too careful, Freda. Not every man is as nice as he seems.'

'As nice as holy Harry Kirson, you mean,' said Freda.

'Who?' said Margaret, then realised Nellie was blushing. 'Is that *your* young man, Nellie?'

'Yes'm, but he's quite respectable. A postman. I only do church things with him: Mum won't hear of us going off on our own yet. He's not going to kidnap me and take me off somewhere, never to be seen again.'

Freda rolled her eyes. 'Doctor, have you any post? I'm just going to the box.'

'To meet *him*?' said Nellie.

'Not that it's any of your business, Nellie, but no.'

'I haven't anything,' said Margaret. 'And couldn't your letter wait until tomorrow, when hopefully the fog's cleared? I saw a girl knocked down in Marylebone Road yesterday when I took Mrs King home. The motorist couldn't stop in time.'

Freda blinked. 'Oh no! What does she look like? Was she badly hurt? Where's she from?'

'Not terribly badly hurt,' said Margaret. 'But she's in Dorcas Free for now. She's small, blonde and by the way she talks, from the East End. Are you afraid it's a friend?'

Freda shook her head, her expression relieved. 'No. Don't worry about it, doctor. And I'll be careful with the fog and everything. Nellie's making a fuss about nothing. I can look after myself.'

Three

D r Naylor sat back with a kind but determined smile. 'Before we discuss anything else, Dr Demeray, I hope you'll consider my request now that Edie is better. I believe it would be good for you as well as Dorcas Free if you worked more hours here. Your knowledge would benefit D Ward, and you would refresh your patient skills.'

'Dr Demeray's skills need no refreshing,' said Dr Gesner. 'And she is critical to the pathology department. Another doctor could be obtained for D Ward. Not so much for mine.'

The tiny fire in Dr Naylor's office faltered. It had been lit to drive off the damp of two days of fog, but its warmth reached only a few inches from the grate, which made the rest of the room feel even colder and damper.

'What it is to be in demand,' muttered Margaret, then raised her voice. 'Why is it so hard to fill the vacancy?'

Dr Naylor sighed. 'The board won't employ any more female doctors. The male applicants have mostly been unsatisfactory. We have hopes of one, but his current hospital is reluctant to release him. I appreciate how you must feel, Margaret, but please think about it while you're away at the weekend.'

There was a sharp knock at the door and Matron Russell entered. 'Good morning, doctors. May I discuss Rosie on E Ward?'

'I was just about to tell Dr Demeray about her,' said Dr Naylor. 'Rosie's the girl you saw knocked down, Margaret.'

'I thought she was doing well. I was going to come and see her.'

'Please do, Dr Demeray,' said Matron. 'Physically she's doing as expected, but one can't get much sense out of her.'

'Haven't you found her family?' asked Margaret. 'She seemed quite young.'

'One would guess no more than fourteen,' said Matron, lips narrowed. 'It could easily be two years either side, but she is not physically mature. She says she's forgotten her surname, her age, her address and everything about any family.'

'Do her clothes help?'

'They are plain, unmarked and ready-made,' said Matron Russell. 'No handbag or personal effects were found where the accident occurred. Not even a hat. Do you recall any?'

Margaret shook her head. 'I'm surprised she's so confused. I really didn't think she was concussed.'

Dr Naylor sniffed. 'I suspect it's feigned because she's scared. Apart from the injuries sustained from the collision, Rosie has bruising on her arms consistent with being restrained.'

Margaret leaned forward. 'Really?'

Dr Naylor nodded. 'I requested that a clerk record the details of any marks on the clothes before they were laundered, in case we ever needed to confirm anything to the police.'

'The police?'

'Rosie is little more than a child,' said Matron Russell. 'I would very much like to know what she was running from.'

The image in Margaret's mind altered: now she saw the girl not as careless but desperate. 'Any sign of intimate assault?'

'Not that we could ascertain,' said Matron Russell. 'But the police want to speak with her too.'

'Didn't they do so on Saturday?'

'Only about the accident, not why she was running.'

'There have been more and more cases of procurement in the newspapers recently,' said Dr Naylor. 'And a good deal of press criticism of the powerful getting away with their sordid little pastimes despite backing the White Slavery Bill. The police wish to be seen to take action, and are threatening to charge Rosie with attempted suicide if she won't cooperate, yet she won't budge. Has that changed, Matron?'

'It may have. This morning she suddenly asked for the lady doctor from St J's, so I put a call through to their Matron Johnstone and discovered that the only female doctor St Julia's Hospital has ever had is Dr Demeray. Therefore, one assumes it's Dr Demeray the girl wants, which again raises doubts as to whether her memory is really gone. She has a marked East End accent and we believe she muttered in Yiddish when she was unconscious. Without a surname, Matron Johnstone couldn't confirm whether the girl or a family member had ever been a patient.'

Margaret frowned. 'I left St J's a year ago and I worked solely in pathology. I only very occasionally spoke directly with patients and don't recall Rosie at all.'

'Maybe she saw you at one of the talks you give.' Matron Russell's stare reminded Margaret of a mathematics teacher who had once refused to let her sit down until she'd recited her thirteen times table. 'You can speak Yiddish. That might encourage her.'

'I can't speak Yiddish,' said Margaret. 'I know a few greetings, a few insults and what I suspect are swearwords, most of which I learned because they've been addressed to me. That's pretty much all. Everyone thinks Yiddish is the same as German, don't they, Dr Gesner? But it isn't.'

Dr Gesner nodded. 'I can't speak a word.'

'Something is amiss, Dr Demeray,' said Matron Russell, 'and I don't know what. If someone was procuring Rosie, I don't want to be responsible for effectively returning her to them when she's discharged. I'm sick of sending girls and women to infectious disease hospitals, or watching them bleed to death from botched operations, or treating them when they've been beaten and abused but won't say who did it, then discharging them to return to a life that will kill them, one way or another. Whether this girl is twelve or sixteen, whether she has already surrendered her virtue or had it taken from her, she seems very young. Maybe you can help and maybe you can't, but please will you try?'

Rosie sat bolt upright, eyes narrowed, mouth clamped shut, her uninjured hand clenching the bedclothes across her chest. She watched Margaret approach then glared at the woman in the next bed, who was observing with unveiled interest.

But Rosie's defiance was thin. Her gaze flickered about the room – into corners, towards the windows and door – before it returned to Margaret.

She suddenly seemed very young: a girl at the start of adolescence with a fractured arm, in a ward of grown women whose broken bones had been caused by falls, faulty mangles, and 'accidents' they wouldn't explain. Margaret had a good memory for faces, but small, stick-thin Rosie, with her pale freckle-dotted skin and plaited ash-blonde hair, was a mystery.

'Good morning,' said Margaret, 'I'm Dr Demeray. I used to work at St Julia's. I understand you want to speak with me.'

'You helped me on Saturday.'

'I did. It must have been very frightening.'

'I got a cough,' whispered Rosie. 'I heard you was good at that sort of thing.' She made a hard wheezing sound and put her hand over her mouth. It was not a real cough, but sounded like she was replicating something she often endured.

'I am,' said Margaret, 'but Dr Callendar is in charge of treating chest disease here. She's a woman, if that helps. I have a different job here and I did at St Julia's, too.'

'A friend said you know how to keep mum.' The words were sharp but a plea seeped through the scowl. 'She said you helped her.'

Margaret turned to Matron Russell. 'I'd like to examine the patient. Could the bed be screened, please, and a stethoscope brought, and could someone send a message to Dr Callendar that I will speak with her later.'

'Yes, doctor.'

Matron waved a hand at two nurses who scurried off to fetch the screens while Margaret looked at Rosie's file. Dr Perch had confirmed a fractured forearm, damaged ribs, concussion, cuts and grazes, and a badly sprained ankle. Rosie had only reluctantly exchanged her clothes for hospital-issue nightwear. It had been difficult to undertake more than a cursory examination. *Bruising on torso and legs consistent with accident*, the report said. *Additional bruising on upper arms perhaps a day older, but inconsistent with accident.*

When the screens had been placed, Margaret held up the stethoscope. 'If you want me to examine your chest, you'll have to drop the sheet a little.'

'You ain't gonna make me take my clothes off, are ya?'

'It's not necessary.' As far as could be seen under the starched cotton gown, Rosie's chest was still almost flat. Her heart was steady and sounded healthy. Her lungs were a little congested and there was a slight catch in her breath but that was all.

'Have you any other symptoms?'

'I'm wheezy. My bones ache something rotten. I go hot and cold. I—'

'Are you like that now?' said Margaret.

'Not exactly.'

'Are you like it when you're doing your normal job?'

Rosie narrowed her eyes. 'Maybe.'

'I diagnose byssinosis.'

'Do yer?' A moment of childish interest sparked in Rosie's eyes. 'Coo. Fancy.'

Since Matron couldn't see, Margaret sat on the bed. 'Who is the friend you mentioned?'

'Anna Balodis.'

Margaret nodded. That made a little sense, if not much. Anna was a seamstress she'd met in Whitechapel two years before, half-Jewish, half-Gentile, angry with everyone and everything. Anna hadn't struck Margaret as having many friends, and certainly not one perhaps ten years younger.

'Don't take it as meaning anything in particular,' said Rosie. 'Anna's lived all over London. Just cos she's from Whitechapel don't mean I am.'

'Of course not.' To Margaret's knowledge, Anna hadn't lived in more than two other London boroughs in her life, and then only briefly before leaving the country. Wherever she'd been, however, she'd been as linked to the rag trade as the chest condition called byssinosis. Rosie had described the symptoms perfectly. If they'd eased, it was because she hadn't breathed in cloth dust for several days.

'Will you tell me your surname?' said Margaret, her pencil poised over the girl's notes. 'It would be nicer than being Rosie Unknown.'

The girl settled against the pillows, her pale hair and skin fading into them. From a distance, all you'd be able to see of her was freckles.

'Go on, Rosie.'

Nothing. Beyond the screens were the sounds of the ward: the tapping of shoes, soft voices, a rattling trolley.

'All right, it's Levene. But there's a million Levenes in London and my lot don't want me.' Rosie's mouth wobbled.

'How old are you?'

'Fourteen.'

'Truly?'

'Give or take a month or so.'

'Thank you. Will you tell me how you know Anna, and why you wanted me in particular?'

'I worked with her at the soup kitchen last year,' said Rosie. 'We weren't friends exactly, but she pointed you out once when you were traipsing about Ravel Street. She said you was tricksy but fair and you gave the bluebottles a run for their money.' Rosie's expression became one of near-adoration. 'I wish I could talk to her again. Does she write to you?'

'No.'

'Yeah, well, why would she? She's got a new life in New York.' Rosie drew a slightly wheezy breath, her expression wistful then suddenly sad. 'I hope *hers* turned out all right.'

'So do I,' said Margaret, wondering where Anna was, but certain it wasn't anywhere as safe as New York. 'Have you been looking for a new life?'

Rosie's eyes brimmed with tears and she nodded. 'The ad said – it said...'

Margaret reached for Rosie's hand and the girl let her take it. 'What did the ad say?'

'They wanted a likely girl to learn seckertarial work. No experience needed. No stifficates. Just a good head for numbers and willingness to learn. Maybe I don't sound like it, but that's me. I fancied being a shop girl, but I had to leave school too soon. The job I got made me sick.'

'Sewing for a sweatshop?'

'Yeah.' Rosie slumped. 'That byssiwotsit you said I've got. What is it in English?'

'Cotton lung. You're right: better working conditions would help. A different job would probably make it go away for ever.'

'People don't like factory girls, they think we're not re-spectable. When I leave here I wanna start again, only I don't know who to trust. Anna said you suggested somewhere for her, but I can't remember where.'

'Maria's, perhaps. It's a dressmaker's and very well-run. Maria only employs girls over fourteen, though.'

'Told you. I'm fourteen. But...' Rosie lifted her broken arm. 'I can't run a machine like this.'

'Maria learnt to operate a machine with a damaged arm a good many years ago,' said Margaret. 'Her business specialises in giving opportunities to women like her. Your arm will heal completely in time, but meanwhile, Maria could find something for you to do. And there's a class I know of where they teach girls like you the things they didn't have the chance to learn at school.'

Rosie's face clouded.

'I'll speak with Maria, shall I?' said Margaret. 'She may know somewhere safe for you to lodge if you really don't have a family to go back to.'

Rosie's face held a shred of hope. 'All right.'

Margaret helped her pull the covers up. 'When you were knocked down on Saturday evening, you looked as if you were running from something. Will you tell me what?'

Rosie shook her head.

'Did someone hurt you in a nasty way?'

A harder shake.

'You ran away before they could? They tried to stop you but you got away?'

A nod.

'Don't you want them to be arrested?'

Rosie shook her head violently, tears spilling as her eyes widened. 'I ain't gonna peach – I can't! They'd kill me. I-I never knew there was people like that up west.'

'Will you let me guess what you're talking about?' said Margaret. 'Someone offered you a job you thought was respectable and more pleasant than seamstressing, but it turned out to involve your body being used in a way you didn't want.'

'I don't know,' said Rosie, with a catch in her voice. 'But whatever they wanted me for, I knew I didn't want to find out. Don't make me peach, Dr Demray, but... Anna said you know a different sort of bluebottle. Tell him. It's happening round this way and I'm afraid my friend Violet will apply and I don't know where she'd end up.'

'I need names and addresses, Rosie,' said Margaret. 'He won't know where to start without them.'

Rosie's face closed. 'I don't know where Violet Brahms lives and I don't know where I was and I can't remember any names except Broad. But if your fellow can't work it out, he ain't much of a bluebottle, is he?'

Four

F ox shook out the newspaper, nearly knocking the milk jug over Margaret's sketchbook. Margaret caught the jug in time, put it as far away as possible and looked around the small café again, pencil poised. Outside, it was overcast and drizzling. Inside, electric lights and mirrors were doing their best to illuminate the room. The aroma of coffee was overwhelmed by the smell of damp overcoats. The more delicate scent of tea had no hope.

'Tingling yet?' said Fox.

'No,' said Margaret. 'And I bet you aren't either. I can't see what we'll gain from this.'

Fox lowered the paper. 'I'm not having one of your patients doubt the powers of your personal bluebottle.'

'I expected you to pass her information to a real policeman,' said Margaret. 'The trafficking of women has nothing to do with military intelligence.'

'Not generally,' said Fox. 'But it's good to have a change. Not to mention that if I weren't here, you'd probably do this alone.'

Margaret wrinkled her nose. 'Rosie isn't well enough to run any distance,' she said. 'So when she ran into the road, it must have been from one of these streets. But there are so many, and I've no idea whether Violet is here or elsewhere. I'm not sure sitting in a café will help.'

'You have no idea how much of my job is spent sitting in cafés, bars, hotels and parks, watching for things or people that don't quite fit,' said Fox.

'You sound like Juniper watching for mice in the shrubbery.'

'Juniper's prey can't sneak up behind her with a cosh.'

'Haven't you met a London rat?'

He snorted. 'Juniper isn't stupid enough to tackle a London rat.'

'What have you found in the paper?'

'Small advertisements never cease to entertain,' said Fox, running his finger down the page. 'Modern artistic dress, boneless corsets, ancestors as Christmas presents, ladies' eyebrows grown in one month. A single-handed kitchen-maid wanted, right next to an advertisement for cheap sets of china. And here's my favourite: Boy Scout's astronomical calculator – a simple device which enables the scout to find his way in strange parts by night. Can I have one for Christmas?'

'Only if I can have the Girl Guide's version.'

'Certainly not. You're not wandering in strange parts at night without me.'

'You'd need me to protect you.'

'Not in context, perhaps.' Fox's moment of humour had passed. 'Here. This looks like what Rosie saw.' He turned the paper for Margaret to read. '"Young girl, 12-17, wanted as clerk-assistant for female secretary working for a lady. The less experience the better as training will be provided. No school certificates required. Opportunity for advancement for ready learner. Apply to Post Office Box etcetera." It could simply have said "Young girl wanted as clerk-assistant for a female secretary. Training provided. Opportunity for advancement". The rest is superfluous, and would have cost another shilling.'

'Spendthrift or sinister?'

'What do you think?'

Margaret perused the print more thoroughly. 'I've never heard of this newspaper.'

'It's from Berkshire. Searching through London ones didn't bring up anything like what Rosie described. So I thought I'd look at some country ones.'

'Where would Rosie get a country paper?'

'That's a question for Rosie. I'll have Elinor look into the post-office box while I see if this ad is running in other papers. Where's Rosie from?'

'If she's not from the Whitechapel area, I'm a tabby cat.'

'Hmm.' Fox took Margaret's sketchbook and scanned her drawings. 'This man...'

'What about him? It's just a lightning sketch. He left shortly after we came in.'

'There's something familiar about him.'

Margaret twisted her head to consider the sketch. 'I don't recognise him.'

'Mmm,' said Fox. 'Can I take it and see what Bert thinks?'

'Please do.' Margaret tore the page from her sketchbook and watched Fox fold it inside the newspaper. He seemed oddly intent on such a simple task. 'You're still churning over what Gil said, aren't you?'

Fox tipped his head on one side. The scar on his temple had healed into a grey line, as if someone with little skill had drawn it with a pencil. 'Which particular thing?'

'About my keeping away from your job.' Margaret restrained herself from touching her shoulder blade. It ached a little.

Fox gave her a rueful grin. 'It would be easier to keep Juniper from the cream than you from my work. I try, but you sneak back in.'

'It's your own fault for approaching me in a tea shop in 1910 and asking a peculiar question. If you'd taken no for an answer...'

'It was a nice tea shop,' said Fox. 'And you were lonely. How could I not?' He clasped her hand. 'And if I'd taken no for an answer, we both know what would have happened. Since then, apart from both of us occasionally losing various pieces of skin, some blood and an awful lot of dignity, I'm not sorry. Are you?'

'No.'

'And now, since you've helped me before, I'll see if I can help track down Rosie's procurer and Violet, and we'll pass on what we discover to the local police.'

'Yes,' said Margaret. 'But we don't tell Gil.'

Fox squeezed her hand. 'Not until you've taken that job in Switzerland, where you needn't do anything more dangerous than learn to ski.'

'There's more chance of me becoming a cat who doesn't like cream than doing that, Fox.'

'Skiing?'

'Taking a job in Switzerland.' Margaret rose. 'I have to get back to Dorcas Free. If Elinor finds the address, we'll know where Rosie was hurt, and if we can establish where she's from, maybe we can find Violet. I've written to Captain Blanchett – do you remember him? The Salvation Army officer who helped us when we first met?'

'Will that stop you from wandering the East End without an escort?'

'As to that, dearly beloved,' said Margaret, picking up her handbag. 'I make no promises.'

In Dorcas Free, Miss Upton greeted her from the clerk's desk. 'The police are bringing a body to the Other Place shortly.' With a slight wrinkle of the nose, she indicated the extension built in late summer to keep the less savoury corpses away from the main laboratories. 'Dr Gesner's with Dr Innes and says not to wait. He's asked Miss Buckram to assist as part of her studies. Here are his notes.'

'Thank you,' said Margaret, opening the file. Her colleague's handwriting was neat, but letters formed in the German style took a moment to decipher. Once she had, she grimaced. 'I'll prepare Miss Buckram for what to expect.'

'Capital idea.'

Margaret found Polly sitting on a stool, so engrossed in a book that she jumped when Margaret spoke and clasped it to her chest, eyes wide. 'Oh, doctor, you scared me so! This is so thrilling that I quite forgot where I was.'

'*Clinical Pathology In Practice*?' said Margaret.

Polly blushed. 'No, it's *The Beetle*. I couldn't resist reading another chapter. Have you read it, Dr Demeray?'

'The novel about a resurrected Egyptian princess and a murderous, metamorphosing fiend?'

'Yes.'

Margaret blinked. She'd assumed Polly would prefer romance, but here she was reading a book full of supernatural horror, demon possession and implied immorality. 'My friends and I preferred it to *Dracula*. I didn't think it would be your sort of book at all.'

'My brother dared me to read it,' confessed Polly. 'Please don't tell Dr Gesner.'

'I won't.' Margaret sat down beside her as Miss Upton entered with more paperwork and handed it over. 'But please put it away and listen before we prepare the laboratory. This post-mortem won't be pleasant. You need to brace yourself.'

'A bomb?' Polly's face paled.

'A stabbing,' said Margaret. 'But he's been dead for several days. Thank goodness it's been so cold.' She shuddered, hoping the stench would not be marked and there wouldn't be maggots.

The body arrived before Dr Gesner returned. It emitted no marked smell except for stale blood, which was puzzling. Even in

November, if the man had been dead for some time there should be more of an odour. Inspector Coulter from the local division had accompanied the corpse. He had grudgingly endured Margaret on the few occasions they'd met, but he seemed affronted by Polly. 'What's a girl doing here?'

'Miss Buckram is a student,' said Margaret. 'She needs to learn.'

'The chap's near enough naked.'

'Miss Buckram studies anatomy and goes to art galleries,' said Margaret. 'I'm sure she won't get the vapours.'

'It's not proper.' The inspector indicated for his constable to remove the sheet. 'This is Hector Radden, aged forty-one. Trader in objay dart according to his business cards, though I suspect that means bits of tat that'll be out of fashion in a twelvemonth. If that means he's also a fence, he's not come to our notice so far.'

Hector Radden wore a knee-length nightshirt. A cut on his temple had bled into one eye. Dark hairs on his cheeks, forearms and calves were stark against skin like grey-green marble. A purple tint on the right side of his body indicated how he had been lying when he died, and where blood had subsequently pooled.

But Mr Radden had had little blood left to pool. A kitchen knife was deep inside his abdomen, the nightshirt stained brownish-red. His eyes were half-closed, his tongue swollen and protruding. Inasmuch as Mr Radden had an expression, it indicated quiet despair.

'Aren't you going to do something?' said Inspector Coulter. 'He's not going to wake up and talk.'

'First impressions help a good deal with establishing facts,' said Margaret.

'I'll save you some time. He's dead.'

'Thank you. So helpful. What caused that triangular wound on his head?'

'Handle of a screwdriver from a set that was in the parlour, we think. The tool itself is missing, presumed chucked elsewhere. Let's get on with it. The poor chap's been dead since Thursday.'

Margaret bent to peer at the body. 'Thursday? There's little decay, little apparent build-up of internal gases, no evidence of insect infestation.'

'The weather being what it has, he'd have been warmer in a refrigerator,' said the inspector. 'He's got a whopping hole in his stomach to let gas out, and any insect with sense is hibernating.'

'Nevertheless, I suspect he died on Saturday or Sunday. Some information about how he was found would help.'

'His sister, who lives with him, went out of town on Thursday evening with a pal and that was the last time she saw him. No one's sure of seeing him after that, but he kept to himself and so do the neighbours. There was a postcard from his sister postmarked Friday lying on his body. The char's theory is that he was coming downstairs with the knife then tripped and fell on it, knocking himself out on the corner of the hall table. He died behind the front door, mucking up her clean tiles and, as I say, getting the mail dropped on him. I ought to point out that there's no blood on the corner of that table.'

'Why would he have a kitchen knife in his bedroom?' asked Polly.

Inspector Coulter gave her a pitying look. 'If you want to be a doctor doing house visits, missy, you'll have to anticipate things in bedrooms that would surprise a drug-addled poet.'

Polly blushed and bent to scribble in her notebook.

'Please address Miss Buckram with respect,' said Margaret. 'Is there any likelihood that the char is right?'

'A little. I believe he was whacked on the head and stabbed in his bed. There's blood on his pillow and a fair amount on the sheets and covers. There's more on the floors of the bedroom and landing and on the stairs, suggesting he tried to go for help, and a whole river in the hall, where he died. Murderer's mistake number one: there's no object present that could have injured his temple like that, which suggests it was taken away. Mistake number two: the house was locked, so Mr Radden couldn't get out, but the key is missing, so the murderer must have taken that, too. Like I said, the last confirmed sighting of him was when he waved his sister goodbye on Thursday. I need you to confirm that's when he died so I can arrest my suspect.'

'We'll confirm what's there,' said Margaret. 'Not what you tell us to.'

The inspector stared at the constable and jerked his head at the door. Once the constable had left, he faced Margaret and opened his mouth just as Dr Gesner entered.

'Please accept my apologies for being late,' said the doctor.

'At last,' said the inspector. 'A man.'

Dr Gesner raised his eyebrows and turned to Margaret. 'Could you summarise?'

'May I?' said Polly.

'Of course,' said Margaret.

Her face red, Polly read from her notes, then concluded, 'We must try to ascertain whether the head wound rendered him unconscious, disoriented, or both. We need to establish from what direction and with what force the knife was applied and also the extent of the stomach wound, though from initial observation it appears the stomach and intestines were missed and the liver sustained the damage. It's possible he was too weak to remove the knife, though if he had he would have died even more quickly – but that is supposition. We need to establish a likely time of death. Allowing for the cold, rigor has passed, which means he has been dead a good deal more than a few hours. However, everything else so far indicates less than four days.'

'Three days, eight days, what's the difference in November?' snapped Inspector Coulter. 'Dr Gesner, I expect you to take control. And maybe get a male student in.'

'Miss Buckram has summarised everything perfectly,' said Dr Gesner. 'You may stay if you wish, and you can follow the thinking behind our conclusions by reading the book Miss Buckram has with her.'

'He means *Clinical Pathology in Practice*, not *The Beetle*,' whispered Margaret, seeing panic on the younger woman's face.

The inspector sat down. 'If it wasn't Thursday, I might have to review my chief suspect. But let's get on. We've got motoring incidents to investigate, a punch-up at the workhouse, a woman drugged at the theatre with intent to kidnap, and a family of paupers found dead of cold in a doorway.'

'In that order?' said Margaret.

Inspector Coulter eyed her coldly. 'In whatever order keeps the peace. Let's start with an actual crime, shall we?'

Five

'Oh! I'm sorry, ma'am.' Coffee spilled from the pot as Freda placed it on the breakfast table.

Fox had left and Margaret was dawdling over the newspaper. Surprised by the uncharacteristic clumsiness, she looked up and realised Freda been reading over her shoulder.

'It's just a few drops,' said Margaret, conscious that she wouldn't be the one getting the stain out of the tablecloth. 'What's wrong? You look upset.'

'It's the paper, ma'am. I heard someone nearly got kidnapped in a theatre and Dinah said there's been a murder, but I didn't know they were both as near as Marylebone. What—'

Margaret proffered the paper. 'Please take it.'

'Thanks, ma'am.' Freda read aloud. '"Mr Hector Radden, trader in..." What do those words mean, ma'am?'

'Objets d'art? Small decorative ornaments and pictures.'

'Dust gatherers?'

'Well, yes. He bought at auctions on behalf of rich clients and made his living from commission.'

'"...was found dead by his charwoman. The victim's widowed sister, Mrs Vidler, is being comforted by friends on the south coast, with whom she had been staying since Thursday." She had a lucky escape.'

'She did.'

'"The inquest will take place on Friday. Anyone who saw anything suspicious in Tibberton Street at the weekend should inform the police."' Freda made a subtle snort. 'It says the same about that lady who got drugged in the theatre. No one could have seen anything in that fog, could they, ma'am?'

'It misdirects and it conceals,' murmured Margaret, remembering what she'd said to Gil a few hours before seeing Rosie's ghostly form dash into the road.

'There's hardly anything about the woman who was drugged.'

'Sometimes it's important to keep details out of the press,' said Margaret.

'Girls ... women ... *people* need to know what to look out for.' Freda recollected herself. 'Sorry, ma'am. I didn't mean to bother you.'

'You're not,' said Margaret. 'What's really worrying you? The murder or the attempted kidnap?'

Freda swallowed. 'Kidnap. I was worried about my little cousin Evie.'

Margaret thought of Rosie and her palms became clammy. 'What happened to her?'

'Nothing, as it turned out, ma'am. When I say little, Evie's sixteen, but a bit flighty. We thought she'd run away from home and been kidnapped. That's why I was meeting with the man Nellie saw. It's my cousin Joe, Evie's brother. He's a footman in Hampstead. We were trying to work out what to do.'

'You should have told us!'

Freda shrugged. 'Joe wasn't keen, but I was about to. Then Evie wrote to my aunt and it seems an earlier letter had gone astray. She's working as a typist in Highbury and lodges with a nice family. Me and Joe are hoping to meet up with her soon, but all three of us being free at the same time isn't easy to organise. When I heard about that woman in the theatre, it reminded me of all the dreadful things me and Joe were thinking. It's just so easy for girls to be fooled.'

'Oh, Freda, it is,' said Margaret. 'Are you sure Evie's all right?'

'Yes, ma'am.'

'If you want time off, please just ask, or invite her here for tea if you like.'

'Thank you, ma'am. Let me pour your coffee, else you won't be set up right for work. And you're out to dinner tonight, aren't you?'

'Yes. Miss Pendleberry's.'

'Very good, ma'am. And thank you, ma'am. I told Joe you'd understand.'

'We're still wrangling with the Post Office,' said Fox, on the way to Phoebe's that evening. 'By the time we discover who that post-office box address belongs to, any replies to the advertisement will have been collected and the box closed. Any news from Captain Blanchett?'

'Getting information out of people in Whitechapel isn't any quicker than getting it from the Post Office. Rosie's still keeping quiet. One piece of good news: I thought Freda's cousin had been caught up in the same thing, but it turns out she wasn't.' Margaret described the discussion over breakfast. 'So Freda can come to Weymouth and enjoy herself, and hopefully she and Nellie won't bicker.'

'Which means we'll have more time to enjoy ourselves.' Fox reached for Margaret's hand.

'You'll be on your mission.'

'As I said, my missions often involve watching the world go by. This is one of those.'

'Once again, you manage to make your job sound like a holiday. I'm surprised Hare doesn't have you following the Archduke Francis Ferdinand on his royal visit instead.'

'Hare's managing that himself,' said Fox. 'Hopefully, any threat to the archduke will be staying in Austria-Hungary, but we'll be glad when he's gone home.'

'So what are you doing?'

'Being observant. Weymouth is a nice bit of seaside to do it in, like Eastbourne. Don't you remember 1910 – cafés, cinemas, promenades, you winning Mr Tod on a hoopla stall? Perhaps we can win a Mrs Tod.'

'You've forgotten we're taking Father with us.'

Fox squeezed her hand more tightly. 'And *you've* forgotten that Katherine has arranged for your father to spend Saturday at the museum in Dorchester with a professor friend. You and I will be tourists in Weymouth, taking in the sights.'

'What are we looking for?'

'*We* are looking for Mr Tod's new missus. *I* am looking for people stealing information about Whitehead's torpedo factory at Wyke Regis. The weapons testing the navy did off the Dorset coast the other weekend was of great interest internationally.'

'Wasn't that the point of sinking that ship so publicly?'

'Of course,' said Fox. 'There's nothing like a bit of sabre rattling. But someone has been trying to get into the factory. Whether it was to sabotage or steal information isn't known, because the guard couldn't catch him. My job is to potter about for a day and a bit with my family, watch for things that don't fit and maybe play hoopla.' He began to sing. 'Oh I do hope to win a plaster vixen, oh I do hope to find a foreign spy, oh I do hope to walk along the esplanade, watching my lovely wife go for a healthy bathe.'

Margaret laughed. 'No amount of flattery will get me in the sea in November.'

'Coward.'

She sobered. 'Is it safe to take the children and Father?'

'If I thought it wasn't, I wouldn't take you,' said Fox. 'Anyway, here we are. I'm surprised Phoebe invited Maude and Geoff as well as Etta and Percival. Maude and Etta loathe each other.'

'It's not that bad,' said Margaret, trying to convince herself. 'Maude thinks Etta's self-centred and lazy and Etta thinks Maude is self-centred and irresponsible. But it's not a suffrage meeting, so they ought to be civilised.'

Taking her seat between Geoff and Percival, Margaret saw that Gil had been right. Phoebe had lost a little of her plumpness and her calm smile seemed fixed.

However, the dinner party began with the usual discussion of the news: the archduke's visit, an earthquake in Peru, a ship sunk in the Great Lakes, the launching of a new dreadnought, the dangers of flying. Then Maude lightened the mood by mentioning an illustrated article in the *Sketch* about the tango. 'Let's try dancing it after dinner.'

'Certainly not,' said Etta, who was sitting on Phoebe's left. 'I saw the paper on a newsstand and the female dancer's leg was visible to her knee. If Percival and I were to do anything like that, his political career might be destroyed. We can't have accusations of an indecency scandal on top of everything else.'

'Are your legs that hideous, Etta?' said Maude.

'You know that isn't what I mean.'

Maude was unrepentant. 'If a bare calf is all it takes to bring down a government, I shall suggest all suffragettes wear short skirts till we get the vote. But we're in private here. Let's do it.'

Etta pursed her lips.

'I haven't the right gramophone record,' said Phoebe. 'Next time, perhaps.'

'The very idea,' sniffed Etta. 'Percival must protect his dignity.'

Twenty years before, people – including Margaret – had said Percival was so idle that he'd allowed Etta to talk him into marriage so she could organise him and add to his wealth. Nowadays, Margaret realised that whatever reason had led Percival to marry Etta, it was not idleness. He could have lived a life of comfort without working, but had chosen to stand for election in one of the poorer north London seats instead, trying to improve things there and speak up for suffrage from the back benches. Dignity had never really worried him.

The second course was cleared and the general conversation broke into smaller discussions. Etta turned to Fox, who offered to explain the origins of the tango without going into immoral detail. She became so mesmerised that her mouth fell half-open. With her viridescent dress and his expressive hand gestures, they resembled snake and snake charmer.

'Etta's never forgiven me for dancing with my constituents to a ditty called "Knees Up Mother Brown",' murmured Percival to Margaret, as the third course arrived. 'It's the most interesting thing I've ever done. My job is so much duller than yours.'

'The most interesting thing I've done recently is a post-mortem on a man who bled to death from a stabbed liver,' said Margaret.

'It wasn't in the House of Commons, then,' said Percival. 'The stabbing there is always in the back and bloodless.'

'Who's coming to the WSPU rally on Wimbledon Common this Sunday?' said Maude loudly.

Etta shook herself free of whatever Fox was saying. 'Is there any reason to?'

'A former factory inspector, Mrs Davies, will speak about inadequate housing conditions and women earning a living by sweated working in those homes,' said Maude. 'I thought you'd be interested, Etta. It's the sort of thing Percival campaigns about.'

'Oh, um...'

'I'll be there,' said Percival. 'I imagine Etta will be caring for the children.'

'Quite right, dear.'

'Perhaps we could go together, Maude and Margaret?' said Phoebe.

Margaret shook her head. 'I'll be in Weymouth. Will *Athene's Gazette* report on it, Maude?'

'It certainly will.'

The next course arrived and Margaret turned back to Percival. 'Talking of poverty, is there much trouble in your area with women and girls being lured into vice? I'm speaking in your constituency tomorrow morning and might bring it up.'

Percival pulled a face. 'No more than there ever was. I'm hoping the White Slavery Act will stop people being shipped out of the country and sold. And now those living off immoral earnings can be sentenced to a flogging, at least there's a deterrent.'

'Surely the victims won't report it, for fear of reprisal?'

'Then what's the answer?' said Percival. 'There's more than one kind of procurement to stamp out. Everyone says a person living off the earnings of a prostitute is immoral. But if a man makes a profit from employees working themselves to death, he's hailed as a successful businessman. And the very name White Slavery is ridiculous. The bill is supposed to protect people of every colour, but you can be sure people only think of one.' Percival sighed. 'I apologise. This isn't dinner-party talk.'

'I started it,' said Margaret. 'Let's discuss something else.'

It wasn't until they were in the drawing room with the gramophone playing that Phoebe addressed her guests. Standing by the fire, she was as self-contained as ever, but Margaret noticed tension in the hands clasped at the waist of her green velvet gown, and an unfamiliar catch in Phoebe's voice, as if it wouldn't take much to make her cry.

'I have been sued for withholding my taxes as a suffragette protest. I anticipate the bailiffs may visit at any time.'

'But our family can't have *bailiffs*!' exclaimed Etta.

'I shan't contest the judgment,' Phoebe continued. 'I am making a point. Some of my heirlooms are hideous and I'll happily hand them over.' She took a breath. 'However, as supporters of the school, you need to know that I am selling it. Telling you together feels less painful than telling you separately.'

Etta gawped. 'But Elfrida is due to commence next September. At a discount.'

Maude turned a glare on her. 'Is that all you care about?'

'Elfrida will have her place,' said Phoebe. 'The school will continue preparing girls to be female leaders one day. I will not see that destroyed because of me, or have anyone say that the payment of my fine comes from school funds.'

'Who would think that?' exclaimed Geoff.

Phoebe's hands clenched. 'My personal secretary has resigned to distance herself from me. Others will follow. I don't care about myself, but I will not sacrifice the education of my girls.' She attempted a smile. 'I wish I had some tango music to play. I have brought down the mood.'

'Never fear,' said Maude, rising and giving Phoebe a gentle pat on the shoulder. 'I had your staff telephone mine during the dessert course and one has been brought over. I shall both raise the mood and lower the tone. Come along, Etta, you can dance with me if you think it's too scandalous with your own husband. I promise no knees will be bared.'

Ignoring his wife's protestations as she was hauled from the sofa, Percival turned to Margaret, his expression intense. 'Is there any particular reason you spoke of procurement earlier? Has someone come forward with allegations?'

Margaret, startled by his change of subject, hesitated. The police had released no information about Rosie, other than to say that an unnamed girl had been knocked down in the fog and was recovering.

'There just seems to be a lot of it in the press at the moment,' she said. 'For example, the woman who was nearly kidnapped from the theatre the other day.'

Percival's staring eyes creased into a twinkle. 'Oh, *that* story,' he said, rising and offering a hand. 'It's utter nonsense. One can't believe everything one hears. Separating fact from fiction in a constituency is half of my job. Shall we dance?'

'The tango looks very complicated,' said Margaret. 'And I'm too full. Dance with Phoebe and cheer her up instead. Fox and I will try shortly.' She watched him approach his sister, feeling oddly uncomfortable.

She told herself she hadn't wanted to make a fool of herself with an unfamiliar dance, but deep down she knew that sort of thing never bothered her. Something which had been said that evening felt wrong, and she wasn't sure what it was, or who had said it.

Six

S t Mark's parish hall was in the poorest district of Perci-val's constituency. It was within easy walking distance of mansions owned by people so rich they probably didn't know how many rooms they contained. It might as well have been on another continent.

'I'm afraid we're in the Sunday School room,' said the vicar's wife, Mrs Tomlinson. 'Members of the railway union are having a strike meeting in the main one. I hope it won't get too loud. And I'm sorry about the furniture.'

'Please don't apologise,' said Margaret, contemplating a chair designed for a child. She decided to stay standing rather than risk getting stuck.

The room was warm, well-lit and bright with coloured prints of Bible stories. Moses frowned as he held stone tablets aloft, like the chairman of a hospital board declaiming the rules for female doctors. Little Samuel's mother delivered him to the temple with infinitely more joy than Margaret could have mustered in the same situation. Dropping his nets, Peter turned a head framed with wild dark curls towards the stranger on the shore. He reminded Margaret of her nephew Ed, with his face full of impetuosity and a rock-steady certainty that was yet to be tested.

The room took Margaret back to Sunday afternoons squirm-ing on a wooden seat and trying to recite memorised texts, but also to the vicar's daughter, who overlooked errors but rewarded success with pear drops, and taught rousing, bombastic hymns which appalled the older congregants. That vicar's daughter was probably a suffragette or social reformer by now. Margaret ought to look her up.

Now, however, she had a talk to give. Her audience, aged between teens and middle age, entered and sat down. Three women made no bones about spreading their broad hips across two chairs rather than trying to balance on one. Most sat with arms folded and expressions blank, giving every appearance of cracking mental knuckles. Later, they would have to catch up on the housework, piecework and laundry they'd put aside to listen, and they wouldn't be pleased if their time was wasted.

'Oh no.' Mrs Tomlinson was wringing her hands. 'They've come.'

A group of men was congregating by the door. Most were threadbare. A few were smarter, with one or two in uniform, while an even smaller number, standing slightly apart, seemed well-heeled and in the wrong place entirely. Most looked angry.

Mrs Tomlinson cleared her throat. 'Good afternoon, ladies and, er, gentlemen. May I introduce Dr Demeray of Dorcas Free Hospital, who will speak about keeping hearts and lungs healthy, so that you and your children can avoid going to hospital – or worse, a sanatorium.'

'I ain't worried about chest disease,' sniffed one of the matriarchs who had commandeered two chairs. She had a large bust so uplifted by corsetry that a cat could have lain on it, and a feathered toque perched behind a curled Alexandra fringe. She started to rummage under the high collar of her dress.

Realising what the woman was doing, Margaret addressed the room. 'Educated women like you won't rely on old wives' tales and superstitions, I'm sure.'

The matriarch's hand paused. 'Like what?'

'Blue beads to protect against bronchitis,' said Margaret. 'Strange things can be true.' The woman looked smug. 'But they're often not. I'm sure none of you modern women would rely on a talisman over science, cleanliness and common sense, would you?'

The matriarch's hand moved to scratch her ear.

'The air is definitely cleaner here than in some parts of London,' said Margaret. 'We are a good deal closer to open country than people living in, say, Whitechapel. But I'm afraid—'

'Dirty lazy East-End gets,' remarked a woman in a brown coat. 'Foreigners, most of 'em.'

'The dockers ain't foreign,' said a timid-looking young woman. 'Not usually.'

'The tailors are, Ruth,' said the woman with the blue beads. 'And they're from who knows where. Litnia, Lathuavia, Lancastria – all them places. *And* half of them are arsenics too.'

'I think you mean anarchists, Mrs Wantage,' said Ruth.

'You want a clip round the ear, young woman? Everyone knows it's an arsenic what keeps stirring strikes up, and they may be behind all them girls getting kidnapped and never seen again. The country's going to the dogs. Bring in the army, that's what I say.'

There was a general muttering of agreement.

Margaret attempted to steer the subject back to health. 'There are many reasons why there's unrest, Mrs Wantage, but a lack of blue beads isn't one of them.'

'Don't knock 'em till you've tried 'em,' said Mrs Wantage. 'Doctors don't know everything. Even women ones.'

'*Especially* women ones,' called one of the men. 'Ain't you one of them suffragettes what squeaks in Hyde Park?'

The women turned to look at him. Margaret met his scornful gaze. 'Sometimes. But I am not here to talk about suffrage today.'

'Yeah?'

The women turned back to assess Margaret.

'I'm here to talk about how your heart and lungs work,' she said, 'and how you can do your best to keep them running smoothly.'

Ruth sniggered. 'You mean my insides are like machinery?'

'Exactly,' said Margaret. 'Your body is a mechanism and you have to look after it, just as you do a stove, a sewing machine, a mangle or anything else. Now, I have some diagrams which will help explain.' She turned over a sheet of paper to show the outline of a woman's upper torso with heart and lungs displayed within.

'You can't show that!' shouted another man. 'It's – it's rude.'

'Innards?'

'The outline. You can see her... her shape.'

'There's a good deal less "shape" here than there is on the girl in a bicycle advertisement.'

'Yeah, but that's art, not my missus.'

'But this is—'

'What's wrong with showing the top half of a *man's* body?'

'If you invite me to speak to your group, I'll bring different pictures.'

'Not on your nelly. And keep politics out of this, or we won't be answerable.'

'I'm speaking of how you might improve your health. If anything needs to be done which is outside your control – improving the condition of your home, for example – you can act accordingly. But for now—'

'So you're attacking landlords,' called a tall, blond, well-dressed man. 'Houses round here are fine if the tenants are decent, clean-living people. Changes mean rent rises.' He turned to the poorer men. 'She's stirring up your wives. Women don't understand money. Their lungs and hearts might be the same as men's, but their brains aren't. Everyone knows that.'

The poorer men exchanged glances.

'You're a suffragette,' said another well-dressed man. 'Never mind bodies, a bomb's a mechanism. Have you set one, eh? Shame on you!'

'No, I haven't, and—'

Mrs Wantage levered herself up on Ruth's shoulder, and turned to the men. 'Let the woman speak afore she explodes,' she bellowed.. 'Never mind your brain, mate, *my* brain is capable of listening and deciding. There's women here scrub every day but the black mould keeps coming back. Who's fault's that? The landlord's.' She turned back to Margaret. 'Men's brains *is* different – full of beer and how's yer father. I'd like to see them feed, clothe and house a fambly of ten on what my ole man gives me when he's not on strike – let alone when he is. Now, doctor, keep off the vote and let's see if you can explain how my chest's like a sewing machine.'

With a grunt, she descended into her chair. Several of the men shrugged and left, while the rest leaned against the wall, arms folded.

The talk continued as planned, with only a few objections from the men. Most of the women quelled them, but some looked anxious and a few sidled out, heads bowed, eyes averted. Margaret's heart sank as a girl in her late teens limped away, cringing as one of the men muttered something then followed her outside.

Male or female, most of the audience was coughing with the resigned regularity of those for whom it was as natural as breathing. Some were clearly very sick: a baby was wheezing, a pregnant teenage girl doubled over when she coughed, clutching her belly with one hand and covering her mouth with the other.

Many of the women bore bruises on cheekbones or eye sockets. Towards the end of the talk, after giving out details of savings plans for medical expenses, Margaret mentioned reporting assault to the police or seeking refuge. The audience's expressions ranged from blank to derisive, knowing that nine times out of ten the police would send a woman home and tell to her not to annoy her husband again.

Margaret hadn't intended to do more than give leaflets about Lucy's classes to Mrs Tomlinson, but the dispirited women had made her angry. They deserved a chance to help themselves out of poverty.

'I want to tell you about some day and evening classes in Archbold Street,' she said. 'They teach reading, writing, arithmetic and first aid to women who finished school too early to have much choice of a career. Perhaps some of you might—'

'Who wants to be bossed around by posh ladies with no idea about nothing?' said Mrs Wantage.

'The instructors come from many walks of life,' said Margaret. 'They want to help others find the confidence to improve their lot.'

'I ain't having my missus getting ideas,' said one of the men. 'I need looking after and so do the kids.'

'Girls should know what side their bread's buttered,' said another man.

Two of the women shifted in their seats, studying the floor. But others leaned forward. 'What's it cost?'

'Sixpence a class,' said Margaret. 'But there's a fund to help anyone who can't find the money.'

'I ain't gonna get rapped on the knuckles with a ruler and told to stand in the corner!' There were sniggers and guffaws.

'That won't happen. The idea is to learn so that you have more opportunities in life. If you don't like it, you needn't stay.'

'Perhaps you should go, Ruth,' said Mrs Wantage. 'Then you'll learn that I'm right about the arsenics.'

As soon as the meeting was over, Margaret urged the pregnant girl and the sick baby's mother to consult a doctor, then found Ruth hovering nearby. 'Can I help you?'

'If you'll be at that class on Friday afternoon, I'll go,' said Ruth, in a hurried whisper.

'All right,' said Margaret, wondering how she'd manage that along with preparing to go to Weymouth. 'I shall.'

More men than women were outside when she went to collect her bicycle. One sidled past, leaning down to whisper 'Watch your step' before stalking away to watch at a distance. Margaret tried to reassure herself that she could outpace them, provided they didn't have bicycles too. *But what if they surround you before you can get going?* whispered a treacherous inner voice.

A private motor car drew up on the opposite side of the road. For a second, Margaret thought it was Percival and felt a sense of relief. But when the driver removed his goggles, she realised it was a stranger. He scanned the scene, his eyes settling briefly on her. Then he looked at the men she thought were landlords and beckoned one over.

The inevitable group of boys and men appeared from nowhere to admire the motor car. Mrs Wantage cuffed two heads, then stomped up to Margaret as the motorist climbed out of the car. His gaze flickered towards her again.

'Who's that?' said Margaret.

'Enddles. New bloke what's inherited half the houses in this street, including the ones not fit for rats to live in.' Mrs Wantage stared at the motorist until he looked away. 'He oughta be paying attention to the news.'

'What do you mean?'

Mrs Wantage wasn't listening. 'I'm sticking to me blue beads,' she said. 'Belt and braces, ain't it? But I'll hand it to yer, Dr Demree, you gave a good talk and kept your nerve and stood up to them fools at the back.'

'What do you mean about Mr Enddles needing to read the news?' said Margaret. 'And about girls being snatched? Has that happened round here? I was wondering—'

'That's a lotta questions.' Mrs Wantage scratched her nose. 'No girls been snatched from here. Some of the girls work nights, but I ain't going to be the one to suggest the police should be interested in *them*.'

'I'm interested in their wellbeing, not what someone might call their morals. I know it's not that simple.'

'I believe you.' Mrs Wantage made a tiny gesture with her head towards the women who'd been told to remember which side their bread was buttered. 'They earn better money doing that than doing piece work or seamstressing or charring, but someone else gets most of it in return for a roof over their head and meals. If they're allowed to go to this class, that don't mean they'll be allowed to change their job. And landlords like Mr Enddles cram girls together like rabbits, taking a cut but pretending they don't know what it's from. Then there's the ones whose job it is to snatch the girls who never intended to do the work and force them into it.' A wicked grin crossed her face. 'Mind you, one of them's got his comeuppance ain't he? Butchered.'

'Who—'

But Mrs Wantage had stopped listening. 'What's my sons doing gawping at that car instead of doing their sums?' She grabbed two lads by the ear and dragged them along the pavement.

Mrs Tomlinson joined Margaret. 'I'm so sorry about those men. I hope it won't put you off returning.'

'I'm used to it,' said Margaret. 'Could I ask about Mr End-dles?' She nodded as discreetly as she could towards the motorist.

'Mr...? Oh, Mr Endsleigh. I don't know a great deal.' Mrs Tomlinson pursed her lips. 'He plans to improve things without raising rents. One likes to be charitable and hopes he will.'

'Has there been a murder round here recently?'

'Around here?' Mrs Tomlinson looked towards the skulking girls with genuine distress. 'What kind of murder? If you mean a deliberate attack with malice aforethought, not that I know of. But if you mean someone destroyed by a disease they didn't choose to contract, dead after bearing a child no one wants, or frozen to death in a rented house not fit to live in, then all the time. They're just as much of a murder, in my view.'

'How very true, Mrs Tomlinson,' said Margaret. 'I couldn't agree with you more.'

Seven

By the following morning, Margaret's throat felt scratchy.

After breakfast, she prepared for Mr Radden's inquest, trying not to think of her coughing audience the previous day. The post arrived while Fox went to answer the telephone. There was a brief letter from Captain Blanchett.

There are a lot of Rosies, Rosas, Roses, Rosamunds, and Rosalinds, it said. *There are many Levenes, but few will readily talk to me. So far, I have not found Violet Brahms. Sweatshop workers are reticent. However, rabbi friends from reformed synagogues, with whom I often have theological discussions, might be able to assist.*

I will write again when I discover something.

Fox returned as she was replacing the letter in the envelope. 'Bert will drive us to the coroner's court.'

'Why need you attend?'

'I needn't,' said Fox, his face serious. 'I want to talk with you on the way. Incidentally, I forgot to ask how your talk went yesterday.'

'It felt futile,' said Margaret, packing her briefcase. 'How much can those women do without decent housing or money for medical care? There I was, bleating away before coming back to my nice home, fresh clothes and someone else making my lunch. I might as well prescribe blue beads.'

'I don't know what blue beads mean,' said Fox. 'But your talks allow for their constraints. If nothing else, you explain the importance of doctors' saving schemes and hospital funds.'

'One of the women said that a local procurer had been murdered. She seemed happy about it. Mrs Tomlinson didn't know what she meant.' Margaret looked up to see Fox frowning. 'Is it something to do with your work?'

'I'll explain on the way.'

Once they were in the car, Fox said, 'Can you tell me briefly what you know about Mr Radden.'

Margaret considered. 'He traded in small pieces of art. He lived with his widowed sister. From the photographs of the house, knowing Tibberton Street a little and ignoring the blood, I formed an impression that their life was comfortable but not wealthy.'

'Because?'

'It was decorated in a tasteful, modern way and there were books, but the house is relatively small. I imagine they are much less financially comfortable than us and hugely less so than Maude or Phoebe. They had a char, but I'm not sure if they had any other domestic help.' She wondered what Fox wanted. Presumably, he too had seen the photographs. 'From something Inspector Coulter said, I wondered if he initially thought the sister had murdered him before leaving with her friend on the Thursday, until he realised Mr Radden had died after she'd gone.'

'Could a woman have killed him?'

'Definitely. Especially as he was asleep.'

'Drugged? Drunk?'

Margaret shook her head. 'There were no traces of alcohol and only a small trace of narcotic, which is accounted for by a new bottle of Chlorodyne at the house from which one dose had been taken.'

'Chlorodyne has laudanum in it, doesn't it?'

'Along with cannabis indica, chloroform and goodness knows what else,' said Margaret. 'It's supposed to cure just about everything, but the post-mortem indicated Radden had a cold so he'd presumably taken it for that.'

'And taken enough to render himself unconscious?'

'Only enough to make himself sleepy, maybe.'

'So...' Fox leaned forward.

'So I think Radden was asleep but the murderer struck him to stop him from waking, then stabbed him. No great force was needed, simply determination. The blade was inserted more or less centrally, up under the ribs. It missed bone and pierced the right lobe of his liver.'

'Just the liver.'

'That was all that was needed for him to die. There was only one stab wound. They stabbed Mr Radden, then left him to bleed to death. If they'd removed the knife then death might have been quicker, but not much.'

'Do you think they were aiming for his heart?'

Margaret shrugged. 'They stabbed to the right, not the left, and it seemed like a confident murder, if you know what I mean.'

'A medical professional?'

'I'm not speculating that far.' Margaret secured a loose strand of hair, trying not to think of one of her colleagues standing over a vulnerable human with a weapon and expert knowledge. 'But in my view, the murderer knew the liver might be easier to reach than the heart and how to do so without hitting a rib. Or they knew that pretty much any stab wound in that part of the body could kill, particularly if the victim was left inside a locked house with no hope of getting help. Or possibly it was sheer luck they hit an organ that would bleed so much.'

'No frenzy?'

'None.' Margaret straightened her hat. 'It was calculated. If it was normal burglary, why not just steal the item or, if necessary, knock him out and burgle in peace? Why murder him?'

'Bert got wind of something that might explain it,' said Fox.

'What?'

'And we've obtained information about the post-office box. I wanted you to know before you went to the inquest. And I wanted to ask whether Rosie Levene could have been running from Tibberton Street.'

Margaret thought back. 'Possibly. Why? Rosie was running from someone who'd tried to assault her.'

'That's what she says.'

'She was definitely running and afraid.'

'Two witnesses say they saw someone slender in a longish coat enter Radden's house on Saturday afternoon,' said Fox. 'One says it was a girl. Another that it was a youth.'

'It could have been a giraffe. No one could tell in that fog.'

'Was there blood on Rosie's clothes, apart from what she might have had from the accident?'

'I don't know.' Margaret frowned. 'What is this? Are you suggesting Rosie was burgling that house, nearly got caught, then... No, I'm sure she's been telling the truth. And assuming she wasn't and lashed out with a knife in fear, the wounds would be entirely different.' She contemplated him.

Fox drummed his fingertips on the window frame. 'Mmm.'

'Why is Bert interested in this? Why are you?'

'Mr Radden's main profession was exactly what everyone thinks,' said Fox. 'But some of the objets d'art went abroad in a way that worries Bert. Hence the possibility that it's to do with us, but that's by the by. Mr Radden also traded in a different kind of pretty thing – young girls.'

Margaret gasped. 'You mean the house was a brothel? Or women were kept there against their will? That didn't show in the photographs.'

'The house, as you said, is pleasant and respectable, with an attic full of empty suitcases and a cellar full of coal,' said Fox. 'There's no evidence that anyone but Radden and his sister lived there. He kept his procurement activities completely separate from her, and encouraged her to go away on a regular basis. However, he left a few clues.'

'What?'

'A half-burnt envelope, addressed to the post-office box connected to those advertisements, was in the fireplace, and on a blotting pad it was possible to discern part of a letter from Radden arranging to meet someone at a tearoom for an interview,' said Fox. 'Exactly the sort of thing someone like Rosie would think was safe.'

'Never mind someone like Rosie,' said Margaret. 'You first approached me in a tearoom, then asked me to join you in another, after we bumped into each other during a bicycle ride. I didn't know you at all, yet I agreed. It's that easy to trust someone who seems respectable.'

'I am.'

'None of it was as accidental as you made out, though.'

'Perhaps not, but I had no improper motive. I wanted information and you wanted justice.'

'True. But what's this?'

'As far as we have worked out so far,' said Fox, 'he lured girls to places where they'd feel safe, then presumably arranged for them to be taken who knows where for who knows what illegal purpose. That may have included Rosie.'

'And you think she escaped, tracked him home and killed him? An undernourished, terrified girl of fourteen?'

'That's why I asked about the attack,' said Fox. 'If Rosie – or a girl in her position – had done it, I'd expect it to be more frenzied and less like an execution.'

'Quite.' Margaret wasn't sure if she was glad or not that Fox had given her this information. If she was called to give evidence, could she stop herself from divulging what she now knew? She had pitied Mr Radden. Now she despised him. His murder had seemed shameful, but now it seemed defensible.

'One of them's got his comeuppance, ain't he?' Mrs Wantage had said after talking about women forced into prostitution. 'Butchered.' And she'd smiled in a way that suggested she thought justice had been done.

Had she meant Radden? There were less than three miles between the two districts. The murder had been in the paper, and word of a vengeful murder could have travelled by word of mouth.

Margaret fiddled with the strap of her briefcase. 'Rosie said nothing bad had happened to her yet. She just feared it would. And you said no girls were kept at that house. Even if she went there to kill him, rather than run away, surely she wouldn't have angled a knife and forced it into the liver. That's not instinctive. Instinct, terror or anger would make you stab blindly.'

'I believe you. And as for what I've told you about Radden's illicit activities, none of that will be made public yet.'

'Then why tell me?'

Fox cleared his throat. 'The police know that Rosie was knocked down not far from Tibberton Street. They guess something happened to her, and it might not take long for them to work out a possible connection.'

'No one will get anything useful out of her if she's arrested,' said Margaret.

'Agreed. And she may still be in danger. Whoever Radden traded Rosie to will want to know where she is, and if she witnessed the murder, the murderer may know that. So someone may want her silenced. If the coroner asks if a girl could have killed Radden, say yes, but emphasise how unlikely it would be for the reasons you just gave me. In the meantime, I'll have a word with the police about a hiding place.'

'Rosie might be prepared to go to Maria's,' said Margaret, then realised Fox was looking blank. 'My dressmaker.'

'Ah.'

'It's the last place anyone would expect someone who's run away from seamstressing to hide.'

'Good idea, I'll speak with the police.'

Bert parked outside the courthouse and Fox handed Margaret out of the car. At the entrance, Dr Gesner was checking his pocket watch. Nearby, a slightly built woman in mourning, supported by another, wiped her eyes under a heavy black veil. Two men on the pavement, heads close in conversation, turned as Fox bade Margaret goodbye. One was Inspector Coulter, his face sulky. The other was Inspector Silvermann, who touched his hat to her.

'You've finally turned up,' said Inspector Coulter. 'I thought you might be too contrary, like you were at the post-mortem.'

'Watch your lip, Coulter,' said Inspector Silvermann. 'If you don't treat Dr Demeray with respect, I'll have even more words with your super. This wouldn't be a Yard matter if you'd done your job properly in the first place.'

Inspector Coulter swore under his breath and stalked towards the courthouse.

'Good afternoon, Inspector,' said Margaret. 'What have I done to earn your praise?'

'Possibly nothing,' said Inspector Silvermann. 'But if anyone's going to give you a hard time it'll be me, not some halfwit from D division. You might be a thorn in my side, but you're my thorn and it's my side, and now this is my case. I've read your report, and can tell you now that we have witnesses who think they saw Radden on Friday. I know I always tell you I don't want supposition, but this time I do. So go on.'

Margaret held his gaze. 'The attack wasn't frenzied,' she said. 'Whoever killed Mr Radden knew exactly what they were doing. An execution, an assassination – take your pick. But it wasn't emotional. It was business.'

'Does Dr Gesner think so too?'

'He'd probably express it differently, but yes.'

The inspector nodded. 'Me too. I'll avoid calling you because I don't want any accusations of feminine sentiment.' He held up a hand. 'Not *my* accusations. We both know how the press twisted your completely unsentimental evidence last time, and it would muddy the already filthy waters that I'm trying to clear. I'm sorry. But justice is more important than pride, isn't it?'

With a sigh, Margaret nodded.

'Good. So can you ask Dr Gesner to make this clear: it was one wound, inflicted in a way that indicates skill and knowledge. Leave the rest to the press's cursed imagination.'

'All right.'

'I won't ask what your old man told you,' said the inspector. 'But people can't take the law into their own hands, whether from fear, for revenge, or taking care of business. Coulter's been considering the girl at your hospital as a possible suspect, but...'

'I don't believe she'd kill in that way.'

'No. But it's possible she was there and could identify who else was. If so, she's at risk. I need to find a place for her where she's safe and unlikely to abscond.'

'I've suggested somewhere to Fox. Speak with him.'

The inspector rolled his eyes. 'I knew it would be wasting my breath to tell you to keep out of things. Do you know anything else that's useful?'

Margaret gave Dr Gesner a little wave to indicate she'd join him shortly. 'Two things: Rosie knows someone called Violet Brahms who might apply for the same job. A Salvation Army officer is trying to find her in Whitechapel, as well as Rosie's family. Secondly, I gave a talk in St Mark's parish hall yesterday morning. One of the women mentioned with relish the murder of a man who trafficked girls. I didn't connect it at the time because I didn't realise what sort of person Radden was.'

'Good luck to your Sally Army chap. He'll need it. As for your woman, she won't talk to the police, more's the pity.'

'Well...' Margaret pondered. 'I might be able to ask a class in Archbold Street this afternoon and find out what they know.'

'Is that all you've got?'

'So far,' said Margaret, 'I'm afraid it is.'

Eight

'A verdict of murder by person or persons unknown was expected,' said Dr Gesner, as he and Margaret walked back to Dorcas Free after the inquest. 'But I felt the police were withholding something. Perhaps Mr Radden had a secret. An unmarried man of that age might be supposed to have a mistress, which would bring his moral integrity into question. Perhaps they wanted to spare his sister's blushes.'

Mrs Vidler was the last word in respectability. Apparently in her mid-thirties, a pillar of the local church, she and a bosom friend were encouraged by her brother to visit pleasant seaside towns where they stayed at better-class temperance hotels and through letters of introduction from their own church visited other churches, filling their days and evenings with pleasant, refined activities.

She had explained the setup of their home, which they had bought jointly with money inherited from their parents, and how her income from monies and property, bequeathed by her husband, fed into the household. In addition to the char there was a daily cook-general who lived out. However, the cook-general was always given leave when Mrs Vidler was away, Mr Radden saying that he would shift for himself.

'We're decent people,' Mrs Vidler had gasped through her sobs. 'Why should such a thing happen in our lovely home?'

'You're probably right,' said Margaret. 'She may be in for a shock.'

'*Lügen haben kurze Beine.*'

'Lies have short legs?'

'Or, as your Shakespeare would say, truth will out.' Dr Gesner indicated she should enter the hospital before him. 'Won't it?'

Margaret glanced about: no one was in earshot. 'I gathered from Inspector Silvermann that Mr Radden was not in any way a decent man. He died not far from where Rosie Levene was running. I think the police want to establish if there's a connection.'

'Ah,' said Dr Gesner. 'From what I have heard of Miss Levene, I would have said that she was scared rather than guilty. Do you agree?'

'I do.'

'Perhaps there's evidence in the hospital which will stop them harassing a frightened girl.'

'Checking the clothes she was wearing on admission may help.'

'They'll have been laundered for when she leaves.'

Margaret smiled. 'Don't you recall? Dr Naylor said she had the details recorded in case of any prosecution. It won't take long. I'll say someone wants to know if Rosie's clothes are fit to be worn. They'll think the Lady Almoner is asking.'

'I'll order tea,' said Dr Gesner. 'We'll review the evidence in case we're needed again and then, since you're here, prepare for next week.'

Margaret put her things in her office, then went to the laundry. Somewhat surprised, the chief laundress went through the ledger until she reached the entry for *Unknown, Rosie*. No one had amended it with the proper surname.

'Here you go,' said the laundress. She started to read laboriously. '"Thin knitted black gloves. Calf-length black coat mired with road oil and dirt." Lucky there weren't any horse apples, hey? "Otherwise clean. Good quality once. Boots sturdy, a little too big. Soles worn but uppers polished. Stockings and underwear inferior. Corset didn't fit right." What is all this? It's normally just a list. Oh, now I recall. Dr Naylor had some nurse probationer write it all down. Wish she hadn't. All this reading's making my head hurt.'

Margaret thought hard. The murderer would be likely to have the victim's blood fanning up the sleeve of whichever hand they had used. If she could be certain that didn't apply to Rosie's clothes, it would be a step forward.

The laundress ran her finger along the next line in the ledger. '"Calf-length grey skirt, grey cardigan, white blouse."'

'Any blood?' said Margaret.

'Course not. We're experts. You should know that, with the amount of muck you get on your things, and we get them back to you like they was fresh from the shop.'

'Before laundering, on Rosie's cuffs?'

The laundress looked at Margaret as if she were several drums short of a marching band. 'She had gloves on, din't she?' She peered at the ledger. 'But if you want proof, this says "Blood on blouse and stockings, around elbows and knees, where the skin broke on impact with motor car." I never seen so much stuff recorded.'

'One doesn't argue with Dr Naylor.'

'Hmm.' The laundress looked as if she might.

'It might be needed if the police prosecute the driver who knocked her down.'

'Poor kid.' The laundress shook her head, then brightened. 'Reckon the Lady Almoner can find Rosie Unknown a liberty bodice? She doidn't need a corset yet from what I gather.' She prodded herself in the waist. 'Not like us, eh, doctor, what with the revenges of time. Perhaps I need more keeping in and you need more keeping up, but either way, a liberty bodice wouldn't do nothing for neither of us. Meaning no offence, acourse.' She smiled blandly and closed the ledger.

'None taken,' said Margaret, and added a shilling to a collection tin for the laundresses' Christmas treat.

After leaving the laundry, it was all she could do not to seek a floor-length mirror to check what the 'revenges' of time had done to her. She returned to the mortuary wing, surreptitiously measuring her waist with her hands.

Miss Upton hailed her from the clerk's desk. 'Got a tummy ache, doctor?'

'What? Oh no. Just checking my clothes were sitting neatly.'

'A gent's here to see you.'

'But I'm not supposed to be here today.'

'He didn't know that,' said Miss Upton, handing over a card. 'And since you *are* here, I thought he might as well stay. I didn't quite know what to do with him. Luckily, Dr Gesner took him into his office. He's ordered extra tea.'

Margaret read the card. It said *Augustus Endsleigh, Esq.*, and gave the address and telephone number of a gentlemen's club in Mayfair.

'Oh my,' she said.

In office, both men stood as Margaret entered. Mr Endsleigh shook hands before they all sat. Up close and without the motoring clothes, he was a tall, attractive man with warm, friendly eyes.

'Mr Endsleigh would like to hear how Dorcas Free strives to help the poor,' said Dr Gesner.

Margaret accepted a cup of tea and nodded as if the mortuary wing was the normal place to find out. Mr Endsleigh's polite expression gave no indication that they'd locked eyes across a road full of rundown houses the day before. She had no similar inclination for pretence. 'Did I not see you yesterday, outside St Mark's parish hall?'

'You did,' said Mr Endsleigh. His accent was as immaculate as his clothes and bearing. He embodied Savile Row, Jermyn Street and Mayfair, and looked almost as out of place in a hospital as he had in a rundown district. 'I'm partly here to ask about your talk. I fear my agents reported it inaccurately.'

'Indeed?' said Margaret. 'What did they say?'

'That you were a suffragette encouraging women to be improper, to be disobedient to their husbands, and to make unreasonable demands of landlords. They thought you might burn something down or blow it up.' His eyes twinkled. 'In that neighbourhood, it would probably improve things if you did.'

Margaret struggled to keep her expression neutral. 'The talk was about women keeping themselves and their families as healthy as possible, specifically in relation to respiratory illness. The "impropriety" relates to my showing them diagrams of the *inside* of a female torso. This offended some of the men's delicate sensibilities because the outline – and I *mean* outline – was female. I was in no way political, other than by saying that if they felt their housing was inadequate and causing them sickness, they should tell their landlord.'

'As I thought,' said Mr Endsleigh. 'They reported your talk in the light of prejudice rather than fact. Perhaps the woman who spoke with you did the same with regard to me. I mean the stout woman, not Mrs Tomlinson. But I'm sure you wouldn't believe anything without evidence.'

Margaret could feel her face warming, and sipped her tea in the hope that any blush would be attributed to that. 'Of course not.'

'I recently inherited some properties in that district which I intend to improve. They are woefully inadequate: insanitary at best, death traps at worst. Several families may live in houses designed for one, and in some dwellings illegal and illicit activities take place. I regret that the person who bequeathed them to me was happy to profit regardless. He and I share the same name, of course, so possibly your informer assumes we're one and the same. But we aren't. What did the woman say?'

'Pretty much what you assume.'

'Then, one hopes one has put that right.'

'I'm glad you're making improvements in the neighbour-hood,' said Dr Gesner. 'This is not a chest hospital per se, but the chest ward is always full. Dr Demeray and I undertake many post-mortems after death from respiratory disease. And there are patients on the fracture ward who have fallen down un-safe stairs or through rotten floorboards. Much local housing is shockingly substandard.'

'Not everyone on the fracture ward is the same, surely,' said Mr Endsleigh. 'I gather you admit those who are knocked down in the street too.'

Margaret took another sip of tea. 'What makes you say so?'

'Something in the paper. One doesn't want to be blamed for *every* patient.' He smiled and leaned forward a little. 'I *shall* improve those houses. Immoral activity *will* cease. The area *will* become pleasant and safe. But it is not simple. Decent, respectable occupants have to live somewhere, yet one can't improve or rebuild with them in the house. If one evicted them meanwhile – where would they go? Places like Devil's Acre were cleared, what, sixty years ago, and rebuilt. The areas are transformed – pleasant, respectable, healthy. But the original tenants weren't allowed back after those infernal slums were destroyed, were they? Now they're in Whitechapel and the like, existing in even worse conditions.'

Margaret remembered Anna saying that her grandmother had been evicted from a rookery with nowhere to go but Whitechapel, along with countless displaced others to swell the population of an already overcrowded area which had been the settling-place of immigrants for generations. Once it had been Huguenots, later those escaping famine in Ireland, now Jewish families fleeing Russian pogroms. Added to those were sailors and clerks from Indian, African and Caribbean colonies, looking for work in the Empire's capital. Perhaps it wasn't surprising that Mrs Wantage's assumptions about Mr Endsleigh were as skewed as his land agents' were about Margaret. Mrs Wantage feared eviction more than she feared black mould.

'If you encourage your tenants to form a residents' committee and discuss things with them, maybe it's simpler than you think,' said Margaret. 'The illicit activity is a harder matter to deal with, I know, but—'

Mr Endsleigh sniffed. 'Quite immoral. The police are failing in their duty.'

'It's not simple.'

'It's criminal,' said Mr Endsleigh. 'I have no compunction in putting those debased women out on the street. Then I can improve the properties they were infesting so that my respectable tenants can move into them while I improve the next set of houses. I have no intention of evicting anyone decent and moral.'

'I understand what you're trying to do,' said Margaret. 'But the women you'd call indecent may have little choice in how they make their living and need a different kind of help. Some are little more than children.'

'Then they should go to a reformatory.' Mr Endsleigh took a breath and smiled again. 'However, your idea about a tenants' association is a good one. I shall ask Reverend Tomlinson to set up a public meeting. Perhaps one or both of you can come.'

'The Member of Parliament will help,' said Margaret. 'Mr Percival Pendleberry.'

'Really?' said Mr Endsleigh. 'He owns properties too, you know. And then there are all the rumours. I hope they're as unfounded in his case as mine.' He rose and bowed. 'Now we've cleared the air, I'll bid you adieu.'

Dr Gesner rose and escorted him from the room.

I thought Etta was being ridiculous to worry about Percival's reputation, thought Margaret. *What if she was serious and that was why I felt uneasy at Phoebe's dinner?*

'Had you heard anything about Mr Pendleberry?' she asked, when Dr Gesner returned.

Her colleague paused as if weighing up what to say.

'One doesn't like to repeat rumours without substantiation,' he said, at last. 'But I've heard that Mr Pendleberry is profiting from slum dwellings, despite his avowed principles. He has denied it. But it is merely a whisper. I've seen nothing expressed publicly, which suggests someone trying to slander him. But...'

'People believe what they want to.'

'He is a family friend is he not? I'll trust your judgement over anyone else's. Back to business: what did you discover at the laundry?

'There's no record of blood stains suggesting Rosie stabbed anyone. Perhaps we should look at the clothes ourselves.'

'It's too late,' said Dr Gesner. 'She was discharged while we were talking with Mr Endsleigh.'

'How do you know?'

'A message was left with Miss Upton. Matron thought you would be interested that a dressmaker called Maria Edwards collected Rosie and will give her a secure place to stay. Although the pressmen who keep telephoning to ask about the girl who was run down, will simply be told she's gone home. Do you have concerns? I'm sure there's still time to fetch her back.'

'Not at all,' said Margaret. 'I know Mrs Edwards and think it's an ideal solution.'

'Is she a relation of your friend, Miss Elinor Edwards? Her mother, perhaps?'

'No relation whatsoever,' said Margaret. 'It's a common name.' She relaxed a little. 'Since Rosie's safe, shall we discuss next week's work, as you suggested? Then I must make my way to my cousin's class. I promised one of the young women from the parish hall I'd be there. I hope she turns up, because I'd rather be at home supervising the packing for Weymouth and don't fancy listening to my cousin teach Shakespeare.'

'"Study is like heaven's glorious sun",' said Dr Gesner.

'I bet when Shakespeare wrote that he didn't know he'd be the one people were studying,' said Margaret. 'I'd very much prefer a penny dreadful.'

Nine

S hortly before two, Margaret crossed the road to the building where the class would be held, having had a pleasant lunch in a small restaurant opposite. She had watched the young women entering the building with interest. Their ages ranged between fourteen and perhaps twenty. Many appeared to be maids on their half-day, out of uniform and dressed in an approximation of the latest smart fashion. Then there were a few young women like Ruth or Rosie, not as smartly dressed, and in the main carrying string bags rather than handbags to hold whatever notebooks and pencils they had.

The two groups didn't mingle if they arrived together, but they had the same look of determination and anticipation. *Presumably Shakespeare doesn't daunt them*, thought Margaret. *Perhaps studying it as adults, rather than stumbling and droning through it as a child, makes it more pleasurable. It'll be fun to see how Lucy manages any saucy passages.*

She made for the building just as Ruth came down the street, glancing around as if worried that someone she knew would see her. Whether that was because they'd jeer or because they'd tell her she didn't belong was hard to tell. She had the cowed look of a mistreated cat or dog that wasn't sure it could trust a new owner. Seeing Margaret, she smiled and walked faster, her demeanour more confident.

'How do, doctor,' she said. 'Glad you could make it.'

'Likewise, Ruth,' said Margaret. 'Shall we go in? I shan't stay for the whole lesson: I need to get home to my children. Oh, and is your name really Ruth? Mrs Wantage does seem to muddle things.'

Ruth chuckled. 'It is. So's hers. I think that's the only reason she can remember mine.'

She became shy again when handing over her sixpence and giving the simplest of details for registration, then walked across the hall and up the stairs alongside Margaret. She entered the classroom first, her hand trembling a little on the doorknob.

The classroom was warm, a low fire burning in the grate. Warmer, in fact, than Margaret remembered the school for which her uncle had paid a good deal of money. It seemed happier, too. There were times tables and alphabets on the walls, but also prints of different types of art, and sketches and written work by students.

Lucy stepped down from a small dais equipped with a black-board, which faced rows of tables behind which young women sat with notebooks, slates and pencils at the ready. They all looked at Ruth as she entered and smiled. One waved from the far side of the room. 'Yoohoo, Ruthie!'

'That's my cousin Mary!' gasped Ruth, before Lucy could finish her welcome. 'She's a char over Tottenham way. I haven't seen her in months, but she's a sight for sore eyes now. If it's good enough for her, it's good enough for me. Can I sit with her, Miss Frampton?'

'Sit wherever you like,' said Lucy. 'All I ask is that you wait your turn to speak and that if you're bored or have to go, you leave quietly without disrupting the others. Dr Demeray might prefer to sit at the back. I shan't be tempted to ask her questions that way.'

Margaret grinned. 'I'll sit by the door so that I can slip out in half an hour. If she's teaching Shakespeare, mine is rather rusty.'

Lucy laughed. 'It's just as well I'm not teaching it, then.'

'Aren't you?'

'Not in this class. I use short stories – anything funny or thrilling, and as many as I can with women as capable and interesting human beings. I do some of the reading and others take turns if they're comfortable. Their confidence grows, you know. They start off feeling alone. Then they realise they all want the same thing – to increase their opportunities – and start helping each other. When they progress to another class they'll do more difficult books and plays, but not yet.'

'I really am proud of you,' said Margaret. 'It's hard to remember you're not quite twenty-one. That finishing school must have been worthwhile, though you hated it.'

'Huh,' said Lucy. 'That was all about finding a husband. An utter waste of money.'

'Your parents meant well.'

'Huh.'

'Do you mind if I sketch while I'm here? More to the point, will the class?'

'They're used to it: Reuben is here quite often. He's helped us with advertising, making posters for nothing.'

'Reuben?'

'Your friend. *You* know, the artist.'

'I thought you were only acquaintances through me.' But Lucy had already walked back to the dais and was starting the class.

Margaret sat down near the door, puzzled. Reuben was a young artist she'd met two years previously and occasionally invited to family celebrations, where he'd met Margaret's family. She'd never noticed him talking to Lucy in particular, nor realised they'd kept in touch.

Apart from working as resident artist for a moving-picture company in which Margaret had invested a small amount of money, Reuben also illustrated for magazines. Presumably he'd come to know of the class through the latter – although how he could afford to make posters for nothing was a mystery. It was a few months since she'd last seen him, though. Perhaps something had changed.

She concentrated as Lucy publicly welcomed Ruth, explained how things ran, then announced the name of the story they'd be discussing and started to read it aloud.

'"Madeleine Dupont had been missing for two days before her brother consulted the Baker and Clark Detective Agency. He declared that she had vanished into thin air yet the police had done nothing, and—"'

'Well, we all know where *she* went,' said Ruth's cousin Mary.

'At least one of the bastards what snatches girls has been got,' said another girl. 'Stuck like a pig, I hear.'

'What's that like, then Nance?'

'I ain't a country bumpkin like some, but it doesn't take much to work out.'

Lucy rapped on her lectern. 'I'm happy for us to have a discussion instead of reading,' she said. 'If so, can we remember this is a lesson and keep to facts.'

'I want to hear the story, not listen to gossip!' said another girl rolling her eyes. Her whole posture so far suggested she was waiting to hear something she didn't already know but anticipated being disappointed.

'Give over, Sadie,' snapped Nance. 'It's not gossip. It's fact.'

'I don't know what you're talking about,' said one of the youngest girls.

'Then you should,' said Ruth's cousin Mary. 'It could be you next.'

Lucy rapped the lectern again. 'I have a suggestion. I'll jot any facts Nance can tell us on the blackboard. Then I would like you to spend ten minutes writing an article on the subject, as if it were going in a newspaper. When you've handed them in for marking I'll read the rest of this story and we can discuss it.'

The girls looked at each other and shrugged.

'If you like this idea, raise your hand and we'll follow the majority – that is, what most people want.' Most of the hands went up. 'Then that's what we'll do. Now, Nance, tell us succinctly – that is, simply and briefly –where the girl in the story might have gone and why, and I'll write that down. Then I'll come to you, Mary and ask you what *you* meant and why. Please answer without using sensational language, and without adding details you can't possibly know. I'll write that down. Then I'll ask anyone with something to add or ask to raise their hand, and I'll write *that* down.' She glanced sideways at Margaret. 'Please don't lie, exaggerate or say anything to us that you ought to be telling the authorities.' Low muttering greeted this. 'I know many of you don't like the police and I understand why. If you do know something important, tell me afterwards and I'll help you get that information to them without being inconvenienced or embarrassed. Perhaps you know something which could save another girl from disappearing.'

'They take all sorts, Miss Frampton,' said Mary. 'Even ladies. One nearly got nabbed in the theatre the other week. You just got to be what they want. A pretty girl like you would be right up their street.'

Lucy blinked then held her chalk up to the board. 'Let's start with facts, shall we. Come along, Nance: I'll time you. Sixty seconds and no frills, please.'

Margaret sat forward, her own notebook ready, and listened as Lucy guided the class, jotting down only the barest information before setting a task of turning it into an article.

Supposition and regurgitated tales of white-slave traders and foreign harems were mingled with facts. These included the names of girls who'd disappeared or been found dead, references to Jack the Ripper who'd terrorised East London ten years before they were born, and, to Margaret's horror, the fact that a Marylebone man responsible for trading in girls had been stabbed and his body taken to a local hospital afterwards. To her relief, they seemed certain the post-mortem had taken place in St Mary's, undertaken by 'that bloke what got Dr Crippen arrested.'

Lucy was trembling a little as she left them to write and sat next to Margaret. 'How much of that is true?'

'If you take out the embellishment, a good deal,' said Margaret. 'If afterwards someone says something that might need passing on, will you let me know? Anything about advertisements offering jobs that don't exist perhaps. Don't prompt them, just see if it comes out.'

'Yes, of course.'

'I ought to go before someone asks me about post-mortems. We did one on someone who was stabbed, but nothing in the press suggests he was anything other than an innocent victim of burglary. I'd like to hear what your pupils think they know.'

'It's hard to separate fact from fiction.'

'That's what Percival said. It's true.'

'I never know how this class will go,' said Lucy. 'First aid is much less trouble. Although this lot might ask how to deal with someone stuck like a pig.'

'Probably,' said Margaret. 'Please do take care going home. Take a cab please. Or I could come back for you.'

'Not today: a friend is collecting me. Next week, perhaps. I'll write if anything more comes of this.'

Closing her own front door behind her, Margaret felt drained. The family would be taking a late train to Weymouth shortly after Fox came home, so that they had the whole of Saturday to enjoy. Just now, though, she wished they weren't going at all.

The sense of relief she'd felt about Rosie going to Maria's had been drowned by what Lucy's class had said, and the cold, damp November air as she cycled home had made her chest feel tight. She changed into a loose tea-gown and went to the nursery to play with the children.

After a few minutes of crawling around with them and their toys, she lay down on the rug in front of the low, well-guarded fire and let them crawl over her instead.

'Mummy a lion!' said Alec, pulling Margaret's hairpins out, then spreading strands of hair across the carpet.

'Mummy's a sleepy lion,' said Margaret. 'Why don't the cubs cuddle up and go to sleep?'

'Mummy a road,' said Edie. 'Beep beep! Neigh neigh! Choo choo!'

Something rolled over the hills and dells of Margaret's face and body. It had wheels, and even with Edie's jerky handling, it felt oddly relaxing till it got to Margaret's stomach. Whether it was the cream of mushroom soup from lunchtime or the 'revenges of time' now free of a corset, the rolling and prodding made Margaret feel queasy, then want to cough.

'Enough, darling,' she said, opening her eyes and sitting up. She removed the remainder of the pins, put them in her pocket and let her curls fall loose.

'Mummy pity hair,' said Edie, dropping a wooden train to stroke it.

'That's much nicer.'

'Edie brush?'

The thought of a brush tugging at her waist length hair made Margaret wince. 'Not today. Come and cuddle up and sing me a lullaby.'

'Alec read a story?' said Alec.

'Yes, please.' Not that he could read, of course, but Alec liked to pretend, repeating what he could recall of his favourite stories and making others up.

She lay on the rug with Edie and felt a curl being twiddled. What was probably a picture book was rested against her and over Edie's tuneless crooning she heard Alec's voice. 'Unssaponatime Alecanedie anmummyandaddy annellieanfreda went on a pickanicka...'

'She shouldn't sleep like that, sir. There's a draught.' Nellie's voice sounded more anxious than disapproving. 'Especially with that cough.'

'What cough?' Margaret opened her eyes and found herself staring into Fox's face. 'Has Edie started again?' She sat up, small toys falling off her as she did so. The children were putting things away in a box and their tea awaited them on a low table.

'No,' said Fox. 'But *you* were coughing a little.' He was grinning as he helped her to her feet. 'I expect you'll want to change before we take the train, but I think you look very fetching. I wasn't sure about the zoo on your tummy, but I like the folderols in your hair and the addition to your decolletage, and you have a becoming flush.'

Margaret reached up and felt ribbons wound inexpertly round her curls, then looked down at the socks tucked into her chemise. 'One does one's best to be à la mode.' Her throat felt raw, her bones were chilled. But Nellie was right. Falling asleep on the floor wasn't sensible.

She kissed the children, then tidied herself in the bedroom and followed Fox downstairs.

'Thank you for taking up my suggestion that Maria might offer a safe place for Rosie,' she said.

'Inspector Silvermann's doing,' said Fox. 'He doesn't think Rosie's guilty of murder, but if she knows something useful, he's hoping she'll tell Maria. I've arranged for a female clerk to work in the house as a maid to make sure Rosie doesn't disappear again. Oh yes, and I had someone look into Endsleigh. He's recently inherited, he's made noises about improving his properties and he has no record of any former impropriety, so I think what you heard was either malicious gossip or a misunderstanding.'

'I know.'

'Good.'

'So everything's under control.'

'Completely,' said Fox. 'There's nothing more for you to do.'

Ten

When Katherine was born, the nursemaid hired for her mother was a girl called Ada, who later looked after Margaret, then became the family's cook-general, then later Katherine and James's cook-general. Despite being offered a sizeable pension at sixty, she only agreed to retire when Katherine conspired with Ada's niece in Weymouth and explained that Ada's expertise was essential to running the niece's small hotel.

Fox had hired the whole place for the family for the weekend; largely, he said, for the pleasure of watching Margaret being admonished by the only person who could get away with it.

Rocked by the train journey, the children were fast asleep when they arrived, and stayed asleep all night, but not having seen them for a year, the following morning Ada greeted them with delight. 'Miss Edie has exactly the same contrary expression as you did, Miss Meg,' she said. 'She'll be climbing out of windows before you know it.'

The little girl in question gave Ada a huge grin, squeezing her eyes shut.

'It was Kitty who climbed out of a window.'

Ada snorted. 'You both did. You tried to make me mend your drawers once, saying you'd torn them climbing over a stile. As if we had stiles in Fulham. Not that I did it, of course, Mr F. I made her darn them herself, and make it pretty too.'

Fox's mouth twitched. 'I should hope so.'

'Really, Ada.' Margaret's face burned.

'This young chap looks like the sensible one.' Ada patted Alec's head. 'What do you like, young man?'

'Daggons,' said Alec.

'Dragons?' said Ada. 'Well, there are plenty in Dorset.'

'Do you mean people, or fossils?' said Fox.

Ada tapped her nose and winked.

'You needn't have given up your sitting room for Father,' said Margaret. 'He could easily manage with us in the one for guests.'

'It's full of things he and Miss Kitty gave me from the house in Fulham. It's nice to feel at home when you're old.'

'You'll never be old, Ada.'

'I didn't mean me. Take the twins to him. I'll bring something to eat and drink. His friend won't be collecting him until eleven, but I know you and Mr F want to go for a walk. Nancy will help with the children if needed.'

Margaret and Fox found her father in Ada's light-filled upper sitting room, sitting in a comfortable chair with a view of the quay. On a low table was a special box containing 'treasures' – buttons, bobbins, thimbles and finger puppets – which Margaret's late stepmother Thirza had assembled to keep small children entertained. When they bored with that, Margaret's father would send them to find a wooden set of dragons he'd had made when Ed was two. Seventeen years ago, the hunt had taken place in a park. Nowadays, a sitting room had to suffice.

'Ampa! Box!' demanded Alec. 'Ampa! Daggons!'

Margaret turned to the maid, who was jigging in her excitement to take the twins. 'Just a moment, Nancy: Alec at least is rather damp. I'll—'

'Let me, madam. It'll be a pleasure, the little angels.'

'Pleasure? Angels?' Margaret looked at her offspring in doubt. 'It's like wrestling with eels.'

'Pshaw,' said Nancy. 'They're no match for me. I likes a challenge.'

Margaret relinquished the twins with relief, sat beside Fox, then scanned the walls. Alongside photographs of Ada's family, were ones of the Demerays including a picture of Katherine as a prim fourteen-year-old holding hands with five-year-old Margaret, both of them looking as if whatever bribe they'd been offered to look sisterly wasn't worth it.

There were also scenes from the far-flung places her father had visited in the eighties and nineties, in which he stood with his assistant Henry against a backdrop of mountains, forests and obscure villages.

'You should have taken Katherine,' she blurted out. 'She wanted to go so much.'

'Taken her where?'

'On your travels.'

'Oh.' Her father compared the photographs – wild, rugged landscapes and little girls in frills and ribbons.

'Didn't *you* want to go?' said Fox.

Margaret wrinkled her nose. Her father had barely stayed home after her mother died. She'd been a little girl at first, her mother's memory fading as shy Aunt Alice emerged from the shadows to replace people who couldn't be replaced.

The grief and sense of abandonment Margaret couldn't express had come out in bad temper and rebellion against Aunt Alice's soft discipline.

There were occasional parties and balls thrown by wealthier cousins, and to start with, fashionable clothes to wear to them, but even as a selfish teenaged girl, Margaret had sensed Katherine felt she was being briefly let out of a box before being put back in to do her duty.

They had both hung on every word when their father returned with his magic-lantern shows and photographs, but it was Katherine who constantly begged to travel too.

As a child, Margaret had compared those images of dusty, heat-scorched villages and the rough clothes that Father and Henry had worn with leafy Fulham and her own pretty dresses and shoes. She decided she'd rather stay home with Ada and Aunt Alice. Looking back now on that self-centred child, Margaret knew she should grant herself some grace. It wasn't so much a lack of desire to travel, as a fear that if she left all the ornaments and china and embroidery that had been her mother's, Mother herself would fade away entirely.

'Not then,' she said. 'Now I would.'

'Ladies didn't travel,' said her father firmly.

'What nonsense, Father. Isabella Bird was trekking in America before Kitty was even born. Fay Fuller, Gertrude Bell and Mary Kingsley were all travelling the world when Kitty was begging you to let her go with you. If you'd taken her, perhaps you wouldn't have got lost. And if I'd come too, perhaps I'd have stopped being frivolous and self-absorbed a good deal sooner.'

Her father slowly shook his head. 'I'd lost your mother. What if I'd lost you too?'

Before Margaret could respond, Nancy returned with the twins followed by Ada carrying a loaded tray.

'Bikkits!' said Edie.

'Your grandpapa asked me to make them specially Miss Edie,' said Ada. 'I did my best.' She offered a plate of biscuits made using animal cutters, then iced green with red round their mouths. Margaret saw sickly, murderous bunnies, chickens and kittens, but to the children...

'Oooh!' said Alec, inspecting one with glee. 'Daggon!'

'They're perfect,' said Margaret. 'But there's only enough for three, so Daddy and I will do something else.'

'Will you go in a naryplane like Ed?' said Edie, jumping up and running with her arms outstretched. 'I wanna fly a nary-plane all around the whirl.'

'Will you take me?' said Margaret.

'Acourse I will, Mummy. And Alec and Daddy and Nellie and Freda and Juniper and Ampa.'

'Goodness,' said Fox. 'An air-omnibus. But just now we'll go for a walk along the esplanade, and Nellie and Freda will go shopping.'

'Will you be all right, Ada?' asked Margaret.

'Perfectly,' said Ada, her eyes fixed on the twins. 'I couldn't be happier.'

After lunch, Margaret, Fox, Gil and Raoul took a long walk round the harbour. People were milling on the quay as the boat for the Channel Islands prepared to leave.

'Shall we take some photographs?' said Fox.

He, Margaret and Raoul took it in turns with a small camera. Margaret suspected most of Fox's photos would turn out to be focussed on the harbour and ship rather than the people posing in front of him, in case there was something useful to be gained. She was preparing to take a final one of her own when she realised Raoul was smiling at someone behind her.

'Bonjour, Monsieur Andreyev! Ça va? What a surprise to see you in Weymouth.'

She turned to find an elegant man in a smart overcoat, carrying a small leather valise.

'Monsieur Favre. How do you do?' Monsieur Andreyev made a small bow and shook hands. If he was foreign-born, it was impossible to tell from an English accent as cut-glass as Mr Endsleigh's. 'And Dr Trewellan too. And these are...?'

'Dr Demeray and—' Raoul's pronunciation was markedly French-sounding.

'Good day, Monsieur Docteur de Marais, Madame de Marais,' said Monsieur Andreyev. 'I'm afraid I have a boat to catch. My staff and belongings are already there. Are you sailing too? If so, we are all behind.'

'Not us,' said Raoul. 'Bon voyage.'

'Merci. Jersey was one of Marie's favourite places, Dr Trewellan. I am visiting in her memory.' Monsieur Andreyev tipped his hat and departed at pace.

'A friend?' said Margaret.

'No,' said Gil. 'He rented a place from Raoul's family while his wife Marie stayed at the sanatorium. She was nice, but too sick to recover. I didn't take to him. He didn't seem to be greatly affected when she died. But you know what it's like, Margaret. Sometimes they're simply drained from caring. It's easy to be uncharitable.'

'Here,' said Fox, 'let me take the last photograph.'

They posed, then turned away from the sea and walked alongside Radipole Lake towards the swannery.

'Nice fresh air here,' said Fox. 'And hospitals that doubtless need shaking up by a female doctor.'

Margaret breathed deep, then coughed. He was right on both fronts. And the hills ahead of them and the sea behind were beautiful. But it wasn't London.

'Even fresher in Switzerland,' said Gil. 'With a sanitorium begging for a female doctor.'

'Poor Madame le médecin,' said Monsieur Favre. 'She should not be bullied so.'

'Merci, Raoul,' said Margaret. 'I— What's going on?'

Ahead of them a small group of people stood by the lake watching a policeman hunch over a boat. Hands were pointing and gesticulating across the water, and a police whistle shrilled.

Gil and Raoul moved forward, but Fox held Margaret back. 'What about it?' he said. 'Gil has a job for you. The climate's better for Edie. Let's move.'

'All my family is in London. You'd still be away for weeks at a time.'

'I'd always come back,' said Fox, kissing her. 'And you'd be somewhere safe.'

Safe, Margaret thought. *Is safe what I want?*

'Dr Demeray!' called Gil.

The policeman stepped back to reveal a huddled shape in the bottom of the boat: a curled form in jacket and trousers, with an overcoat bundled at the stern. One rowlock was empty. 'It's a poor frozen lad. He must have lost an oar.'

'We're doctors,' said Gil, indicating himself and Margaret. 'Let us see.'

The policeman shrugged. 'There's nothing to be done, sir. He's dead.' He started to prod the body as a sergeant came up the path at a trot.

'Don't do that,' said Margaret, moving as close as she could without miring her shoes. 'The police surgeon needs to examine him.'

'It's obvious what happened.' The policeman addressed the men. 'His clothes are damp and he's cold as ice.'

'Dr Demeray undertakes post-mortems for Scotland Yard,' said Gil. 'You should listen to what she says.'

'That's a bit of a push,' Margaret whispered. 'It's generally just the Metropolitan Police, and only when they can't find any other hospital with capacity.'

'We can't mess with Scotland Yard,' said the sergeant, then muttered something under his breath. 'Better get him to the station mortuary. But the official cameraman is off elsewhere and so are half my men, so you'll just have to remember what you see.'

'We have a small camera,' said Margaret.

'But no film left,' said Fox.

'As we were then.' The sergeant turned his attention to the crowd. 'Move along please. Nothing to see.'

Margaret whispered to Fox. 'You always ask if I'm tingling ... now I am. Would you mind if I tried to find out more?'

'Be my guest,' said Fox. 'I'll take Gil and Raoul back to our place.'

The police surgeon was reluctant when Margaret asked to observe the post-mortem. In the end, it took telegrams to Dorcas Free and St Julia's to gain her admittance. But as she'd anticipated, it didn't take long to find out what had happened to the boy.

She returned two hours later to find Fox playing with the children in the sitting room. 'Where are Gil and Raoul?'

'They've gone to Chesil Beach. They'll come here for lunch tomorrow before we go home. How was the post-mortem?'

'The boy was, at a guess, between twelve and fourteen.' Margaret let Alec climb into her lap and pull down a curl to twiddle. Once, perhaps, some woman had done the same with the boy in the boat, thinking she'd never let anything hurt him. She stroked Alec's soft hair. 'If twelve, he was tall for his age. It looked as if he'd eaten meat and potatoes yesterday evening. His clothes were lower quality, but not the worst by a long way, and with no identifying marks – maker or laundry. He had no money or personal effects. Just like Rosie.'

'How did he die?'

'There's no sign of violence,' said Margaret. 'He'd ingested some chloral yesterday evening – enough to make him drowsy but nowhere near enough to kill. It seems he took the boat out on the lake, lost an oar, went into the water after it, climbed back into the boat, then died of exposure as the boat drifted or possibly just fell asleep and the moisture was dew. Maybe he'd been sleep-walking.'

'Why didn't he have his coat on?'

'Sometimes, when people become so cold they might die, their mind plays tricks on them and tells them they're hot,' said Margaret. 'So they take clothes off, and then...' She sighed. 'If it's any consolation, he probably fell asleep and died peacefully.'

'It's not much of a consolation.'

'No.' Margaret saw the boy in her mind's eye, curling up in the boat under a frozen sky: close to shore but not close enough, rocked to eternal sleep in a treacherous mental lullaby.

'What are the police doing?'

'They've made a sketch of his face, and they're telegraphing all other forces about missing boys so they can send copies if necessary. Some mother somewhere must be wondering where he is.' She pulled Alec tighter against her.

'Maybe there isn't,' said Fox. 'Rosie says no one cares about her. Some people – children included – are all alone in the world.'

'I know,' said Margaret, letting Edie clamber up and snuggle on her breast. 'But sometimes I don't want to believe it.'

Eleven

Before Gil and Raoul arrived for Sunday lunch, Fox and Margaret left the house for a family walk along the esplanade. But as they were shutting the door, Pigeon arrived on a motorbike and asked to speak with Fox.

'You go, Margaret. I'll catch you up.'

'Can Mrs F stay too?' said Pigeon. 'This is to do with how she spent the afternoon yesterday.'

'How did you spend it, Meg?' said her father. 'You never told me.'

'Busy busy,' said Edie.

Freda glanced at Pigeon and appeared to exchange a nod. 'Tell you what, Mr Demeray, sir. Let's leave the master and missus to entertain Mr Pigeon. Nellie and I will come walking with you and the children. You can tell us all about pirates and we'll stop the twins going in the sea.'

'Capital idea!'

In the sitting room, Pigeon, divested of his outer motorcycling clothes, gratefully drained a cup of tea while Fox read the paperwork he'd brought.

'The description of the boy is similar to that of the person who tried to get into Whitehead's Factory in Wyke Regis,' he said.

'Similar, or the same?' said Margaret. 'Is that the only identification there is? He wasn't that distinctive.'

'No,' said Fox. 'But it will take some time for all the other forces to report back about missing people in their area, and as you say, he wasn't distinctive.'

Margaret sat back. Pigeon gave her a kind, unreadable smile. He always looked a little odd without his motorcycling cap and goggles. He had the kind of face that had probably looked old at fifteen, but would look young at fifty, then barely change as he aged. She always had to remind herself that he was only in his early thirties. She wished she knew him well enough to decipher his expressions, but maybe she never would. It was hard enough to read Fox's.

'Now then, Mrs F,' he said, putting his cup down and leaning forward. 'The guard's description isn't clear, and I wondered if you'd like to come with me and Fox while he views the body. He might have information that would help.'

'Yes, of course.'

A short while afterwards, in the hospital mortuary wing, Margaret stood with Fox, the sergeant, the police surgeon and a thickset man in his Sunday best, who was crushing his hat brim in his ham-like hands while waiting for the sheet to be drawn back.

'The pastor led us in prayers for this lad this morning,' he said. 'I didn't expect to have to look at him. Is he very dead?' Despite a frame that looked as if he could fell an ox with a prod of his finger, the man was trembling.

'Nothing worse than you've probably seen before,' said the police surgeon. 'It wasn't a violent end, and he's been very cold from the moment he expired.'

'All right.' The guard gripped his hat. 'Go on.'

The sheet was pulled back to reveal the boy, waxen and pale, eyes shrunken under their lids. He was thin, his features fine. The face was changing from boyishness to manliness, with a fair fuzz on his upper lip. His thick mop of brown hair was arranged over his brow, to hide the stitches from when they'd looked inside his skull.

'Is this the fellow that tried to get into Whitehead's?' said the sergeant.

The guard waggled his head. 'Maybe he is and maybe he isn't. Depends what you mean. Poor soul: he's just a lad.'

The sheet was pulled up again and the guard taken to a side room.

'What do you mean, maybe he is and maybe he isn't?' said the sergeant, nodding at Margaret to pour the tea.

Sacrificing her dignity for the sake of the anguished guard, she did so, and handed it round to everyone but the sergeant, leaving the cup just out of his reach.

'All I can say about the boy who tried to break in a bit that it was a tallish, slimmish person with brown hair, who dodged like a boy could and a man probably couldn't and wasn't shaped like a girl,' said the guard. 'But a boy looking exactly like this one tried to get into Whitehead's on Thursday. Not in a sneaky way, mind. He thought he could walk in to ask for a job.' The guard stroked his chin. 'I didn't think he was so desperate he'd drown himself.'

'He didn't drown himself,' said Margaret, before the police surgeon could intervene. 'He died of cold.'

'I didn't know he was so desperate for shelter he'd sleep outside either. I thought he had somewhere to live. I'm sure he said he did.'

The sergeant stretched to get his tea, then opened a notebook. 'Tell us what happened on Thursday.'

'I was on the gate, like always. This lad just marches past. I says—'

'What was he wearing? What was his mood?'

'He was wearing a cap and a suit. Grey, nothing fancy – the sort a clerk wears rather than a factory man. He had a tie on, but it didn't look like he was used to a tie except on Sundays. That's what it looked like to me, anyhow. Mood?' The guard shrugged again. 'In a rush. Keen. Or maybe desperate. I said I'd take his details and find out if we had any vacancies and if so, what he needed to do. That's when it got a bit odd. We thought maybe he was a bit wanting.'

'Why?'

'Well he *said* he was from Hart-ford-shy-er.' The guard enunciated the word slowly, with every vowel stretched to its limit and every R elongated. 'Wherever that is. He said he was fourteen and prenticed to a cobbler and he was good with his hands, but he was good with his head too and wanted to use that more.'

'Hertfordshire,' repeated the sergeant as he jotted, marginally more quickly. 'Didn't he give a name?'

'Sorry sir, didn't I say? Kay Rowlands. Is Kay short for Christoper? Or is it a name itself? Anyhow, I asked how far away Hertfordshire was and he said "Miles and miles, but I'm here now and I've come from Camelot." and waved his arm about. That's when my mate came out and said "Kay from Camelot? What you done with King Arthur?" The lad went a bit pale and said "Where can you get the train to London?" and we said "Well, Wyke Halt's just there." It's not like the station isn't obvious. They pretty much built it for the factory. Then he said "Apart from that one" and I didn't know what to say, because it was a stupid sort of question but my mate said "The one down in Weymouth of course". The lad asked if he couldn't come in and ask the boss about jobs. My mate had had enough by then and told him there was jobs at the swannery on Radipole Lake, even though I dunno if there are. I felt more kindly and told him I'd ask about jobs, and if he still needed one Monday, he should come back.'

'And that was the last you saw of him?'

'Arr. My mate said maybe there's a couple of boarding houses called Camelot hereabouts. I mean here and Wyke and even Portland, maybe.' He spoke of Portland as if it were further away than Hertfordshire, rather than within walking distance. 'I felt a bit sorry for the lad. He looked kinda scared. The last thing he said was "I don't want to go abroad no more", so I wondered if this here Hertfordshire was foreign.'

'It's north of London,' said the police surgeon.

'Arr.' The guard nodded, confirmed in his suspicions.

Margaret tried to remember the Weymouth area as a map, but apart from Portland, she couldn't place anything. 'Could Kay have borrowed a boat and tried to get to Radipole Lake that way?'

The sergeant raised his eyebrows. 'Do you know where Wyke Regis is in relation to Radipole Lake, doctor?'

'No.'

'Let's say it'd be quicker and safer to walk than go by sea.'

'Even if you didn't want anyone to see you, because you're scared of someone?'

'Especially if you didn't want anyone to see you.'

Fox touched Margaret's shoulder. 'It's true. The walk would take about three-quarters of an hour. Rowing would take someone who knew what they were doing maybe two hours, and that's assuming the tide was running the right way. He'd have been lucky to get across the harbour, let alone through the north channel into the open sea beyond the breakwaters, then up the Wey into the lake.'

The police surgeon shook his head. 'Maybe he walked from Wyke and found there was no job at Radipole. Perhaps it was late and dark and he was afraid of getting lost on the way back to wherever he was lodging, so he decided to shelter in the boat, got wet and died. It looks like you're right, sir. He was a bit lacking.'

Lunch was sufficiently subdued that even Margaret's father noticed. He stopped interrogating Pigeon about his motorcycling exploits to peer at Margaret while passing her the vegetable dish. 'Has anyone upset you, Meg?'

'Me? No. I'm sorry,' she said, taking the dish from him. 'I just feel sad about the boy they found at the lake yesterday.'

'The one they said prayers for in church?'

'Yes.'

'Any ideas who he was?' said Gil.

'The police have a possible name,' said Fox. 'I imagine it'll take them a few days to see if that turns anything up. I don't suppose you've seen any guesthouses or houses called Camelot in the area, have you?'

Raoul and Gil looked at each other and shook their heads.

'Cornwall, surely,' said Margaret's father.

'Not necessarily,' said Margaret. 'There's a Blandford Street not far from Maude in Marylebone, and the house two down from ours is called Inverness. People name places after other places all the time.'

'Ah, but Camelot is special! Galahad! Tristan! Bedivere! Aren't those the names of Maude's children?'

'Phoebe's nephews are Gawain and Lancelot, which must be fun for them at school. Etta said she was very keen for her boys' names to be from British mythology. I'm not entirely sure why she chose Elfrida.'

'Elfrida was our first crowned queen!' said her father. 'Albeit reputedly a murderous one. In fact, she allegedly did the dastardly deed at Corfe Castle, not so far from here. Have you visited it yet, Gil?' He leaned forward. 'They say that in the right conditions you can still hear medieval ghosts calling from the dungeons and civil war ghosts crying from under the fallen walls. Both were after Elfrida's time, of course. I think her victim—'

'Percival's Elfrida is only ten years old, Father, and despite her mother, rather sweet. Shall we not talk about murder over lunch?'

'Let's speak of travelling instead,' said Raoul. 'When I saw Monsieur Andreyev today, I thought how nice it would be to travel to Vaud via Jersey. But it's too roundabout and I don't have his wealth to meander aimlessly about Europe.'

'Oh, but you can travel very cheaply if you try,' said Margaret's father. 'There's nothing like an aimless meander. Is there, Pigeon?'

'Indeed not, Mr Demeray,' said Pigeon, helping himself to more potatoes. 'Though I have to say, Weymouth to Jersey to Russia is peculiar.'

'Andreyev lives in the Hauts-de-France,' said Gil. 'It's where his wife was from. Perhaps, as I say, I was doing him a disservice and he's mourning her in his own way.'

'We all have to,' said Margaret's father. 'But in the end the joy of life wins through, doesn't it, Meg? Don't worry about the boy in the boat: he is at peace now. Let's hope they find his loved ones and they can come and pay their respects at the funeral.'

'If not, we shall,' said Gil. 'Now, let's discuss something else entirely. How about skiing – is that something you ever tried, Mr Demeray? I can imagine you did.'

'Funny you should say that,' said Margaret's father. 'Now, when I visited Norway in, I think, 1882...'

The journey home on Sunday afternoon was nowhere near as relaxing as Friday's journey to Weymouth. Margaret's threatening cold, which had called a truce in the fresh sea air, began threatening again as soon as they boarded the train.

'It's a shame it turned into a sad trip,' said Fox after they'd settled the family into a compartment and were watching the children wave at Ada from the window. 'We didn't even get Mr Tod a wife.'

'We'll have to look elsewhere,' said Margaret, trying to find some humour in an otherwise awful day. 'At least the sun shone and presumably you have some useful photographs in which the only visible part of me will be the edge of my hat.'

'Possibly not even that,' said Fox. 'I'm a terrible photographer. Whether it was worth it is another matter.' He looked as miserable as she felt.

'Do you think Kay Rowlands was the one trying to break into Whitehead's, as well as the one trying to get a job?' she whispered, even though it was unlikely anyone would hear her over the train whistle and quickening engine.

'Possibly. Since breaking in failed, perhaps he thought if he had a job he could access information. We may not find out until we know who he is for certain, where Camelot is, and whether it's relevant. Hertfordshire constabulary may have a job on their hands. Kay is an unusual name, but Rowlands isn't.'

'Kay suggests a romantic mother to me,' said Margaret. 'Someone who'd read about the court of King Arthur. Poor woman.'

The train pulled out of the station and Ada, to all intents and purposes, disappeared. Edie let out an anguished cry, then burst into loud sobs and Alec followed. 'Wanna Ada! Wanna seaside!'

They barely let up for the entire journey home.

Margaret, Nellie and Freda took it in turns to walk or carry the twins up and down the train corridor to settle them. It was futile. An hour into the journey, as Edie wailed at almost exactly the pitch for bursting eardrums and other passengers glared through the glass doors of their carriages, Margaret wished she'd sent the twins home in the panniers of Pigeon's motorcycle. Better still, she wish she'd escaped on it herself before anyone could stop her.

Twelve

At breakfast the following morning, Margaret drank honey, lemon and aspirin instead of coffee or tea. Her throat was raw and her head throbbed. She toyed with her food and took the morning mail from Freda in the hope that she could actually concentrate on it.

'I'll get the photographs developed and wait for more information,' said Fox. 'What about you? What's waiting at Dorcas Free?'

'I can't recall,' said Margaret. 'I thought I'd go to Maria's first and ask how Rosie is doing.'

'She won't be there.'

'I know. But I want to know that at least one lost young person is all right.'

'You sound hoarse.'

'I'll be all right in a bit.'

Margaret rifled through the mail and passed Fox's across before opening a letter from Lucy which she'd posted the night before and had somehow managed to be delivered with the first post.

Dear Margaret,

I'm afraid not a great deal came from the discussion after the lesson.

The girl said they didn't want to embarrass or offend me because I was too fancy to know what happens to girls who get lured into a life of immorality. Not that they phrased it that way.

Another girl said I was the type that would get drugged in a theatre and end up in a harem in the east living the life of Riley and they should be so lucky.

Another one said a harem was as bad, you just died slower, and maybe worse because you didn't get paid and had no chance to get away.

Yet another said it wasn't all selling your body. It was piecework and factory work too, sometimes locked up in the kind of place you wouldn't wish on rats. Most agreed that someone who was recently killed deserved to die because he'd sold girls.

Two remained silent throughout, looking at each other or the door. I thought they'd leave at one point. Perhaps if I keep calm, one will tell me something useful sooner or later.

I went with a friend to the WSPU rally on Wimbledon Common today, much to Mother's disapproval. She thought it would be too damp, and she doesn't agree with suffragettes, only suffragists, so she rarely attends anything run by the WSPU.

I was shocked by the talk. It explained what the girls in my class meant about how piecework could be sweated work. I'd always imagined embroidered panels and collars and whatnot being made by happy women quietly working in a cosy home, at a sensible pace, with a decent meal waiting for them afterwards. I never considered that their homes might be dark and cold, and that they'd be the ones making the meal and keeping home after several hours stitching in bad light. Sometimes I feel such an ignorant fool.

With love, Lucy.

After breakfast, Margaret made her way to Maria's Dressmakers. Most of her bespoke clothes had been made there since the mid 1890s, and the establishment felt as familiar as a friend's home.

Maria Edwards, after whom the business was named, was now in her sixties. Although she still oversaw the business, it was her married daughter Martha, a small woman in her early thirties, who ran things nowadays, keeping her maiden name for business purposes.

Martha's designs were innovative and her standards high, and she'd kept to the principles her mother had started with. No girl under fourteen was hired unless in a strictly after-school capacity, with proof required that she attended school regularly. Women down on their luck, injured, and struggling to find employment were welcomed. All seamstresses were offered support in obtaining additional training at the technical college and if, ultimately, they set up on their own, they were sent off with a gift of money.

'It's good to see you, Dr Demeray,' said Martha, her face anxious, 'but I don't have you down for an appointment. I'm sure I can fit you in, but you may have to wait.'

'I wanted to ask how a former patient is doing.'

'Ah.' Martha relaxed. 'Actually, she's here today.'

'I thought she was at your house.'

'She would be, normally,' said Martha. 'Ma's teaching her to sew with her left hand, which would be a slow process even if the girl wasn't as edgy as a cat. But Ma's had to visit a bereaved friend, so I brought Rosie here. The clerks can show her some office work. Let me take you through.' She hurried out of the public part of the shop and led Margaret down a corridor. 'I'd help her myself, but it's one of those mornings. I've a particular type of customer due at ten and I need to prepare. I'd rather Rosie didn't watch me engage in a polite battle of wills, so she'll just have to rest with some old school primers. She tires very easily. I imagine that's her body healing itself.'

'Rest is what she needs.'

'Yes, but unlike my ten o'clock customer, who would recline on her sofa declaring that girls like Rosie are idle layabouts with no drive, girls like Rosie don't know how to sit still. Rosie's very frustrated.'

They passed the workroom and Margaret peeked inside. Maria's had complied with good working practices long before the tailors' strike had improved regulations. Workstations were well spaced, and it was as warm, well-aired and light as possible on a misty November morning. One of the seamstresses was reading aloud from a book, her voice barely audible over the clatter of the treadles.

In the office, a female clerk was typing, pausing from time to time to refer to a ledger beside her. She acknowledged Martha and Margaret with a smile and nod.

Wearing a crisp white blouse and navy skirt, Rosie sat at another desk, attempting sums on a slate with her left hand. She chewed her lower lip in concentration and looked even younger than she had in hospital.

When she saw Margaret, the chewing stopped and her pale face became even whiter, though the scowl remained. 'What's up?'

'Nothing,' said Margaret. 'I just came to see how you were.'

'I'm all right. I'm not usually here.'

'I know. And you should be resting.'

'I'm bored of resting.' Rosie glanced at the clerk. 'But I can't do much with one hand yet. Miss Edwards, can I read out loud in the workroom for a bit later on?'

'What about the thread dust?' Martha's question was more to Margaret than Rosie.

'I looked inside the workroom,' said Rosie. 'It's like the dust's scared to settle. You should see what I'm used to.'

'What's the book?' asked Margaret.

'*The Wonderful Wizard of Oz*,' said Martha. 'They're part way through, so it might not make much sense to you.'

'I don't care,' said Rosie. 'As long as no one laughs if I don't know a word, or they think I talk funny.'

'No one will laugh,' said Martha. 'No one knows all the words in the world. Do they, Dr Demeray?'

'I certainly don't.'

Rosie smiled, stroking her bandaged arm, then picked up the slate pencil with a sigh. 'Twelve pence in the shilling, twenty shillings in the pound. Who thought that would make sense? Not anyone who had to add it up, that's who. But I told— I said I could do it, and I can.' She straightened her back and peered down her nose at the primer.

'How's your alphabet, Rosie?' said the clerk. 'I have some index cards you can put in order for me, if you like.'

'Go on then.'

Margaret bent over to examine the bandages and dropped her voice. 'I'm sure you'll be fine, but tell Miss Roberts if anything worries you. She'll look after you and have someone here quick as anything.'

Rosie shook her head. 'I'm all right,' she whispered. 'I don't want no one knowing I've been talking to coppers. It's not natural. And I never saw nothing.'

Martha glanced at them and asked the clerk to speak with her in her private office, leaving Margaret and Rosie alone.

'Who did you tell that you could do sums?' said Margaret.

'Someone in a posh café. You know the sort of place: ladies in fussy hats, fancy cakes, different types of tea to choose from, like you need more than one.'

'A man, or a woman?'

'*He* wasn't the problem. He seemed kind. I ain't saying no more. I'll be all right here: everyone's nice. You needn't worry, doctor.'

'Won't you say his name? Or the name of the café? Or what he looked like?'

Rosie bit her lip and rubbed her head. 'I can't remember is the honest truth. He was Radley I think.'

'Radden?'

'Yeah. How did you know?'

'What about the café?'

'It had a flower name. They gave me something later. I was fuzzy most of the time and then I ran and I banged my head and I can't remember.'

'Is that the honest truth?'

'Yeah.'

'And you don't remember anything about the people who kept you locked up?'

'They were all right to start,' said Rosie. 'A lady was teaching me this sort of thing.' She waved around the office. 'Filing, writing letters properly and so on. I was going to learn simple accounts with some feller next. The lady was nice and said I had a head for numbers. You're going to ask what she looked like and what her name was. Thing was it was always a bit dark, I was always a bit fuzzy and she had some sort of stupid name you can't remember – Board I think.'

'What was the house like?'

'So many rooms instead of just one. Somewhere just to sit down on one side of the front door; somewhere just to eat on the other; a classroom towards the back near the kitchen where …'

'What?'

'I overheard some bloke I hadn't heard before call me something. Not my name. Something.'

'What?'

Rosie's face went a dark red and her mouth set. 'I wouldn't dirty my mouth saying it. My family didn't leave everything behind to come here and have to listen to that sort of word again. You wouldn't understand anyway and I don't want to translate.'

'I'm sorry,' said Margaret. She could guess the sort of name. Presumably Rosie's family like Anna's had endured violent persecution in the Russian Empire, but name-calling and prejudice were everywhere. 'Was that what made you escape?'

'I said I'd changed my mind about the job and wanted to leave. That's when...' She rubbed her arm where the old bruises were. 'One of the staff got rough. I started being careful what I ate and drank and listened at doors. They said I was good enough to do the first job and I needed to do it sharpish, and after that, I looked young and pretty and skinny enough to - what did they say? - appeal to a certain type and make good money. That was when I guessed what was coming. I don't think Mr Radden what interviewed me knew, and I'm not sure Miss Board did either. She wasn't there when they were talking.' Rosie shivered. 'I told the perlice most of this.'

'I'm not the police,' said Margaret. 'I'm just trying to work things out so I can help you and maybe help Violet too.'

'You and your bluebottle got someone looking for her?'

'I have. Knowing what happened might help.'

'Yeah?'

'Can you tell me which newspaper you saw the advertisement in?'

Rosie frowned, but her expression was one of genuine uncertainty. 'I dunno – I got it off Violet. She was up from the country, dossing with her big sister, and hadn't got round to applying. I think it was from wherever she was from. Essex, maybe.'

'Why didn't she want the job?'

'She did, but her sister got sick and she said she'd try again another time. I left the paper with her but copied the stuff dahn. I wish...'

Listening to her, Margaret was suddenly conscious that she might have misheard before. 'You did say Violet's was Brahms didn't you?'

'Brahn,' said Rosie. 'I said Brahn.'

'I'm not criticising the way you talk Rosie, but can I be clear – do you mean the colour? Brown like... like the desk?'

'Yeah. But I might be wrong. They're from the country and talk funny.'

'And her sister's name?'

'Daisy.'

'Thank you. But you've no idea where they kept you?' said Margaret.

Rosie shook her head. 'After I spoke with Mr Radden, I went with a lady and a gent. It was dark by then. They took me in a motor car. I don't remember much immediately after that. Like I said, fuzzy. I wasn't when I escaped.'

'How did you escape?'

'There was a kerfuffle. Shouting. Someone had told someone something and everything was going to pot and someone would pay. They were so busy arguing in the kitchen they forgot about me. But I wasn't going to wait and see if it was me who'd be paying. They'd forgot to lock the front door. So I legged it. But it was foggy and I was scared. I didn't even know which way to run. I don't know how long I ran. I just ran. You know the rest. Find Mr Radden – maybe he'd know.'

'He's dead. Someone murdered him.'

'Gawd.' Rosie fell silent, squaring up the index cards. From the distance came the clack of sewing machines. 'Was he the one what paid?' she said at last, in a low voice. 'Daisy nearly got nabbed herself when she came to London. She thought the job

Violet saw was kosher, so she was pleased. But it wasn't, was it? You gotta find her.'

'You'll have to tell me where she lives,' said Margaret.

Rosie stared unseeing at the index cards, then looked up. 'I don't know the address. But they've got a room near Ravel Street in Whitechapel. That doesn't mean –'

'It doesn't mean you're from there,' said Margaret. 'I know. But I'll pass the information on so she can be found.'

'I hope it's not too late.' Rosie cleared her throat and laid the cards out as best she could with one hand.

'I'm sure it's not,' said Margaret. 'Mr Radden died shortly after you met him. It's far too soon for someone to have taken over his job.'

Thirteen

When Margaret arrived at Dorcas Free, Dr Gesner was unnervingly pleased to see her.

'Good morning!' He put a cloth over the jar he had been examining and shook her hand warmly. The effusiveness of his greeting startled her, and she braced herself for a hug.

'Good morning, Dr Gesner – you seem very jolly. Has Miss Black recovered, against the odds suggested by the sample we analysed yesterday?'

'She is fighting on, but I am happy about something else. Two somethings, in fact. One to please me and one to please you, perhaps!'

Margaret waited. Dr Gesner's expression normally had little range. If pleased, there was a slight smile; if joking, a different slight smile; if angry or sad, a slight hardening of the jaw – but you had to know him well to notice. Now, however, there was no mistaking the joy in his face. She wondered if she should have paid more attention to the news that morning. Was Archduke Francis-Ferdinand of Austria's visit important to Dr Gesner? Surely if it was of more political concern than usual, Fox would have mentioned it. Maybe Dr Gesner didn't have a view, other than to hope it indicated more chance of peace. As for what might please her, she had no idea, unless it was that Dr Naylor had lost interest in having Margaret work more hours.

'Soon you shall meet my wife Ilse,' he said. 'She arrives in a few days and she will be making us a home here. I wanted it to be a surprise. A house will be ready for us soon, but first we will stay in a hotel. My lodgings are not nice enough for a lady.'

'That's wonderful!' said Margaret. 'But does that mean...'

'Ach no. My father-in-law has not died. As I said, he may outlive us all. But my sister-in-law has convinced Ilse that her place is with me. You will like her, I know.'

'I'm sure I shall.' Now Margaret did want to hug him: he seemed so overjoyed. Presumably he'd no longer have to travel between England and Germany so often and worry Fox. She wasn't altogether sure how well she'd get on with Ilse who, from what Dr Gesner had said, seemed supremely domestic, but perhaps they'd find something in common. 'I'm delighted for you. And you say there's something else?'

'Ah yes. I think you'll be pleased to know that a new doctor has been appointed to fill the vacancy. A young man from Wor... One of the cesters. There's a bottled sauce named after it, I believe.'

'Worcestershire?'

'I believe so. Ach, English place names. Four syllables, only three pronounced, and none of those how they're spelt.'

'I think it's Saxon,' said Margaret. 'So as a German, you share the blame.'

'Let's split the difference and blame the Angles.'

'At any rate, that's good news too. I assume Dr Naylor won't want me to work on the chest ward now.'

'I assume not. But the main point is that I believe you know him. Dr Algernon Hardisty.'

'Algie!' Margaret exclaimed.

'He was once your assistant at St Julia's, was he not?'

'He was. And he has a sort of understanding with one of my young cousins.' Margaret chuckled, imagining Albert's face when he knew that his daughter Bee's suitor was no longer more than a hundred miles away. Then she frowned. Algie had kept up a spasmodic correspondence: she'd understood he was going into pathology. Did that mean he would replace her? She erased the frown. Surely that would not happen. 'He'll be a boon to Dorcas Free. I look forward to seeing him again.'

At eleven, Inspector Silvermann arrived.

'Is Dr Gesner busy?'

'He is,' said Margaret. 'Would you prefer to wait and speak with him?'

'You'll do. I want...' Inspector Silvermann scowled. 'Need, not want. I don't care that Radden's dead, God rot his soul, but I can't have people taking justice into their own hands and if I've got to send someone to trial for his murder, I want it to be the right person. Can you elaborate on Radden's time of death?'

'I'm not sure what I can add to what we said at the inquest,' said Margaret. 'He had been dead at least twenty-four hours, but not as long as forty-eight. In other words, it's most likely he was killed between Saturday afternoon and Sunday morning. Rosie Levene – in case it's relevant – is accounted for after about six on Saturday afternoon. Mr Radden appears to have been in bed when he was attacked. Six o'clock is very early, although it's possible he was trying to sleep off his cold by taking Chlorodyne. Of course, I suppose he might have had a visit from a lover.'

'Lover sounds too romantic for a bastard like Radden,' said the inspector. 'But knowing you're a married woman saves my blushes, since I won't have to explain. There was no evidence of that sort of activity in any bed or any room whatsoever. For a relatively young man, he had dull habits. He'd laid his clothes out neatly for the next day and tidied his toilet things, and he'd been reading *Around the World in Eighty Days*. Neither the char nor the police found any lights on when they arrived, nor had the bedroom candle burnt down. I agree with you and Dr Gesner. The chlorodyne on the night stand suggests he had a cold and went to bed early, and was possibly asleep when the attack happened. If there was any light, the murderer brought it or turned it off afterwards.'

The door crashed open. One of the new young orderlies dashed forward with a tray and dumped it on Margaret's desk. Milk and coffee sloshed from their pots onto the biscuit plate. 'Oops! Sorry, doctor. I'll get a cloth, shall I?'

'Don't worry on my account, lad,' said the inspector. 'Saves me dipping my biscuit. Although I expect the lady's too refined for that sort of thing.'

'It's all right, Hal,' said Margaret, opening a drawer. 'I have something somewhere... Ah, here it is.'

The orderly gawped. 'That's not – that's not from the operating room, is it?'

Margaret waved a large white handkerchief. 'Never fear, Hal. All the bloodstains are washed out – see? And I'm sure the inspector isn't squeamish.'

'B-but—'

'I'm joking, Hal. It's a perfectly innocent cloth which has never touched any body parts or surgical instruments.'

'Phew, doctor. You had me going there.' Hal backed out, with a smile on his lips but doubt in his eyes as he watched her mop the biscuit plate.

'I promise I just use this to polish a magnifying lens,' said Margaret, after he'd gone.

'Wouldn't bother me either way,' said the inspector, making his choice. 'Like you, I've been in this game too long to be squeamish. Fancy biscuits, these.'

'I made them. Will you risk one?'

'Nice to know you can. Is it jam inside, or gore?

'Which would you prefer?'

'A copper's always hungry. As long as there aren't pips or gristle, I couldn't give a rat's behind.'

'Coffee?'

'Please. No milk or sugar.'

Margaret poured, passed the cup and saucer, then sat back.

'You don't look quite the thing, if you don't mind my saying,' said the inspector. 'And you're a bit wheezy. You need cleaner air.' He contemplated her. 'What's going through your head? Something is.'

'I spoke with Rosie this morning.'

'Yes? Do you think she's told you more than she told us?'

'I don't know what she told you.'

The inspector dipped his biscuit in his coffee then rattled off a few short sentences. 'She was interviewed by someone she called Radley. She went somewhere in a car but isn't sure where. It sounds as if she was drugged. She was taught some simple clerking skills. She got frightened. She waited till they weren't watching and escaped. I don't know what made her frightened. She says they didn't touch her except to move her when she was being slow. I don't know why she couldn't get out sooner. Do you?'

Margaret explained what Rosie had said.

'So she overheard someone saying someone else would have to pay,' said the inspector. 'Mmm. I can guess the insult she overheard. I presume it was Russian or Latvian... I don't suppose you had to suffer name-calling in the kind of school you went to.'

'I had my fair share,' said Margaret. 'I had a strange name, my mother was dead, my father was an eccentric, then after a while we had very little money and my clothes became unfashionable and a little shabby. Girls can be thoroughly unpleasant even in the nicest of schools. And since then, I've endured all sorts of name-calling for being a woman in a man's job and, as you know, as a suffragette. But... for my race or religion? No.'

'Hmm,' said the inspector. 'Well, I won't report what she said about that - yet. It could be used against her. But it confirms where she's probably from, where her family originated, and what she's possibly had to put up with in her short life.'

'There are a lot of Levenes and Rosies in the area I think she comes from,' said Margaret.

'Is the Sally Army looking in Whitechapel and thereabouts?'

'Yes.'

Inspector Silvermann put his empty cup down and Margaret refilled it. 'Tell them to try Raisa.'

'What?'

'It's a forename. Commonly shortened to Rosie for fitting-in purposes, like Freddy for Fishel.'

'Is that your name?'

'No.'

'Why aren't you telling me to keep my nose out?'

'My heart isn't made of stone. Maybe Rosie's family's dead, or maybe she did something that made them reject her. I know you have a hard time in your job, being a woman. But I bet you anything you like that even if you did something that shocked your family to the core, they'd find some way of coming to terms with it.'

'Perhaps you should write my biography one day,' said Margaret. 'You know me so well.'

'Thank you: perhaps I shall.' He leaned forward. 'Look, where Rosie's from isn't important. She's one of hundreds of poor kids who get tricked into a form of slavery. I could write their biographies as easy as I could yours. Easier, in fact: I grew up in the same world. What's important is who she saw with Radden, who she was passed on to and where she was kept.'

'She can't remember,' said Margaret. 'Or she never really knew.'

'Didn't you say you were observing a class of girls like Rosie on Friday? Anything come of it?'

'A number of girls there seemed to know that Radden was dead and had no high opinion of him,' said Margaret. 'That's all so far. I'm hopeful one of them might be able to tell my cousin something useful. In the meantime, I wish I knew which café Radden was meeting them in. Rosie mentioned a flower name.'

The inspector drained his cup and put it on the saucer. 'It's the Daffodil Café in Daffodil Street. Someone reported Radden a while back for suspicious activity there. It was filed away as spinster fussing until he died and someone remembered and I told them to start digging.'

'Daffodil Street sounds vaguely familiar.'

'It's not far, that's why. There's a fancy bookshop in Daffodil Street. You probably know it. You like books don't you?'

'Yes, but I don't recall that one.'

'Yes, well, Daffodil Street is parallel to Twentyman Street which is quite different in character. The former is very refined, the latter very much not. An alley dead opposite the café joins the two.'

'I suppose the café's irrelevant now and if Violet Brown applied after Rosie, she's bound to be safe. It's Brown by the way, not Brahms. She has a sister called Daisy.'

'Let's hope whoever worked with Radden doesn't just try a different tack,' said the inspector. 'I'll note Violet's surname and do what I can. As for your cousin's class, I bet her students won't say a peep, but if they do, it could be helpful. In exchange, I might as well tell you my thoughts and assume you think I'm wrong. That'll save time all round.'

'Please do.'

'I believe Radden was the middleman for a gang: the respectable person who met young people and passed them on to someone else. It's more sophisticated than women being drugged at the theatre, which is what the papers bleat on about even though it's hardly ever happened and the last report turned out to be nonsense. But it's not necessarily unconnected.'

'Go on.'

'My informant only knows so much – or at least, he's only saying so much. It's possible Radden didn't actually know what he was doing, any more than he realised that the Regency silver he bought on behalf of Lady Fancytoes for eighty quid was in fact electro-plated tin worth ten shillings. So ... what if he found out?'

'He could have told the police.'

'And risk getting flogged? Nah. But if he "accidentally" let the goods escape to get word out?'

'Rosie?'

'Could be.'

'She doesn't mention him being at the house.'

'Doesn't mean he wasn't. Perhaps he wanted to stop it, or to distract them while he worked out how to escape the situation himself. He was definitely planning something. Enquiries made about tickets for him and his sister to sail to Australia, letters from property agents wanting to value the house. But he played the wrong game and when someone worked out who was doing it... As you say, assassination.'

Margaret sat back. 'Rosie said Radden was nice.'

'In some jobs, it pays to be nice,' said Inspector Silvermann. 'Never worked for me. Just now, all I need is someone who saw Radden alive after six on Saturday.'

'Are you sure Radden didn't know what he was doing?' said Margaret. 'A woman I spoke with last week suggested that he did, and so do the girls in my niece's class.'

'Did they name him?' said the inspector, rising and collecting his hat. 'They didn't, did they? And besides, you know what those sort are like: gossips, scandalmongers, give a dog a bad name then hang him. Maybe Radden knew –but what if he didn't? In that case, he was a hero who could have led us to the gang. And now he's dead.'

Fourteen

A letter from Captain Blanchard was waiting when Margaret returned home that evening.

Your telegram helped me trace Miss Levene. She was known as Rosie at board school, but her given name is Raisa. Her grandparents lost everything in the pogroms that drove the family to Britain. Soon after Rosie was born, her parents died. The grandparents wanted to keep Rosie within their community. She wanted a life outside it. They told her she'd bring disgrace on them, but now they want her home. I'm hopeful that with the help of their rabbi, I might be able to encourage them to speak with her. Whether she wants to speak to them, of course, is another matter.

As for Daisy and Violet Brown, there seem to be as many Browns as Levenes, and they're less tied in to a community that I can speak to, especially if they're up from the country. If they're seamstresses too, talking to sweatshop owners might help, but it will take time.

'He's right,' said Fox, over dinner. 'Brown is the second or third most popular surname in London, according to Elinor. As for Daisy, it's yet another shortening for Margaret, isn't it, along with Polly and Molly and Peg and Meg... I've never quite worked out why. She's a needle in a massive haystack. Or the urban equivalent, a splinter in an ash heap, I suppose.'

Margaret's head throbbed. 'Is there nothing that can be done?'

Fox put down his knife and fork, then laid newspaper cuttings and his notebook from his case onto the table. 'We can stop it from happening any more.' He turned his notebook for her to read.

There was a list of newspapers with ticks and crosses against them. Five ticks related to newspapers printed in country towns situated around London.

'Someone up from the country might not know where to look for safe work in the city,' said Fox. 'Seeing a direct advertisement in a newspaper for a legitimate job with prospects would encourage anyone who had enough sense not to pitch up and hope for the best. Each paper I've spoken to only received one single advertisement, but it's been going on for months. I can't find any of the same kind since late October, and all papers have been warned to watch out in future.'

'What a lot of palaver,' said Margaret. 'How would Radden know the girl's family wouldn't smell a rat and report him.'

'I imagine he'd pick interviewees carefully from what they'd said in their application – aiming for those who might not trust the police and without loving families. Perhaps the clerical work was relevant in some way.'

'Surely it was a blind? Rosie gave the impression that she was kept under lock and key while being "trained". Doesn't that mean they were destined to be sold to the highest bidder? She said they thought she was good enough to do the first job and her looks would appeal to a certain type and make good money in the second.'

'That's two jobs,' said Fox. 'One apparently legitimate, the other very much not so. It's easy to work out what the second job probably is, but what's the first?'

Margaret put her knife and fork down. 'I'll visit Sullivan's sweatshop on Thursday,' said Margaret. 'I'm sure Rosie worked there: maybe Daisy does.'

'That might be as much as you can discover,' said Fox. 'Rosie may have come *from* the East End but nothing leads to it. I'm not sure how Sullivan can help.'

'I have to try. Rosie knew Anna. Daisy lives in Ravel Street. Sullivan's is at least a possibility.'

'I'll come with you.'

'What about the mission?'

'I don't have to return to Weymouth until Friday and a mission that possibly links to it is under someone else's supervision. It's not a quick job.'

'What's the link?'

Fox dropped his voice. 'Two huge cases of arms have been intercepted at Belfast docks, both coming from the continent. I need to know who paid for them and how. Each was destined for opposing sides in the dispute about the Irish Home Rule Bill. I want diplomacy to have a chance, and I also want to stop anyone making money from selling arms.'

'Then surely you need to resolve that, not come with me.'

'You'll be at work tomorrow. I have to leave early for Weymouth on Friday and I won't be back till Saturday afternoon. I'd like to spend the day with you on Thursday, even if some of it is in Whitechapel.' Fox squeezed her hand.

'Have the arms anything to do with that dead boy - Kay Rowlands?'

'I don't know. No one has yet found out who he was.'

'Is Dr Gesner aware of any of this?'

'Dr Gesner isn't on Hare's staff, Margaret.'

'That's not an answer.'

Fox poured more coffee. 'Intelligence suggests money is going to the continent via one set of ports and arms arriving via others. It's not clear if the money is only paying for arms and if arms are only destined for Ireland. In this particular instance, however, the cases destined for opposing sides came from the same source, which means the seller is more interested in profit than principle.'

'That sounds like the sort of thing Abney would have done.' Margaret recalled the man whose crimes had brought her and Fox together in 1910.

'Yes.' Fox stirred his coffee, frowning.

'Abney died five months ago.'

'*Someone* died. They couldn't be fully identified.'

'But...' Margaret ran fingers round her temples. 'But the trail on him went completely cold. Abney can't have just disappeared.'

'He could with the right help.'

'I don't want to think other people have the same despicable ideas,' said Margaret, 'but they do. Abney *has* to be dead.'

Fox squeezed her hand. 'I don't know whether to hope he is or isn't. I always wanted him to stand trial. As for Weymouth, there's still the possibility that documents from Whitehead's or copies of them are being smuggled out, whether or not Kay Rowlands was involved. I'd take you again, so we'd appear to be on a day's excursion rather than rooting around, but you're giving another talk on Friday, aren't you?'

'Yes.'

'So on Thursday we'll visit Ravel Street and see if professional pride will make Sullivan point us to less "respectable" enterprises.'

'Then we should visit the Daffodil Café and see if they can tell us anything. We'll have to wear different clothes for each, of course. You could raid your office dressing-up box for Whitechapel clothes, then change into something respectable afterwards.'

Fox rolled his eyes. 'I live for the day when the solution lies in a nice quiet pub.'

Wednesday passed calmly at the hospital. Margaret taught a class of third year students, and spoke with Dr Naylor about her ideas for future work that might not involve increasing her hours or leaving Pathology. She could only hope she'd come across as passionate rather than belligerent and it would have the desired effect.

Fox arrived home at dinnertime with news of Kay Rowlands.

'He went missing from a Hertfordshire village late on the thirtieth or early on the thirty-first of October. He had the sharpest brain the schoolteacher had ever seen. If you gave him a list of numbers, he could add them in his head in seconds without seeing them or writing them down. He could sketch a wall including every single brick. He could remember details from every grave in the churchyard in any order you gave him: alphabetical, date, age. He was the sort of person who's completely failed by a world in which money rather than intelligence guarantees you a university education. He was the sort of person Hare would hire like a shot. And so would any enemy intelligence unit.'

'And you?'

Fox poured gravy on his roast beef. 'He'd be invaluable for his skills, but I'd want to be sure that his opinions couldn't be swayed. The world isn't black and white, but sometimes people whose minds work like his can be convinced that it is. Hare would say "We convince him that we're right and everyone else is wrong and he'll do whatever we say". I'd say "What if someone else tells him we lied and he has to undermine us for the greater good?"'

'I see.' Margaret cut a slice of carrot. 'Did he have a family and were they missing him?'

'His mother is distraught,' said Fox. 'His father apparently seemed to find Kay a disappointment: bookish and somehow "lacking", as the guard put it. Not a proper boy. Even his mother admits Kay didn't have much common sense, the sort who might get lost and climb into a boat for the night rather than seek shelter indoors. But I had the impression Kay's father had been trying to beat common sense or normality into him for most of his short life.'

'Poor Kay.' Margaret pushed her plate away. The food was scratching her throat, anyway. 'What about the Camelot reference?'

'Books about King Arthur in Kay's bedroom that might have been his mother's once, but no other reference. But when Kay's photograph was put in a Weymouth newspaper, the owners of a house near Nothe Fort recognised him as someone who'd moved into a rented property nearby and ran down the street early one morning. Nothe Fort doesn't look like Camelot to me, but it might have to Kay.'

'And the property itself?'

'It's rented out for short periods to families wanting a holiday. The agent had let it to a married couple and their manservant. They were due to leave on the Saturday we were there. He'll provide the details if we provide a warrant. I have a feeling...'

'That Kay was the servant, but the rest will come to nothing?'

'Mmm.' Fox took a mouthful of food. 'Aren't you going to eat anything? Feed a cold and starve a fever, and all that.'

'I'm not terribly hungry. There's still no news on Violet. And here's poor Kay Rowlands, another youngster looking for a better life, miles from home and dead.'

'In Weymouth, not London, though,' said Fox. 'Otherwise, I take your point. I'll see what I can find out about Hertfordshire newspapers. In the meantime, hopefully Rosie took the advertisement with her, so Violet had no one to apply to.'

'No. Rosie copied it.'

'Oh,' said Fox. 'Well, we'll find her anyway, Margaret.'

'Hare would say you have spies to catch.'

'And since when have either of us cared about Hare?'

The doorbell rang just after they'd settled in the sitting room and Margaret was sipping honey and lemon wondering whether it was too early to go to bed.

Freda ushered Phoebe in. She was apologetic and looked more drained than Margaret felt.

'I'm sorry to barge in unannounced,' she said. 'And I know I'm coming for dinner on Saturday, but I need some advice. It's about Percival and he'll be there on Saturday too. I'm sorry. I'm gabbling.' She sat down and drew a breath. 'Have you heard any rumours about him?'

Margaret exchanged a glance with Fox. It felt like a betrayal to even mention what Mr Endsleigh had said. 'I heard his name used disparagingly the other day,' she said. 'I assumed the person was expressing political disapproval.'

Phoebe gave Margaret a headmistress stare. 'Please be specific. Who said what?'

'A gentleman called Endsleigh intimated that Percival profits from being a slum landlord.'

'I hadn't heard *that*.' Phoebe's poise began to slip. She twisted her hands. 'The rumours I was made aware of today were about misappropriation of political funds: small amounts of money moving from heading to heading, then disappearing. This parent suggested Percival might be using me or the school. I spoke to Percival about it and he says he's done nothing himself but there is a problem with the accounts. He anticipates an investigation. He suspects someone in his office made the information public but doesn't know who or why. It's quite absurd. Percival doesn't have a mathematical mind, any more than he has a devious one. Someone needs to do something.'

'He and you should inform the authorities,' said Fox.

Phoebe looked blank. 'I'm telling you.'

'I'm in quite the wrong department.'

'I'm not a fool and I never have been.' Phoebe's voice was sharp, but under its acerbity was an edge of uncertainty. 'There might be a connection between this and your work. I know what Special Branch cares about.' Phoebe turned to Margaret. 'This Endsleigh: the name sounds familiar. Was he simply accusing Percival of hypocrisy?'

'I think so, but he was on the defensive. His predecessor, to all intents and purposes, was profiting from immoral earnings. He might argue that by taking rent from dwellings inhabited by night walkers and brothel keepers, Percival is doing the same.'

'Hmm,' said Phoebe. 'Well, he isn't. But if he were, that's different from embezzling funds.'

'Where did this parent say the money is rumoured to be going?' said Margaret.

'The implication is that it's funding something damaging to the country,' said Phoebe. 'Percival's opponents would suggest a working man's revolt. But Percival wants reform, not revolution. This parent says he's probably using me or the school to move money. The school accounts are quite public, but mine... I no longer have a secretary to counter that sort of thing and even if I knew where to start myself, I wouldn't have time.'

'I might have a solution for that,' said Fox. 'You know my senior clerk, Miss Edwards – we nickname her Miss Hedgehog?'

Phoebe's face flushed a little. 'Very well. Elinor and I often meet at social events and have shared interests. We occasionally attend new exhibitions at the Science Museum together, or take tea at the Gardenia. I had wondered about offering her the job, but I know how much you rely on her.'

'She's due some leave,' said Fox. 'Several years' leave, probably. She was threatening Hare with resigning the other day. She could take some, then work for you. She'll see off any nonsense.'

Phoebe almost slumped in relief and her face flushed. 'That would be lovely,' she said. 'If she likes, I can have a room made up for her in the house while she's working as personal secretary. Might she come with me to your dinner on Saturday?'

'Of course,' said Margaret. 'I was going to invite her anyway.'

'Well then, yes. That would be wonderful.'

Fifteen

As they emerged from Aldgate tube station on Thursday morning, Margaret felt a pang, knowing that if she turned a corner she'd be outside St Julia's Hospital and continued for a while in silence, weaving through the people on the pavement, avoiding newspaper boys and people handing out tracts and leaflets.

When Fox paused to light a cigarette, Margaret wafted the smoke away and gestured at the grubby, unwelcoming buildings. 'Any one of these could house the sort of place we're looking for. *You* might get into a brothel but not an illegal factory. I'd never get into either, even if someone needed a doctor.'

'Have you never treated anyone from those sorts of places?'

'Occasionally, if a lucky one was dumped at a workhouse.' Margaret hugged herself, remembering the worn-out, shattered humans she'd helped treat, ghosts even before they'd died. 'Afterwards, more often than not, they go back to what they nearly escaped.'

'And for the unlucky ones, the river's not far, the sewer's under our feet, and there are plenty of vehicles taking rubbish and manure out of the city in which anything – anyone – might be hidden.'

'Exactly,' said Margaret. 'Then there are the ones in plain sight but trapped by the people running them, too scared or ashamed to find a way out. There are some in Lucy's class. It has to stop.'

Despite the drizzle, a group of women winched up lines full of washing to dangle above the street, their babies left to the care of barefoot toddlers and small girls. Boys who ought to have been in school lolled against the wall, smoking and watching.

An old woman muttered and dribbled on a doorstep, her head against the wall. She stretched out a trembling hand. Fox bent and put two sixpences into it. 'Shall we take you to the workhouse?'

'Umm-mmm-mmm.'

'My old mum don't need charity,' said a man, from behind them, taking the money from the woman's palm and pocketing it.

'She's getting cold and wet.'

'I'll get her coat if you pack off.'

On the next step, three lacklustre adolescent girls sat leaning against each other and smoking. The door behind them was open, the hallway dark. One had a black eye, swollen shut. The loose blouse of another revealed bruising across her upper chest and there were marks on her wrists. The youngest drank from a pewter mug, her gaze unfocussed.

Margaret crouched down. 'I'm a doctor. I—'

The girls looked up at the man, stood unsteadily and went inside, slamming the door.

'Maybe not this time,' said Fox, taking Margaret's arm and picking up the pace. She didn't demur.

Eventually they arrived at the building where Sullivan's was. Fox looked up in doubt.

'There's a factory on every floor,' said Margaret. 'Mr Sullivan's is at the top.'

'I know,' said Fox. 'I had people watching you last year. They didn't tell me it was a deathtrap.'

'Just don't cough while you're inside.'

'You're the one coughing.'

Sullivan's sweatshop was as hot and noisy as ever. It had been almost tidy when Margaret had last seen it. Since then, workstations that had been removed to comply with new regulations after the tailors' strike had been brought back in and lint lay in drifts across the floor again. One of the tailors sitting cross-legged by the window nodded in recognition. The machinists glanced sideways without changing pace, but a bellow from across the room made one jump and swear, pausing to lick a finger caught by the machine. Mr Sullivan, hat on the back of his head and cigarette clamped in his mouth, stormed over.

'What you doing here, Dr Thing? Everyone's still alive and kicking, as you can see ... even if they're slacking!' The last words were a shout. He scanned Fox from head to foot. 'Who's this?'

'My friend.'

'Another busybody?'

'I had a subtler introduction in mind, Dr Demeray,' muttered Fox.

'We'd like to have a word about your staff and your competitors,' said Margaret.

Mr Sullivan scowled, then jerked a thumb towards the corner of the room. 'Either get out, or come and tell me what you're gabbing on about in my bureau de business.' He strode across the room without a backward glance, yelling 'Them clothes won't sew themselves, more's the flaming pity. Get cracking!'

'I'll be upfront, Mr Sullivan,' said Margaret, when they were sitting in the tiny room beyond the machinists, watching him shove documents into an overstuffed cupboard. 'My friend is a researcher.'

A ledger slipped from Mr Sullivan's hands and crushed the cigarette he'd put in a shallow tray. 'If you mean journalist, you can sling your 'ook! A reporter's no better than a peach.' He dug around for another cigarette and swore to find the case empty.

'He just wants the truth, Mr Sullivan.'

'Truth my arse. Reporters are worse than narks – they writes the lies down. Get out, or I'll ventilate the bloody workroom by shoving you both through the bleeding window.'

'Even less subtle, Dr Demeray,' said Fox. He offered a cigarette from his own case and Mr Sullivan accepted it with a grunt.

'Please hear me out,' said Margaret. 'I know none of your staff are coerced into working here. I know you pay them the lower end of the going rate. I know their hours are just about legal.'

Mr Sullivan sat back in his chair, then turned his attention to Fox. 'You could have told him to type that up without bringing him here in some secondhand coat as a disguise. I can see the cut of the trousers underneath, you know.'

'I'm glad you like the trousers,' said Fox. 'But the doctor's right. I'd like to know about people who don't run their businesses as legitimately as you, who maybe buy gullible young people to work for them.'

Mr Sullivan snorted. 'I'd like a million quid and a title, and I got more chance than you have. Look...' He leaned forward. '*Maybe* there are people who nabs kids up from the country looking for work, and if they're not pretty enough for one job, they shove 'em in another. *Maybe* there are people who'd slit my throat for mentioning it and yours for asking. But I don't know nothing about them and don't say I do.'

He stood up and passed behind them to open the door. 'Oi! Bessy, get on with your job, or so help me...'

Margaret followed his gaze. The pinched face of the little girl she'd seen the previous year, sweeping indifferently when she should have been at school, reminded her of Rosie, even though the features weren't the same. 'I also wanted to ask if anyone called Rosie or Raisa or Daisy ever worked here?'

Mr Sullivan frowned. 'A Raisa who went by Rosie ditched us for bigger and better things. She was friends for a bit with a girl called Daisy who was up from the country.'

'Is Daisy still here?'

'Nah. She got sick just before Rosie ditched us. I figure she went home. I doubt I'll see her again.' His face contorted a little. If it was pity, it was causing him pain.

'Do you have her address?' Margaret nodded at the ledgers.

Mr Sullivan grabbed them to his chest. 'Who are you, a tax collector? They come and go, seamstresses. What's the point in wasting ink on that sort of thing? But hang on... You're not telling me Rosie or Daisy have been nabbed?'

'I've met a Rosie Levene who used to be a seamstress. She's safe.'

'Good.' Mr Sullivan's concern disappeared. 'If it's the same one, she got 'fluenced by that Anna Balodis during the strike. I hope she's not bad-mouthing me. If you want to stop kids getting into trouble, stand at a station and nab them coming up from the country expecting the streets to be paved with gold before someone else does.' Mr Sullivan sniffed. 'Better still, go home to things you understand or find some other poor sod to pester.' His face twitched into what might have been a smile. It was worse than being threatened with violence.

'Sullivan was my best chance,' said Margaret, over a pot of coffee in the Daffodil Café. 'I wish I could write to Anna Balodis, but I don't know where she is. Do you?'

'No,' said Fox. 'But I suspect she'd agree with Sullivan. It'll be near impossible getting entry to any of those places. But intelligence men and Special Branch are watching for people stashing arms in the area: they might be able to.'

'Are the arms for anarchy, or something else?'

'In London, mostly the former. But not entirely.'

'How many anarchists are there in London?'

'A good many. Just like Anna. She probably still supports anarchy. That, or revolution.'

Fox stared into his cup as he poured more coffee. Margaret told herself that he was talking possibilities, not certainties. She didn't want to think of which country's revolution Anna might be tangled up in. None of them would spare her life if she was caught.

'I tried to encourage her to fight for suffrage, but she said they didn't want to win a vote within our corrupt political system.'

'Which one can understand,' said Fox. 'But I have to hunt anarchists down.'

'Fox, don't be absurd. Not *all* of them. The *Freedom Press* publishes from a known address and anarchists give speeches in Trafalgar Square. Not every anarchist is a bomber or criminal: the majority aren't. You only track down those who intend to harm others.'

Fox leaned close and whispered as if he was speaking endearments. 'I track down whomever I'm told to track down. But I promised you to help find Violet and I will.'

Margaret itched for a notebook or sketchbook to doodle on to clear her thoughts, but with the change of clothes, she'd brought the wrong bag. 'By the way, did you ever find out who the man I sketched in the other café reminded you of?'

'He's a Russian going by the name of Petrov whom Hare has under surveillance. Bert was expecting him to be in Portsmouth ready to receive documents and was surprised that he was in London being irreproachable instead.'

'Why would Russia act against us? Russia's our ally.'

Fox shrugged. 'You know how it is. Alternatively, Petrov may be working for two sides, or simply be like Abney, providing information to the highest bidder. His nationality may be irrelevant. He may not even be Russian. But ports are part of the intelligence. Hence going back to Weymouth tomorrow.'

Margaret looked through the windows at the view outside. Daffodil Street was just as the inspector had described, very refined with several businesses catering for a discerning middle-class clientele. The alley to Twentyman Street ran alongside the bookshop, shadowy and unappealing.

Most of the café's customers were female, with a few middle-aged couples and two small children being treated to cake by their grandparents. She wondered how many times Radden had interviewed applicants here, and which of the bustling waitresses had reported him to the police.

She rose, intending to stop the most motherly looking waitress and ask whether the shop had a lavatory for customers. It was unlikely, but she could do a lot of coy whispering and maybe hint about Radden. But as she did so the door opened and Mr Endsleigh stepped inside followed by a male companion. He raised his hat, scanned her dark-mauve costume briefly, then turned his gaze to Fox, who was wearing a smart houndstooth suit. A tiny smile appeared on his lips.

'Good day, Dr Demeray,' he said, as the other man closed the door and asked for a table.

'Good day, Mr Endsleigh, this is—'

As Margaret hesitated, looking at Fox for confirmation as to how he wanted to be identified, and heard the door burst open with a bang. A woman screamed. Someone grabbed Margaret. The tearoom fell silent apart from gasps and a tinkle of china.

Margaret turned slowly. A short man in shirtsleeves was gripping her arm with one hand. He brandished a bloodstained knife with the other. His face was white, his eyes wide. 'Where's the back way out?'

Time slowed. Margaret was aware that Fox was near, that Mr Endsleigh was reaching out, but she brought her fist down on the arm holding hers, hooked her foot round the assailant's ankle and pushed him hard. The knife clattered to the floor and the man fell backwards against the counter, knocking off a cake-stand. Before he could regain his balance, Fox had dragged him upright and restrained him.

'My man and I will get the police,' said Mr Endsleigh, hurrying through the door.

'Stop him!' cried the assailant. 'I don't mean the lady no harm.' He twisted and pulled, appealing to the room. 'You don't understand! They'll pin it on me. It's not even my knife. I just went to help and I picked it up. Why would I hurt Lizzie? Let me go!'

He slumped as two constables entered the shop, one taking handcuffs from his belt, the other extracting a notebook.

'Higgins?' exclaimed the first. 'This isn't your usual caper. Someone object to being burgled?'

'Be quiet!' said Fox, extracting his warrant card with an effort and showing them. 'It sounds as if a woman's been hurt. She'll need help.'

'Hurt?' said Higgins. His eyes sparkled with tears. 'She's dead and so's the other one.'

'Who are?' said the constable. 'Where?'

'My Lizzie and the woman what she worked for. In the yard off that alley—' Higgins nodded towards the door. 'Back of our lodgings in Twentyman Street. But it wasn't me. I just heard yelling and looked out the window. There was this bloke running off and a knife left behind and—'

'Course there was,' said the first constable. 'You can explain all that at the station.' He exchanged glances with his colleague. 'Someone needs to see what's what, but...'

'I'll help escort the prisoner,' said Fox. He mouthed 'Are you all right?' to Margaret.

She nodded, then turned to the constable. 'I'll come with you to see the victims.'

'You?' The constable blinked and scanned her outfit.

'I'm Dr Demeray from Dorcas Free. Someone should alert them to expect casualties.'

'Lumme.' The constable stared round the room. 'Any of you gents doctors?' The few male customers shrank back in their seats. 'She'll have to do, then.'

Sixteen

As Higgins was marched to the police station, Margaret and the constable hurried down the alley. The yard of the house in Twentyman Street backed onto the yard of the bookshop on Daffodil Street. Its gate was open onto the alley and two boys were peering inside. On mossy, slimy cobbles, under a line of flapping laundry, lay two women. One, in gabardine skirt, striped calico blouse and large apron, lay on her back, her blank eyes open to the skies. Blood pooled on the ground and her apron was saturated with it, darkest of all where her heart would be. There was no hope of life.

The other woman lay crumpled on her side. She was all in black with a long coat. Her hat had come partly loose of its pins. One hand was at her shoulder. The coat was darker there, but it was above her heart and signs of bleeding were minimal. There was a slash in the coat around waist level, but any blood must have soaked into the wool.

Margaret dropped to her knees.

'Watch your dress,' said the constable.

'Don't be ridiculous,' said Margaret. 'Send one of those boys for an ambulance and the other one to get blankets. We need to get these women to Dorcas Free.'

'Our usual police surgeon—'

'He can come too. Quickly. I think this woman is alive.' Margaret removed a glove and placed her fingers gently on the woman's throat.

The woman groaned and her eyes opened. She stared at the cobbles in confusion, then turned her head. 'That man! What's he done to Lizzie? Watch out, he has a knife!'

'He's been arrested,' said Margaret. 'I'm a doctor, and we're taking you to Dorcas Free.'

'Both of us?'

'Yes. Just lie still. The ambulance won't be long.'

The woman struggled to sit up. 'People are saying terrible lies and I thought maybe Lizzie knew why. And then…' She started to sway.

'Lie down,' said Margaret. 'Help is on the way.'

The woman did as she was told, then put a black-gloved hand over her eyes. Something about the gesture and the hat seemed vaguely familiar.

The constable came back with the blankets. 'Oh! She's—'

'She's simply fainted,' said Margaret.

'I know that,' said the constable. 'I meant that I recognise her. That's Mrs Vidler, Radden's sister. I mean Mr Radden. The one who got stabbed. What's going on?'

At Dorcas Free, Margaret accompanied Mrs Vidler to the accident ward and explained what had happened to Dr Perch.

'I didn't want to expose her to more cold or dirt than necessary,' she said. 'It seems as if the assailant aimed for Mrs Vidler's stomach but hit the clip of a chatelaine at her skirt waistband, which was hidden by her coat. She slipped as she tried to get away. He then aimed for her chest, cutting her shoulder – hopefully, not too deeply. She fell and knocked herself out. She said she started screaming when she saw Lizzie stabbed. I can only assume that the assailant wanted to stop her, then thought she was dead and dropped the knife and ran when Higgins looked out to see what the screaming was about.'

'Does she know Lizzie is dead?'

'I thought you'd like to treat her first, in case her wounds are worse than I presume. I didn't want to add to the shock, and she was drifting in and out of consciousness.'

'Thank you,' said Dr Perch. He stared at Margaret's outfit, the muddy hem of her embroidered skirt, the mossy slime on her sleeve where Mrs Vidler had grasped her. 'Next time you come across an injured woman, do it on a working day, when you're in plainer clothes.'

Margaret gave him a rueful smile. 'I'll try,' she said, then hurried to the mortuary wing.

When she arrived, Dr Hughes the police surgeon was scratching his cheek as he looked down at Lizzie's body. She looked like a marble statue that someone had dressed in housework clothes then painted red. On a stained tea towel beside her head was the knife Higgins had brandished. Dr Gesner was in a corner, frowning as a sergeant murmured.

'Good day, Dr Demeray,' said, Dr Hughes. 'Thank you for your help thus far. You needn't stay: I'll take over from here. Besides, your dress might become more soiled.'

'I have a spare hospital outfit in my office,' said Margaret. 'I want to know what happened.'

'So do we,' said the sergeant, 'but Inspector Silvermann said Dr Hughes should do it. Besides, you look peaky. I've always contended that women doctors ought to stick to babies and children. Too much gore is difficult for natural feminine delicacy to endure.'

'I take it you've never attended a birth, sergeant.'

The sergeant blinked at her. 'Er, no.'

'The inspector will arrive soon,' said Dr Hughes. 'Why not wait for him by the desk? We won't start till he gets here, and if he's agreeable, you're welcome to assist us.'

'Assist you? This is my laboratory. *You* are the visitor.'

'Dr Demeray and I work as equals,' said Dr Gesner firmly. 'You would be assisting us.'

Margaret left the room with her head held high. She paced for a while in front of Miss Upton's desk, then realised she felt weary and went to her office. Feminine delicacy aside, she was cold, her clothes were damp and she'd had little to eat or drink since breakfast. It was nearly five p.m. and getting dark outside. The streetlights would shortly come on. Her urge to help with the post-mortem was now motivated more by the desire to make a point than anything else. If Fox came to collect her soon, she would be tempted to leave without waiting for the inspector.

But the inspector arrived first. 'Go home, get out of that wet coat before you catch your death and go to bed. You look well under par.'

'I'm perfectly fine. I want to find out how Lizzie Jackson died.'

'Dr Hughes is quite competent. You're allowed time off. I was half-minded to have the body sent to St Mary's, but they're busy and I'd rather there were no delays.'

'I still want to take part in the post-mortem. It didn't look like a frenzied attack on Lizzie, just accurate. Was the murderer the same person who'd killed Radden? Call it professional curiosity or call it wanting a consistent comparison. I want to know.'

'You look sick and I call it bloody-mindedness.' The inspector dropped down into a chair. 'I'm concerned that as you have a connection, this would be used by the defence in any trial.'

'What connection?'

'For a start, Higgins threatened you at knife point in the café. Apart from that, you've helped shelter Rosie Levene, who's a suspect for Radden's murder even if a highly unlikely one.'

'I simply suggested where Rosie might go. The decision to send her there was yours. You're not suggesting she murdered Lizzie Jackson? The fact that Radden's sister was there is surely coincidental.'

The inspector shook his head. 'According to Higgins, Lizzie charred for them sometimes. Mrs Vidler told you that she'd gone to see if Lizzie knew why someone was spreading rumours about her brother. Lizzie who lived with a known burglar who steals the sort of goods Radden traded. Funny how before Mrs Vidler can find out what Lizzie has to say, she's attacked, Lizzie's dead and Higgins runs off with the knife.'

'Someone who runs into a café full of witnesses with a bloody knife doesn't seem like the calculated murderer who killed Radden and possibly Lizzie,' said Margaret. 'Maybe Higgins is telling the truth.'

'Or he's bluffing, or he's full of remorse. He's good at the former, and the latter isn't impossible.'

'Either way, it's nothing to do with Rosie because I don't believe she killed Radden for a minute.'

'But she might have seen who did.' Inspector Silvermann leaned forward. 'You keep forgetting that the night Radden died, a girl and/or a youth was running in the area.'

'It was foggy. And Higgins isn't a youth.' Margaret frowned as she said it. Higgins was perhaps in his late twenties, but he was short and very slight. On a dark, foggy afternoon, bundled in coat and cap...

'Fog drifts. You get clear patches,' said the inspector. 'Herb Higgins is built for burglary and has a record twice as long as he's tall.'

'For procurement?'

'Maybe he's branched out,' said the inspector. 'What if Higgins was working with Radden and Lizzie knew, and he didn't want her to spill the beans to Mrs Vidler?'

Dr Hughes accepted Margaret's presence without question. They worked together on Lizzie's remains while Polly wrote down their observations.

Leaving the body on its back, they unbuttoned the blouse, cut off the corset cover, unhooked a modern, lightly boned corset and cut away the chemise. There were no defensive marks on the victim's arms, no cuts on the fabric of her sleeves. Two stab wounds to the heart corresponded with the knife. Both had been well aimed, but had been impeded by what corsetry there was and by Lizzie's ribs.

'There's something odd here,' said Dr Gesner. 'Do you not both agree?'

'It's as if she went like a lamb to the slaughter,' said Dr Hughes. He looked at Polly, then strode purposefully towards her, scalpel held up. Her eyes widened and she shrank back, holding up the notebook as a shield and nearly falling off the stool. 'Sorry, Miss Buckram. But do you see the point?'

'Yes, doctor.' Polly reseating herself with dignity. 'If you look at my notes, I'd written that down. "Why didn't she try to protect herself when someone came at her with a knife?"'

'Or run,' said Margaret. 'It's not the only thing, is it?'

'Ummm.'

'Come and look at the wounds.'

Polly put her notebook down and came over to peer. 'I don't follow. Her heart was stabbed twice. She screamed. She died.'

'She wouldn't have died immediately from those wounds,' said Margaret. 'She could have moved away, but she didn't.

She wouldn't have got very far, but you'd be surprised how far stabbing victims can go. The desire to live, to get away from the assailant is astonishingly strong, even when the brain must know there's no hope.'

'Did anyone take photographs of the scene?' Dr Hughes asked the sergeant.

'Yes, sir. After Mrs Vidler and the doctor had gone to the hospital and before we moved this body here. We'll have them in an hour or so, I imagine.'

Dr Hughes turned to Margaret. 'You saw the body in situ. What were your observations?'

'It looked as if she'd pretty much dropped dead where she stood. I was concentrating on Mrs Vidler because there were signs of life. I assumed the person stabbing Lizzie had been lucky and ruptured her heart so effectively with one thrust that it simply stopped, but...'

'Realistically, that would be unlikely,' said Dr Gesner. 'Unless she stood there waiting to be stabbed and then lay down to die.'

'When we open her up, we might see if there was anything else that killed her,' said Dr Hughes. 'An underlying heart condition. A bleed on the brain. Ingestion of poison or drugs.' He peered into Lizzie's sunken, cloudy eyes.

'There may be something else,' said Margaret. 'Let's turn her over.'

They carefully turned the body and removed the remnants of her clothes. They had soaked up much of the blood and mud beneath her.

'Well well well,' said Dr Hughes. 'Inspector, Sergeant – come and look at this.'

On the underside of Lizzie's body, behind her heart, was a large hole.

'Shot?' said Dr Gesner. 'Someone came up at close range and shot her, then they stabbed her to make it look like a knife attack? We need to look at the clothes very carefully to see what the mud and blood is concealing.'

'Get someone to do another search,' Inspector Silvermann told the sergeant. 'Search the yard for the bullet and everywhere you can think of for the gun. And tell the clerk to let the doctor on the ward know that once this post-mortem is over, if she's even half awake, I'll be interviewing Mrs Vidler.'

Margaret spent the journey home staring out of the window, waiting for Fox to ask about the post-mortem and her conclusions, though she wasn't altogether certain what they were. He didn't, and his silence was somehow warm and calming. Her thoughts formed, dispersed and reformed like waves on a river, facts bobbing to the surface to float with supposition for a while, then disappearing to be replaced by others.

She shivered and knew it was only partly the shock of Higgins holding a bloodied knife in her face coming out. Pulling the blanket further up didn't seem to help. Home seemed a long way away and then... the car stopped outside the house and unbearably hot.

Inside, Margaret examined the dirt on her clothes with mild depression. Goodness knows if it would come out, and if so, what the laundress would charge.

Removing her hat, she caught sight of herself in the hall mirror. Her face looked grey and unhealthy. Her forehead and neck felt hot and clammy, even though her bones ached with cold again. No wonder everyone had been making comments. She poked her tongue out at herself, asked Freda for a hot water bottle, made her apologies to Fox and went straight to bed.

She cuddled under the covers to the sound of distant voices: the children, the maids, Fox and felt guilty. She'd spent no time with the twins and Fox had taken a day away from his mission to spend with her and nothing good or useful had come of it.

Sullivan had revealed nothing they didn't already know. Lizzie would have been murdered and Mrs Vidler stabbed whether or not they had been there. They might as well have gone somewhere nice for the day.

Margaret tried to recall what Fox's mission was and as she grew hot again and threw the covers back found her thoughts swim and swirl: a passenger steamer in Weymouth became a rowing boat, a technical design of a torpedo became a newspaper cartoon of an angry Russian hiding a crate of guns in Lizzie's washing basket. She felt she should tell someone, but no one was there and she felt too sick to care.

Seventeen

Fox left for Weymouth at six thirty the following morning, and Freda came with a tray of tea at eight fifteen.

How do you feel ma'am?'

'A good deal better thank you,' said Margaret, sitting up. 'The fever's broken. I'm just a little tired now.'

'I hope you'll stay in today ma'am.' Freda's expression was firm. 'You won't get better by gadding about.'

'You sound like Ada.' Margaret grinned. 'I'll be fine after that tea and a bath. I'm made of stern stuff. I have a talk to do later this morning and then I'll be good and stay home.'

At ten, Margaret was in a pleasant church hall, ready to address her audience. The women were a social rung above the ones she'd addressed the previous week. Any husbands were in more settled jobs. Most had lodgers and their houses were likely to be marginally less damp and draughty. They could afford more coal, and maybe a few hours' paid help if they didn't have too many mouths to feed. But they were not even close to being financially comfortable. The husbands had been striking on and off for years.

Margaret was a little surprised to see Mrs Wantage in the audience, since she lived some miles away and had heard the talk already, but she gave her a nod of acknowledgement before getting underway. At least no men were there to interrupt, no landlords to complain, and no reference was made to recent suffragette militancy.

At the end of the talk, after mentioning Lucy's class, Margaret warned her audience of the dangers of jobs which seemed too good to be true. She added that anyone who'd been duped into a life they didn't want to lead could tell her, or write to her care of the hospital, and she would do what she could to help them.

As the audience departed, however, it was only Mrs Wantage who came forward to speak with her.

'How nice to see you, Mrs Wantage.'

'My sister lives this way: she told me you'd be here. She couldn't come, but I fancied listening to you again. You're better without interruptions. All the same, ducky, you can't blame those men for all of what they said last week. Suffrages ain't exactly helping themselves, what with bombs on the tube and places burnt down. You ever seen the muck left by a house fire? It ain't no joke, and it's women like me what have to clear up after. And you're worried about my chest? You should try breathing that stuff in.'

'I understand. But some women feel it's the only way that anyone will ever listen.'

'You?'

'Not me.'

'Good-oh,' said Mrs Wantage. 'But you wanna watch your back, Dr Demree. Cos the men giving you grief just know you stand on boxes bellowing alongside of someone who probably has.'

'Did you come to warn me about that?'

'No. I came because you care about girls in trouble. I've heard of a kind of hidey-hole you might want to know about. I'm not much for writing, so when I find out where, I'll get Mrs

Tomlinson to send you a postcard. That's as long as you don't get the girls arrested.'

'I wouldn't.'

Mrs Wantage nodded. 'There's another thing.' Mrs Wantage twisted round to check no one was hovering in earshot. 'Your hospital cut up Radden, didn't it?'

'We undertook the post-mortem, yes.'

If Mrs Wantage realised the word 'we' was literal, she took Margaret's involvement in her stride. 'If he was done in by someone he'd sold on or someone getting revenge for someone he sold on, then none of us'll help the police.'

'I'm not—'

'But if it was someone stopping him from telling what was going on, that's another matter. Maybe Radden was a leopard who'd turned over a new spot.'

'Er, yes.' This was what Inspector Silvermann had suggested: the possibility that Radden had either been unaware of what his interviews led to until recently, or had developed a conscience and was about to inform. 'What makes you think he might have?'

'A girl called Lizzie who was a daily got killed yesterday and her missus too. Maybe the missus is alive: I dunno. Anyway, they've arrested Lizzie's fella. Goodness knows Herb Higgins probably pinched the midwife's wedding ring while he was being born – but a murderer? My sister says nah. Everyone reckons they're dead, half-dead, or whatever it is because of what they didn't know they knew about Radden.'

Margaret could feel herself squint as she tried to work out what Mrs Wantage meant, and wondering if she should explain that Mrs Vidler was still alive.

'The missus was Radden's sister,' said Mrs Wantage. 'Mrs Viper. Very proper, apparently, almost like a lady. Anyway, they say Radden never took the girls home but met them hereabouts, then handed them off to the abbess. That's why his sister never met them. But she might have seen them and so might Lizzie.'

'An abbess?' said Margaret. 'They were being sent to a convent?'

'Cor lummee, doctor! It's slang. Abbess, abbot – people who find girls and run them from a knocking shop. Thing is, Lizzie and Mrs Viper might not have thought nothing of any woman they saw Radden with, but now people are talking. If Mrs Viper wanted to blame someone, she and Lizzie might put their minds back and describe the abbess. Someone didn't want them to. So *anyone* who could describe her had better watch out.'

There was something urgent in Mrs Wantage's expression. A pain, almost, that she couldn't say something as directly as she wanted to.

'Do you mean someone in particular?' said Margaret. 'Will you say a name?'

'I was a seamstress once,' said Mrs Wantage, tapping her nose. 'I got friends who still are. Girls come and girls go, but they don't often end up doing sums in the office. If my pal saw someone like that, she'd notice it. And so might someone else. I wanted to tell you cos I think there's been enough blood, don't you?'

Did Mrs Wantage mean Rosie? Or was there someone else in the same position? Margaret felt appalled that Maria and Martha might be in danger, as well as Rosie. Had she been seen at Maria's business or Maria's home? It sounded more like the former.

As soon as she could, Margaret sent a telegram to Fox's office and another to Inspector Silvermann, then went home to wait.

She played absently with the twins and greeted the inspector when he arrived with a relief that surprised him. 'Could you take the children to Nellie, please, Freda,' she said. 'This shouldn't take long.'

'Tea, ma'am?' said Freda, eyeing the inspector narrowly.

He tipped his hat at her, then removed it. 'No thanks, Miss Mead. As the doctor says, this won't take long.'

Freda sniffed, gave a sharp nod and left the room with the children.

Margaret explained the gist of Mrs Wantage's assumptions about Lizzie's death.

'It's possible,' said Inspector Silvermann.

'But surely Herb Higgins can't have been behind the enterprise Radden was running.'

'I don't think Radden was running it either. And Higgins is a conundrum.'

'Did you find the bullet and the gun?'

'The bullet wasn't far from where Lizzie dropped dead. There's no sign of a gun even though every bit of litter and dog mess in the alley was searched. Not that we could have got any fingerprints if it had been the latter.'

'How revolting.'

'You weren't the one looking.' The inspector grimaced. 'Mind you, due to the privileges of rank, neither was I. Herb Higgins freely admits to burgling to get nice little bits and bobs for Radden to sell on. He also admits he'd made a copy of Lizzie's key for Radden's house. He'd been stealing from there, too – sometimes the stuff he'd sold to Radden in the first place. He said that Lizzie knew Radden was a fence, but otherwise thought he and his sister were as dull as everyone else she worked for, only with more stuff worth nicking. Anyway, he had the means to be in Radden's house on the day he was murdered and has no alibi that a court would believe. Maybe he was there and did the deed, and Lizzie knew and was going to peach on him.'

The inspector paced the room, peered out of the window, then came to sit down, turning his hat over in his hands.

'It makes a sort of sense,' said Margaret.

'Things that make sense aren't necessarily right. I could just about see Higgins killing Radden in a panic, but Radden *wasn't* killed in a panic. Lizzie's different. I've seen murderers – especially men who've killed their women – weeping and wailing and grieving when they're responsible for their own grief. But... The gun, maybe. Attack Mrs Vidler because she's a witness? Maybe. But shoot Lizzie dead then stab her? Why?'

'To be certain?

'It's a flipping palaver, handling a gun and a knife. A good burglar needs to be dextrous, but someone who can juggle two weapons at a time ought to be on stage.'

Juniper jumped into Margaret's lap and Margaret ran her hands through the soft fur, visualising what the inspector was saying. 'The same principle applies in reverse,' she said, after a moment. 'Something that's right doesn't necessarily make sense. People do very odd things. Maybe he did kill Lizzie, and Mrs Vidler appeared at the wrong time.'

'According to the statement she gave, Mrs Vidler had suspected someone was burgling the house and mentioned it to Lizzie,' said the inspector. 'When she found out Lizzie was living with a burglar, she put two and two together and decided Lizzie was spreading the rumours to stop people taking any burglary allegations seriously. So Mrs Vidler went round to remonstrate with her.'

'Did Lizzie know about the procurement?'

'Higgins says they'd heard things, but never seen anything to back it up. On the other hand, according to what everyone says, Lizzie was just a char, Radden never brought anyone home and Lizzie wasn't the teashop type. Mrs Vidler *is* the teashop type, but hadn't even heard the rumours until after he died.'

'And what did Mrs Vidler see in the yard?'

'She says she entered the yard and Lizzie was hanging out the washing. The assailant came from nowhere, bundled up in mackintosh and muffler, killed Lizzie before she even had a chance to scream, stabbed her on the ground, then went for Mrs Vidler, who had just started screaming.'

'Did she hear a gunshot?'

'You know they're not as loud as people think, especially when the gun's shoved into a chest covered in four layers of clothes. Mrs Vidler says she was frozen to the spot in terror and had no chance to run before the assailant attacked her. But he misjudged his aim and she fell and knocked herself out.'

'And what does Higgins say?'

The inspector's mouth twisted into a wry grin. 'He says he knew Mrs Vidler was there to talk to Lizzie and thought he'd keep out of it. When he heard the scream and went out to see what was happening, he saw someone legging it out the gate and two women in a state of collapse. He picked up the knife to follow before realising Lizzie was dead. He says he tried to revive her, but... The rest you know.'

'And their descriptions of the assailant?'

'Mrs Vidler says the man had flashing dark eyes. Higgins says he had fancy foreign shoes. I suppose a thief might notice that sort of thing. It's useless, either way. Mrs Vidler has concussion, so her evidence is questionable. *Anything* Higgins says is questionable. He's admitted to burgling the house, so we might have to go back through the inventory and Radden's paperwork to see if we can prove or disprove that much. Although from something he let slip, it's possible that Higgins killed Radden for a completely different reason.'

'What?'

'He said Lizzie didn't deserve to die like Radden did. He said people like Radden had been responsible for what happened to a girl he knew when he was a lad – someone he was fond of. I had someone do a bit of digging. A fourteen-year-old girl from Higgins's manor was snatched, then found abused and murdered a few weeks later. She and Higgins were by way of being sweethearts and Higgins was briefly under suspicion, but he had a solid alibi. The culprit was never found. If Higgins discovered the rumours about Radden were true, he might have decided on rough justice. But proving it is another matter. And it doesn't explain Lizzie.'

Juniper jumped down and went to the inspector, curling round his legs. Margaret expected him to recoil, but he reached down and scratched between the cat's ears. His expression before he looked down had been sad, angry, unnervingly human. Margaret wondered how many similar cases he'd dealt with in his time. How many culprits had gone free.

'Mrs Wantage hinted at something else,' she said. 'Something about Rosie.'

'Yeah?' The inspector looked up, his normal, neutral expression in place.

'She thinks someone knows where Rosie's hiding. She said, more or less, "Seamstresses don't often end up working in the dressmaker's office. My friend noticed someone who did, and so might someone else."'

'Damn.' The force of the inspector's voice made Juniper dash under the sofa. 'Damn, damn, damn. Leave it with me. I'll tell you as soon as I've got Rosie somewhere else, but I won't give you the location. It'll be less risky for both of you.'

'Understood. But promise you'll keep her safe.'

'I promise.' The inspector cleared his throat. 'I'll be frank. As I said before, I don't think Radden was running this whole enterprise but I think he was running part of it. If his death wasn't rough justice seen through by Higgins, then it was an execution by someone who didn't want him to talk. So your Mrs Wantage is right. Anyone who might have seen something that would identify the others is under threat. That meant Lizzie Jackson, and now it means Rosie, Mrs Vidler and maybe Herb Higgins.

And given where you were yesterday and your connection with Rosie, it might mean you.'

Eighteen

Leaving early enough on Saturday morning to cycle the area where Rosie had been running, including Daffodil Street, was a simple enough task, and the fresh air helped clear the sleep from Margaret's head. She'd heard that all was well with Fox and Inspector Silvermann had rung to confirm that Rosie was safely elsewhere. She'd taken comfort from the assurances and slept well, feeling a good deal more healthy on waking than she had for days.

The streets were coming to life: shutters rolling up, signs turning. Shopkeepers placed boxes of wares on the pavement. Butchers hung rabbits and pheasants from rails in front of the windows. Florists, tea shops, bakers and bookshop owners came out to inspect their window displays.

Delivery boys' bicycles were three deep outside shops and newsagents. The boys themselves yawned, jostled and swapped cigarette cards, blowing into their cold hands as they waited for their orders. The working world stretched itself awake: commuters scurrying, carts and motor vans unloading.

The scene was familiar enough, but now she was seeking something specific. The number of cafés, tea shops, and bakeries with tables was depressing. How long would it take to ask in all of them? And how likely was it that Radden always met the interviewees in the same area?

Margaret bought a copy of *The Daily Mirror* from a news-stand, partly to look normal and partly out of curiosity, as the cover portrayed a woman in a short dress undertaking exercises. It turned out that the article aimed to improve a woman's posture and discourage her from adopting a fashionable 'slinker slouch'. Margaret looked forward to showing Maude sometime. Perhaps, that evening, she could even shock Etta with the bare knees.

She propped the bicycle against the wall near the bookshop in Daffodil Street and watched one of the waitresses put a sandwich board on the pavement outside the Daffodil Café. The waitress was small and slight, the board three quarters of her height, but she moved it as if it were made of paper. Then she stood, hands on hips, surveying the window. If Margaret hadn't encountered a possible murderer brandishing a weapon in the café, she could have asked questions. Now someone else would have to do it.

Margaret turned to the bookshop, wondering if someone working there had noticed anything. Cafés were busy, the waiting staff focused on their customers' demands. Bookshops, on the other hand, were pleasantly idle places where purchasers became lost in words and the staff, perhaps, could sometimes watch the world go by.

A bookshop assistant might possibly recognise Margaret as the woman who'd followed the constable to the alley. However, they were more likely to have seen Radden regularly meet people at the tea shop and to note what happened afterwards.

The shop had just opened. A small selection of popular novels was displayed in a bookcase outside, to tempt commuters on their way to work. But they were all romances, which would narrow their appeal.

Inside, a young man was altering the window display. He smiled warmly as she entered and asked how he might help.

Margaret tried to recall what he'd been putting in the window so that she could start with a logical question, then noticed what looked like a ream of paper on the counter. She saw scrawled writing, words crossed out, arrows and circles, sentences scribbled up the margins. It was a little like one of her own manuscripts, and a good deal more like one of her father's or James's. 'You have a wonderful view of the street from here,' she said. 'It's the perfect place to watch the world go by and describe it afterwards.'

The young man followed her glance and blushed, but it was a proud blush. 'Indeed it is. I confess, sometimes…'

'It's frustrating to break off from your writing to serve a customer?'

'I don't mean—'

'Truly, I understand. What is your novel about?'

'Oh … I can't really explain. There's a shy man and a brave girl, and beings from another world who— It's not a bit like *The War of the Worlds.* The beings may be benign: it's the humans who display the very worst behaviour and, er, impropriety. Subtly described, of course … it'll be quite raw and realistic. Although some are affected by a sort of mania and others are quite underhand. And there's the psychological effect on the young man as he tries to protect— Because of course the girl is quite independent, fighting for the rights of, well, everyone. She doesn't realise he— He's very brave inside, but finds it hard to express. Of course, it's not a romance. It's a drama, with an underlying theme of, er, outsiderness. I'm not making it sound very… I wish I could ask some advice.'

'I'm sure it'll be marvellous,' said Margaret, tempted to pat his arm to calm him. 'I gather it's been busy around here recently.'

'Thursday's murder? Oh yes. Not that we heard or saw anything useful from the police's point of view.' He glanced at his manuscript. 'If one of us had been in the upstairs back room, we might have, but we weren't. We saw the murderer run past with the knife, then into the tea shop. And we saw the police arrive and then the murderer was taken away and another policeman and a woman passed and went up the alley.' He frowned at her for a moment, then appeared to dismiss whatever he was thinking. 'Of course, the murder was really in Twentyman Street. We don't have that sort of crime in Daffodil Street.'

'What sort of crime do you have?'

'I, er... Well, theft from shops, obviously. And Dotty – I mean one of the waitresses across the road – said that someone lured girls and boys away to do improper work for bad employers. I'm not sure what she means by that.'

'Yet your novel's going to be raw and realistic?'

'Er, what? I mean pardon?'

'Never mind. Which waitress is Dotty?'

'Oh, she's gone.'

'What? Is she all right?'

The young man stared at her. 'Why wouldn't she be? She started a new job nearly two weeks ago. I'm, um, I'm glad she wasn't here on Thursday. The ladies in the café were very upset and some of their customers may never return.'

'I imagine Dotty is made of stern stuff, though. Quite independent. Fighting for rights.'

'Oh yes, indeed. She's rather, um...'

'Frightening?'

'She's very feminine and ladylike ... but yes.'

'What did she say about the luring?'

'She said young people arrived to have tea with someone they clearly didn't know, then afterwards they crossed to the alley where a man or woman – generally a woman – led them away. It all looked above board, but she said it happened too often. The chap they met was a customer of mine. I wonder if he'd been hired by some questionable people.'

'Your customer?'

'He was called Mr Radden. You may have read in the paper that he was murdered recently. Dear me, I've just realised. Two murders.' The young man became lost in thought and his gaze drifted to the manuscript.

'What was he like?'

'He liked fantastical fiction,' said the young man, as if this precluded an inclination to lure people or be murdered. 'He seemed very nice. He was a little agitated the last time he came in. He'd ordered a copy of *The Lost World* – I remember, because we had quite a discussion when he ordered it, and it was dark when he came, nearly six o'clock. We were about to close. He paid, then asked for some paper, sat in that chair and scribbled for a bit, then he left. He treated the book rather more roughly than he usually did.' The young man squinted. 'I *think* that was the day when Dotty said "Someone didn't turn up."'

'What did Dotty think of Mr Radden?'

'She couldn't decide. She doesn't like the people in the alley, but she never saw faces. Just people who looked very respectable, by their clothes and the way they stood and that sort of thing. I don't like to ask what she thinks they're doing, in case she has to say something indelicate and she's embarrassed.'

'Perhaps you should,' said Margaret. 'If not for the sake of showing her that you care, then for your novel's sake. Has Dotty told the police about the people who lure people?'

The young man shook his head. 'She says it's best not to be involved and she couldn't identify anyone anyway.'

'Well, if Dotty does decide she wants to tell someone, and she doesn't want to speak to the police, she may write to me.' Margaret handed over her business card. 'Incidentally, why not put some detective novels on the stand outside? They'd probably sell better, especially just now.'

The young man blushed again. 'Isn't that rather improper?'

'It's good business sense,' said Margaret. 'Detective stories are popular even when there hasn't been a murder in the neighbourhood.'

The young man glanced down at the business card. 'Oh! Are you any relation to Mr Roderick Demeray? He's one of our best customers. He bought a most wonderful book here last December and quite made my day: a first edition of *Rural Rides*. Very valuable, you know.'

'I do,' said Margaret. 'He gave it to me for Christmas.'

'I'd like to ask his advice about my novel, but...'

'You should.'

'Really? Oh! I hadn't seen him come in. He doesn't look quite the thing. Sir, are you all right?'

Margaret turned and saw an elderly man with a cane come round the end of a bookcase, staring into the next section as a child might look at a shelf filled with jars of sweets. It took Margaret seconds to realise who it was. 'Father! Whatever—'

'Meg! Darling! Have you seen this edition of—'

'What are you doing here at half past eight in the morning? Does Katherine know you're out?'

Her father pouted. 'Why shouldn't I be? And why need Kitty know? She's not my wardress. She doesn't tell me when she's going off on one of her jaunts with Connie.'

'I'm sure she has breakfast first,' said Margaret. 'Did you?'

'One had some tea before one left,' said her father, with dignity. 'And one may patronise one of the cafés, after one has made one's purchase.'

'You don't have anything in your hand.'

Her father was oblivious, still happily staring at spines and covers, his head on one side. But he was swaying a little and he was paler than paper.

'Come along, Father,' said Margaret. 'Let's get you home. Return later. The assistant wants to pick your literary brains, but just now you need breakfast.'

'Don't rush me, Meg, I'm making a choice. You know I need to choose not on looks alone, but by becoming acquainted with character, mood, intellect and deep expression of the same things I hold dear.'

'Father, you're buying a book, not finding a wife.'

'That's unkind, dear. Thirza's passing was less than a year ago.'

'I'm sorry.' Margaret felt a pang at his stricken face and tucked her arm into his.

'Besides...' He peered down at her with a puzzled expression. 'You don't look well yourself. You remind me of your mother when... Oh dear me. Perhaps we should visit the churchyard in Fulham and—'

'I'm not that sick, Father. I've had a feverish cold, but I am on the mend.'

'It's not so easy to visit your mother's grave these days.'

'We three shall take flowers for her soon,' said Margaret. 'Let's decide a date when I get you home. Kitty will be worried sick. I understand that you have every right to go where you want, but do try to see it from our point of view. Now, let's find a cab that'll take my bicycle as well as us.'

'I could go on my own.'

'I don't trust you,' said Margaret. 'You'd double back as soon as I was out of sight.'

'Really,' said her father, his sadness eclipsed by a grin. 'What a dreadful thing to suggest. Although I do seem to recall that was the sort of thing you did as a small child.'

'I must have inherited something from you, then.' She squeezed his arm.

'A good deal more than that,' said her father. 'Do let's go to a tea shop or bakery. We can buy some buns to assuage Kitty's wrath.' With a wave at the young man, he led her from the shop.

With some difficulty, Margaret steered him from the Daffodil Café towards a fancy bakery a few yards down the street. Like the more humble one where Margaret used to have lunch when she worked in St Julia's, it had tables inside, and she made her father sit as she waited in the queue.

Early customers who presumably didn't have work to go to were having a light breakfast while reading newspapers. A woman was buried in the *Marylebone Mercury*, its front page dedicated to advertisements. If Lizzie Jackson's murder had been reported, it would be somewhere inside. Perhaps that was what she was reading.

The front page of the *Globe* obscured its reader's face with densely packed articles relating to Archduke Francis-Ferdinand's visit, which Hare so longed to be over.

But it was the *Illustrated London News* which caught Margaret's eye just as she was about to reach the front of the queue. The front page displayed a large photograph of officers on what appeared to be a ship's bridge, looking through an enormous telescope. An inset photograph showed a battleship under way. The reader let the paper slip as he turned the pages and the feverish thoughts Margaret had had on Thursday evening came back. She was certain it was the man whom she'd sketched in a different café a week or so before: the man Bert knew as the Russian agent Petrov.

She bowed her head as far as she could to obscure her face and adopted the slinker slouch before turning to the counter, bought a far wider selection of buns than she needed, collected her father and left.

Nineteen

Fox arrived later than expected that evening. 'Thanks for the message you sent the office about Petrov,' he said, as he dressed for dinner. 'Did he notice you?'

'I don't think so.'

'Good. Hopefully, it's coincidental.'

'How was Weymouth?'

'There were no signs of arms going through, but rumours something else is. Military plans, people or both? The harbour staff watch for anyone being escorted under duress and check a percentage of the packing crates too, but have found nothing lately. If people are being taken abroad from there, they must feel safe to begin with. Perhaps that's the first part of the job, or whatever Rosie said. Bert and Pigeon are following up other leads along the Thames now.'

'Don't you need to join them?'

'Not yet.' Fox checked himself in the mirror then turned to kiss her, running a finger down her cheek. 'You look lovely.'

'Not peaky?'

'A little tired, perhaps, but that's hardly surprising.'

'Maude telephoned to ask us to go for a walk with them in Regent's Park before lunch tomorrow,' said Margaret. 'I'd have said no, but she has something she wants to discuss with you.'

'Me?'

'Apparently. I hope you don't mind too much.'

'Not at all.'

Margaret straightened his tie. 'Did the police find out any more about Kay Rowlands?'

'A house near Nothe Fort was rented for three days to a Mr Arthur, who gave his normal address as a villa called Camelot in a street in Islington.'

'I bet there's no such place.'

'Exactly,' said Fox. 'It's all smoke and mirrors as usual. But Kay's fingerprints were found on various sills in that Weymouth house, as if he'd climbed from windows, and he was seen several times in the vicinity of Whitehead's, possibly once at the station and almost certainly at the quay. One thing he didn't do is ask for a job at the swannery.'

'So that's a mystery.'

'I'm afraid so. Incidentally...' He handed her an envelope which contained a few photographs. 'These are the snaps from our weekend in Weymouth that came out.'

Among the photographs was one of Margaret with Gil and Raoul. In the background, a stream of people headed towards the ship. One person had half turned at the moment the shutter went: Andreyev. 'Did you show this to Bert?'

'Why?' said Fox. 'Because that man has a Russian name and Gil doesn't like him?'

'Because he was in Weymouth, about to board a ship where staff were waiting. What if he's Mr Arthur and the missing person was Kay?'

'Could be,' said Fox. 'I'll telephone Bert and tell him to look at the negative.'

Phoebe, Elinor, Percival and Etta arrived half an hour later. Phoebe wore a dark-peach velvet dress which warmed her face. Her honey-coloured hair was dressed in the latest style, with a russet ribbon threaded through, and she wore carnelian jewellery in a Rennie Mackintosh setting. Elinor was wearing a simple navy-blue costume, her curly hair under its usual net, with a cameo brooch pinned to her bodice.

Etta wore the same dress she'd worn at Phoebe's dinner. That surprised Margaret, who'd always suspected her of having a system to ensure that she didn't repeat clothes too often. She and Percival, a little dark under the eyes, stayed close together, but managed to avoid touching each other. It was as if they were restricted by their own orbits, irresistibly connected yet equally irresistibly repelled. They spoke with the politeness of mere acquaintances, with infinitesimal thorn-sharp pauses where terms of intimate affection should be.

Etta's manner to everyone else, however, was the same as usual.

'I gather my sister-in-law has employed you, Miss Edwards,' she said, as they settled in the dining room. 'Are you one of the Berkshire Edwardses? I heard that one of the branches is – ahem – encouraging its female members to take on paid work. Is your father the squire of anywhere I know?'

'I'm an Edwards from Carmarthen, via Tiger Bay and Jamaica,' said Elinor.

'All those places? Tiger Bay sounds exciting. Is it in India? You make it sound as if both your parents were called Edwards. Does the Jamaican branch have a plantation?'

'A plantation was involved,' said Elinor. 'Ownership is another matter. Names are another matter, too. Margaret's dressmaker is called Edwards and she isn't a relation.'

'I believe the Welsh didn't have surnames until long after everyone else,' said Etta, putting on a sing-song voice as Freda placed oysters before her. 'You don't sound Welsh.'

'Whereas you, Mrs Pendleberry, sound precisely what you are.'

'Jolly good,' said Etta, with a happy smile.

Phoebe turned a snort into a cough.

Percival forced a smile. 'I'm delighted that you're assisting Phoebe, Miss Edwards. I've never been good at figures. Etta runs rings round me.'

'One has a large establishment to run,' said Etta, spooning condiments onto an oyster.

'You make your house sound like a department store,' said Phoebe.

'How amusing, dear. My financial expertise is quite domestic.'

'What nonsense,' said Percival, as the oysters were replaced with chicken consommé. There was no humour in his voice. Phoebe nudged him, but he shook it off.

Margaret decided she had no intention of her dinner party being ruined when it had barely begun. 'Did you see the article about how to avoid the slinker slouch, Etta? I thought you might have a view on the skirts.'

Etta's scowl smoothed into indifference. 'One would never slink or slouch, Margaret, nor use slang. Incidentally, how many courses have you ordered? This is rather more delicious than I had exp— Did your maid get it sent from Fortnum's or Harrods?'

Freda, standing by the door, scowled.

'Just six courses,' said Margaret. 'And Freda has cooked absolutely everything. One day I'll lose her to a large establishment, just as one day I'll lose Nellie to Norland College.'

'Maude says you spoil your staff,' said Etta. 'Why would they leave?'

'By the way, Etta and Phoebe,' said Fox, with a warning glance at Margaret. 'What do you—'

Whatever he said next was inaudible to Margaret, but seemed to amuse the women he was speaking to and relieve the tension.

'I'm so sorry,' said Percival to Margaret. As Freda collected his soup plate, he apologised to her, too. 'I have very little appetite just now. It's no reflection on your skills, more on ... other things.'

'Very good, sir. Perhaps the Dover sole will help.'

'And after that?'

'Roast duck with dressed vegetables and Parmentier potatoes, then Waldorf Pudding, then cheese and nuts.'

'Excellent. Please don't be offended by those who speak before they think.'

'No, sir.'

'Nor you, Miss Edwards.'

Elinor inclined her head.

'I also owe you a different apology, Margaret,' Percival added. 'Life has been unexpectedly busy recently, with unforeseen matters arising, and I've failed to answer the question you raised at Phoebe's dinner party. The trade in question is a sensitive subject, and so far I have little concrete information.' Percival shifted his cutlery about. 'I'm likely to remain busy with the unforeseen matters I mentioned earlier. But if I hear anything useful, I shall let you know.'

'You mentioned a funny article, Margaret,' said Elinor. 'They're few and far between. Was it the one about the cat?'

'No. What did it do?'

'Disrupted the tramway in Kennington for a quarter of an hour, then rode quite happily on the motor beneath the tram all the way to Blackfriars Bridge. I wondered if it was Juniper.'

'Probably,' said Margaret. 'Several miles and crossing the Thames wouldn't stop Juniper if she had a mind to get away. It wouldn't stop me, either. Hiding on a nice warm electric engine sounds positive bliss.'

'Doesn't it,' said Percival, quietly. 'I wonder if a disgruntled husband would fit.'

As the next course was served, everyone joined in a general conversation and the atmosphere lightened.

Afterwards, they rearranged the sitting-room furniture so that some could dance to the gramophone while others chatted by the fire. Etta and Percival sat close together, their heads nearly touching, but whatever they were saying appeared neither affectionate nor even friendly. Briefly, Margaret and Fox were the only dancers. He held her close as if they were alone, his hand warm in the small of her back, his heart beating against hers.

'Despite everything, Phoebe looks happy, doesn't she?' whispered Fox. 'You always say she keeps everyone else's secrets, but she's half-revealing her own.'

Margaret looked across the room. Phoebe was showing Elinor dance steps. They held each other at a distance and looked down at their feet, faces flushed. Elinor's normally solemn expression and Phoebe's sensible one had been replaced by girlish grins. They both looked ten years younger and ready to giggle. It was fascinating to witness, and at the same time, intrusive to watch.

Something Margaret had only half realised in twenty years dropped into place. *What a fool you are*, she thought. She felt happy for Phoebe, but uneasy. Scandal didn't just come from breaking the law, but also from breaking society's rules.

'What Percival said about Etta is interesting,' murmured Fox.

'Etta has a massive house in London and a small manor in the country, at least twenty inside servants and six outside ones, plus the governess, the dancing master and who knows what else. I struggle enough with two staff plus Dinah, a jobbing gardener and a house that's comparatively tiny.'

'That's not what he meant.'

The record came to an end and Fox released Margaret to start another. In the silence, Etta's voice was suddenly clear. 'I'm no more skilled with money than you.'

'Nonsense,' snapped Percival. 'I've seen you look at the constituency accounts with Bloom in your guise of financial-idiot wife, when you're nothing of the sort. You treat him like dirt as you query every sum. You interrogate our man of business about our investments in such a way that I half-expect you to bring out the pincers. And when you scrutinise your family's Irish estate papers you ask questions no one else thinks of.'

Etta made no attempt to keep her voice low. 'One has to be vigilant about Irish estates: the rebels won't honour agreements. If they'd acknowledge that an independent Ireland would be best ruled from Ulster, I might trust them more – but they won't. Thank God, the Unionist movement is growing. We will not stand by to be trampled on.'

'They're republicans, not rebels,' said Percival. 'Let your accursed family sell that Irish estate and let the Home Rule Bill go through. I don't need any more accusations that I'm involved in the despicable treatment of the poor.'

'The Irish Citizen Army is arming its men. They say it's to protect strikers, but I don't believe it. This is a matter beyond your dreary little constituency, with its whining paupers, loose moralled girls and thieving men whose lives aren't worth a penny candle.'

'Not worth a penny candle?' said Percival, rising and looking down at her. 'All these years of being my wife, and that's what you really think?'

'There are things that are worth investing in, no matter the cost, and the Union is—' Etta blinked as she realised that there was no music and her voice was the only sound.

She swallowed and turned to the room. 'I apologise, Margaret. How rude of us. Do start dancing again. I have a slight headache, er... Do you have any sort of garden where I might take some fresh air?'

Margaret counted to ten in her head while she rang for Freda. 'The garden will be dark and foggy. Freda, please take Mrs Pendleberry to my study and bring her aspirin and water.'

'Very good, ma'am.'

'Thank you,' said Etta, as she left the room. 'I wouldn't like to ruin the evening.'

Percival's jaw clenched for a second, then he managed an enigmatic smile and took Margaret's hand. 'Once more, I apologise profusely,' he said. 'Despite our discourtesy, would you do me the honour of a dance? Perhaps Fox might put a waltz on the gramophone: something to calm my beloved wife, should it filter through to the study.'

Another half hour passed as slowly as that waltz – the dancing, the polite conversation, the subdued card games.

It was more than a relief when Phoebe mentioned the eight o'clock Sunday-morning service at church. In all the time Margaret had known her, Phoebe had happily stayed up late on Saturday yet gone to the early service at church on Sunday. Percival, taking her hint, said that he and Etta would also leave.

When they embraced to say goodbye, Phoebe whispered 'I am utterly mortified by my family. I am so terribly sorry.'

'Don't blame yourself,' Margaret whispered back. 'It's not your fault.'

Margaret and Fox had waved them goodbye, shut the door and were staring at each other in disbelief when the telephone rang.

Fox answered. 'Hallo... Excellent. And...? Ah.' There was a short pause as he listened then 'Interesting... Yes. Goodbye.'

He replaced the receiver and led Margaret into the sitting room. 'An agent's found out where the Brown sisters live. The house is crammed with people who come and go, some more criminal than others. Daisy and Violet owe rent for their tiny room and haven't been seen for a few days. The landlord expects them back, though, and someone will keep an eye out, so we're on the right track.'

'That's good news.'

'Hopefully.' Fox went to check in the hallway, then returned. 'The other thing is that your hunch was right. Bert recognised Andreyev in the negative. He knows him under a different name through friendly agents based in north-eastern France and Flanders. Andreyev's a suspected spy who specialises in obtaining copies of secret documents and plans. In answer to your next question, his only personal allegiance seems to be to money. So his presence in Weymouth when Kay was trying to get into Whitehead's seems unlikely to be a coincidence.'

'So you'll be going back?' Margaret tried to sound as if she didn't care.

'I've been there too often recently,' said Fox. 'Bert will go. I want to know what Maude has to say, then I'll have to go back to the office to see if I can find a link to Abney.'

'He's dead.'

'Hopefully,' said Fox. 'But that doesn't mean the people who worked with him have stopped his work, does it?'

Twenty

They drove to Regent's Park at eleven the following morning.

'If you need to be elsewhere, I can find out what Maude wants,' said Margaret, even though what she longed for was a normal family Sunday.

'It's all right,' said Fox, changing gear. 'I wish I could get Elinor inveigled into the constituency office to look at the accounts tomorrow, but they'd never accept a woman to do it, even if they thought she'd be intellectually capable. Government offices are too afraid of suffragettes.'

They passed along Daffodil Street. Margaret peered down the alley beside the bookshop, wondering what Dotty had seen and whether it was worth trying to speak with her.

'It's a slow process,' she said.

'Investigation usually is.'

'I mean the way they're taking these young people. Rosie was adamant there was no assault, yet it's often the first thing that happens so that they're brutalised into prostitution. Instead, they trained her for clerical work and treated her well. It was only after a few days that she became afraid.'

'A pleasant prison is still a prison.'

'Maybe it's a subtler operation than usual.'

'Some men will pay good money to destroy absolute, trusting innocence,' said Fox. 'It's a disgusting world. Thank you for saying I could go, but it would be nice to have a few hours of normality. If Hare needs me, he knows where to send someone.'

The fog had largely receded everywhere else, but in Regent's Park it drifted in waves, making walkers appear to be wading through waist-deep water. Apart from Becca, the children zigzagged along the path like otters in a stream, the twins barely visible.

Here and there, bedraggled men and women huddled on benches, coughing. Margaret wondered how many had slept in the park overnight, unable to find the wherewithal for lodgings, unwilling to go to the workhouse, obscured by fog from wardens and police. Maude said she wanted to speak with Margaret first, so Fox and Geoff strode ahead, herding the children.

The damp air tickled Margaret's throat and she tucked her muffler tighter. 'What's wrong?'

'Goodness,' said Maude. 'Can't one be social first?' She took Margaret's arm. 'It's good to see Edie whizzing about like that.'

'She's pretending to fly a naryplane like poor Ed.'

'*Poor* Ed?' said Maude. 'I'd love to fly an aeroplane.'

'He's nursing a broken heart.'

'Ed? Oh... Do you mean Lucy?'

'Katherine says Lucy's explained that she simply sees him as a cousin who's also a good friend. At the moment, Ed thinks that's worse than death.'

'You were like that when some boy wasn't interested.'

'Tosh,' said Margaret, her voice recovering. 'I always bounced back and Ed will, too. He just needs to find another girl.'

Maude chuckled. 'How was last night's dinner party?'

'Absolutely dreadful. Etta was rude and snobbish from the off, then ended up shouting at Percival. It was awful.'

'In public? What about?'

'Home Rule. Percival's lack of political ambition.'

'Etta's staunchly Unionist, isn't she?' said Maude. 'And Percival opposes her. He grasps the issue more clearly as he takes trouble to discover why people are discontented. I can't imagine Etta bothering.' Maude's face was troubled. 'But Percival's reputation is being damaged by rumours, isn't it?'

'What have you heard?' Margaret kept her voice low even though no one was near.

'Embezzlement of funds and taking rent from substandard housing under a false name. Someone asked *Athene's Gazette* to investigate.'

'That's tricky,' said Margaret, grimacing.

'He's the brother of one of my best friends. I'd feel like a hound. I legitimately said that I had plenty of other things to investigate and asked for some evidence for the rumours' validity. It went quiet, so presumably they're groundless. But you know what people are like. I'm surprised no one's accused him of having another woman somewhere.'

'I'm not sure I'd blame him,' said Margaret, wondering what Maude would think if she knew Fox was investigating the claims of fraud himself. She coughed again.

Maude patted her back. 'You should take more care of yourself, Demeray. Breathing in dead people isn't healthy.'

'I do wish everyone would stop nagging. I'm minded to paint my face to stop everyone insisting I move to Switzerland.'

'I can lend you some rouge.'

'Thank you.' Ahead of them, Sam had dropped back to walk with Becca, swinging her hand. Geoff walked on Becca's other side, her arm tucked into his. Fox had Alec on his shoulders, while Edie and Johnny ran in circles round him.

'Becca's growing up,' said Maude. 'Suddenly, one understands why everyone was so overprotective when we were young. I understand how papers work, but as a mother I'm terrified when I read that another girl has disappeared, died or had a narrow escape. Half of it isn't true, but... This is why I want to speak with Fox.' Maude stopped walking.

Margaret's skin prickled. 'Go on.'

'Do you know how I manage the letters received by *Athene's Gazette*?'

'Two staff choose letters for possible publication, then pass them to you for approval. You'll publish anonymous letters if the writer requests it, but only if they provided their name and address.'

'Even if they don't, if there's cause for concern – threats perhaps, or a cry for help – I might print an article providing helpful information, or pass the letter to a private investigator to see what can be done. Very occasionally, I tell the police.'

'I see,' said Margaret.

Maude withdrew her arm from Margaret's and peered about. The fog had almost gone and their surroundings were quiet. The children sat on a bench in age order, lined up like steps. Fox and Geoff had paused to light their pipes. 'I've had a letter that may need to be reported, but I think it might be more Fox's thing than the usual policeman's.'

'Does Geoff know about it?'

'Yes. Come on.'

They joined the men. Maude handed the letter to Fox and Margaret and stood nearby with Geoff, keeping half an eye on the children.

The letter had been sent from France, the postmark Bayonne. It was written in neat, precise handwriting and signed simply with 'A Reverend's Wife'. It began by saying that the writer's husband was rector of an English church in a French town popular with tourists. She explained that along with the normal duties of an Anglican church, they also assisted any English speaker who found themselves in difficulties abroad.

Sometimes girls come to us for help after having been seduced and abandoned; others to escape a life of vice. It takes either young woman a great deal of courage, and I do everything I can to assure them I will assist with compassion rather than judgment.

This kind of thing has happened for millennia, of course, but a short while ago a girl came to me whose story was a little different. This is why I, as an avid reader of Athene's Gazette, am writing to you.

The writer described what had happened to a girl of seventeen called Hilda who, without family or prospects in her small town, had sought a better life. Her experience had been just as Rosie had described: the advertisement in a country paper, the interview at the Daffodil Café, a 'training school', and a vagueness in detail which suggested some sort of drugging.

But unlike Rosie, Hilda had not been the only 'trainee'. There had been a girl of sixteen called Eveline and a boy of fourteen called—

'Kay,' whispered Margaret to Fox. He nodded, his face sombre.

A Miss Board trained them in copying or typing 'all sorts of gobbledegook', as a test that they could do it quickly without having to understand the words. Arithmetic, and draughtsmanship by way of copying diagrams and maps, were taught by a Mr Quill.

Eveline left to work in Belgium for a Miss Bull, then Kay left, uncertain where he was bound, to work for a Mr Arthur.

'Why are you two twitching?' said Maude. 'You seem to be half expecting this.'

'Do you remember that a dead boy was found when we were in Weymouth?' said Margaret. 'His name was Kay.'

'Oh God. Do you think... Never mind, keep reading.'

Left alone, Hilda listened at doors. She heard two men say that selling two things at once made better money and they sniggered about how buxom, pretty Eveline was 'bound to be good in the second stage of her work'. Kay, it seemed, was destined for a different second stage, and they hoped he was as strong as he looked as 'there's no factory act there'.

Margaret clenched her fists. 'So they're going out of the country thinking they're clerks, then the girls are sold into prostitution and boys into a different sort of illegal industry?'

While the lasciviousness with which they spoke of Eveline upset Hilda the most, sadly it did not surprise me, the letter continued. *However, something else did. Tourists may come to a resort to forget current affairs and politics, but those living here cannot. Hilda also says she overhead people discussing whether 'it was right to support both sides', but concluding that 'a gun is only deadly if it's used'. This concerns me. She was possibly under the influence of some drug, but I believe she remembers the essence of what was said.*

There followed a long explanation of Hilda's attempts to escape, which were foiled at every turn. Finally, she was provided with new clothes and a small valise and escorted onto the boat train at Waterloo to meet her employer, a woman with the unlikely name of Mrs Stitch. At Dover, she went to the lavatory and looked in the case to see if anything useful was in there. Well buried, she found jewellery and a map of some barracks. Before she could do anything, though, Mrs Stitch found her and took her to the boat, where she was given something to help with seasickness which made her drowsy.

For a few days after arriving in France, Hilda undertook simple clerical work for Mrs Stitch. There was nothing in the valise when she next looked and she concluded that anxiety had made her imagine things. She began to enjoy herself a little. Her work was interesting and Mrs Stitch took her about and made a foreign land seem delightful. Hilda was happy, although she felt increasingly under the weather, which Mrs Stitch said was a consequence of getting used to foreign water.

Then one day Hilda was given something to help her sleep. When she woke, it was in a strange bedroom, with a view from the window she didn't recognise. A woman came in to say that she should expect a visit from a man shortly and it would be more bearable if she didn't make a fuss. The woman didn't allow clients who liked resistance, and Hilda should be grateful for that.

She was promised a bath and a good meal at the end of her evening's work, when she could meet the other girls. She was assured that in no time she'd learn to enjoy her work, but if she tried to escape she would be killed.

The room was on the third floor, but Hilda escaped before the man arrived. I am not sure if I will ever know quite how, since she was still under the influence of something when she was brought to me, thinking she was asleep and in a nightmare, badly grazed from a fall and running barefoot through the street. I suspect she may have injured the woman in order to escape, but find it hard to care. It has taken several days of patient kindness to get the information I have given you.

She cannot or will not describe the house nor the madam, and all she can recall of Mrs Stitch was that she seemed fancy, while the woman who'd taken her to the 'training school' was quite young and wore cosmetic.

Hilda only gave me her Christian name. She is terrified of being discovered. At present, she is being nursed to health before we try to find safe work for her under a new name. I fear her body will be easier to heal than her mind. But she is angry too, and I think would, if the perpetrators were arrested, give evidence against them.

Was Hilda given a respectable job initially, and only afterwards sold on? Are guns relevant, or is Hilda simply confused? And where are Eveline and Kay? I have no evidence to take to either the French or British police. But if you could alert your readers to this ruse, it might prevent another young person from experiencing the horror Hilda faced.

'Thank you, Maude.' Fox folded the letter and put it in his wallet. 'I think this is indeed my sort of thing.'

'It's what she overheard about the gun, isn't it?' said Maude. 'They're buying arms to sell, using the sale of stolen information and smuggled people, aren't they?'

'It looks that way,' said Fox.

'It's elaborate but potentially foolproof, if they don't do it for too long,' said Geoff. 'Customs won't think a junior member of staff with an old case and secondhand clothes will be carrying anything valuable.'

Maude swallowed. 'And there's Ed, learning to fly for the war which the papers keep hinting that Germany wants to start.'

'It might not be that war,' said Margaret.

'What, then?'

'Ireland,' said Fox. 'Anarchists. Revolutionaries in Russia. There are any number of groups who'd pay for arms. This group is prepared to sell to any or all of them. Thanks, Maude.'

'Do you know of anyone else caught up in this who's still out there?'

'We're trying to find someone called Violet Brown who might be,' said Margaret.

'I'm publishing an article about this ruse in the next issue of *Athene's Gazette*,' said Maude. 'I'll mention her.'

'Don't,' said Fox. 'Not yet. Too much detail may hinder attempts to find the whole gang.'

'Very well,' said Maude. 'I'll make it general enough to make a point, but sufficiently clear for the vicar's wife to know it's due to her letter and write again. I just hope it's enough.'

Twenty-One

With Fox in the office on Sunday afternoon, Margaret and the twins danced to gramophone records, played with building blocks, and scribbled with stubby pencils on scraps of paper.

At three, Nellie requested leave to go for a walk with some young people from her church – presumably including Harry Kirson – and Margaret agreed. 'You can go too,' she said to Freda.

'With the holy of holies? No thank you, ma'am. I'd rather black the stove.'

'You're not going to, are you?'

'Hardly, ma'am,' said Freda. 'I've got letters to write and a library book I've been saving, if you don't need me.'

'I don't, thank you,' said Margaret. 'Why not go and visit your cousin in... Highbury, wasn't it?'

'Joe had a letter,' said Freda. 'The family she lodges with are taking her to Margate to get some ozone. But we're all going to meet up for afternoon tea on the second when I have my half-day, if that's all right with you.'

'Of course it is.'

As the twins slept, cuddled under a rug on the sofa, Margaret sketched them. She thought it would keep her mind off things, but as she looked at their soft, round faces she recalled what Maude had said about Becca.

One day, Edie would be on the verge of puberty too. What would she be like in 1923? Would she be growing up in a fairer society where a woman could vote, get a university degree and do any job she chose? Would girls and women be able to exist without fear of assault? Or would Margaret worry about Edie as Maude did about Becca? As Fox did about her?

She turned back in her sketchbook to the rough impression she'd made of Kay. What would he have done after he left the country? Prostitution was as much of a possibility for boys as it was for girls, but what Hilda had said about the Factory Act suggested that wasn't Kay's destiny. And just as the White Slave Bill hadn't yet stopped the international traffic in people, the Factory Act couldn't guarantee that every factory and mine was safe.

Perhaps Kay was to work in some illegal operation in Britain, or perhaps he was simply meant to die in Weymouth.

The thought made Margaret feel angry, nauseous and helpless. Ensuring that there were cushions on the floor in case the children rolled off the sofa, she telephoned Inspector Silvermann's office. To her relief, he was on duty.

'Has Fox told you about the Browns?' she said.

'Yes. They've done a flit. I hope they're on their way home to Pitsea.'

'Where?'

'Essex. It's getting on for thirty miles from Whitechapel. If they're walking, it might in theory take two days, but if they're keeping off main roads to stay safer it'll be longer. I'll let you know if we find them. You're really ringing about Rosie, aren't you?'

'Partly.'

'She's safe, I promise. If it makes you feel better, she's getting a school education now. If you telephoned only partly about her, what else did you want?'

Margaret fidgeted with the telephone. 'How many places do you think operate outside the Factory Act in Britain?'

'Outside it? Factories? Sweating shops? Mines? Shipping companies? Think of a number between one hundred and ten thousand and triple it. Why?'

'Because people aren't just trafficked for one thing, are they?'

'No.'

'If Radden was selling people on for illegal factory work in Britain, where could they go?'

The inspector sighed. 'Your kids would be great-grandparents before we exposed every place we know about, let alone the ones we don't. Just trust me, Dr Demeray. I'm doing everything I can to find out what Radden was up to and stop it.'

Fox returned home at four, cuddled the sleeping children and listened to Margaret's thoughts about Kay.

'I think you're right that he wasn't the only boy being recruited,' he said. 'But keeping him in Britain would fall outside the pattern for this organisation.'

'So he was supposed to have sailed from Weymouth.'

'Presumably,' said Fox. 'Bert followed your suggestion. Andreyev did rent the house under the name of Arthur. though he wasn't there a great deal and his alleged wife not at all. His name wasn't on the passenger list for the ship, but his description matches a Lord Antony who was supposed to be accompanied by an unnamed secretary, but in the end sailed alone. We're following that trail now.'

'What makes you think that boys as well as girls were going through Radden's hands?'

'His numerous ledgers. I've worked out that if you know what you're looking for, they cross-reference, and the innocuous becomes disturbing. Without Elinor, it's been a long slog.'

'Are you relying on Smith?'

'No, thank God. None of it's in another language.'

The door to the sitting room opened and Nellie entered. 'Shall I take the twins, ma'am?'

'Yes, please. Did you have a nice time?'

'Yes thank you, ma'am.' Nellie's voice was prim, but there was a misty look in her eyes. The soft smile on her lips as she lifted the children faltered as she paused in the doorway. 'W-would you let me have Harry— Mr Kirson for tea in the kitchen on Wednesday if Freda chaperones us, ma'am?'

'Goodness,' said Margaret. 'I suppose so, if Freda's willing. Though I shall be at work, so you'll have to be chaperoned by the children too.'

'Thank you, ma'am.' Nellie jigged the children and grinned. 'And that's all right. Harry likes children. Thanks ever so.'

Fox waited till she'd gone before turning to Margaret. 'Are you going to tell her mother? We know nothing about this Harry Kirson. Being a churchgoer proves nothing except that he goes to church. I could do without any more young women getting into difficulties under our noses, or unknown strangers in our house.'

'I hadn't thought of that,' said Margaret. 'I'll tell Nellie to tell her mother herself. She won't disobey me: she's not made that way.'

'If I can spare Pigeon for an hour I'll send him round on some pretext – mending that wretched vacuum cleaner, or designing some sort of kitchen gadget. Freda can reward him with cake.'

'She'll probably be glad of his company if Nellie and Harry are as pious as they make out. Piety's not Freda's style at all. But never mind that now. What were you saying about Radden's ledgers?'

'The trade in valuables has been going on for years, with some clever paperwork mixing legitimately purchased items and fenced ones,' said Fox. 'But for a few months there's been another business which, if I'm right, involves procurement. There's mention of flowers and machinery, and a regular income, but no evidence Radden had anything to do with floristry, gardening or engineering. Flowers are reported to "grow well", "need pruning" or sometimes they "didn't thrive". Machinery "runs as expected", "needs adjustment" or "failed". I'm taking the flowers to be girls and the machinery, boys. We're cross-referencing everything again to see what we've missed.'

'Does Herb Higgins come into it?'

'Not that we've found.'

'Not even in his diaries?'

Fox shook his head. 'His diaries describe an utterly respectable, boring life. Nothing suggests any doubt about what he was doing or who he was working with.'

'With or for?'

'That, my dear, is the burning question.'

The following morning, Fox drove Margaret to work.

'I forgot to tell you that Percival's constituency accounts are being investigated,' he said. 'I shall find a way of discovering the outcome.' He stopped the car outside the hospital and cleared his throat. 'I'm afraid I have to ask you this, Margaret. Do you think Hilda's "fancy" Mrs Stitch could be Etta pretending to need a secretary, showing Hilda a little bit of France, then coming home totally unaware of Hilda's intended destiny.'

'Why ever would she?'

'Whatever else was behind that argument, debt surely is. My money – if you pardon the pun – is on Etta being the one in financial difficulties.'

'She'd never allow herself to be employed.'

'If the proposal was phrased so that it didn't feel like employment and someone said she'd be supporting the Unionist cause, don't you think she might? On the other hand, if she rarely leaves the country, it can't be her.'

'Will you inform Inspector Silvermann?' Margaret felt sick. She had a vague feeling that Etta did go abroad now and then, but where and when was another matter. She wouldn't say so without being certain. She didn't like Etta, but had no intention of throwing her to the lions without evidence.

'If Radden's nasty little enterprise connects to money for arms, I may have to,' said Fox, climbing out of the car to hand her onto the pavement. 'I'm sorry. I don't want to think that Etta would knowingly be involved in such a thing, but if she did it unwittingly, her evidence might be critical.'

The doctors' morning meeting went through its usual business, with a brief reference to Mrs Vidler, who had been discharged into a friend's care as her concussion was mild and her injuries not of great concern, before confirming Algie's arrival in the new year.

'His area of work is yet to be decided,' said Dr Innes. 'As you know, the vacancy is on the gastric ward, but Dr Hardisty is highly skilled in both the treatment of chest disease and pathology. Therefore, some rearrangement of staff might be considered. We will come to a decision before Christmas.'

Margaret felt her stomach clench. When, before everyone returned to work, Dr Howe asked if she could discuss something professional in private, the feeling of foreboding increased. Sylvie Howe was becoming a close friend, but they never usually talked about medicine. Margaret's knowledge of obstetrics was rusty, so why would Sylvie seek her advice or opinion? Was she warning Margaret that she would be assigned to the obstetrics ward to refresh her knowledge, while Algie took over in pathology? Margaret loved Algie, but the thought hurt. None of that was Sylvie's fault, though, and she forced herself to sound encouraging. 'Of course. How can I help you?'

'You've had a lot more to do with the police than I,' said Sylvie, when they were alone. 'Generally, I stay away from them, especially when I'm smashing windows and gluing suffrage literature to doors.' She smiled briefly. 'I wanted to ask your advice about Mrs Vidler.'

Margaret frowned. 'I had no idea she was pregnant.'

'She isn't,' said Sylvie. 'But we were worried she might be. They anaesthetised her to stitch the wound in her shoulder. When the anaesthetic started to take effect, she muttered something like "What about the child?" Mr Dupré had the anaesthetist stop and asked me to make an assessment before he continued. You know how he prefers not to dabble in things which he thinks are beneath him.' Margaret expected an eye roll, but Sylvie was frowning.

'And?'

'Unless she's so early in gestation that it's hard to confirm and she doesn't know, Mrs Vidler isn't pregnant. Mr Dupré wondered whether she meant Lizzie. But Dr Gesner said Lizzie wasn't pregnant, either.'

'No, she wasn't. But perhaps Mrs Vidler thought of Lizzie as a child. She was barely twenty. Did anyone ask Mrs Vidler when she came round?'

'I did, in case there was an early pregnancy, which I couldn't confirm without asking questions,' said Sylvie. 'Mrs Vidler's response was odd. I expected her to be insulted that I thought a respectable widow could be expecting. But she went blank. After a moment, she said that Mr Dupré had misheard and she'd been talking of china, because she was worried about what Higgins had stolen from the house.'

'But you didn't believe her.'

Sylvie spread her hands wide then stood up, collecting files from the table. 'It's not so much that I disbelieve her as that I'm worried for her. According to Mr Dupré, the injury at her waist was merely a slight bruise, since the knife thrust was thwarted by a chatelaine and any amount of underwear. The wound on her shoulder needed stitches, but was quite shallow. Maybe her slipping on those mossy cobbles made a difference, but those stabs seemed inept or panicked. I understand that those that killed Lizzie weren't.'

'They were clean and accurate, just like the wound that killed Mrs Vidler's brother.' Margaret prepared to follow Sylvie out. 'But it was a bullet which killed her.'

'Really? Then Mrs Vidler was very lucky. Perhaps they didn't have any more bullets, or the gun jammed and they were left with a knife. Maybe they'd have finished her off if Higgins hadn't turned up. Unless he's the perpetrator.'

They paused in the doorway. 'You don't think Higgins is guilty?' said Margaret.

'All I know is that he hasn't been charged with murder yet, which suggests the police don't think so.'

'Or they don't have enough evidence yet.'

'The point is,' said Sylvie, 'if I were Mrs Vidler, I wouldn't have asked to be discharged. I'd have stayed here, where it's safe. Someone wanted her dead. If she *is* protecting a child, she might lead them to it. And what might she mean by child? I heard the rumours about Rosie Levene.' Sylvie's lips pursed and she waved one of her files. 'This belongs to a tiny girl of thirteen who gave birth last week. I thought she'd die before she delivered and I'm desperately trying to stop her from ending up on the table in your wing. Whoever's responsible for her situation deserves more than a birching.'

'Had you heard what Mrs Vidler's brother was allegedly doing?'

'Of course.' Sylvie opened the door and ushered Margaret through. 'The women on my ward would have hanged him on hearsay. They aren't sure if he had rough justice or if he was murdered by someone in his own gang, but either way, they're glad. Now, I want perpetrators shamed and imprisoned with people who understand about the lives they've ruined. But whether Mrs Vidler knew what her brother was doing or not, I think she's in danger. And this child she's speaking of might be too. Someone needs to warn her.'

Twenty-Two

Margaret telegraphed Fox before returning to the mortuary wing. When he arrived, she explained what she had heard. 'Is there any indication that Mrs Vidler is involved?'

'So far, none,' said Fox. 'She might really have meant china.'

'And she might not.'

'I'll contact the inspector and see if we can visit her at home,' said Fox. 'Will you come, as the person who helped save her, concerned she might yet die from infection?'

'If she'd shown signs of that, they wouldn't have let her go home.'

Fox winked. 'Time to bring out your acting skills.'

'I don't have any, remember. I have dissection skills, and I need to teach them to a class of students.'

A telegram arrived as she was leaving to buy lunch: *In hand. Collect 5.30. F*

Trying to distract herself as she sought somewhere to eat, Margaret walked further than normal. She found a small tea-room down a side street, and paused on the pavement outside. A poster for a new moving picture had been pasted on a wall nearby, and she wondered if Reuben had drawn it.

As if she'd summoned him, inside the tearoom was the man himself, talking intently with a woman in a ruby-red costume whose face was obscured by a large hat. They made an attractive couple, of similar build and colouring, their heads close as he took her hand and smiled with an intensity Margaret hadn't seen before.

Before she had decided whether to stay or leave, Reuben noticed her. His smile faltered a little. 'Doctor!'

The young woman turned. It was Lucy. She released Reuben's hand and gave Margaret a bright, unnatural smile.

Margaret wasn't sure what to do for the best, although it probably started with closing her mouth. 'How lovely to see you both,' she said, when she'd gathered her wits. 'I understand you've been drawing Lucy's class, Reuben. I thought you'd be hard at work designing more posters. A new moving picture seems to come out every five minutes.'

'Believe it or not, I have a slight lull. Drummond's films are getting longer, so there tends to be more of a gap. And I've been trying other things.' Reuben patted his sketchbook with shy pride. He could draw an excellent likeness: bring out the inner strength and lost prettiness in a haggard flower-seller's face, or the cruel indifference of a classic beauty who'd never lifted a finger in her life. 'I want to help bring about change by drawing the truth. I know photographs can do that, but sometimes art can be more real.'

'It can.'

'Er, incidentally... I assure you that Miss Frampton's quite safe with me, doctor.'

Lucy rolled her eyes. 'Oh, honestly.'

'I didn't doubt it for a moment. May I see?'

'Of course.' Reuben handed over his sketchbook. The first drawings Margaret saw were of suffragette rallies, just a few lines capturing the passion and fury of speakers and audiences. One was juxtaposed with images of women sewing in dim light. *Wimbledon, Sunday 15ᵗʰ Nov* was scrawled alongside.

Ah, she thought. So Reuben was the friend who'd taken Lucy to the rally.

Other sketches depicted slum streets, barefoot children, a very young woman with a black eye, holding a scrawny baby in her shawl. In one, a man had collapsed in a doorway and a small boy reached for the empty bottle at his side. Did he intend to refill it? Or take it to a shop and claim a coin for its return? In another, a tailor sat cross-legged by a window, squinting in the fading light. In yet another, a speaker at a rally declaimed with his fist raised, the visible faces displaying the differing moods of his audience: cynicism, desperation, fanaticism, anger, doubt, fear. The drawings were as far removed from the fantasy of moving-picture posters as Margaret could imagine.

'They're excellent,' she said. 'Are they for a book?' She wondered if books still wanted illustrations, rather than photographs. Which were easier and cheaper to reproduce? But it was hard to portray this sort of reality in a photograph. People tended to pose as soon as they saw a camera.

'Or a magazine, or a newspaper,' said Reuben. 'After what happened two years ago, I decided to look deeper into things. I returned to Myrdle Street and obtained permission to visit a workhouse.'

'That's not always easy if you've no official business.'

'No, but once I promised I wanted to show the good as well as the bad, they let me in. Those sketches are further on.' A classroom full of children, a workroom, a laundry. Nothing told a negative story, but it wasn't a positive one either: the wary faces of the children looking up from slates, the adults' closed expressions. 'Then someone told me about the classes. I was asked if I could teach mathematics, calligraphy, draughtsmanship, that sort of thing, and then Miss Frampton and I became better acquainted. I've been able to do some sketching there, too.'

Margaret turned another page. Girls and young women between fourteen and eighteen sat poised over notebooks, their eyes focussed on someone near Reuben. 'Is this one of your classes, Lucy?'

'Yes. That's from a Wednesday afternoon a few weeks ago. Every one of them wants a copy.' She tapped the seat next to her. 'Come and sit with us, Margaret. I was asking Reuben's advice. You might have some thoughts, too.'

'Yes, do,' said Reuben, with a shade less enthusiasm.

Margaret kept her face straight. 'You should find a proper market for your other work, Reuben. I'm sure you recall my friend Maude: she runs a journal called *Athene's Gazette*. Write to her. She might have some commissions.'

Reuben smiled. 'I'd love that. Perhaps Lucy – I mean, Miss Frampton and I – could do an article about the classes.'

Lucy glanced at her watch. 'Oh my. Look at the time. Mother will make a fuss if we're late.'

'I'll pay the bill while you ask Dr Demeray's advice,' said Reuben. 'Then I'll escort you home.'

'Don't trouble the waitress to come over,' said Margaret. 'Tell her I'd like the vegetable croquettes and a pot of tea.' She waited until he'd walked off, bracing herself for an outpouring of romantic nonsense or worse. 'So, what sort of advice do you need?'

'Um... You know I'm adopted, don't you?' There was a slight catch in Lucy's voice.

Margaret blinked. 'Oh. I wasn't expecting that. But yes, I'm aware, although I've thought of you as a blood relation ever since you joined the family. I wasn't sure if you knew.'

'When I was about twelve, I asked why I was tall and dark when Father was short and fair and Mother, Katherine and you are short and red-headed.'

'I'm not red-headed, I'm chestnut.'

'Go on with you, Margaret. Your hair isn't as carroty as Katherine's, but whose is? You're auburn. Anyway, they told me then and explained how much they'd wanted me.'

'That's perfectly true.'

Lucy's voice wobbled a little. 'When I was eighteen, Mother gave me a letter that my ... my real mother had left for me. She wrote that she loved me so much. She said she was married to my father but h-he wouldn't own me. I suppose that means she'd been in an intrigue with someone.'

The old-fashioned words made Margaret want to smile, but she didn't. 'Yes. You have two mothers. One who gave you life and loved you, and the other, who carried on what the first one started.'

'Yes, but my father – my *real* father must have thought I wasn't his child, even though my real mother said I was. Don't you think he'd have cared about me, just in case?'

'If he didn't, then he's not your real father other than by biology. Uncle Donald was.'

'I miss Father so much,' Lucy whispered.

'Of course you do. And Lucy... Even if Aunt Alice isn't your "real" mother, you were meant for each other. Her personality and yours fit perfectly together. You both love dressmaking. You both care about other people and use your skills to make the world better. Your mother at birth couldn't have asked for a better person to take her place, even if her family didn't step in. In fact, if they didn't try to, you're better off without them.'

Lucy gave a brief chuckle. 'You're both right and wrong.'

'What do you mean?'

'Yesterday, Mother had a letter saying that I should stop mingling with the poor and give up my ambition to become a nurse, as it was unseemly. They said there was still time for them to find a sponsor so that I could be presented at court, do the London Season and make a suitable match, which would remove me from my bourgeois life and bluestocking cousins. I assume they meant you and Katherine.'

'Well, I doubt they mean Ed,' Margaret said, with a grin. 'How do you know what the letter said?'

'Because I was there when Mother read it and saw her reaction. I thought she'd have apoplexy. She burst out "I already said no. How dare they?" I was so concerned that I took the letter from her.'

'Who was it from?'

'The trustees of a fund set up by my grandfather – my other mother's father. That's where the money for finishing school came from. I thought it was Father's, but it was mine.'

'Oh, I see.'

'Then it all came out.' Lucy pushed her cup and saucer about. 'Apparently, when I was tiny, my real grandfather offered to take me in as a sort of impoverished distant cousin, to be brought up as a mutual relation's companion, provided no one admitted who I really was.'

'That's appalling.'

'Yes. Since the cat was out of the bag, Mother showed me the letters she'd received when she first took me in. I could tell that Mother had said that if I wasn't going to be brought up as a member of my own family, I would be better off in a humbler home where I was loved and cherished. I think my grandfather was relieved. In any event, he set up a fund for me, asked that I be suitably educated and said he'd pay for finishing school when the time came.'

'Oh, Lucy.'

'Until recently, I'd hardly ever thought about being adopted,' said Lucy. 'But suddenly it hurts that my ... my other mother's family think I am an embarrassment who can be bought off. It hurts that my other father didn't care what happened to me. It hurts that he's never tried to find me, to see if I look like him now that I'm grown up. It just hurts. Now, whenever I see someone who looks a little like me – like Reuben, for instance – I wonder if they're my half-sibling, or cousin, or...' She caught Margaret's expression. 'I've asked Reuben and he says he isn't. He's from a different horrible rich family and would rather make his own way than take their money. I'm not sure what to tell Mother. Or what people might think if they knew.'

'Tell your mother you're glad you belong to a lovely family,' said Margaret. 'And that Reuben is a decent young man who values your family and, presumably, you. But ultimately it doesn't matter what people think, if you're doing the right thing.'

Lucy flushed, but kept her eyes fixed on Margaret's. 'Doesn't that depend on who they are? Today, a gentleman was waiting outside the class as I went in. He said a lady shouldn't be teaching' – she dropped her voice to a whisper – 'tarts. I was so shocked that I could feel myself babbling, and he went away looking pleased with himself. Reuben told me to ignore him. Some of the girls who were there said he was their landlord, and others used terms I shan't repeat to express what they thought of what he'd said. I don't know what I'll say if he comes back. And I don't know how I want Mother to reply to that letter. What would you do?'

'I wouldn't let anyone tell me what to do with my time, unless what I wanted to do was harmful to someone else.'

'Would you refuse the money?'

'I don't know,' said Margaret. 'Why not ask Albert's advice about the terms of the trust?'

'And you think I should follow my dream?'

'To be a nurse? Why not?'

'I'm not sure if that's still the dream.'

'Then find a new one, Lucy. You want to change the world for the better. Don't take advice from a person who abandoned your natural mother, or someone with the same point of view.'

'Do you suppose the gentleman who spoke to me today is family? He looked so respectable.'

'As Nellie would say, "Man looketh on the outward appearance but God looketh on the heart."'

'Nellie's a wise woman,' said Reuben, returning to the table. 'And a lisp is always endearing.'

'It's from the Bible,' said Lucy.

'The Book of Nellie?' Reuben grinned. 'I don't recall that one.'

Lucy wagged her finger with a mock frown. 'Don't be naughty. And it's true. I'd rather trust the girls in the class than that man.'

'I wouldn't trust *all* those girls.' Reuben exchanged glances with Margaret over Lucy's head, then reached for his bag.

'I don't suppose any of them have come forward about missing people after the lesson I attended?' asked Margaret.

Lucy shook her head. 'I'm sorry.'

'Wait a moment,' said Reuben. 'I didn't know you were interested in missing people.' He extracted his notebook and showed Margaret a sketch of another classroom. She scanned each row of desks and saw a girl who looked like Rosie.

Lucy peered. 'That's not my class.'

'It's mine,' said Reuben. 'Arithmetic.' He tapped the sketch of Rosie. 'That girl is called Rosie Levene. I haven't seen her since the day I drew this and I've been hoping she's all right. She's very capable. Maybe she doesn't need us any more. It was a Saturday. She boasted that she was being interviewed for a clerical job on the Thursday and she'd tell us about it later, but she hasn't returned.'

'I don't suppose you remember the date,' said Margaret.

'I don't have to,' said Reuben. 'I wrote it on the page.' He pointed. *1ˢᵗ November 1913.*

Margaret took the book and checked her pocket diary. It was a week to the day before Rosie had run into the fog.

Twenty-Three

At half past five, Margaret found Fox's official car waiting outside the mortuary wing. Bert, in a sergeant's uniform, was driving. Margaret sat between Fox and Inspector Silvermann, who greeted her with 'Here's a thorn between two roses,' and grinned.

'Better the official car than our own,' said Fox. 'Someone may be watching the Radden house.'

'I completely agree,' said the inspector. 'But for different reasons. I'm not sure what you're after, but everyone seems to have forgotten that Radden was murdered. I don't mean that I don't care about Lizzie Jackson – far from it. But she's dead because he is, I'm sure of it.'

'Are you still convinced it's not Higgins executing rough justice?' said Margaret.

'Whether it's Higgins or not, I don't think it was rough justice. I think Radden was killed because he was about to betray whoever he's working for.'

'A leopard turning over a new spot.'

'A what?'

'Something someone said.'

'Oh, and by the way, why did no one tell me about the letter Mrs Holbourne received until this afternoon? Just because she and I crossed swords a few months ago, that doesn't mean I'd have dismissed it.'

'That was my decision,' said Fox. 'You want to find out who's procuring girls. I want to find out who's taking valuables out of the country. It's delicate.'

'You think I don't know that? I'm sick of collaring men like Radden and never the people who pay them. All we ever do is prune the tree and we need to dig out the root. It's the same for you, isn't it? But I think they mis-stepped this time.'

'You have the details of the letter now,' said Fox. 'Does it help?'

'Rosie confirms most of it.'

'I find it strange that Rosie was training alone when Hilda wasn't,' said Margaret.

'Yes,' said Fox. 'If I'm right about the records, when the new business started, the flowers and the machines were batched in overlapping twos and threes. So why wasn't Rosie?'

'We're missing something,' said Inspector Silvermann. 'And when we find it, I reckon it'll explain why Radden was about to peach, and that might lead us to who paid him.'

'They'd have destroyed the record when they killed him,' said Margaret.

'No: they left in a hurry. That's why they took the key.' Inspector Silvermann scratched his chin. 'We've been through every bit of paperwork in the house. It was organised better than a government ministry. Radden could have been high up in the civil service if he'd stayed on the straight and narrow. You might find what we missed, Superintendent, because you're looking at it from a different angle.'

'You can call me Fox in private. I'm not a superintendent and you know it.'

'All right.' The inspector turned to Margaret.

'You can call me Dr Demeray,' she said.

'Ha!'

'Did you look through his books?'

'A constable did and found nothing. Why?'

Margaret explained what the bookseller had seen. 'People seem so confused about Radden. On one hand, local women seem convinced he's a procurer. On the other, the people he met in cafés and shops say how nice he was.'

'No one goes willingly with someone who's obviously up to no good,' said Fox.

'But they didn't go with him. He just—'

'Passed them on like a package to someone just as nice,' said the inspector. 'Perhaps, as this Dotty says, someone apparently high class and therefore to be trusted.'

'What if Radden didn't know what he was involved in initially?' said Margaret, reminding herself that while Etta might be described as high class, she would never be described as nice. 'What if he genuinely thought he was working for a legitimate employment agency until something made him realise the truth?'

'Let me tell you about Radden's illustrious career, as discovered painstakingly over the last few days,' said Inspector Silvermann. 'He was born in Deptford in 1872, five years after his sister Bertha. Four siblings died before the age of fifteen. At twenty-one, Bertha married a ship's steward and moved to Southampton. Meanwhile, Hector started as junior clerk at a London shipping office. He was highly valued and destined to get on. A year later, he resigned. We can't find out where he went next, although that original employer thinks it was to similar work.'

'That all sounds perfectly respectable,' said Margaret.

'Until 1890, apparently so.'

'And then?'

'Aged eighteen, Radden comes before the quarter sessions in Dover, charged with assisting another man to procure destitute men to be employed as sailors and thereafter obtaining their advance notes.'

'Procuring them to do what?' said Margaret.

'They collected down and outs from workhouses, dressed them in sailors' uniforms and put them on ships. When the down and outs signed up they were issued notes in respect of their first month's wages. The down and outs gave the notes to Radden and his accomplice, who pocketed the money. Radden and pal were caught because some of the men were rejected as unfit and the truth came out. The accomplice was fined five pounds and Radden was acquitted. They said it was the first time they'd done it and it was a misunderstanding. Who can say if it's true.'

'That's a bit different from what happened to Hilda,' said Fox.

'Hmm,' said the inspector. 'In 1892 he was up before the bench in Swansea, charged with procuring a girl of sixteen for immoral purposes by posting an advertisement for domestic servants. The girl in question had been making her living on the streets for three years, but even though her evidence was therefore considered unreliable, Radden was found guilty and sentenced to two months with hard labour. Maybe he used that time to think about how to improve his operation. Or maybe someone decided he was worth training up.'

'I presume he didn't stop there,' said Fox.

'He did not. Eight years later, in Leeds, Radden's charged with assisting in the procuration of boys for an illegally run factory through a bogus labour exchange. Acquitted. Then in 1907, in Plymouth, he's charged with procuring young women for immoral purposes via advertisements offering matrimony through a bogus marriage bureau.'

'What happened?' said Margaret.

'Again, acquitted. He was happy to assist the police, horrified at what he'd been involved in, manipulated by those he considered his betters... I could go on, but I'd be sick. If he was just a clerk, I'm a duck. And guess what, seems I can't quack. He'd have been convicted if there'd been solid evidence to prove beyond reasonable doubt that he knew exactly what he was doing. But there wasn't.'

'I imagine it took a long while to gather all that,' said Fox, with the bitter gloom of experience. 'I wish there was a simple way to link records across the country.'

'Don't we all.' Inspector Silvermann closed the notebook. 'I don't believe for a moment that Radden was a model citizen in the gaps between offences, and look how he moved about. I suspect that now I've sent out to all the forces in the country they'll find other records of similar activity, becoming more and more sophisticated.'

Margaret pondered as the car turned the last corner. 'His sister must have known all that.'

'*I* didn't know all that till I went hunting,' said Inspector Silvermann. 'They lived some distance apart till she was widowed a year ago and they bought the house in Tibberton Street. He moved to London in 1909 though and neither the Metropolitan or City police have any records on him, which means that either he got better at it or stopped. I know where I'd put my money. Any reports of court cases elsewhere were buried well within local papers. Unless someone told Mrs Vidler, how could she know? She's a pillar of the community, up to the feathers on her hat in good works and interfering. If she knew, she turned a blind eye to save her reputation, which sums up what I expect from most pillars of the community.'

The house where Hector Radden had died was an end of terrace house. Three steps led to a polished door lit by the lamp‚post directly outside. Drizzle sparkled and danced in the beam of light as they emerged onto the pavement. In the fog, the street lamp would have been drained of its power: a yellow glow in a yellower sea.

On that Saturday, thought Margaret, *it would have been impossible to make out anyone's features – barely possible to make out their shape.*

Even now, when there was nothing but a little rain, Fox's face and no doubt hers were shaded by their hats as the light shone down, their clothes monochrome. She doubted any of the curtain twitchers would be able to describe them accurately if asked. Come to think of it, looking back to the day when Rosie had been knocked down, Margaret couldn't now describe the motorist, the man with the lamp, or anyone who had come to help. It wasn't just that she'd been concentrating on Rosie: it had been impossible to make anyone out properly. Even Katherine and Ed had been hard to distinguish, emerging and disappearing as the fog swirled.

A stout woman of perhaps forty, wearing a well-fitting, highly fashionable dress with buttons from shoulder to hem, opened the door. 'I'm Mrs Vidler's friend, Mrs Warner,' she said, shaking hands. 'I've been trying to persuade her to come home with me. Is one of you the doctor?'

'I am,' said Margaret.

'Fancy. This way, please.' She spoke as if the house was a mansion rather than a three up, three down.

Margaret hesitated. Despite having visited murder scenes before, she didn't relish entering. In her mind, the hallway behind the polished door would be as it had been in the photographs – awash with blood, with bloody handprints on wall, stair-rails and door. She wondered how Mrs Vidler could stand to stay, knowing what had happened to her brother. It was her home, though, and selling it might prove hard.

But when Mrs Warner ushered them into the hall, there was no evidence that anything had ever happened there. It smelt of fresh paint, new wallpaper and beeswax. The tiles were sparkling, the staircase bare of carpet, the wood lighter where it had been.

In the parlour, Mrs Vidler sat by the fire mending stockings. She rose to shake hands, acknowledging Inspector Silvermann with a nod. Her gaze flicked between Fox and Margaret in confusion, then settled on Margaret. She smiled. 'You saved me! You're the doctor.'

'I am.'

Mrs Vidler shook Margaret's hand. 'I can't thank you enough.'

'I wanted to see you before you left Dorcas Free,' said Margaret. 'I was surprised you came home so soon, and I wanted to see for myself that you were all right.'

'And to think people disapprove of women in the medical profession. I started to train as a nurse once, you know. But then I married and that was that. I wasn't suited to it, though. I don't like mess and suffering...' She paled and glanced at the ceiling, then closed her eyes briefly and forced a smile. 'I'm glad you're a stronger woman than me. Than I. Please sit.'

The parlour was decorated in a relatively modern way, with lamps and knick-knacks dotted about and a small modern bookcase containing around twenty volumes behind a globe on a stand. Margaret itched to see what was there.

Some of the ornaments and pieces of small furniture were old, perhaps Georgian, with some items possibly even older. Even though they didn't match, the effect was attractive and tasteful. It wasn't hard to imagine that Mrs Vidler might fret about her belongings and might go to remonstrate with someone for allegedly stealing them.

'This room is delightful.'

'Thank you. I take pride in it. All but two of the books are Hector's and I confess that to me, they're untidy dust collectors.' She coughed, as if to make a point, and pressed a hand to her bruised stomach, where the knife had stabbed but not penetrated.

'Do sit down,' said Margaret.

'I'm all right. I get rather weary but otherwise I am well, and I much prefer to be surrounded by my own things. I feel as if the house has been under siege, what with the police, Lizzie betraying me to Higgins, and Higgins murdering Hector in his own bed. I want to bring it back to normality.'

'There's no evidence that Higgins murdered your brother,' said the inspector.

'You've yet to find any evidence at all,' snapped Mrs Vidler. 'It's been over two weeks. Nothing.'

'We can't charge a man without evidence, madam.'

'Ridiculous. It was all to do with burglary. The items in this room may not be worth much, but the things Hector bought and sold were. A man like Higgins, however, will probably steal anything.'

'And what about the girl who was reported as running around at the time?' said Mrs Warner. 'Where's she got to?'

Mrs Vidler frowned at her. 'That must have been Lizzie. He knew she'd been here and she'd eventually realise he killed Hector.'

'I thought—'

'If I'd realised Lizzie was living with a man out of wedlock I wouldn't have hired her. And if I'd realised that man was a burglar, I'd have reported them to the police. But what would they have done? Nothing, no doubt. How many weeks do you suppose Higgins was coming in here with a copy of our own key, taking our belongings and the things Hector needed for his business? My faith in the police is sorely tried. I could have died, if it hadn't been for the doctor's quick thinking. That constable had already decided I was dead. He'd have left me in the mud.' She contemplated the inspector with a vicious glare, then dropped into the chair and looked up at Fox. 'Might I be introduced?'

'This is Superintendent Foxcroft,' said Inspector Silvermann.

Mrs Vidler's expression became more neutral. 'I assume you're taking over because this case needs someone competent. Are you here to find out who killed Hector, Superintendent? Or to besmirch his name?'

'I want to know who killed your brother and why.'

'Good,' said Mrs Vidler. 'Then I shall do everything to help. What do you wish to know?'

Twenty-Four

F ox gave Mrs Vidler a winning smile. 'I understand that you believe Higgins stole some of your belongings. I know the police have already been through your brother's books, but now I'd like to compare them with your household inventory. That would make it easier to gather evidence.'

'I see.' Mrs Vidler smiled at Mrs Warner, who muttered something about tea and went out. 'Come to the study. Please stay here, Dr Demeray: there's no fire in the other room. You could look at the keepsakes in that glass-topped table. You'll like the netsuke. It's damaged, so of little value, but it represents a doctor and patient – neither female, I'm afraid. Higgins probably thought it was bakelite, which is why it's still here, unlike a rather nice gilded china tea set which isn't.'

'Thank you. May I look at your brother's novels, too? I love books.'

'Please do: I shall be selling them shortly. You'll have to bear in mind that the police went through them for any paperwork Hector might have left. I hope you don't count that as contamination.'

'I don't. Thank you.'

'It seemed an intrusion to me.' Mrs Vidler rose to lead them to the study. 'The police aren't operating a proper investigation. *I* was the one who found out about Lizzie and Higgins.'

'You should have informed us about that, rather than go round and confront her,' said Inspector Silvermann.

'I wanted to give Lizzie the benefit of the doubt. However, Higgins intervened to shut us both up.'

'You said it was a foreign-looking stranger who attacked you and Lizzie.'

'Whoever it was was muffled up, but he had dark eyes and a criminal look, like Higgins. And he attacked us.'

'With a knife.'

'Of course with a knife.' Mrs Vidler touched her shoulder. 'He got very close to Lizzie and she started screaming, and then she just dropped down. Then he came for me. I've told you all this. Are we looking at the inventories or aren't we?'

'After you,' said Fox.

As they left, Mrs Warner entered and placed a tea tray on a low table.

'Mrs Vidler said I could look at her collection,' said Margaret, walking to the glass-topped table and peering in. There was a locket containing a Celtic knot made from dark-brown hair; matching miniatures of a Regency couple; a silver snuff-box engraved with a swirling pattern; a tiny pair of heeled shoes made from china and decorated in gold; the charming jade netsuke. Margaret suspected they were of little monetary value, but they were attractive: the kinds of things her father would appreciate and turn into stories. 'They're lovely.'

'I prefer a china shepherdess and a toby dog on the mantlepiece, myself,' said Mrs Warner. She hugged herself. 'I don't like it here.' She cast her eyes upward to what was presumably Hector Radden's bedroom. 'I want to look after Bertha in my home.'

'I'll see if I can help persuade her.'

'Thank you.'

'Mrs Vidler said I could look at the books too.'

'Hector lived for his books. It was all he was interested in.'

'No best girl?'

'Never. You don't want to listen to those wicked rumours.' Mrs Warner pursed her lips. 'It's ruining Bertha's life. Hector was most gentlemanlike. There was never any girl brought here, and if he spoke with some while taking tea, it was to provide guidance. He was a kind, caring man. I don't know where the talk has come from.'

Before she could look into the case, Margaret needed to move the globe. It was old, judging by the territories on its slightly battered surface, and the hoop round its equator was damaged. It felt heavier than it looked, but was of less interest than what was behind it. On a lower shelf was a battered copy of Mrs Beeton's *Household Management*, which must be Mrs Vidler's, along with a pristine illustrated nursing manual which was presumably from her truncated training.

The others were clearly Radden's: *The Lost World, The Machine Stops, A Princess of Mars, Master of the World, Looking Backward* ... Book after book, with beautifully decorated covers protected by almost as beautiful paper dust jackets. Margaret wondered what Fox would do if she asked to have them. Perhaps she should suggest he send one of his men as a secondhand book dealer.

Mrs Vidler had thought the police ridiculous for searching through them. Was that because she didn't think there was anything to find, or because she knew there wasn't? If she wanted to keep up the pretence of his innocence, she would be keen to destroy any evidence of what he'd been doing. Maybe she hadn't said 'child' or 'china' to the anaesthetist, but something else.

The only word that came to Margaret's mind as sounding vaguely similar was 'wire'. Maybe there had been a telegram which unquestionably connected Radden to procurement and

Mrs Vidler wanted it destroyed. But the more Margaret thought about it, the less 'wire' sounded like 'child'.

Margaret pulled out *The Lost World*, which Radden had bought the day before the murder.

'He asked for a piece of paper and scribbled on it,' the bookseller had said. 'He treated the book a little more roughly than he usually did.' What had he been scribbling? A resignation? A warning? A confession?

The pages were stiff and clean, but the spine felt looser than was usual in a new book, while at the same time looking perfectly normal. Or did it? She smiled at Mrs Warner. 'This is one of my favourites,' she said.

'Not my cup of tea at all, doctor. Talking of which, shall I go see if they've finished in the study?'

'Please do.'

As soon as she'd gone, Margaret inspected the book under a lamp. The paper lining the inner cover felt normal, but tightly packed inside the spine was a piece of paper, folded to look as if it was part of the spine itself. Someone who rarely read a book might not notice. Someone who loved them would.

Using a hatpin, Margaret pierced the paper and eased it out. Her silent prayer that no one would come in before she had extracted it was answered when there was a rattling at the front door, then Mrs Warner's voice greeting whoever was there.

Margaret buried the paper in her pocket, replaced the book in the case, and was standing by the glass-topped table as the others entered.

'What do you think of the netsuke?' said Mrs Vidler, standing beside her.

'It's delightful.'

'The superintendent's taking my inventories away.' Mrs Vidler rolled her eyes. 'I don't have a great deal of faith. All I want to do is distance Hector's name from any reference to procuring girls.'

'It's a terrible trade, Mrs Vidler,' said Inspector Silvermann.

'Yes, but it's nothing to do with us,' snapped Mrs Vidler. She turned to Margaret. 'I shall give you a book to thank you for saving me, doctor. Which would you like?'

'I couldn't possibly choose,' said Margaret.

'Well, in that case...' Mrs Vidler pulled out *The Time Machine* and handed it over. 'This was one of Hector's favourites.'

Mrs Warner entered, her round face troubled and an envelope clasped in her hand. 'I think it's another of those vile letters, dear.'

'I'll take that,' said Inspector Silvermann. 'If you're receiving unpleasant mail, Mrs Vidler, you should have told me from the off.'

'What can *you* do?'

'Do my best to see justice done. You must leave here.'

'It's my home.' Mrs Vidler's calm was gone. She glanced to the ceiling as Mrs Warner had done earlier. 'Even if—'

'I agree with the inspector,' said Margaret. 'Stay with Mrs Warner, where no one can send you letters or do worse.'

'Worse?'

'Never mind the tea,' said the inspector. 'Pack up the essentials. I'll order a cab for you, then make sure a constable watches the place for a day or so.'

At home with Fox, the inspector and Bert, Margaret opened the piece of paper Radden had hidden.

It was dated the seventh of November, a day before Hector Radden's death, and set out in rows. Each started with a date, the first being the twenty-seventh of August.

27th Aug, RW f 15, 30th Aug, Ger, Jwl, <u>Doc</u>, EMP: BLN F̶ <u>X</u>

'Wait a moment.' Fox opened his notebook and flicked pages. 'This is when Radden's work subtly changed... Yes, he recorded buying a flower called Rosa Vincula that day. There's no such plant.'

Margaret and the inspector looked at him blankly.

'Townies,' said Fox. 'So it looks as if RW was a girl of fifteen sent to Germany with jewellery and documents in her case. Then employed in... Berlin? I wonder what the F stands for. Or why it's crossed through. And then the X underlined.'

'Three final letters keep repeating,' said Margaret. 'F, M, B, and four of them crossed out and followed by an X.'

'Bet you a pound to a penny that B is for brothel,' grunted the inspector. 'If the small F stands for female, that seems to be where most of the girls were destined. If small M stands for male, they seem to be mostly going to capital F and capital M. Factories and mines? X hopefully means escaped, thank God.'

Between the twenty-seventh of August and the thirteenth of October, the entries were bunched together in twos and threes, a fortnight or so apart, a record of twelve adolescents who'd been sent abroad. It seemed heartbreaking that so many people could go missing without anyone reporting their disappearance, but it was perfectly possible. Rosie thought her family had rejected her. Hilda said she had no family. Kay had run away from a job he hated and a father who beat him.

'If we can find the ones who escaped, that could be all we need,' said the inspector. 'But how can we, without putting something in the papers that might alert this gang?'

'Let's work up from the bottom,' said Margaret. 'We know the names Rosie, Kay, Eveline and Hilda.'

'The last six are closer together,' said Fox, turning the paper. 'Raising money more quickly? Slicker operation? But yes... It looks as if those names are there, as well as two people who didn't appear.'

'The people who should have trained with Rosie!' said Margaret.

'Must be,' said Fox. 'So this is a list of people he invited for interview and what had been planned for them if chosen.'

30th Oct, EY f 16, 3rd Nov, Bel, Sil, EMP: AMS B?

31st Oct, KR m 14, 4th Nov?, Swi, Chi, Flm, EMP: URLS M

1st Nov, HU f 17, 5th Nov, Fra, Jwl, Doc, EMP: BIRZ B

~~5th Nov, PR f 16, 10th Nov, Ger, EMP: MSC F (Did not arrive)~~

6th Nov, RL f 14, 11th Nov, Ger, Sil, EMP: BLN B

~~7th Nov, CP, m 17, 12th Nov, Swi, Tim, EMP: ZUR B or SIB M (Did not arrive)~~

Underneath, Radden had written, in capitals: ENDS. AM NEITHER TRAITOR NOR MURDERER.

'KR,' said Margaret, swallowing. 'Kay Rowlands. Disappeared from home on the thirty-first of October.'

'And destined to smuggle china,' said Bert. 'Though I can't imagine how without breaking it.'

'Very small items, well wrapped, buried in clothes in a valise carried by someone who's perhaps never had a nice case before and will treasure it,' said Margaret.

'EY, HU. Eveline something, Hilda something,' said Fox. 'Whatever they expected Kay to do on the fourth didn't come off, although it looks as if it involved film – presumably from inside Whitehead's.'

'Film might be turned into Stanhope photographs that could be hidden in something small – like a hollow china ornament?' suggested Bert.

'Maybe that's why he stayed in Weymouth until the fourteenth, to give him time to get them. Then he was destined for Switzerland, and thereafter...'

'Mines in the Urals?' said Margaret. 'When Radden was murdered, Kay was still alive.'

'RL is Rosie Levene,' said the inspector. 'Your friend Reuben said Rosie Levene was going to be interviewed on the sixth.'

'PR and CP didn't turn up,' said Margaret.

'We spoke to Dotty the waitress,' said the inspector. 'She warned off a girl who turned up early.' He sat back and scratched his nose.

'It's a shame she didn't report him earlier.'

Inspector Silvermann grimaced. 'She did. No one took it seriously. I've had words with Coulter, but I'm afraid too many of my colleagues consider women hysterical and irrational.'

'Mmm,' said Margaret.

Bert pointed at the row starting with the twenty-sixth of November. 'Working on the same principle, Eveline went to Belgium with silver and was destined for an Amsterdam brothel, but there's a question mark. Perhaps a plan changed, like it did for Kay, but Radden wasn't sure how. Hilda, as we know, went to France with jewellery and ended up in a brothel in ... BIRZ?'

'Biarritz?' Margaret suggested. 'The woman who wrote to Maude posted the letter in Bayonne. That's just up the coast.'

'Sounds about right,' said Bert. 'Then Rosie was supposed to go to Germany with silverware and then was destined for a Berlin brothel. What kind of punishment would Radden have got if he'd been convicted?'

'For procurement?' Fox shrugged. 'Maybe a birching under the new law, on top of perhaps three years' hard labour.'

'Gawd. I wish he was still alive so I could kill him myself.'

Fox grunted in agreement. 'They took documents and plans as well as jewellery, silverware, gilt items, and timepieces, all small enough to go in a maid's battered valise. And potentially Kay's hollow china with film inside.'

Margaret turned the paper, running her finger down all the initials, and felt sick. Even if they could all be tracked down, who knew what condition the victims' minds and bodies would be in. 'None of this helps find Violet. Radden would have been dead before she applied.' She turned to the inspector. 'Please find her.'

The inspector's jaw clenched. 'Do you think I'm not trying?'

'You need to hide Dotty the waitress,' said Bert. 'If we can find Eveline she'll be another witness. Though if she's in a Berlin brothel, that could take years. How could Radden say he wasn't a murderer? What did he think happened to the kids he procured?' He sat back in disgust.

'Maybe Radden viewed the whole thing as a mental exercise,' said Inspector Silvermann. 'Maybe the moment he realised the consequences and felt some compassion, he became too much of a risk to leave alive.'

'Maybe it wasn't compassion,' said Fox. 'He wrote "traitor" first. Let's hope no one else dies before we work out why.'

Twenty-Five

At seven, Margaret woke on Fox's side of the bed, contemplated by Juniper, regal in an Egyptian pose on the nightstand.

Even after washing, dressing and descending for breakfast she could taste the sourness of dreams, see a swirl of their frantic colour, feel them snatch at her mind then fade. And she hadn't said goodbye to Fox, who must have already gone to work, taking the ledgers and his copy of Radden's note, to await reports on Andreyev and perhaps the Pendleberrys.

'Good morning, doctor,' said Freda, placing a pot of coffee on the table as Margaret entered the dining room. 'The master says he might not be back till late but he'll be back in time, if you get his drift. He made himself an omelette before I could stop him but at least he used the right pan. If he ever gets fed up of Special Branch, perhaps he could open a café. Or help me with tonight's dinner party.' She chuckled.

'It's not a dinner party, exactly,' said Margaret. 'Don't fret too much. Dr and Frau Gesner will be much more polite than ... you know what I mean.'

'Then it'll be a pleasure to cook for them. I'll ask the German butcher for some ideas. Frau Gesner's bound to be homesick.'

'You're wasted on us, Freda,' said Margaret. 'You ought to start your own restaurant.'

'Nah,' said Freda. 'Never mind what Mrs Pendleberry says. You're a fair employer who sometimes likes simple and sometimes likes fancy, and that suits me well.'

The morning at work passed without incident and at lunchtime, Margaret met her sister in a café.

'Everything's a bit frenzied,' said Katherine. 'The case Connie and I are working on is at a critical stage and we're catching the two p.m. train to Birmingham. Meanwhile, James is in Senghenydd again, then he's going to Dublin to report on the locked-out workers, the army that's been set up to protect them, donated food not getting to their families and Mr Bonar Law's Unionist meeting at the Theatre Royal, where he'll say that Home Rule won't go through without a fight.' The corners of Katherine's mouth turned down. 'James is over fifty now. This is a young man's game.'

Margaret touched her sister's hand. 'He'll be all right.'

'I hope so. He says he'll report on injustice until he can no longer lift a pen.'

'Good for James.' Margaret raised her teacup. 'To peace and fairness.'

'To peace and fairness.' Katherine clinked cups, then put her head on one side. It meant she was about to ask a favour.

Margaret sighed. 'What is it?'

'While James and I are away, Father will be unsupervised. I suggested he stay with Aunt Alice, but she seems preoccupied. Father tells me I'm treating him like a child.'

'You are.'

'What do you suppose is on Aunt Alice's mind?'

Margaret explained.

'Ah,' said Katherine. 'That's why Lucy's arranged to speak with Albert. Connie and I thought it was something to do with Bee, since Bee's been more than usually bouncy recently.'

'Algie's coming to work at Dorcas Free in January.'

'Oh my!' Katherine chuckled. 'And there was Albert hoping that after three years his romance with Bee would fizzle out.'

Despite her disquiet about Algie's return, Margaret grinned. 'Now there will be intimate dinners for two in candlelit restaurants.'

'Albert will hire us to follow them to ensure propriety.'

'Tell him you and James managed romantic dinners with propriety before you married.'

'I'm not certain you and Fox did.'

'Nonsense. Fox did nothing more than chastely kiss my alabaster cheek.'

'Of course not. Anyway, going back to Father...'

'I have no time to prepare. Why can't Father stay at your place? It's not as if he's in his second childhood.'

'You found him in a bookshop before breakfast on Saturday.'

'What can I do if I'm at work? I can't ask Nellie and Freda to mind him. And even when I'm not at the hospital, I have research and teaching preparation to do at home.'

'You just don't want to spend time with him, Meg.'

'That's not true.' Margaret heard her voice rise, took a savage bite of her sandwich and washed it down with tea. 'That's not true,' she said, in a calmer voice. 'But you find him easier.'

'When he did all that travelling he was grieving, Meg, just as we were,' said Katherine. 'He never meant to lose himself. If he'd returned as planned, maybe I could have persuaded him not to go away again.'

'We were so miserable and worried and angry and you had to get a job.'

'Which was the best thing I ever did.'

Margaret scowled into her empty teacup. She had a sudden recollection of herself as an angry teenaged girl, watching Katherine walk into the driving rain to spend the day typing for half the pay a man would have received. She'd felt humiliated.

Working wasn't for girls like them: they ought to be too well off. But Katherine was right. If it hadn't been for that job, Katherine wouldn't now be a private detective and Margaret probably wouldn't be a doctor.

'You'll have to forgive Father eventually,' said Katherine. 'Besides, the things you find irritating in him are some of your own characteristics.'

'What utter tosh! Father and I are nothing alike.'

'If you say so.' Katherine refilled Margaret's cup. 'All the same, please will you have him to stay? It'll put my mind at rest.'

Margaret sighed. 'Very well. If Father wants to, and only if he does, tell him to come to my house after lunch tomorrow. That'll give Freda time to prepare, and he can play with the children in the afternoon. I've told Nellie she can have her young man to tea in the kitchen. But warn Father that I might not be home before six thirty and he must behave, and not wander off on a whim and get himself into trouble.'

'I'd say the same about you,' said Katherine. 'Only you're nothing alike, are you?'

Before Dr and Frau Gesner arrived, Fox put waltz music on the gramophone and drew Margaret into his arms to dance.

'The dates in the document correspond with dates of advertisements in various country newspapers,' he murmured, 'and also with the purchase of ornaments and jewellery which were never sold on because they had been assessed as too low in value, but are not recorded as being stored anywhere. They just disappeared. Some appear to have been fenced, so are possibly linked to Higgins.'

'So valuable items were described as valueless then smuggled out of the country,' said Margaret, resting her head on his shoulder.

'Yes. Incidentally, Inspector Silvermann is another person who wants Lucy to stop teaching in case she's asked the class too many questions.'

'She won't.'

'She should. If Radden's colleagues suspect Lucy knows something critical about Rosie, she could be in danger.'

'I'm sure the gentleman who told her to stop was Endsleigh.'

'Endsleigh's what he purports to be,' said Fox. 'He has no record. His father was once a country solicitor, who came up in the world to become someone with private means and a higher social standing when Endsleigh was a youth. The father's money may have come from renting out buildings which were houses of ill-repute, and therefore effectively living off immoral earnings, but maybe it also came from speculating in property. He bought some of it from the Pendleberry family.'

'Really? Where is it?'

'It's a small row of houses near Archbold Street which Phoebe's father had planned to renovate before becoming sick. Endsleigh junior owns those, along with the ones around St Mark's, plus warehouses in Poplar and Limehouse which he purchased himself.'

'I don't like him.' Margaret tucked herself closer into him.

'That's not evidence.'

'What about Etta?'

'Percival's constituency accounts are being audited,' he said. 'Without a warrant, it'll be impossible to look into the Pendleberrys' personal finances. However, Elinor's found nothing linking Phoebe's accounts to Percival's, nor any sign of questionable accounting.'

'Phoebe wouldn't do anything illegal.'

Fox hugged her tighter. 'I agree, but I don't think she'd have come to us without realising that we might find something out about Etta. So she must have suspected something.'

'Maybe. But she hadn't said so.'

The record came to an end and there were voices in the hall. It was time to greet their guests.

Frau Gesner was just like her photograph: a pretty woman in her late twenties with pale-blue eyes and dark-blonde hair. 'This is such a delightful room, Dr Demeray.' Her accent was a little stronger than her husband's but her English was as good. 'Some houses feel like museums or displays of wealth, but yours feels like a home and as if every item has a story.' She went red. 'I am sorry, I do not mean to suggest that your things are worthless. I am not expressing myself well. Please do not take offence. I feel at home here – that is what I mean.'

'No offence taken,' said Margaret. 'What a lovely thing to say. Thank you.'

She scanned the room herself and felt her heart warm. Only a few of their things were valuable: some Georgian silver candlesticks she had inherited from a grandmother, a seventeenth-century Dutch painting of a woman reading that Katherine had given her as a twenty-first birthday present; one or two books, including the first edition her father had given her for Christmas.

Otherwise the room was decorated with her own sketches, photographs, two funny little Swiss bears Fox had bought in 1911 and Mr Tod, the battered china creature for whom they'd failed to buy a wife in Weymouth. There were rows of well-thumbed books and various items that she and Fox had bought purely because they were amusing or pretty.

'I'm glad you feel at home, Frau Gesner,' she said. 'And I hope you'll enjoy dinner. We'll have a light soup followed by a winter salad, *Schweinebraten* with red cabbage and potatoes, then

Apfelkuchen with cream and finally some cheeses. Freda felt you might miss Germany and has done her best to prepare things she thinks you'd like. I know you'll be a few miles away, but she can tell your cook-general where the best German butchers, bakers and grocers are, if that's of any help.'

'Thank you, Dr Demeray. Everything is so different from Wuppertal and I have yet to appoint any staff. Ernst did not think of it. I don't even know whether to hire an English cook or a German one. Everyone is so kind.' A moment of sadness crossed her face. 'But I fear the days will feel long.'

'*Sei nicht traurig, Liebling,*' said Dr Gesner. 'Don't be sad. Your Papa is happy with your sister. Perhaps, when he hears that you are happy, he will join us.'

'I'll introduce you to my aunt as soon as I can,' said Margaret. 'She'll be much better able to help with your domestic questions. And if you're missing a father, you can borrow mine. He travelled in Germany in the early eighties. I think he was mostly dragon hunting in the Black Forest but I daresay he went to Westphalia too.'

Frau Gesner looked blank. '*Schwarzwald in Baden-Württemberg*? Surely even there dragons don't exist.'

'If you meet him, you'll understand,' said Margaret. 'Tell me, what is your new house like?'

'Please come for coffee next week and find out,' said Frau Gesner. 'Bring your father, the children and your aunt if you wish.' Her face was a little pleading. 'At the moment we are, um ... *da haben wir den Salat.* How is that in English?'

'We'd say "we're at sixes and sevens",' said Margaret. 'Goodness knows why.'

'Who knows why it's salad in German, either. But I promise to only offer cake.'

'I'll certainly come,' said Margaret. 'I'll bring the others when you're more settled.'

'That will do well.' Frau Gesner sipped her sherry. 'I was so afraid there would be feeling against us. The newspapers can be so worrying, with their talk of torpedoes, zeppelins, warships and guns to support civil war. My formal education stopped when I was fifteen, Dr Demeray. I am in awe of you and perhaps I do not quite understand, but it all seems wrong. Our countries belong together. Our emperors are cousins, we share ancestry. Who tries to drive us apart?'

'One should always strive for peace,' said Margaret. She could sense Fox's tension without looking at him. 'People have more in common than not.'

'That is so true. But one feels for those who are being arrested without cause. Even young English boys, accused of spying when they say they have escaped, er, *Sklaverei*?'

'Slavery?' said Margaret, more loudly than she'd intended. 'English boys? I mean... I apologise, it's just that—'

'I knew nothing of this.' Dr Gesner's voice had an edge and he looked first at Fox, then back at his wife. '*Wie viele Jungen, Ilse? Wo?*'

Frau Gesner stared quizzically at everyone. 'Just one boy, found asleep in bushes outside a naval building near the Kaiser Wilhelm Kanal. Why should you know, Ernst? *I* only know because my friend Elke heard it from an aunt who lives in Brunsbüttel. So many people are being arrested, and this turned out to be nothing in the end.'

'How nothing?' Dr Gesner's voice had softened again. 'He was not a spy?'

'Who can say?' Frau Gesner shrugged. 'Apparently he was first arrested for vagrancy, but when it appeared he could speak only English, they charged him as a spy, because that is how things are these days. Things looked bad for him. But he was ragged, sick, starving, rambling. The magistrates said he should be in an asylum, not prison, and that's where he was sent. Poor lad.'

'I'll have someone look into it,' said Fox.

Frau Gesner looked anxiously from him to her husband. 'I, er... It may not be quite true. Elke's aunt likes to... um... exaggerate. Or perhaps he *is* a spy and I am betraying my own country.'

'Don't worry, I shan't mention any names,' said Fox. 'But if there's a boy who needs diplomatic help, I'll make sure he gets it.'

'Is that part of your job, Superintendent?'

'Sometimes,' said Fox. 'I'll join you in the dining room shortly. If you'll excuse me, I have a telegram to send.'

Twenty-Six

Margaret was sent home an hour early the following evening. She'd wanted to stay at work where she was busy, rather than sit at home, wondering what Fox had found out while trying to keep her father entertained. However, Dr Gesner wouldn't hear of it.

'Your father is visiting for a few days. Go home.'

'But we need to write up our findings from the second opinion St Oswald's asked for,' she argued, 'and we haven't finished analysing the latest samples from the thirteen-year-old on Dr Howe's ward.'

'A student can assist with the former, and Dr Howe planned to help with the analysis on her patient anyway, as she's the one responsible for treating her. Go home.'

'Work is the only place where I can focus when—'

'When there are many things to worry about,' Dr Gesner finished. 'I understand. But for now, go and enjoy someone you won't have for ever. I wish I could spend an evening with my papa once more.'

An image of her father slumped in the chair at the bookshop entered Margaret's mind and filled her with shame. Not many reached the age of eighty-four. Those long, dreadful years when she and Katherine had thought he was dead had been bad enough. One day, there would be no coming back.

'If, by any means, I hear about the boy in Germany before Fox does, I promise to let you know,' said Dr Gesner. 'But in the meantime, you will have a lovely evening, I'm sure.'

For all his assurances, Margaret still wasn't at ease when she arrived home. She knew something was awry before she'd even finished removing her hat. From the sitting room came the sound of her father talking and the twins answering. They should be in the nursery by now, calming down before bedtime.

Freda appeared at the other end of the hall, strode towards her and pulled a face. 'I'm glad to see you home early, ma'am,' she said. 'It's been a peculiar afternoon, what with odd people coming and going. Now Nellie doesn't know how to get the children to bed. And I—'

'Odd people? You mean Nellie's Harry?'

'Oh, him,' said Freda. 'They're both so wet that I didn't need to chaperone at all. Mr Pigeon and I designed a spinning shelf for my pots while the lovebirds stared into each other's eyes, talking about the language of flowers and I don't know what. But talking of flowers, the master's on his way home and—'

'With flowers? He must be celebrating. Thank goodness.'

'No, ma'am. They're—'

A loud squawk came from the sitting room. Alec was overexcited and overtired. Laughter would turn to tears in seconds. 'Explain later,' said Margaret. 'Let's rescue Nellie.'

In the sitting room, her father sat on the carpet, playing with a wooden train. Alec appeared ready to stamp on a carriage. Edie lay on the hearthrug with her thumb half out of her mouth, reaching for the engine and at risk of being trodden on. Nellie stood to the side, wringing her hands.

'Hello darlings!' called Margaret, lifting Edie from the floor. 'It's time for bed.'

'Aw Mummmmeeee...' said Alec, yawning. 'Going Cossipopple.'

'We haven't arrived in Constantinople yet.' Margaret's father pointed at a chair leg. 'Need they go now?'

'I'm afraid they must.' Margaret kissed Edie then handed her to Nellie. Freda swept Alec up and pinned him squirming under an arm.

'Mummy do bedtime,' muttered Edie.

'Nellie's the expert,' said Margaret. 'Say goodnight to Grandpapa.'

'Goonight Ampa,' murmured Edie through her thumb. But Alec let out a yell, kicked his legs and pummelled Freda's stomach.

'Stop that immediately, Alexander David!' said Margaret. 'Say sorry to Freda this second.'

'Shan't.' Alec's bottom lip wobbled.

'Then you shall stay in the nursery all day tomorrow, while Edie and Grandpapa and I make the train go to Constantinople and then go to the park with Aunt Maude and Johnny.'

'But *I* wanna.'

'Then you'd better go upstairs with Nellie and Freda and say sorry. I'll come up once you've settled down and see that you have.' Margaret watched the children leave, then helped her father up from the carpet. He was unexpectedly light, as if his bones were hollow, and his hand was fragile, its skin delicate in hers. Looking up into a face that was always younger in her mind than in reality, the shame she'd felt earlier flooded back. She hugged him.

'Are you quite all right, Meg?'

'Yes, Father.' She kissed his cheek. 'If you're going to play trains, you should do it on the dining table.'

He pouted. 'It's more fun on the floor.'

'Yes, but draughty. Sit by the fire and tell me about your day while I tidy up.'

Her father settled in the armchair, readjusting the cushions to make himself comfortable. 'I went back to the bookshop in Daffodil Street because I remembered you'd said the young man wanted advice about the novel he's writing. It appears that the heroine is now annoyed with the hero and has gone to work outside London, but she won't say where and he's not sure how to resolve things. I told him to add more monsters.'

'Always good advice.' Margaret knelt to put the train in its box, relieved that Dotty had been intercepted by Inspector Silvermann's men and sent somewhere safe, even if Dotty herself was not so happy.

'Then I had coffee and cake in the little café opposite, which was rather noisy. A nice girl on the table next to mine looked very nervous.'

Margaret paused. 'A nice girl? What was she like?'

'Oh, I don't know. Nearly forty, I suppose, in a silly hat.'

'She's hardly a girl if she's forty.' Margaret finished packing toys into a box.

'Any woman under seventy is a girl to me. I suppose she was nervous because the boy was asking everyone a lot of questions about the bookshop, or rather the alley next to it, which I hadn't noticed till he asked. He wrote our answers in a notebook and gave out cards.'

Margaret wondered if he was one of Fox's men or one of the inspector's. 'Was the boy about forty too?'

'Don't be silly, dear. He was around twenty, I suppose. Then I lunched at Katherine's, then a cab brought me here. Anyway, you can't argue about the *other* girl.'

'What other girl?' Margaret put the box on a side table and dropped into the chair opposite her father. It felt easier to unpick the secrets of a sick patient than to follow her father's thought processes.

'The strange girl who brought the flowers for you.' Her father pointed at the mantlepiece, where a china vase held three chrysanthemums.

'Father, do I have to shake you? Did she bring them here or to Katherine's? Who was she? How old was she? Fifty? Thirty? Ten? What sort of girl? Well-to-do? Middling? Poor?'

'An "asking me if people actually read books" sort of girl.' The pout returned. 'She said yours looked quite the mishmash, even if some must have cost a pretty penny. I told her I have four times as many and they're even more mishmashy. She asked if I were a librarian. I said the British Library has a million times more and she laughed as if I'd made a joke. Quite peculiar.'

'Father, what was her name? How old was she?'

'Sadie Taylor. She was fourteen, perhaps. Maybe sixteen. Possibly twenty. Definitely a girl.'

'How did she find my address? Where is she now?'

'She's gone, but she said she knew Lucy. Perhaps she's one of her Girl Guides.'

'Lucy wouldn't tell anyone my address without asking my permission.'

'Mmm,' said her father. 'Well, I told her you were at Dorcas Free, but that she could wait if she liked. However, she said no and left and said she was sure you'd catch her up.'

Margaret began to wonder if she might be asleep and dreaming of Alice's Looking-Glass Land. She leaned forward. 'Please help me to understand, Father. You went to the bookshop after breakfast, then the café, then you went back to Katherine's for lunch before coming here in a cab?'

'Yes.'

'Then you wrote or played with the children or both, and Sadie arrived with a bunch of flowers.'

'I'd hardly call them a bunch.'

'Did you tell Pigeon?'

'I'm not sure why I should have,' said her father. 'But he and Nellie's young man had gone by five.'

'You mean I've only just missed her? What time did Sadie Taylor turn up?'

'Fifteen minutes ago.' His mouth was downturned, his eyes sorrowful. 'Why are you interrogating me like a policeman?'

Margaret reached for his hand, searching for the right words. 'I'm sorry, Father. I just wish I'd been here.'

'I explained that I was sure you'd be home early since I'm visiting, but she still wouldn't wait. She said you'd understand if I gave you a letter.'

'Oh, Father, why do you only ever start at the beginning when you're writing a book? What letter?' Margaret stood up, checked the mantlepiece, then scanned the room. An envelope lay on a side table.

Dear Doctor, I wrote this before I came, in case you weren't in and I had to explain. You came to Miss Frampton's class and afterwards Miss Frampton asked if anyone knew about girls who'd gone missing because they got fooled by someone. Then a friend who works near St Mark's said you asked the same question at the parish hall and my friend asked my advice.

A girl from her village called Violet something came up to London a while back and was living in the East End looking for work. My friend said this Violet went to 5a Playhouse Yard this afternoon to be interviewed for a job and if she gets it, she's going abroad tomorrow.

My friend thinks it sounds wrong, but won't tell the police. I don't want to either, so I thought of you. Violet's only young and someone needs to rescue her. I'm going there to see what I can find out. Maybe you can help. If I get scared I'll stay at the station and wait for you. Sadie Taylor

'Damn fool,' said Margaret. 'You should have waited!'

'Meg! Language! And I *did* wait.'

'I don't mean you, I mean Sadie. She's gone to Blackfriars.'

'But it's dark! And Blackfriars is—'

'Father, I promise I'll spend the evening with you later, but first I must find Sadie.'

Her father sat upright and prepared to push himself up with his cane. 'I shall come. I must protect you.' His hand looked frail on the handle, the wrinkled skin blotched with liver spots.

Margaret put her arm round his shoulders as she heard the front door open and a familiar voice call out. 'You must stay here and protect the children,' she said. 'I'll have to make do with Fox.'

'I came home early to keep your father company, in case you couldn't,' said Fox, as she stepped into the hall. He gazed up the stairs, where Alec's crying could just be made out. 'What's happening?'

'Nellie's routine is out,' said Margaret. 'And someone visited just before I came home.' She handed over Sadie's letter.

'Dear God,' said Fox, reading it. 'Please tell me you weren't about to head off after her? I'll go now.'

'*We* will.'

'I will.'

'Sadie's expecting me. She might not trust you, nor might Violet. If we can't find the house, I promise we'll tell the police. But if they go now, they might scare away whoever is behind this.'

'But this letter is vague and specific at the same time, and—' Fox stopped as Freda descended into the hall.

'Freda, we're going out,' said Margaret. 'But I'll go and see the children first. Did Alec apologise?'

'Just about, ma'am. I'm warming milk for them. When you come back, can I ask you about something?'

'Of course, Freda. I'm sorry everything's so topsy-turvy to-day. I hope we won't be very long.'

The children were sleepy and subdued in flannel dressing-gowns when Margaret entered. Alec's sobs had subsided: he submitted to a cuddle and mumbled 'Sorry Mumma' into her hair. Should she really leave them and her father while she chased after strangers? But she'd never forgive herself if Violet ended up like Hilda or Kay or the boy in Germany when she could have prevented it.

Fox was in the study and looked up from consulting a map when she entered. 'I telephoned Lucy, who says Sadie occasionally attends her English class and is bright and sure of herself. She gave a description, which Freda and your father corroborated and added relevant detail to. She's fifteen, medium size, nice features, large eyes, brown hair, long dark-grey coat, blue hat, black boots.'

'I think I remember her,' said Margaret. 'Not very well, but hopefully enough to recognise her.'

'Good. It's around five miles for us. Assuming there's not much traffic and we don't get stopped, it should take us twenty minutes or so. But I also telephoned Bert, who was less than a mile away from Blackfriars at that moment and has a motorcycle. I'm hopeful he'll intercept her at the tube station, assuming that's what Sadie meant about where she'd return if she became afraid.' Fox tapped the map, touching the railway bridge and pier on the Blackfriars side of the Thames, then tracing the routes across the river to Southbank and then into Lambeth. 'Crossing here, it's a very short trip to Waterloo for the boat train – perfect for transporting things or people. I've men in the area looking for smuggled arms and documents, and I'd rather not compromise them by appearing, but if this is connected then I shall have to. Maybe no one will spot me, since it's a mass of wharves, alleys and courts. Look at Playhouse Yard: it's more or less in a warren.'

'We'll manage.'

'I'd rather you stayed here. Someone's on his way to watch the house.'

'Pigeon?'

'No.'

Margaret secured the reinforced black toque Katherine had bought her with an extra pin. 'This came about because of my questions. It's my responsibility.'

'It isn't.' Fox folded the map, his face serious. 'But very well. We'll get there as fast as we can, park by the station, then walk to Playhouse Yard. If at any point I say *run back*, do it without question just as Bert would and raise the alarm. It's called following orders.'

'But I have to—'

'Follow orders, Margaret. Doing it won't kill you. Not doing it just might.'

Twenty-Seven

I t was hard to converse as Fox drove to Blackfriars, exceeding the speed limit where he could, concentrating as he dodged pedestrians and other vehicles.

Margaret recalled an evening in 1911 when she'd headed for Whitechapel after dark against good advice. That was perhaps the first time that she let common sense take control and turned back. Then, she had only had herself to consider. Now, she had Fox and the children.

But somewhere in Blackfriars there was at least one girl in trouble.

Just as Fox had said, Sadie's letter was both vague and specific. Sadie didn't know Violet's full name but did know an address. Was the other girl Violet Brown, or the name a coincidence? Or was the missing girl a fiction used by Sadie's friend to kidnap Sadie herself?

The car rattled as they passed from affluent areas to comfortable ones, then east of Temple into overcrowded, gloomy districts where Fox slowed sufficiently for them to talk.

'Is there any news about the boy in Germany?' said Margaret, hoping a positive answer would reduce her anxiety.

'It'll take a while,' said Fox. 'We have to be careful how we ask in case it looks as if we're helping a spy evade justice. He's safe enough where he is for now.'

'Do you think Sadie's caught up in the same thing too, and Radden's group has moved to a different area?'

Fox shrugged. 'I don't know. It all feels odd.'

'If only I'd been home when she arrived.' Margaret clutched the handle of her handbag. 'If only I'd taken today as leave to spend with Father.'

'It's not your fault. No one could have predicted this.'

They parked by the station, but there was no sign of Bert or a girl who matched Sadie's description, so they walked towards Blackfriars Lane.

The fog on the river darkened as it merged with chimney smoke, obscuring the night sky. From the dock, Margaret heard the rattling of rigging on unseen masts; the slurp of waves around ships and jetties; murmurs, chatter, banter, dispute. Every choking breath she took was filled with the odour of mud, coal, oil and horse muck.

A few women walked the dockside pavement, drifting back and forth with the fog, eddying into groups then drifting apart. It was impossible to make out their faces.

There were several men. One disappeared with a woman; others watched from the shadows; most talked, smoked and strolled along the pavement. Some followed Margaret and Fox with their eyes, while others seemed to follow on foot. Margaret walked close to Fox and hoped the men were his undercover agents, considering whether to stop what they were doing to act as a guard.

Fox paused to peer about. 'We need to take the next turning on the right. I hope she isn't—'

'Don't, Fox.'

When they arrived at Playhouse Yard there was no sign of anyone, which meant they'd have to investigate the alleys. Even though the fog had thinned, there was little light in the narrow, twisting lanes. But posters had been ripped from a wall, leaving bare brick. '5a' and an arrow had been chalked where they would be most visible.

'I don't like this,' muttered Fox. 'Would anyone really follow that?'

'We have to find out. Hopefully, Bert was moments behind her.'

They trained their torches along the alley. A pair of rats oozed out of a hole then ran ahead of them, their paws making little flashes of light as the torches followed their scurry. They were unafraid, knowing that they owned the area and the humans were the infestation.

A woman who'd been slumped against a rotting door stepped into the alley and leaned against the wall.

'Has a girl passed this way?' asked Fox.

'Lotsa girls.'

'Recently, I mean,' said Fox. 'Medium height, young, long coat. Maybe a man in a cap shortly after.'

'There was a girl not that long ago. Asked where 5a was.'

'Where is it?'

'Dunno.' Thin shoulders shrugged and the shawl dropped from a head of grey hair. Her pin-prick-pupilled eyes were as disinterested as her voice. 'Men? None interested in doing business. Are you?'

'No,' said Fox. 'But here's a shilling. Please buy food and shelter with it.'

'Ta.'

'She won't buy food,' Margaret whispered, as they hurried away.

'Who am I to judge?' said Fox. 'She hasn't long to live, has she, whatever she uses it for.'

The alley opened onto a square of old, grubby houses. What looked like a large bundle of clothes lay on the ground just beyond a puddle of light from a street lamp.

'Oh God! Sadie!' Margaret started to run.

From behind them came a clatter of footsteps. She didn't turn, but heard Bert's voice. 'Mrs Fox, what are you— '

Margaret ran ahead then crouched by the bundle. What she'd thought was a person was nothing but a large, sodden, heavy overcoat. She heard Fox and Bert calling her name, and running feet.

She started to turn and stand at the same time and—

A heavy blow caught her on the side of her head. Hearing and vision distorted, faded, disappeared...

...then returned confused and blurred.

She could smell the stench of wet cloth, could hear sounds which she knew were words but couldn't decipher. When she opened her eyes, she could see nothing but a white glare.

'Drop that, you fool,' said Fox. 'You're blinding her. Margaret... Margaret, can you hear me?'

She found herself staring up at Fox, a constable with a torch and the man she had seen going around with Endsleigh. She let Fox help her sit up, his arms tight round her. 'Who...?'

'Bert's gone after him,' said Fox. 'He was waiting in the shadows, hit you before we could get there, then ran. How bad is it?'

'How long was I unconscious?'

'Seconds.'

'All right, then. Sadie...?'

'Gone,' said Endsleigh's man. 'You're the doctor who gave the talk, aren't you? The one who was in the tea shop. How'd you know Sadie?'

'She came to my house and said she was coming here to rescue someone and needed help.'

The man sucked his teeth. 'I didn't know that was your house or that that's what she was doing. I'd have come and had a word if I had, instead of keeping on following her. Not that I'd have expected you to believe her without bringing the police.'

'I don't understand,' said Margaret. Her head was fuzzy. 'Why were you following her at all?'

'The boss had me do it. Sadie tried to lure Miss Frampton this evening.'

'What?' said Fox.

'Miss Frampton's a do-gooder who teaches a class Sadie goes to,' said the man. 'My boss has been warning her to stop: he knows the kinds of girls they are. Fortunately, Miss Frampton was escorted home by a male teacher and probably never realised what might have happened. But I followed Sadie afterwards, all the same. We're trying to stop this sort of caper.' He shook his head. 'Miss Frampton's lucky she's not halfway to hell by now, cos that's where Sadie Taylor would've sent her. And you're lucky that cosh didn't do more damage. What's your head made of, apart from naive ideals?'

The journey home seemed to take years, but eventually Fox settled Margaret in his study, away from her father's chatter, while he collected water and aspirin.

She curled up in Fox's chair, struggling to piece together what had happened, feeling as if something important was just beyond her mental grasp and sick with fear for Violet and Sadie. But her thoughts burst apart when Freda crashed into the room with tears streaming down her face.

Margaret stood up too fast and steadied herself on the chair. 'Oh goodness, Freda, you wanted to tell me something and I forgot. What's wrong?'

'When I asked, it was just about a postcard,' sobbed Freda. 'Now it's Evie, ma'am. Joe's just come. He got a telegram and went to look then came to tell me. It wasn't true.'

Margaret's head swam. She couldn't recall who Evie and Joe were. 'What wasn't true?'

'That she was safe in Highbury,' said Freda. 'My cousin, do you remember?'

'Oh! The one who got the ... typing job.' Margaret felt blood drain from her face. 'Oh God, Freda. What's happened?'

'I'd told Joe about the postcard I was going to show you. Then he got a telegram from his father and showed the butler, got leave and went to the address we thought she was at. It's empty. The neighbours say the postman puts letters through the door, but if anyone collects them, it's at night. Evie was never there. And now she's dead. And it's my fault!'

Fox entered the room halfway through the speech. 'I'll take over from here, Freda, Dr Demeray needs to rest.'

'No,' said Margaret. 'I need to know.' She forced herself to concentrate. 'Go on, Freda.'

'The police found Evie's coat in the harbour in Ostend, in Belgium. And a body in the sea. She's drowned and it's all my fault. I should have told you before, then the master might have found her in time.'

Margaret began to feel sick. 'Told us what? You said you were receiving letters.'

'Not me. Joe and his parents did. But I couldn't work out why we couldn't meet up no matter what I suggested. I should have trusted my own instincts at the beginning.'

'Please, Freda,' Margaret caught the twisting hands and held them tight. 'Please explain.'

'Evie wanted a telephone or telegraph job in the city.' Freda's voice dropped. 'Joe and I must've made London sound better than it is.'

'I'm sure you didn't,' said Margaret.

'She saw this advertisement. It said they'd pay for her to come to London and she could make her fortune.'

Margaret's heart went cold. Why hadn't she thought to ask how Freda's cousin got her typing job? But why would she, when Freda seemed so sure her cousin was safe and it was a perfectly normal job to have? Katherine had been a typist for years. She'd been bored and frustrated, but she'd always been safe.

'Do you know when and where Evie saw the advertisement?' said Fox.

'October, in the local paper in Buckinghamshire. I wrote to say that girls get caught out like that all the time, but Evie wrote back and said it was above board. They sent her a travel warrant to London and everything.'

Margaret swallowed.

Freda's voice was barely audible. 'So then I wrote and called her stupid. I told her to tell me what time the train was coming in to Paddington, and even if I lost my job, so help me, I'd meet her there. I skived off work to look for her because she was more important than my j—' Freda cleared her throat. 'I mean—'

'Don't worry,' said Fox. 'Go on.'

'Then my aunt and Joe got letters from her and we thought it was all right. I wasn't surprised she didn't write to me, since I'd called her stupid. I just hoped that when we met I could apologise. I was happy enough she was writing to Joe. Then this morning I had a postcard from her. That's what I wanted to show you, because it doesn't make sense.'

'Slow down, Freda. Do you have it with you now?'

'Yes'm.'

Freda handed it over. 'It sounded different from the letters Joe got, but more like Evie, if you know what I mean, and I started to wonder...'

On the front of the postcard was a picture of a kitten with flowers. On the reverse was a second-class British stamp, postmarked in Dover on the twenty-fourth of November. On the back, every available space had been filled with tiny handwriting.

Dear Freda, I hope someone on the boat puts a stamp on this and posts it for me. Sorry I haven't written, I never seem to have time. It's been a rum few weeks. To start with, I wondered if I should have heeded your advice, but Mr Quill, my teacher, is such a nice gent with eyes you can trust, like a deer. I went to Antwerp on the third. The crossing was ever so exciting though it made me sick. They'd said I'd be staying for a while, but someone let my employer down so we came back to England then went out again twice, through different ports. The foreign water doesn't half make my head feel funny, bit like whatever disagreed with me in the training school. I've been lonely and wanted to give notice, but they said a girl called Violet is joining me on the 3rd of December and we'll work together. As soon as I can, I'll give you my address. Maybe you and Joe could join me too. Love Evie.

'Is Evie's surname Mead like yours, Freda?' said Margaret, already sure of the answer.

'No, ma'am. She's properly Eveline Young.' Freda broke into sobs. 'It's all my fault. If I'd got to Paddington earlier that day. I could have—'

Margaret pulled Freda into her arms and let her weep. 'It's not your fault. And so help me, we'll find out who's responsible for Evie's death.'

The doorbell rang.

'I'll go,' said Fox, 'I expect it's Bert. Will you speak with the police, Freda?'

'Anything, sir.'

'Will you be all right for a moment while I ask Nellie to make some tea?' said Margaret.

'I haven't finished making d-dinner, ma'am. Mr Demeray will be hungry.'

'Don't worry. We'll manage.' Margaret led her to the chair then stepped into the hallway.

Bert was just inside the door, whispering urgently with Fox. He paused when he saw Margaret.

'What is it?' she said.

Fox turned, his face grim. '5a Playhouse Yard doesn't exist. But Bert and the police found a rundown building which locals said had had a lot of odd activity recently. Inside, there's a book listing all the current sailings to the Continent, a marked 1913 calendar, one of Radden's business cards, a package of old jewellery in a cupboard and an empty gun crate in the cellar. There's evidence that people were kept in an upper room: clothes, belongings, blotting paper with half-written letters ... rope, blood, the initials VB scratched on a skirting board.'

'Then if you can find the owner...'

Fox said nothing. He couldn't meet her eyes.

Bert heaved a sigh. 'I'm sorry, Mrs F. The owner is Percival Pendleberry.'

Twenty-Eight

'We've found Sadie,' said Inspector Silvermann. He stood grim-faced, arms folded.

Margaret's headache lingered. She'd heard Freda sobbing during the night and had wept herself, imagining Evie's body tumbling with Violet's, even though one was in the North Sea and the other perhaps in the Thames. If only she'd asked Freda more questions. If only she'd tried harder to find Violet.

The door to the sitting room opened and Margaret's father entered. 'Meg, will you— Oh! I don't believe—'

'This is Inspector Silvermann, Father,' said Margaret. 'He went to some of your magic-lantern shows in his youth.'

The inspector stood up and shook hands. 'I remember them with pleasure, Mr Demeray. If only life were really so magical.'

'But it is,' said Margaret's father, in surprise. 'Should I give illustrated talks again, Meg? Your police friends are as serious as Kitty's.'

'Let's discuss it later,' said Fox, steering him through the door. 'Perhaps Nellie or Dinah can help drive the train.'

'I wasn't entirely sure about that girl with the flowers, you know, Fox. I wish—'

The door closed and his voice faded.

The inspector sat down. 'Sadie is very sorry. She says she didn't know what would happen. She's in desperate straits.'

'How?' said Fox, sitting down again.

'Sadie says she was dismissed from her position as a house-maid recently,' said the inspector. 'She was given two months' wages in lieu of notice. A constable's been round to the address to confirm. According to the mistress, Sadie was loose in her morals and a liar. According to Sadie, she lost her job for accusing the son of promising marriage to get what he wanted until she found herself in the family way.'

'She's not even sixteen. What he's done is illegal, never mind immoral.'

'It's an old story, and her word against his. The court rarely believe the maid.'

'The fact that the employer gave her two months' wages suggests it's true,' said Margaret.

'Mmm.' The inspector leaned forward. 'Doctor, I know you wander about places like Blackfriars all the time, but—'

'I don't,' said Margaret. 'And almost never at night. Was your next question going to be "Why didn't I realise it might be a trap?" The truth is, I did realise, but thought that it might have been a trap for Sadie until Mr Endsleigh's man said it was set for Lucy.'

'It wasn't. Sadie was sent to get you.'

Margaret's confusion mingled with fear. 'Much as I'd like to think I look like an innocent teenaged girl, I don't. What would anyone want me for?'

'Dead, probably.'

Margaret swallowed. 'Sadie told you that?'

'No. She was just told to get you under the pretext of saving someone called Violet, even though she had no idea who that was.'

'Hardly anyone knows I'm looking for Violet,' said Margaret.

'You were asking about Violet's sister at Sullivan's, remember,' said the inspector. 'Besides, Radden might have noted who gave Rosie the advertisement, and given how many queries the hospital has received, I think they guess that Rosie was admitted to Dorcas Free on the eighth.'

'That doesn't mean I—'

'You started asking awkward questions at local talks a few days after the accident. Every innocent person who knows or guesses what Radden was up to and might reveal his colleagues is at risk.' The inspector blew out his cheeks briefly. 'His sister has reported several attempted assaults, one of which was witnessed by a constable, although without an arrest. The threatening letters that keep arriving at their house for her would make a hangman feel sick.'

'So you're hiding her?'

'Not yet. She'd be safe enough if she stayed at her friend's house.' He leaned forward. 'The alternative is that they didn't want you dead – yet. Maybe they just wanted to borrow you and persuade you, ever so nicely, to tell them where Rosie is. They don't know you don't know.'

Fox put his arm round Margaret. 'How did Sadie get involved?'

'Two months' wages isn't much to live on when your chances of getting a decent job are scuppered by having no reference and being pregnant,' said the inspector. 'She asked the wrong person for help. They gave her a choice. If she could get you to help find Violet, she'd be given a nice sum of cash. Alternatively, she could make a regular income providing comfort to lonely men. Unsurprisingly, she didn't fancy the latter.'

'How did she know where I live?'

'She says the person who gave her your address said they'd got it from the telephone directory. I'm surprised you allow your wife's details to be published, Fox. Yours aren't.'

'They shouldn't have been,' said Fox. 'Someone—'

'It's too late now,' said Margaret. Her skull thudded. 'If the point of going to Blackfriars was to take me there, why not wait until I got home from work?'

'She says she genuinely believed in Violet and wanted to save her. She says she made for the address, but was pulled through the doorway then knocked out – with a drug, not a cosh.' He glanced at Margaret's head. 'The next thing she knew it was dawn and she was back in her lodgings with a note saying "*You'll get the blame*", which she burned.' The inspector scratched his nose. 'That's what Sadie *says*, but all I *know* is that she was found wandering in Paddington by a constable. She told him her side of a story he knew nothing about, assuming he was about to arrest her, and he had the sense to contact the Yard. It's hard to know what to charge her with. Mr Endsleigh's man thinks she's a wrong 'un, but Sadie says she thought she was saving another girl. I'm reluctant to be one more person who assumes the toff is telling the truth and the maid is a liar.'

Margaret's face twisted. 'The plan was stupid. If I'd been home when she arrived, I'd have called the police. As it was, after reading her letter I might not have followed her to Blackfriars at all. Even if I did, I might have gone on foot rather than by car.'

'Then you might have found your hat dented closer to home, possibly by a tube train,' said the inspector. 'Someone knew you well enough to know you'd take the bait. You generally have a bee in your reinforced bonnet about something.'

'I have more than one bee,' snapped Margaret. 'The traffic in young people, including Freda's cousin who—'

'Dealing with procurement is my job. If they've been flushed from that place in Blackfriars, now I have to start again.'

'It's misdirection,' snapped Margaret. 'Hilda, Evie, Kay and Rosie were all trained in a nice house.'

'Those are four names out of twelve,' said the inspector. 'We don't know what happened to the others. Maybe they were too drugged to realise the house wasn't nice at all.'

'Nonsense,' said Margaret. 'Besides, Evie's postcard said Violet would join her on the third. That's Wednesday. If they're following the pattern, Violet's being held somewhere else.'

'I agree with Margaret,' said Fox. 'No one could think the Blackfriars house was "nice" without being so drugged that they couldn't have been trained in anything. It may be where the gang stores arms and goods for smuggling until they're ready for dispatch, while the unwitting smugglers are trained elsewhere.'

'It was sheer luck you found that house, Fox. But it belongs to Pendleberry all the same.'

'It wasn't luck. My men were looking for something similar and your men should have been.'

'They were.'

'It's coincidence.'

'Happenstances happen.'

'I don't like this one.'

'I do. It's evidence.'

Any moment, the two men would square up to each other. Normally, Margaret might have joined in, but it was wasting time. 'How does Sadie describe the man who employed her?'

'It was a woman,' said the inspector, turning away from Fox. 'She was slim, dark, proper. Sadie thought she was a do-gooder, then realised her mistake. With her was a tall, slim, fair, blue-eyed, nice-looking middle-aged gent. I established that proper meant snobbish, middle-aged meant over thirty, and a gent is anyone who doesn't drop his aitches or leer. That means nothing. You can learn that sort of thing.' He stepped into the hall. 'Or maybe you don't need to. I'm sorry to have to point it out, but it describes Percival Pendleberry to a T.'

'Percival has nothing to do with this.'

'Sometimes rumours contain truth, doctor. Mr Endsleigh, whom you dislike for no reason, sent someone to follow Sadie, thereby saving your life. Mr Pendleberry not only owns places he claims to be unaware of but is in waters deeper than the Atlantic. Is he behind Radden's enterprise? I think he might be.'

'Nonsense.'

'A pleasant gentleman, a lady, a nice house. That sums up the Pendleberrys, doesn't it?'

'No one would go off with Etta,' snapped Margaret.

The inspector shrugged. He stood up and made his way to the sitting-room door, followed by Fox and Margaret. 'There's something else. I'm still seeking the original requests for those advertisements to see who placed them. Some papers are cooperating more than others. Some have better filing systems. One of the latter vaguely remembers the name Pendle because their gran came from there.'

'Half a name proves nothing,' said Margaret. 'Show a photograph of Percival to Rosie and Sadie.'

'They're too scared to peach,' said the inspector. 'Let your husband seek money and arms, Dr Demeray. Let me find procurers and murderers. Everyone seems to have forgotten that whoever killed Hector Radden and Lizzie Jackson is still at large.'

Margaret glanced towards the study and lowered her voice. 'As is whoever killed Freda's cousin, Eveline Young. She must be EY on Radden's list.'

'The same thing applies,' said Inspector Silvermann. 'It's my job to find out. Take what happened in Blackfriars as a warning to stop meddling before you make things worse. Good day.' He donned his hat, opened the front door and strode out.

Fox closed the door and turned to Margaret. 'You can't kill him,' he said. 'There's already too much blood.'

'We could have the hall repainted red.'

Fox picked up the mail and ushered her into the sitting room. 'I have to ask. If I hadn't come home early last night, would you have gone off alone?'

'No, and I'd completely forgotten you'd come home early. Was it really to keep Father company?'

'It was chiefly because I thought you'd come home early too. I wanted to tell you in person that there was evidence against Percival, before you heard it another way.'

'What about Endsleigh?'

'Nothing's been found to connect him with anything illegal whatsoever. He and his wife support charities which attempt to steer vulnerable youngsters into safe, respectable work. His father bought houses from Mr Pendleberry senior. Maybe that's why Percival's being connected with specific properties, but it doesn't mean Endsleigh started the rumours. Nor does it mean that Percival is innocent.'

'You suspect yet another of my friends of criminality and treason—'

'I don't,' said Fox. 'The inspector may do. Whoever hired Sadie to lure you to Blackfriars knows that the attempt's failed and the house – whatever it was used for – has been found. But the police won't make any of that public yet. We'd best behave as if nothing happened yesterday evening. And reinforced hat notwithstanding, you should rest.'

'I'm supposed to be going for a walk with Maude.' Juniper coiled round her legs and Margaret picked her up. 'And Violet's still missing.'

'Cancel the walk and leave me to find Violet and do what I can to prove Percival's innocence,' said Fox. 'I'd rather do it without worrying about you. Will you stay at home?'

Margaret caught sight of herself in the mirror over the fire-place. She looked grey, exhausted.

Her father put his head round the door. 'Are you coming to play trains with us before we meet Maude for that walk?'

'Yes, Father. I'll join you in a moment.' Margaret turned to Fox. 'I need some fresh air. It'll look like I'm having a nice quiet day to recover and not investigating anything at all.'

Fox shook his head then handed over some mail. 'I give up. These are for you. A postcard and a letter.'

The postcard was from Phoebe, asking Margaret to visit on Saturday. 'What should I do?'

'Go,' said Fox. 'Phoebe might need you. What about the letter?'

'Let me open it... It's from Mrs Tomlinson.'

'Who?'

'The vicar's wife from St Mark's, where I gave one of the talks the inspector is complaining about.' Margaret scanned the letter and raised her eyebrows. 'Listen to this. "*I daresay you recall Mrs Wantage of the blue beads.*"'

'Do you? I don't.'

'She attended two of my talks.'

'Ah.'

'*She asked me to tell you that a hidey-hole near the Portobello Road has moved,*' Margaret read aloud. '*She will see what she can find out. Apparently Ruth says <u>that man</u> wants Miss Framble to stop teaching because she is a disgrace to her family. Mrs Wantage says <u>that man</u> is a disgrace to <u>his</u> family. This is not quite how she put things, and I imagine Miss Framble is called something else. I hope this makes sense to you. It makes none to me.*'

Margaret handed the letter to Fox. 'The hidey-hole is a refuge for women in danger. "That man" is almost certainly Endsleigh. Mrs Wantage maligned him. I should speak with her again.'

'No.'

'She won't talk to the police.' Margaret thought of Sadie running through the early-morning darkness. 'Do you suppose

Sadie was looking for the refuge when they found her? Can you arrange for us to speak with her?'

Fox raised his eyebrows. 'I can arrange for *me* to speak with her.'

'Why do you only want me to talk to people when it suits you?'

'Because investigating Sadie Taylor is in Inspector Silvermann's jurisdiction.' He touched her head gently. 'Ring Maude and tell her to visit you here.'

'I really do need some air, Fox. A quiet walk in the park will distract Father from quizzing me and keep me from thinking about Violet. I'll come home straight afterwards and rest.'

'If you promise,' said Fox. He kissed her gently. 'And I'll promise that if I can arrange for us to talk to Sadie together, I'll come and get you. That's the best I can do.'

Twenty-Nine

An hour later, Margaret was walking through Hyde Park.

Her father wandered ahead with Nellie and the twins, stopping to inspect fallen leaves and feathers, peering into pruned-back flowerbeds and up at sleeping trees. The park was a little misty and the Serpentine rippled under a light mantle of silver. Maude, Johnny and Johnny's nursery governess were hazy figures in the near distance, discernible by Johnny's frantic waving.

Her father paused while Nellie continued with the children, waited for Margaret to catch up, then pointed at a shrub. 'Look, Meg! A chrysanthemum bush! Perhaps that girl took them from here.'

'You mean stole them, Father,' said Margaret.

'Hmm.' Her father frowned.

'What is it?'

'What happened last night? Should I have made her stay? Was she hurt like you were?'

'Sadie is quite well, Father,' said Margaret. 'There was nothing you could have done. And I'm quite all right. You needn't mention it to Maude.'

His face brightened briefly, then fell again. 'I didn't take to Sadie, you know.'

'Not everyone understands about books.'

'I think she understood their monetary value,' he said. 'Just not their *real* value. She did look quite closely. Which—'

The twins came running back with Johnny and Maude. Alec pointed at the water. 'Ampa! Magic!'

'All water's magic, young man. Have you heard of King Arthur? No? Well...' Margaret's father strode ahead, holding his stick aloft as he told them of Excalibur emerging from the lake. Nellie and Johnny's governess stopped chatting to herd them back to the path, the latter's voice clear and loud. 'If you go in the water, Master Johnny, it'll be an afternoon of sums, even if I have to glue your behind to the chair.'

Margaret's mind started to thud again as Maude chattered. She ought to be somewhere else, doing something. Finding Violet, avenging Evie.

'...really was facetious,' Maude was saying, 'but it was nice to have something to chuckle about for a change.'

Margaret tried to work out if she'd heard anything subconsciously that might help, then gave up. 'Whatever are you talking about?'

'An article in the *Evening Standard* about Antarctic pycnogonids with suffragette tendencies,' said Maude.

'Antarctic what?'

'They're sea spiders whose males carry the eggs for the females, hence the suffragette reference. I'm incorporating the information in *Athene's Gazette* with a cartoon. Would Fox pose for the male spider carrying his children?'

'Hardly. I thought you were writing about Hilda. If you haven't done it yet, I need to tell you about Fre—'

'One has to mix light with dark,' said Maude. She grew sober. 'But it's for next month, anyway. The latest edition of *Athene's Gazette* has already gone to press with the Hilda article and a report on the talk at Wimbledon about sweated working. Your friend Reuben has illustrated both. I hope the vicar's wife writes back—' Her grip on Margaret's arm tightened. 'Wait, I wasn't listening. Were you going to say something about Freda? Please tell me she hasn't got caught the same way.'

'Her cousin Evie has. I think she was the girl Hilda referred to as Eveline.'

'Was?' Maude's eyes widened.

'A body was found in the sea in Ostend.'

'Drowned?'

'I don't know.'

Maude scowled. 'Pen and ink isn't enough. I want to—'

'You can't write about it yet. Fox and Inspector Silvermann are doing everything they can.'

'Silvermann? That man?'

'He's fair and you know it.'

'He's rude.'

'So are you, sometimes. You're still fair.' Margaret pondered. 'Have you heard of any relatively local refuge where girls like Hilda can go if they run away?'

Maude shook her head. 'I'm thinking of setting one up myself. I know you and Phoebe will help. Though Phoebe might prefer you keep the Pendleberry name out of things.'

Margaret swallowed. 'Have you heard more rumours?'

'No,' said Maude. 'But Percival and Etta have gone to Ireland, which smacks of an attempt to escape. I'm not sure I'd go when Mr Bonar Law is stirring up trouble.'

'Etta would say he's talking sense.'

'Etta's an idiot. If Ireland becomes independent and Britain allows it to flourish, it'll be a vital ally. If we foster division, I dread to imagine the outcome. Besides, why go to unhappy Ireland rather than nonchalant France? That's where Etta usually takes her little trips.'

Margaret stopped walking. 'Does she?'

'Of course,' said Maude. 'Paris. You know how ridiculous she is about fashion.'

'So are you, Maude.'

'You're not a great deal better, Demeray.'

'I can't afford to dress like either of you.'

'I'm not sure Etta can just now.'

'The Pendleberry family is hardly short of cash,' said Margaret. 'That's why the rumours make no sense.'

'Which ones? Allowing their properties to be used for illicit activity? I agree. Etta going through money like water? I'm not so sure.'

A yell distracted them. 'No!' shouted Nellie. 'Mr Demeray! Children!'

Ahead of them, Margaret's father, followed by the children, was drifting off the path. His walking stick became stuck in the mud and he wobbled as he tried to free it. The governess helped him while Nellie intercepted the twins as they scampered towards the lake.

Johnny ran onto the path and headed for his mother, barrelling into a woman in black coming the other way. She doubled over but grabbed Johnny, her gloved hand grasping his shoulder as Margaret and Maude rushed up. He squirmed and whimpered but couldn't pull away.

'Madam, I'm so sorry,' said Maude, taking his arm. 'Please do let go. I have him now. John Holbourne, apologise to this lady immediately.'

'Mama, she *hurt* me.'

'Nonsense, Johnny. You have two inches of clothes on. *You* hurt *her* because you were running when you shouldn't have been. Apologise.'

Tears trickled down Johnny's face, but he whispered 'S-sorry, madam.'

'No harm done,' said the woman, straightening up with a hand on her stomach. It was Mrs Vidler. Her expression oozed sickening sweetness but Johnny tucked himself into Maude's side, his shoulders heaving. Mrs Vidler smiled at Maude, then Margaret. 'Oh! Dr, er... I beg your pardon, but I can't recall...'

'Demeray,' said Margaret. 'Are you quite all right, Mrs Vidler? Your stomach...'

'I am recovering well. My... One's shoulder is sorer ... more sore. One's head...' She chuckled. 'It's quite empty, so little to damage. A light tap never does much harm, does it?' Mrs Vidler's voice was softer than Margaret recalled, the accent more refined.

'Oh my,' said Maude. 'Were you a patient at Dorcas Free, Mrs Vidler? I'm so terribly sorry. My son didn't mean to hurt you.'

'Boys will be boys. Please do not trouble yourself, Mrs... Holbourne, did you say?'

'That's right. Here's my card.'

Mrs Vidler waved it away. 'There's no need.' She turned to Margaret. 'I am recovering very well. I daresay one will see you at Higgins's trial, doctor.'

'I didn't know it had been set,' said Margaret, cursing the inspector.

'He was at the police court this morning to have the murder charge added,' said Mrs Vidler. Her face was pale and her voice anxious. 'He denies it. The trial will be in January. One remains scared. If it *was* Higgins, but he's only sentenced for burglary, one day he'll be released. If it wasn't Higgins, might the real murderer try again? No obscene letters can get to me now, but I was followed to the police court this morning, I'm sure of it. Someone tried to push me under a bus. If it hadn't been for Mrs Warner being there to clasp my arm... Maybe someone might even attack *you,* because of whom you might have seen running from the scene of Lizzie's murder?'

'I didn't see anyone,' said Margaret.

'One hopes the murderer knows that.' Mrs Vidler gave her a sympathetic smile. 'Good day to you both. After the trial, one may sell up and move to the coast. London air gets worse and worse, does it not? And surely the further away one is, the safer one would be.' She shook hands and moved on apace.

'Mama, she *hurt* me,' sobbed Johnny.

'Where's my brave little soldier?' said Maude, rolling her eyes. 'I'm sure she didn't mean to.' She cuddled him close and eyed Margaret. 'Care to explain any of that, Demeray?'

'When the children are playing in your nursery. Not before.'

Staring after the bustling figure, Margaret tried to work out what, out of everything Mrs Vidler had said, she had found the most disturbing.

Fox telephoned shortly after Margaret returned home, asking her to tell Freda not to give up hope.

'A coat with Evie's name sewn on the lining was found hooked to a ladder in the harbour,' he said. 'But there's doubt the body is Evie's. A vagrant girl of similar age fell from the harbour wall recently and was swept away. The clothes the body was wearing sound more likely to be hers than Evie's. The people she'd been tramping with are being sought while Mr and Mrs Young travel to Belgium, taking a photograph of their daughter. It's been an expensive exchange of telegrams.'

'Will anyone be able to recognise the body?'

'Possibly,' said Fox. 'Allowing for being in the sea for around forty-eight hours, rocks, and carnivorous sea creatures. But things don't quite add up. If Evie removed the coat in the water to stop herself sinking, the chances of it getting on the ladder by itself are very slim. It's more likely someone put it there so that everyone would think she'd drowned. Possibly she's been murdered, her body is elsewhere and the murderers were laying a false trail. Or possibly she's escaped and made a false trail of her own.'

'And Sadie?'

'I'm trying to pull rank, but no luck so far and unless they charge her with something they'll have to let her go. If anything changes, I'll let you know.'

'Was Higgins before court today, charged with Radden's murder?' said Margaret. 'I thought the inspector said the murderer was still at large.'

'I suspect Inspector Silvermann hopes that indicting Higgins will give the real perpetrator a false sense of security and bring them into the open.'

'Mmm.' Margaret's finger tapped on the telephone.

'Is that supposed to be Morse code?'

'Sorry. I feel agitated. I saw Mrs Vidler today in the park. She says she was attacked this morning and fears for me.'

'Did that unnerve you?'

'Yes. But not enough to stop me doing anything I need to.'

Fox sighed. 'How unsurprising. I'll see you later.'

In the late afternoon Margaret put her work aside, played with the twins, then joined her father in the sitting room to read Frau Gesner's reply to the letter she'd sent earlier.

Thank you for all the local information you have sent.

I hope that the Superintendent can find out more about the boy who was found near the Kaiser Wilhelm Kanal. I am sure it is all a misunderstanding.

Our street seems very quiet, though according to our maid there was a small disturbance early this morning. A young girl was knocking at doors and the police took her away. Our maid says she must have been a troublemaker for the police to arrest her, but this is a very unusual circumstance and not to be worried.

Would you and your aunt like to visit for coffee and cake on...

Margaret sighed. Had the girl been Sadie, looking for shelter and repulsed at every turn? Hilda had been lucky to find refuge with the vicar's wife in Biarritz. How many doors had she tried beforehand?

'You haven't been quite the thing since you went to Blackfriars last night,' said her father. 'Although I shouldn't be surprised that you insisted on going. It was a surprise to find that Kitty had become a detective while I was away.' He said it as if Katherine had made this decision while he popped into a bookshop for an hour, rather than disappearing for so many years that everyone thought he was dead. 'I always thought *you'd* be the adventuress. I have an inkling of your mind, you know.'

'Good grief, Father.'

'It's more like mine than your mother's.'

'I... Really?' Margaret sat on the arm of her father's chair. Her only recollection of her mother was of love, warmth, lavender and silk, of copper-coloured ringlets and soft laughter. An extension of herself, not a person in her own right. And then she was gone. Margaret had afterwards relied on what she'd been told about Mathilda Demeray: shy, godly, houseproud, kind, patient.

'You find me frustrating, don't you?' said her father.'

'Of course not,' said Margaret, putting her arm round his shoulder and leaning her head on his. 'I have a lot on my mind. I'm sorry if I'm impatient.'

'And sometimes you're responsible for so many things that you long to be somewhere else, just for a respite.'

Margaret struggled for a response. Had he found her and Katherine a drain when they were children? Did she find her own children a drain? Did she feel trapped by family life even while loving it?

'I worried about you last night,' he said. 'But I understand. If I were you, I'd do the same. And if the need arises I can protect you, albeit rather slowly and aided by my cane.'

'Are you trying to make me feel better or worse about my responsibilities?'

'I'm trying to make you realise that I can take care of myself and I shall always take care of you. Of all the things you need worry about, you needn't worry about me.'

'Father, if you had the remotest comprehension of how the world works, I wouldn't. But as it is...'

'I go to classes on Saturday afternoons to help me learn,' he said. 'I go this week with new resolve to ensure I come back prepared for anything.'

'Jolly good,' said Margaret, kissing the top of his head and thinking that at least if she and Fox had to go looking for Violet again, her father would not need to know. 'That's one less thing to worry about.'

Thirty

Following orders to behave normally, on Friday morning Margaret visited Dr Naylor at the hospital to discuss research, then Dr Gesner, to find out anything she needed to know for Monday. No one at Dorcas Free knew what had happened in Blackfriars or about Evie, and Margaret was determined to prove that her dedication was as strong as ever, though the effort required was draining.

The only news of any interest was that another telephone call had been received by the hospital, asking for details of the patient knocked down on the eighth of November, including the name of any doctor who'd treated her and where the patient could be interviewed. This time, the caller said he was campaigning for the motoring speed limit in towns to be reduced to fourteen miles an hour again, and was looking for case studies to support this.

Matron had refused to discuss the matter unless the enquirer visited the hospital in person, with proof of their identity and the campaign. No one had arrived. 'Fishing for stories,' Matron declared. 'As if there's not enough real news to report.'

After a quick lunch with Dr Sylvie Howe, Margaret went to a newspaper archive to see whether she could find anything relevant, but the task was enormous. She would have to wade through months of dense newsprint with no clear idea of what to look for. Possessing neither Elinor's knack nor patience, she returned home after a short while with a few notes which were undoubtedly useless.

She was in her study trying to make sense of them when the doorbell rang. She heard footsteps in the hall and a murmured exchange, then Dinah entered the study and handed over a card. *Augustus Endsleigh, Esq.* 'Since Mr Demeray's here, should I let him in, doctor? Or should I say you're not receiving visitors?'

'Has he anyone with him?'

'No, doctor. When is Mr Fox coming home?'

'Shortly, I believe.' Margaret stood up and went to put the card on the mantlepiece. 'All right. Give me a moment to join my father in the sitting room, then show Mr Endsleigh in.'

Dinah leaned closer as they went down the hall. 'Are you sure, ma'am?' she murmured. 'You look peaky.'

'I'm sure.'

'Shall I bring tea, or wait outside the door with a frying pan? Shall I telephone Mr Fox's office?'

'I don't think there's anything to worry about. I'll order tea if he seems likely to stay, but I doubt he will.'

Mr Endsleigh entered a few moments later. As Margaret introduced her father, he looked surprised for a moment before his expression settled back into neutrality. 'I hadn't realised you were related to the famous writer. Nor had I quite realised you had retained your maiden name. How interesting.'

Margaret wished she hadn't let Mr Endsleigh in after all. Hopefully, Fox would come soon. She sat so that the men could sit.

Mr Endsleigh frowned a little, then smiled. 'Thank you for admitting me. I came to see how you were.'

'Very well, thank you,' said Margaret, resisting the urge to touch the tender place on her head. 'I hope you received my message thanking your man for looking out for me. I very much appreciate it.'

'I did indeed. I'm so glad you weren't too badly hurt.' His face was serious, friendly, perhaps eager to please. Margaret realised once more that his looks were attractive: fine bones, thick dark hair, warm brown eyes with thick eyelashes that were almost black. It was disconcerting.

'I'm still confused about why he was following Sadie Taylor,' said Margaret. 'Why were you so sure she had bad intentions?'

'Sadie's an unsatisfactory young woman who lives in a dubious property,' said Mr Endsleigh, blushing a little. 'A week or so ago, my wife tried to help her change direction in life, but Sadie said she had a better offer than kitchen work. After she'd gone, my wife realised the bracelet she'd been wearing before they shook hands was missing, as was a silver inkwell from the desk.' He glanced around the sitting room. 'Are you sure everything here is as it should be?'

'I kept a very close eye,' said Margaret's father. 'One wondered. She was very interested in *Rural Rides*.'

'Rural...?'

'By William Cobbett. First edition. Without meaning to make assumptions, Sadie seemed to understand value more than I'd have expected. She rather turned her nose up at *Cole's*.'

Mr Endsleigh stared at the fire. 'Coals?'

'*Cole's Funny Picture Book*. It was also a first edition, bought by my first wife as a present for Meg, but now significantly more battered than Rural Rides. Though, of course, Meg was very young when she was given Cole's. I shall have to decide what to get you for your next birthday, Meg. Isn't it a significant one? Won't you be—'

'Father!'

'Although it was the time machine she looked inside.' Her father nodded at the side table beside Mr Endsleigh, where the book Mrs Vidler had given Margaret lay beside an ornate, gilded wooden box decorated with coloured glass "jewels".

'Ah,' said Mr Endsleigh. 'It does rather make one feel that if one pressed the right thing, something magical would happen. I can see why you call it that. Very tempting.'

'But empty of all but humbugs,' said Margaret's father. 'She took her time choosing one, but she took it all the same.'

'Hmm. I'm glad you kept a close eye on everything, sir.' Mr Endsleigh inclined his head, then turned his attention to Margaret again. 'Sadie Taylor is an opportunist. I believe you observed a class in Archbold Street which she attended, and of course, you have given talks in the area. I'm afraid Sadie probably thinks of you as a soft touch: someone who has more money than sense. I imagine the intention was to hold you for ransom.'

'Meg definitely has more sense than money,' said her father.

Mr Endsleigh nodded sympathetically. 'I suppose a charity hospital doesn't pay much, if anything. It is good of you to give your time for little or no financial return.'

Margaret cleared her throat. Neither her money nor common sense were his business.

'Meg has very good investments,' protested her father. 'Not simply the ones her grandparents and uncle set up, but she has shares in Verity Moving Picture Comp—'

'I believe your man stopped Miss Frampton from getting into difficulties, too,' said Margaret, before her father started listing what he knew of her finances.

Mr Endsleigh's composure flickered briefly. 'Oh! I was unaware that you and she were acquainted well enough to communicate with each other.'

Margaret could think of no reason why she need explain that she and Lucy were related and willed her father to remain silent. 'Your man told me himself.'

'Ah,'said Mr Endsleigh. 'It's laudable to want to help the poor and ask about missing girls, but one wishes you and she had found a safer way to do so.'

Margaret went to touch her head, and managed to turn it into twiddling an earring.

'You shouldn't have to deal with all those infectious diseases at the hospital, not to mention in those meetings, and Miss Frampton shouldn't be teaching young women with dubious morals. I could help both of you. With good investments, you could have a bigger house, more clothes, more, um...' He glanced round the room.

'More books?' said Margaret's father.

'Why not? And the best schools for your children, and not having to work?' Mr Endsleigh's physical appeal evaporated.

'I love my job,' said Margaret, ' and I'm perfectly content with everything else.' The fact that her work was a vocation, and her need to do it was mental more than financial, was none of Mr Endsleigh's business either.

'One can be rich without being idle,' he insisted. 'There's always a place for unpaid good works. *Noblesse oblige,* and all that.'

'*Noblesse oblige* wouldn't be necessary if life were fair.'

'It's up to the individual to better him or herself.'

Margaret frowned. 'Do you feel I need to better myself?'

'Not at all. I'm so sorry if I offended.' Mr Endsleigh smiled, his dark eyes lustrous. 'I admire you and utterly support the campaign for propertied, educated women to have the vote.'

'Women's suffrage is not just about the vote, but about improving working conditions and housing,' said Margaret. 'It speaks for people, particularly women without a voice. Women's wages are lower than men's, and many endure pregnancy and the brunt of running a home and raising a family while working ten hours a day for six days a week, if not more.'

'They should better themselves and seek better employment,' said Mr Endsleigh. 'Better still, their husbands should better themselves so that their womenfolk needn't work at all.'

'And who will do the jobs they now do?'

'Those who make no effort to better themselves, and who have too many children.'

'Assuming they have a choice in the matter, there's precious little other comfort in their lives than intimacy, and they can't afford to purchase the means to prevent conception.'

'Meg, darling,' interjected her father. 'Really.'

Mr Endsleigh blushed. 'I think we're arguing for the same thing from different angles.' His smile returned. 'Hopefully, once the improvements to my properties are complete, the tenants will be healthier and able to find better work.'

'The local MP, Mr Pendleberry, will support you,' said Margaret. 'He's a man of integrity, and you shouldn't listen to those who say otherwise.'

'As you said before.' Mr Endsleigh pursed his lips. 'I sought a meeting with him, but he's gone to Dublin. He also owns properties in the area, not to mention in Islington, Highbury and who knows where else. I hope that I'm not upsetting any female sensitivities, but I'm afraid a certain sort of business runs out of those dwellings. Sadie Taylor, for example, lives in one of his houses.'

'One full of troubled women?' said her father.

'Fallen women,' Mr Endsleigh replied, his lip curling.

'Fallen?' said Margaret. 'I suggest you stand in their shoes, Mr Endsleigh, and work out whether they chose to fall or whether someone shoved them.'

'Meg has always been passionate about everyone's right to a decent life,' said her father. 'My wife and I brought our daughters up to understand their duty, and not to be afraid of standing up for the needy.'

'Quite right too, sir,' said Mr Endsleigh. He turned back to Margaret. 'I want to eradicate that despicable trade from the area.'

'First, you need to eradicate those who profit from those working in the trade. Secondly, you need to realise that some work in it because their *respectable* job doesn't pay enough to keep body and soul together, while the people who employ them in that respectable job can often afford to dine in the West End.'

'If they choose it, or are weak enough to fall into it, they deserve their fate.' Mr Endsleigh wrinkled his nose again. 'I want to help those who genuinely desire a better life, but I am constantly hampered by people like Mrs Stout confusing me with my father.'

'Who?'

'The stout woman with all the hair who keeps speaking with you. She's prejudiced against me and there's no reasoning with her.'

'Perhaps because you call her Mrs Stout, rather than troubling to find out her name,' said Margaret.

Endsleigh bowed his head. 'That was ungallant of me. What is she really called?'

Margaret felt herself backed into a corner. Mr Endsleigh might be telling the truth about his intentions, while Mrs Wantage's point of view might have nothing to do with evidence. After all, she still held on to her blue beads. But giving Mrs Wantage's name felt like a betrayal. More to the point, how did Mr Endsleigh know she'd approached Margaret more than once?

'A lot of women speak with me,' she said. 'I'm afraid I don't take note of what they're all called. Hopefully, when you address the residents, she'll speak for herself.'

Mr Endsleigh rose and shook hands. 'Yes, of course. Thank you for allowing me to visit. I believe at bottom we want the same things.'

Before he'd even turned, Dinah entered and held the door open for him. In her other hand was a walking stick. He stared before addressing Margaret. 'Are your staff always armed?' His voice was light, but it was a forced lightness.

'What a thing to say,' said Dinah, holding out Mr Endsleigh's hat. 'I'd been cleaning Mr Demeray's favourite stick. I was just bringing it in for him.'

Margaret followed them into the hall, leaving her father behind. Mr Endsleigh's smile seemed friendly and open as he tipped his hat in farewell.

'Was it my imagination,' said Margaret, 'or was he trembling?'

'He was, doctor,' said Dinah. 'But then you were contradicting him something chronic. Not that I blame you.'

'You were listening?'

'Freda showed me Evie's postcard,' said Dinah. 'Evie said the nice gentleman had eyes like a deer.' Her face twisted. 'I know Mr Endsleigh's not the only man like that, ma'am, but what Nellie says about not judging by appearances works both ways, doesn't it? Just cos someone's ugly doesn't make them bad. And just cos Mr Endsleigh's got the sort of face girls fall for, doesn't mean they shouldn't run for the hills instead. A handsome face can hide an evil soul.'

'Yes.'

'If he's responsible for what happened to Evie and I get hold of him, a walking stick will be the least of his worries.'

The telephone rang, making them jump.

It was Bert. 'Evening, Mrs F. Is his nibs there?'

'Not yet. Is it about what you said last night?'

'No. When Fox gets in, tell him to go round the corner from Paddington Station where they do a nice pie and a proper cuppa.'

'It's a bit early for dinner.'

'I haven't had lunch. I've been too busy finding Miss Brown.'

'Violet?'

'Daisy.'

'Paddington's less than a mile away. Bring her here.'

'Fox wouldn't want me to.'

Margaret frowned, wondering what Bert's reasoning was. 'What's the place called? We won't find it without a name.'

There was a pause. 'Might have guessed you'd come too. He'll know it. But maybe bring a brick in your handbag in case Fox needs your protection.'

'From Daisy?'

Another pause. 'A brick won't help with that. See you later.'

Thirty-One

'What do you think Endsleigh really wanted?' said Fox, as they parked near Paddington Station.

'I'm not sure. I can't work out if he was just being kind, wanted to undermine my faith in Percival or was after Mrs Wantage's name. More than anything, I felt I was being warned about whom I could trust.'

'It feels odd. Maybe you're right about him.'

'Maybe I'm not,' said Margaret. 'What have you discovered about that building in Blackfriars? Is it really Percival's?'

'The deeds are a mess,' said Fox. 'But Elinor is putting in extra hours and twisting arms. You know she won't...'

'Falsify information for a friend? Yes I do. But I still think it's nonsense.'

'It's certainly convenient.'

Fox came round to the passenger's side and offered a hand to Margaret. She stepped onto the pavement, took his arm and started to walk. The fine buildings around them varied greatly. Some were smart, occupied by the better off. Others were run-down, housing those with little money and less hope, often doubling as a place of business for women whose other options had long gone. 'Where are we going?'

'To somewhere that's neutral ground for people who work at night, regardless of which side of the law they're on,' said Fox. 'It's hygienic, but don't expect lacy tablecloths.'

Halfway along a street lively with pubs, hot-chestnut sellers and well-lit shops, Fox ushered Margaret into a small restaurant.

It was warm inside, its dark-green tiles sparkling and the air savoury with the scent of rich gravy. Three women in gaudy clothes sat gossiping. One had put her stockinged feet on the opposite chair, a pair of high-heeled shoes underneath. Two cabbies at another table read newspapers while shovelling in food. Some couples at another table laughed and joked.

A plump woman at the counter poured tea from a massive brown pot, then went to refill it as they found a table.

Fox lifted his mug, then put it down again. 'Ah, Sergeant Ainscough,' he said, looking past Margaret.

Bert stood behind her with a hatless girl in her late teens wearing a shawl who looked about to collapse.

'Here you are, Miss Brown,' said Bert. 'This is my boss and the doctor you'd heard of.'

'It's such a coincidence, sergeant,' said Daisy, hunching into her shawl.

'Isn't it,' said Bert. 'Inspector, by luck I happened to take the same route as Miss Brown on the way from Whitechapel. I was on hand when a man tried to bother her, then later when she came over all peculiar in the station. I didn't want her to think I was the same sort of fellow as the one on the tube, so I shouted for the railway officials to put her in a side room and said I'd call a doctor.'

'And then he told me knew a lady one called Dr Demeray,' said Daisy. Her coat drooped on a skinny frame. 'I was that surprised. Fancy you being someone I'd heard of at Sullivan's.'

Fox looked beyond Bert to the door.

'We left by a staff entrance, so as not to have to mingle with all the people at the station,' said Bert, with a discreet wink. 'Sit down and rest, Miss Brown. I'll get us some tea.'

Daisy dropped into the chair, then pushed the shawl back to reveal a very pale face with red blotches. 'I can't afford a doctor. I only came to Paddington to meet Violet, but she's not there yet. Sergeant Ainscough says his friend will bring her here when she arrives.' Her voice was wheezy.

Margaret offered her hand. 'Mr Sullivan thought you'd gone home to the country.'

'Nothing to go back for.' Daisy took a mug of tea from Bert with a smile of thanks. 'And country air won't make me better. My only hope now is Violet.'

'Because she's looking after you?'

'She was. She will be.' Daisy sipped the tea and glanced at Fox.

'I'm a superintendent,' said Fox. 'When did you hear of the doctor?'

Daisy addressed her answer to Margaret. 'I was well enough to go to Sullivan's yesterday. The forewoman had overheard you asking him about Rosie. Rosie's all right, isn't she?'

'Yes, but she's worried about Violet. She said she took Violet's place.'

'Through the ad? Yes, she did. But Vi's all right.'

'Doing what?'

'She's being trained for a clerk's job. She might go abroad, but she'll earn enough to support us both. The landlord'll kick us out if we can't get regular money.' Daisy's face closed a little.

Margaret's heart sank. She felt Fox's hand on her knee and put hers over it. 'You're a long way from Whitechapel and the tube's not free.'

'I meant to come early, but I got pestered on the way.' The blotches on Daisy's cheeks became redder. She took a deep draught of tea and pulled the shawl around her, covering her bare throat. 'Sergeant Ainscough's a gent.'

'Miss Brown fainted soon after she arrived at Paddington,' said Bert. 'It's possible there's been some confusion over meeting her sister.'

Daisy coughed into her shawl, then took a sip of tea. Her lips left a touch of red on the cup's rim, which she swiftly wiped off with a thumb.

Fox met Margaret's eyes and indicated that she should move away. But Margaret shook her head. Daisy's voice was too quiet.

'Maybe I remembered wrong. I don't know who to trust. In Whitechapel, people come and go and it's hard to know if you can trust them. There's Special Branch looking for troublemakers and normal police looking for stolen goods.' She frowned at Bert as if she half recognised him. 'There's crooks looking for places to stash stuff … and maybe stash people. Everyone turns a blind eye except the landlord, if he thinks he can charge extra rent.' Her voice sounded bitter.

'Would you turn a blind eye?'

'Stashing people? Never. It's too...' Daisy blushed, then stared at the table.

Margaret squeezed Fox's hand. He nodded at Bert. 'Let's get some more tea and see what food is on offer.'

'Nothing can shock me, Daisy,' said Margaret. 'I know how girls can be caught out.'

'The forewoman said you'd talked about people making money out of other people. Not a normal factory. Worse than that.'

'Are you worried that's what's happened to Violet?'

Daisy sniffed. 'Vi's all right. It's not the same.'

'Not the same as what? Trust me.'

'The same as what nearly happened to me,' said Daisy.

Margaret remembered Rosie saying that Violet's sister had almost been caught. She waited. Daisy coughed into her shawl, then twisted it in her hands.

'When I came up to London I got a nice job almost straight away through an ad someone handed me at the station. I was companion for an elderly lady. I had the loveliest bedroom and played piano in the evenings and kept house and her nephew came to stay and we fell in love. We were so happy.'

'That's nice.' Margaret kept her voice as neutral as she could. Approaching unaccompanied girls for illicit purposes when they arrived in a new place was one of the oldest tricks in the book. She wondered what would come next. Surely Daisy wouldn't tell a complete stranger something she was ashamed of.

'He was wonderful.' Daisy smiled, her eyes dreamy. 'He said we'd get married and we had cherry wine to celebrate...' The blush deepened and she gabbled her next words. 'He said we were as good as man and wife so it was all right, and after that was the most loved I've ever been.'

'I see,' said Margaret, hoping her doubt didn't show in her face. Had he thrown her over once the novelty passed? Or was he training her up for a different kind of job?

Daisy coughed again as she watched the gaudy women leave. The one who'd put her feet on the opposite chair rubbed them with a grimace, forced them into her shoes, then stood up with the other women. They stretched, put coins on the table then left, their walk becoming a swagger as they stepped onto the pavement.

Daisy looked back to Margaret. 'And then...'

'You don't have to explain if you'd rather not.'

'I need to show you I'm not sinful or stupid.'

'I doubt you're either.'

'I found out I was expecting,' said Daisy. 'I know it's the wrong way round but we were as good as married, so he went away to put up the banns and find a place for us to raise a family. Then the old lady...' Tears started to well up. 'The old lady said she'd find someone to make things right so I didn't ruin my figure. I didn't understand at first. Then I realised what she meant and I didn't want it, but she wouldn't listen. Then she said "Afterwards, we'll get you abroad." '*Get* you abroad, not *take* you abroad. It was like I was a ... a thing. I didn't know who "we" were, cos she couldn't mean my fiancé. But it made me think of a story I heard about some Chinese girls who were bought and sent to Canada in packing crates and died of cold. I don't know if it's true.'

'I've heard something similar.'

'My fiancé wasn't due back for a week. The old lady arranged for someone to sort out my problem the next day and I pretended to be glad. But when I went to get her shopping, I just kept walking till I got to Whitechapel, found Sullivan's workshop, proved I could use a sewing machine and started work. It's dusty, hard and boring, but at least it's respectable.'

'And the baby?'

'He came much too early and didn't breathe for more than a minute.' Daisy wiped a tear away. 'I wrapped him in a scrap of silk I'd taken from Sullivan's to make a hankie, buried him in a corner of the churchyard, then went back to work. Maybe it's for the best. The worst is, my fiancé can't find me and I don't dare go back to find him. Since then, my chest's got so bad Sullivan's won't always let me work. Before Violet came, sometimes I didn't have enough money for the rent and I'd sleep in the graveyard, hoping no one would molest me. Sometimes, I was tempted to... But I didn't. Honest.' Daisy rubbed her eyes. 'Don't never tell Vi. When she came up to London with a little bit of money and the advert she let Rosie copy, it seemed like the answer to everything.'

'Didn't you worry that the advertisement might catch Violet, like you were caught?'

'I wasn't,' said Daisy, baffled. 'I escaped. And the job Rosie and Vi went for is a respectable office job, and Rosie wrote to say she was all right.' She recovered her composure and turned towards the counter. Bert and Fox returned with more tea and two plates of pie, gravy and potatoes. 'Who's that for?'

'You and me, Miss Brown,' said Bert. 'The others aren't hungry.'

'We're not,' said Margaret. 'Miss Brown says that Rosie wrote to say she was all right.'

Daisy mumbled through a mouthful of food. 'I didn't think Rosie knew our address but she must have. She said she would write again soon.'

'Do you have the letter with you?'

'Why would I? Got to light the fire with something.'

'When did Violet apply?' Margaret glanced sideways at Fox, feeling confused. It was two weeks since Radden had died. Had Violet been gone that long? Or was someone else interviewing?

Daisy swallowed. 'Ten, eleven days ago? The interviewer, Miss Board, met Vi in Whitechapel Public Library and I stayed at a distance. She got Vi to copy drawings from a book of patents, then do arithmetic.'

'What did Miss Board look like?' said Fox, pencil poised over his notebook.

Daisy pondered. 'Young. Slim. Really lovely outfit and a toque that covered most of her hair. I didn't see her up close. Violet said she had paint on her face, but subtle. Not like a, um... Subtle.' She scooped up more food.

Fox jotted something down.

'What happened next?' said Margaret.

'Vi was told to meet her outside Islington Missionary College. It has lodgings for female trainees, you see. There was a post-office box address for me to write to.' Daisy closed her eyes, rattled off a number, then sipped some tea. 'Vi and I only had enough money for her to go to Islington, but you can't go wrong with missionaries, can you?

'Mmm,' said Fox, making another squiggle.

'Vi sent a postcard straight away, then a letter asking to meet this evening at Paddington Station.'

'Paddington's a long way from Islington,' said Bert. 'Kings Cross or Euston are closer. So's Liverpool Street, which makes more sense since you live in Whitechapel.'

'I'm sure Vi's letter said Paddington.' Daisy frowned and pushed her plate away. 'What's going on?'

'That advertisement led Rosie into danger,' said Margaret. 'We're afraid for Violet.'

'No!' Daisy's exclamation was loud enough to make the room fall silent for a moment. 'She's coming to meet me. She's just late.'

'I don't think so, Miss Brown,' said Bert. 'I think you've been too good a sister. They want to stop you telling anyone what you know.'

'Who's they?'

'We're trying to find out,' said Fox. 'The fact that you saw Miss Board might help.'

'But the missionary college...'

'Just somewhere to meet,' said Fox.

Daisy's eyes widened as she stared at Margaret. 'They'll put her in a packing crate!'

'I don't think so,' said Margaret. 'I think she'd travel feeling safe.'

'And after that?'

'We don't know. If we can stop her going abroad, she'll be all right.'

'And if you can't?'

'We're doing everything we can,' said Fox. 'You've helped immensely. Now, we need to find you somewhere safe. Maybe—'

'A hospital,' said Margaret. 'Straight away.'

'They'll put me in a sanatorium.'

'Probably,' said Margaret.

'Will I die before I know Vi's safe?' Daisy's voice held only a shred of hope.

Margaret wished she could reassure her, but without treatment in the near future there was no hope at all. 'The sooner you go, the better your chances,' she said, gently. 'I'll take you to the right doctor. Is Violet the same?'

'Not so far.' Daisy coughed and wiped her mouth, tucking the handkerchief out of sight. 'But maybe her fate'll be worse. Is there nothing I can do?'

As Margaret watched Fox write his last note, she had an idea. 'I know someone who can sketch accurately from description. If he comes to the hospital tomorrow, will you describe Miss Board so that he can draw her? If we can find Miss Board, surely we can find Violet.'

Thirty-Two

On Saturday morning, Margaret had to explain what was happening to Dr Callendar before Reuben was allowed to sit with Daisy and sketch from her description. Dr Callendar changed Daisy's surname to the German spelling of Braun in her file, in case anyone looked for her as they were looking for Rosie, but refused to let Margaret observe the sketching, as she had already spent far too much time in close proximity to advanced tuberculosis. As soon as Reuben had finished and X-rays were complete, Daisy would be transferred to Frimley Sanatorium.

Feeling frustrated, and conflicted about the investigation into Percival, Margaret went to Phoebe's as planned, reminding herself that above all else she might simply need to be a friend.

'Elinor's rooted through my books,' said Phoebe. 'Everything is straight. That parent simply linked me to Percival to see what I'd say. Despicable.'

'Yes,' said Margaret, uneasy. 'Talking of Elinor, where is she?'

'Packing to leave.' Phoebe concentrated on her hands, adjusting rings and bracelets. 'She's been good company. But I suppose I'd rather she was my friend than my employee.'

'Could she live here as your friend, so that you both have company in the evenings. Many women do it nowadays.'

'They're usually clerks in lodgings or avant-garde women living in Bloomsbury.' Phoebe blushed. 'I've always been perfectly content alone and so has Elinor. I'm sure she's looking forward to going home to her little flat.'

'I'd ask her, if I were you.'

'Let's change the subject.' Phoebe picked up the latest issue of *Athene's Gazette*. On the front was Reuben's drawing of a Greek goddess protecting a terrified girl while holding aloft a sword. 'Have you read this?'

'Yes,' said Margaret, without adding that she'd done so to ensure it was too vague for Radden's colleagues to be certain it related to them.

'You seem distant.' Phoebe was tense. 'It's because of what you've heard about Percival, isn't it?'

Margaret hesitated. The inspector thought the discovery of the house in Blackfriars was damning evidence against Percival. She and Fox thought it was suspiciously convenient. Would Phoebe know anything about it?

'I'm worried. Fox and I went to Blackfriars the other night to find an abducted girl, but she wasn't there. No one knows where she is.' Margaret realised she was sitting with her hands clenched. Hopefully, Violet was in the pleasant place where Rosie and Hilda had been kept, unless more than the interview process had changed since Radden's death. Maybe she wasn't safe. Maybe she wasn't even alive.

In as much as Phoebe was capable of slumping, she slumped. 'Please say you aren't linking her to Percival. First there were rumours of embezzlement, then running houses of ill repute, now arms smuggling. How could he do all of that?'

Margaret hesitated, then swatted the hesitation away. Sometimes you could only obtain information by divulging information. 'Do you recall Hector Radden, the murder victim from a few weeks ago?'

'What about him?'

'He was definitely involved in procurement and possibly in arms dealing. My maid Freda's cousin is dead because of Radden. And the girl I'm looking for may be, too. Fox is trying to find out who he was working with.'

Phoebe's eyes widened. 'It can't be Percival. He's only...' She closed her mouth.

'Please trust me. I've trusted you with what Fox is investigating.'

Phoebe remained silent.

'Shall I guess from what was said at my dinner party?' said Margaret. 'Etta is in debt and may have taken money from constituency accounts. What would she do to put things straight?'

Phoebe put her face in her hands. 'Surely not selling people or arms,' she said, her words muffled. Then she sat up straight again, pale and tense.

'Even if she were being blackmailed?'

'Who by?'

'The person who started the rumours, perhaps,' said Margaret. 'Could it be Augustus Endsleigh? He doesn't seem to like Percival, even though they theoretically share ideals for the properties which your father sold to his father.'

Phoebe frowned. 'I... Now I remember the name! Papa always regretted that sale.'

'Why?'

'Endsleigh senior was a dreadful man. I bet he managed to confuse the title deeds somehow, and that's why Percival still appears to own them. Maybe Endsleigh junior doesn't realise they are in fact his.'

'Did your father only sell property in north west London?'

'He only had property in north west London to sell,' said Phoebe. 'His heart was never in running estates. He invested in Huntley and Palmers instead, and those are the shares Percival and I inherited.' The answer was confident.

'When Elinor's in her normal job, she can find out whether any deeds have been falsified,' said Margaret.

'Good.'

'What else do you know about Endsleigh?'

Phoebe stood up and paced, picking up ornaments and replacing them. 'He is... Well, to be snobbish about it, he's new money. His father was a country solicitor, I believe. Comfortable, but not rich. Without illustrious ancestry or wealth, most gentry considered him unsuitable for their daughters, until one impoverished, decaying family allowed him to marry their youngest. Then suddenly, Endsleigh senior became rich and could keep her in the style she thought was her right.' She blushed. 'It's a long time ago and all I know is gossip. One shouldn't repeat it.'

'Gossip sometimes has a shred of truth.'

'You're talking about Percival again.'

'I said "sometimes". Unpicking this might help Percival. Where did the sudden wealth come from?'

Phoebe sighed. 'Papa said Endsleigh got it from a squire or baronet with a reputation to uphold.'

'Blackmail?'

'No. Ensleigh was rumoured to have helped the family by concealing a secret, and was rewarded with money and introductions into high society.'

'When?'

Phoebe frowned and stared into the middle distance. 'When Maude and I were at university and you'd left for medical school. So that's, what, twenty years ago?'

'If there were rumours, it couldn't have been much of a secret.'

'I think there was a sinful daughter and an unwanted child. Hardly an uncommon tragedy, but worth concealing, perhaps.

They wanted them safe but kept at a distance. The real sinners, in my view, were the baby's grandparents for disowning them.'

A baby, thought Margaret. She recalled a formal family photograph from around eighteen years ago in which Katherine and Aunt Alice were seated at the front, two-year-old Ed on Katherine's lap, a slightly older Lucy on Aunt Alice's. All those letters Aunt Alice had received, the trust fund, Endsleigh junior being overprotective.

Could Lucy be that unwanted child? Had Endsleigh told her to stop teaching to protect her, in exchange for that family's continued patronage? Was that why he'd sent someone to follow Sadie when he thought Lucy was under threat? Was he innocent of involvement with Radden after all?

'So that's why Papa wasn't happy,' said Phoebe. 'He'd sold the properties believing Endsleigh would improve them, or demolish them to build better ones, but he never did. There were always rumours that Endsleigh senior recruited youngsters for illegal factories and sweated working. This was despite being a fine upstanding churchgoer and a pillar of the community.'

'So are you.'

'That doesn't prove a thing. If spending time in church is all it takes to make you a Christian, heaven will be full of woodworm. From what I recall, Endsleigh senior justified it by saying that if the poor didn't appreciate being found work, they could shift for themselves. Plenty of other fine upstanding churchgoers agreed. But what you're describing is much more complex. Who are these arms for, Ireland? Is that why they're implicating Etta? For which side? Unionist or Republican?'

'Maybe both. Maybe someone else entirely. Whoever pays most.'

Phoebe paled. 'You mean there's no passion or conviction? It's just for profit?'

'Just for profit.'

'Who would do such a thing?'

'The last person I knew like that died in June,' said Margaret. Abney wasn't the only one who'd do it, but he was the only one she'd knowingly met. If Abney was still alive, why hadn't he disappeared into obscurity? Why was his desire for money so strong that he'd try again? The warm room felt stuffy. She wasn't sure if she wanted to cough, or vomit, or whether one would lead to the other. 'Do you mind if I take a turn in the garden?'

'Of course not.' Phoebe looked as sick as Margaret felt. 'I might join you. Shall I order more tea first?'

'Yes, please.'

Margaret stepped through the patio doors, leaving them ajar, and took a deep breath of fresh air. Then she heard familiar voices in the room behind.

Etta had marched in, followed by Percival and by Phoebe's maid, Cora, who spread her hands. Phoebe glanced towards Margaret, looking panicked. Margaret shifted sideways, where she might be obscured by the door frame if anyone looked out, but was still able to see within. Etta's normal composure was completely absent. Her eyes were red and she was twisting the fingers of her gloves.

'I shall be brief, Phoebe. We shan't stay. I've come to apologise.'

Margaret hugged herself. It was too cold to stand outside without a coat for very long, but if Etta really was brief, it might be better to remain where she was.

Through the part-open door, the voices came clear and loud. Phoebe's back was towards Margaret as she looked at her brother and sister-in-law. 'I thought you were in Ireland.'

Etta rubbed her eyes. 'We were. But it was hardly relaxing. Percival insisted on taking me to some tenement buildings in Buckingham Street.'

'Dublin's slums are the worst in the whole of Western Europe,' said Percival. 'You're nearly twice as likely to die prematurely there as in London. It's a disgrace. Etta needs to understand that poverty isn't wearing last year's dress, and face up to why so many Irish want independence.'

'Independence won't make that tenement into a palace.'

'No, but they blame the British government for the poverty that's led to it. The bitterness runs deep and goes back centuries. It won't stay underground a moment longer.'

Etta began twisting her gloves again. 'I don't believe your scaremongering about civil war. I'm here to apologise, then go home.'

'Why apologise for your views?' said Phoebe. 'We've disagreed for a long time about Ireland.'

'I'm not apologising about that. I'm apologising because it may be my fault that the Pendleberry name has been dragged through the mud. The truth is that someone blackmailed me.' Etta looked at her hands.

'Because you've been embezzling Percival's constituency accounts.'

'How did you...?'

Phoebe put her hands behind her back and flapped one of them at Margaret. 'From that mortifying argument you had at Margaret's house.'

'It wasn't embezzlement: it was a brief rearrangement of funds. Everything is straight now.'

'To the detriment of our personal investments,' said Percival. 'And probably my career, and everything I've tried to achieve.'

'What have you tried to achieve?' snapped Etta. 'You've been in politics for twenty years and you're still not in the Cabinet.'

'I never wanted to be in the Cabinet. I only ever wanted to make people's lives better. I never wanted to live a life of extravagance, simply comfort. I never wanted a wife who would lord it over people, but one with compassion. I wish—'

'I know what you wish.' Etta's voice was dull, emotionless. 'And may I remind you that I do not always know what you're doing, either.'

Phoebe cleared her throat. 'Before I accept your apology, Etta, I have to know what you did to square those accounts, and whether embezzlement was the only ground for blackmail.'

Margaret's feet were becoming numb and she felt ashamed to be eavesdropping. If she could find the kitchen, she could re-enter the house, wait for Phoebe to explain afterwards, and—

'I gambled at cards with a new friend, a Mrs Endsleigh.' Etta's words came out in a rush and Margaret stopped thinking about moving. 'I didn't realise she was married to the Endsleigh who's spreading rumours about Percival. I won everything I needed, then thought I'd stay for just one more game and... Anyway, I've paid her back. I suppose I can understand that Endsleigh might slander about money, but not the other things. I can only assume it's because I rejected his request.'

'Did he ask you to be unfaithful to Percival?'

'No!' spat Etta. 'He offered me a job. A job! As if someone like *me* works for a living.'

'What was it?'

'I don't know, because I refused,' said Etta. 'But Endsleigh must be behind what's being said about arms. His wife and I discussed Ireland during that game: a friendly conversation between people who agreed about protecting the Union. But I never suggested anyone should fight.' Etta looked vulnerable and scared. 'If I'd realised what sort of woman she was, I'd have said nothing at all.'

'What sort of woman is she?' said Phoebe.

'The sort who wanders the backstreets of Marylebone and Islington with common girls and a man, assuming no one of importance will notice.'

Margaret wanted to scream. How could she walk in now and ask Etta what she meant?

Whether by mind-reading or chance, Phoebe asked the most obvious question. 'How do you know?'

'I'm not the only one people spread rumours about,' said Etta. 'I wouldn't repeat it outside the family, because I can't say it's true. Some of us have standards. Which include accepting apologies when asked. One would have—' A maid entered with a tea tray. 'Why are there four cups?'

'Oh,' said Phoebe, raising her voice. 'In point of fact, there should be five. Margaret Demeray's upstairs with Elinor. Are you cold? I had the patio doors open to air the room, but I'll shut them and accept your apology in the warm.' She hurried over and pointed Margaret towards what was presumably the kitchen. 'Does that help?' she whispered.

'I think it might,' Margaret whispered back. 'I'll see you in a moment.'

She followed the direction Phoebe had indicated, entering the kitchen via the scullery, to the surprise of everyone but the maid who'd come for an extra cup. It was only as she scurried upstairs to find Elinor's study, wondering how soon she could contact Fox, that something occurred to her. How did Endsleigh know that Etta was embezzling? And who was the man accompanying Mrs Endsleigh?

Thirty-Three

'Thank you,' said Fox, an hour later.

Elinor had come with Margaret to meet him in Dorset Square and sat scribbling notes in shorthand.

'Could Endsleigh know someone in Percival's constituency office?' said Margaret.

'Possibly,' said Fox. 'What was the name of the clerk whom Percival accused Etta of patronising?'

Margaret tried to recall. 'All I can think of is flowers. I'm probably muddling it up with the girls' names. But I think you're on the right track. An indiscreet clerk, or maybe his wife? Mrs Endsleigh seems to have a knack for getting information from people.'

'A "nice" person,' said Elinor. 'The kind Mrs Pendleberry would express her personal political views to. The kind a young person would feel safe with.'

'Could Mrs Endsleigh be Miss Board?' said Margaret.

'Only if she's very much younger than her husband,' said Fox. 'Reuben gave Inspector Silvermann and me copies of his sketch. He says drawing from description is never as accurate as from sight, but both he and the inspector think she seems familiar. What do you think?' He passed over a sketch of a fashionable young woman, intently listening to a girl across a table. The girl, a healthier, younger version of Daisy, was presumably Violet.

The woman in the hat with an encouraging expression, however...

'Another nice woman.' Margaret sighed then frowned, seeing what the inspector had meant. 'Although she does look a little familiar. Maybe this really does get us closer to finding Violet.' She tried to sound more hopeful than she felt. The familiarity was faint, if tantalising. Perhaps Reuben had conflated Daisy's description with someone they both knew.

Elinor perused Fox's copy of Radden's list of initials and dates, scowling at the neat print as if its legibility offended her. 'Are these the other missing people?'

'I believe so,' said Fox. 'But I think critical information that we could cross-reference with this has been destroyed – if not by Radden, then by whoever he confided in.'

Elinor snorted. 'That assumes he trusted that person enough to tell them of its existence. He'd have kept something as insurance, just in case. I'll cross-reference everything myself. It may indicate where that insurance is hiding.'

'Can I help by going through Radden's novels again?' said Margaret

Fox looked dubious. 'We went through them after Mrs Vidler went to stay with Mrs Warner, and found nothing.'

'I might look in a different way.'

'Since Mrs Vidler's planning on selling the house, I suppose we could arrange for someone to pose as a secondhand book buyer wanting to purchase them. But I think it's a waste of time.'

Elinor stood up. 'I'll organise it, though I doubt you'll get the books before tomorrow. I'll also find out about Mrs Endsleigh and the constituency clerk.'

'Aren't you returning to Phoebe's for lunch?' said Margaret.

'There's no work left.'

'But—'

'See you later, Fox.' Elinor strode off without a backward glance.

'Leave them be, Margaret,' said Fox, rising, then walking with her towards the Marylebone Road. 'Let's get you home.'

'I thought we could go out for lunch together.'

'I'm afraid not. I've got to go to the south coast this afternoon, but first, if you don't mind, I need to borrow the photographs I took in Weymouth.'

'Is Weymouth where you're going?'

'Not so far west. I'm going to Southampton and Portsmouth, chiefly.'

'Because that's where Mrs Vidler was when her brother was murdered?'

Fox shook his head. 'Something's missing from a naval base. Deliberately or otherwise is uncertain. Are you having doubts about Mrs Vidler because she unnerved you in the park when you were with Maude?'

'Perhaps.'

They drove home in silence, both deep in thought.

'Sorry about lunch,' he said, as she took the photographs from Weymouth out of the album. She glanced at herself, smiling with Gil and Raoul against an innocuous background, wondering what was there that only Fox could see. It had seemed such a happy morning at first.

The telephone rang as she handed them over. Freda came out of the kitchen to answer it, glum-faced and dressed in black, but Fox had already lifted the receiver.

'You should be resting, Freda,' said Margaret. 'You're on leave.'

'I can't just sit in my room thinking of everything I should have done, ma'am.'

'Please stop blaming yourself. It isn't your fault.'

Freda remained fidgeting at Margaret's side as Fox made monosyllabic responses on the telephone. He flicked a glance at Margaret and tipped his head slightly towards the sitting room.

'Come into the warm and talk,' said Margaret, leading Freda out of the hall.

'Are you going to church tomorrow, ma'am? I don't normally want to go, but now I do. I just don't know whether to go with you or Nellie. St Matthew's is more peaceful, but Nellie's church does louder prayers.'

'Prayers can be silent,' said Margaret. 'Go wherever helps you most.'

Freda hugged herself. 'That's back in time – Paddington Station a month ago. Then I could stop Evie.'

Fox entered. 'I have some news.'

'It's true, then,' Freda's voice faltered. 'There's no hope. Evie's dead.'

'Not necessarily,' said Fox.

'But the coat! The body!'

'Your aunt and uncle have identified Evie's coat. The body is a different girl who drowned by accident.'

'So Evie's been washed away, sir.'

'Hopefully not,' said Fox. 'Maybe she wanted to put someone off her trail and she's hiding till she works out how to get home. The Belgian police are looking.'

'While the people who took her are getting away with it!'

'If we can find Violet, the girl Evie mentioned in her postcard, before she goes abroad, then we'll get the people who took Evie,' said Fox. 'We're getting closer, Freda. I promise we are.'

'I... I...' Freda burst into tears and rushed from the room.

Fox held Margaret's arm as she made to follow. 'Let Nellie comfort her,' he said. 'And sit tight. I'll have someone come to watch the house if I can. I'm sorry about lunch, but I have to leave.'

'Of course. Go.'

Margaret kissed him goodbye, wishing she could think of some way to help, then went to organise a simple meal for herself and her father. She barely ate, letting her mind wander as he chattered. 'If I saw her again, I... Naturally, it's the last thing ... One hopes one's instincts...'

His words drifted in and out of her consciousness and she responded as seemed fit: Yes. No. Maybe.

Afterwards, she helped him into his coat then into a taxi, so that he could go to his club.

The grey sky was blotched with clouds and a brisk breeze made her shiver. Margaret recognised no one in the vicinity and had no way of knowing if they were friend, foe or simply passer-by. *Stay put.*

Back inside, she climbed to the nursery and looked eastwards from the window. Beyond endless roofs, central London was blurry under drizzle. Smoke from countless chimneys angled north east. Damp leaves tumbled past the glass.

'Canna fly a kite?' said Alec, standing on tiptoe to peer through the window.

'Oh no, Master Alec,' said Nellie. 'Let's all stay indoors.'

'I want to go out too,' Margaret muttered.

'Yes!' said Edie. She held up a piece of paper with a crayoned scribble on it. 'Mummy inna car.'

Margaret nodded at the undecipherable scrawl. 'Where am I driving?'

'On a venture,' said Edie. 'Canna come too?'

Margaret suddenly wanted to see the sketch of Miss Board again. She couldn't bother Fox or the inspector, but Reuben still had a copy. 'What a good idea, Edie. Let's go.'

Ten minutes later, Margaret had hailed a cab. 'Verity Moving Picture Studios, Glassmakers Lane, please,' she said to the cabbie, then settled in the back with the children and Nellie. She felt a little guilty not to be staying at home, but if anyone was following, they'd soon realise she was heading towards Piccadilly and hopefully assume she was simply going shopping.

Glassmakers Lane bustled despite a fine, cold drizzle. The surgery door gleamed, the chemist's jars glowed, Soffiato's restaurant tempted, a new sign above Verity Studios indicated that business was good. Only gloomy Nierlings Bookshop, lurking at the end of the lane, brought down the tone.

Margaret paid the cabbie and scanned the area. Another motor taxi pulled up, but no one emerged. Through the rain-streaked window, Margaret saw the driver turn to the passenger within and remonstrate, before shrugging then making a slow turn. As he did so, Margaret could just make out that the passenger was a smartly dressed female. Perhaps the woman had wanted Glasshouse Street, rather than Glassmakers Lane. Perhaps.

For once, Margaret was glad of her father's garrulousness. If the woman had followed her on Endsleigh's instruction, then he knew Margaret had shares in a moving-picture company. Why shouldn't she visit to see how things were and take the children as a treat?

If she couldn't stay put, at least she could look innocent. Smiling as if she had not a care in the world, she led Nellie and the children into the studios.

Miss Isaacs, the receptionist, was rooting in a filing cabinet. 'What a surprise, doctor. Have you all come to audition?' She giggled and the children giggled too, without any idea of the joke.

'Is Reuben here?'

'In his den with Mr Drummond, doctor.'

Margaret led the children down the corridor until she reached Reuben's room. Mr Drummond looked up from poring over a sketchbook. 'Good grief, the circus is in town.' He came over to shake hands and patted the children on the head. 'Nice to see you again, Miss Pinter. Though a bit of notice wouldn't have gone amiss.' He turned to Margaret. 'Any reason why we're blessed with your presence, doctor?'

'I want to ask Reuben about a sketch he made this morning.'

Mr Drummond raised his eyebrows, glanced at Reuben, then leaned out of the door. 'Miss Isaacs!' he shouted. 'Lock the front door, bring me that file, then take the nippers and Miss Pinter to Killick and get him to show you all a film. There's plenty of biscuits to keep everyone quiet. Me and the doctor have something to discuss.'

'It's the wrong time of day for biscuits,' murmured Nellie.

'I promised a treat,' muttered Margaret.

Once Miss Isaacs had handed over a file and led Nellie and the twins out, Mr Drummond waved at Margaret to sit. 'I always wondered who could boss you about, doctor. Never thought it would be Miss Pinter.'

'It isn't,' said Margaret. 'I spend most of my time trying to get her to break with routine, but I'm battling against several textbooks and her mother. Never mind that. I want to see the sketch.'

'Isn't it for the police to follow it up?'

'Yes, but I'm desperate to find Violet,' said Margaret. 'And I've seen Fox's copy. Miss Board reminded me a little of someone, but I can't think who.'

Reuben turned his sketchbook. 'To me, she looks like someone called Sadie Taylor who goes to Lucy's class and mine.'

'You're right!' said Margaret. 'She does.'

'It's been bothering me all morning, but I only realised why a short while ago, so I've been comparing it with another sketch I made of Lucy's class. Look.' He pointed at the front row in the drawing. There was Sadie, confident, head on one side, as if nothing the teacher could say was new. The similarity with the rougher sketch of Miss Board was clear. 'Mr Drummond came to see why I wasn't getting on with his poster and recognised Sadie himself.'

'From her job as a maid?'

Mr Drummond opened the file. 'She's not a maid. She's a nineteen-year-old actress who'd been with some troupe for a year or so and came for an audition in July, when Reuben wasn't here. She's got one of those faces that can look older or younger if necessary.' He flipped over a rejection letter to reveal some photographic stills of Sadie dressed as a fashionable adult and then as a schoolgirl with plaits, her face enhanced with subtle cosmetics. 'I didn't take to her. She asked too much about money, and I got an itchy feeling that I should hide the petty-cash tin. I thought of her as Miss Swag, the pickpocket's daughter, or Miss Coin, the profiteer's daughter. You know, like Happy Families.'

'So you didn't employ her?'

'No, and she wasn't happy about it. That's why I remember her. She made a scene.' Mr Drummond stroked his chin. 'Eventually, she said she had another offer, so I wished her luck, followed her out of the studio and watched till she'd gone. Looking back, I wonder if I should have found someone to talk with her and see what she meant.' He pulled a face. 'It may surprise you to know that sometimes I'm accused of coming across as unapproachable.'

'Who would say such a thing,' said Margaret, in mock surprise. Reuben snorted.

'You, for a start.' Mr Drummond wagged a finger, then sighed. 'I had a feeling she wasn't too certain about the other offer. Perhaps I should have checked what it was. Now, I'm a realist. I know the word "actress" can cover everything from a toff playing Juliet in the West End to a desperate wretch dressing up for immoral purposes in the East End. But Sadie Taylor was at the upper end. She could act. I assumed she meant another studio, or if not, a theatre troupe. I didn't think she'd go into child snatching.'

'Maybe she didn't,' said Reuben. 'I might have drawn Miss Board wrong.'

'Then take the photos and the other sketch to show the girl at Dorcas Free,' said Mr Drummond.

Margaret shook her head. Daisy would be in Frimley by now, worried and scared. 'She's gone to a sanatorium. You'll have to tell Inspector Silvermann and let him arrange it somehow. I'd do it myself, but—'

'Don't tell me you're being watched again.' Mr Drummond folded his arms.

'I can't risk being further exposed to Daisy's illness.' Margaret kept her face as expressionless as possible.

'You work in a hospital.' Mr Drummond scowled. 'I don't believe you. After Miss Pinter and the kids have finished watching the film, I'll take you all out the back way and drive you home myself. That'll confuse 'em. In the meantime, Miss Isaacs can telephone Inspector Silvermann. I swear that drawing is of Sadie Taylor, and I bet she's up to no good.'

Thirty-Four

W hatever Fox felt about Margaret leaving the house, he was too tired to discuss it when he finally returned home. Documents were missing from a naval base, with the person responsible also missing. Elinor had made no more progress, other than to establish that the constituency clerk's name was Bloom and Mrs Endsleigh was in her mid-thirties. There was no more news about the boy in Germany, or about Evie. He was grateful for what Margaret had discovered but it got them no further forward, since Frimley wouldn't let anyone see Daisy until the next day.

They retired to bed early and slept fitfully.

Fox was usually even more inclined to avoid church than Freda, but in the morning he went with the family and servants to the early service at St Matthew's. Despite the risk of heresy, Nellie came too. Freda sat a little apart, expressionless. During the prayers she pressed her hands to her face, shuddering silently, refusing anyone's comfort until Edie cuddled up and reached to stroke her hair.

They'd only been home a few minutes when a telegram arrived for Margaret.

'Oh my word,' she said, staring at it. 'It's from the accident ward at Dorcas Free. Someone tried to kill Mrs Wantage.'

Mrs Wantage sat in a side room, wearing hospital-issue night-clothes and a cotton cap shoved back to free her curled fringe.

'She has deep lacerations to her arms and shallower ones to her upper chest,' muttered the ward sister. 'However, she's insisted a daughter bring her spare corset so that, in her words, she "wasn't flopping about", because she's worn one twenty-four hours a day since she was thirteen, notwithstanding Mr Wantage, ten pregnancies and childbirth. She's not going to stop for a few stab wounds. Good luck.'

'Hallo, Dr Demree,' said Mrs Wantage. She frowned at Fox. 'Who's your feller?'

'I'm Superintendent Foxcroft,' said Fox. 'I gather you don't like the police, but if it helps, I'm trying to stop what Hector Radden was up to.'

'And Enddles, I hope. They were working together.'

'There's no evidence of that.'

'You got these.' Mrs Wantage lifted her arms. Nothing but a clenched jaw indicated any pain. She dropped them again.

'Mr Endsleigh attacked you?' said Margaret, sitting beside her. 'When? Where?'

'One of his men, I reckon. At eightish this morning, down an alley near a knocking shop. He seemed to think I was a pincushion. Stab, stab, stab.' Mrs Wantage shifted in the chair and touched her torso. Her expression indicated terror and shock, then she suddenly grinned. 'Guess what saved me life, Dr Demree?'

Margaret shook her head. 'What?'

'Not wearing a flimsy modern corset, for a start,' said Mrs Wantage. 'Ninety-seven steel bones make a blade bounce right off. That Lizzie Jackson woulda survived if she'd been wearing one like mine, wouldn't she?'

'Not against a bullet.'

'So you say.' Mrs Wantage looked sceptical. 'Second off, he went for this.' She touched her throat. 'What stopped him in his tracks was.... Hey presto! My blue beads!' She hoiked them over the top of her nightgown. 'Told you they worked.'

Margaret forced a smile. 'All right, I'll change my talk to say that they may be useful in unexpected situations. Fair enough?'

'Fair enough.' Mrs Wantage sobered. 'I admit they wouldn't have stopped him for long, if I couldn't shriek louder than a train whistle.'

'Can you say exactly where you were?' said Fox.

'If you promise not to prosercute the girls.'

'I promise.'

Mrs Wantage gave an address, then turned to Margaret. 'I was trying to see if one of the girls knew the refuge I wanted to tell you about. They usually sleep in of a morning, acourse, but it's the only time of day the place isn't watched. The thing was at your talk, Dr Demree. Built like a brick outhouse. He said "You couldn't keep your gob shut. Now I'm gonna shut it for ya".' Again, a flicker of fear under the bravado.

'I'm so sorry, Mrs Wantage,' said Margaret. 'I didn't mean for you to ask for that information.'

'Never thought you did, ducky. But I've had measles, typhers, pneumonithingy and ten kids. Gonna take more than Enddles to see me off. But you, you need to stick to doctoring.'

Fox turned a page in his notebook. 'This is going to sound heartless, but did you ask the girls what you went to ask? I have a feeling you would.'

'No wonder you're a Super. Yeah, I did. Want me to join the force?'

'It would be all the better for women like you.'

'Ain't he the charmer?' said Mrs Wantage to Margaret, then her face fell. 'They didn't know, though some want to. Owner's clearing out his knocking shops, so he looks cleaner than laundry day if anyone cares to check. One of the girls told me she heard the posher clients saying there's a new place abroad and the owner will be sending the best of the best to work there, where they'll be joined by some fresh, innocent blood. The way they said "innocent" made her want to sick up. Actually, one of the clients isn't a client and Blossom, who says he's in politics, isn't posh. He's a quill-driver.'

Fox exchanged glances with Margaret. 'Who's the client who's not a client?'

'Abbot,' said Mrs Wantage. 'Not his job, his name. He visits the house to talk business and pretends he's an inspector. He never dabbles, if you get my drift, but the girls say he looks like he'd happily dabble if he didn't have to pay. They deal with all sorts, but Abbot makes their skin crawl.'

'Are you sure he's called Abbot?' said Margaret, feeling cold again. It couldn't be true.

Mrs Wantage screwed up her eyes. 'Abner,' she said, at last. 'That's it. Abner.'

'Are you absolutely sure?' said Margaret. 'Sometimes you don't quite... Could you have misheard his name?'

'Why are people always saying that?' Mrs Wantage demanded.

'Could it be Abney?' said Fox. 'And the quill-driver – is he called Bloom?'

'That's what I said. Abney. Bloom.'

'I'll ensure someone keeps a watch on you when you leave hospital, Mrs Wantage.'

'Listen, my lads could turn a brick outhouse into a mud pie. Don't worry about me. Worry about Dr Demree. She's been too interested for her own good. And buy her a better corset.'

Fox took Margaret home before returning to work with the information from Mrs Wantage. 'If you can't manage to stay home, please tell me. I already have too many people to worry about.' He kissed her goodbye and left.

After lunch, Margaret collected the children from the nursery and took them to the sitting room so that Nellie and Freda had some time to themselves. Her father was writing at the bureau and looked up with mild irritation. 'Don't talk! I'm in the muse's toils for the boy.'

'Who?'

'Thalia. It could have been Melpomene, but thankfully it's Thalia.'

'Not the muse, the boy.'

'Don't you remember me saying?' said her father. 'There was a young man in the Daffodil Café on Wednesday, asking if people had seen anything untoward in the alley by the bookshop.'

Margaret put the children down and leaned over his shoulder to peruse the scrawl. 'I didn't know you'd seen anything untoward. What was it? People escorting young people away? Or someone in the café taking the young people to them? Or...'

'Goodness,' said her father. 'I've only found the bookshop recently, Wednesday was the first time I'd been to the café, and I hadn't noticed the alley till he mentioned it. I'm making up a story of what *might* have happened. And of course, since Thalia is my muse today, it'll be humorous. That'll cheer the boy up. He seemed sad.'

'Good grief, Father!' said Margaret, as he started writing again. 'You can't send a funny fictional story to a detective investigating a crime.'

'He's not a detective. He's a country reporter following a story about a missing girl.'

'What?'

'Shh.' Her father nudged a business card out from under the sheets of paper, pushed it towards her and bent to his writing.

The front of the card said *Cecil Parkin, journalist*. On the back were the details of a Berkshire newspaper Margaret had never heard of. Underneath, in neat handwriting, were the name and telephone number of a Marylebone hotel and in capitals, *DID YOU SEE MY SISTER TAKEN? CP*

One of Radden's interviewees who didn't turn up was recorded as CP aged seventeen, thought Margaret. She wondered whether she could trust her father to mind the children while in the midst of writing a story, recalled from her own childhood that she couldn't, and took them to the hall while she put a call through to the hotel.

'Mr Parkin's in the dining room, madam,' said the concierge. 'Shall I ask him to come to the telephone?'

'Yes, please.'

During the pause, the twins started to argue. Margaret picked Alec up and juggled him and the two pieces of the telephone, hoping the call would end satisfactorily before she dropped at least one of them.

'Cecil Parkin speaking. How may I help you?'

'It's about the questions you've been asking in Daffodil Street,' said Margaret. 'Have you heard of a magazine called *Athene's Gazette*?'

'I was reading it just now and wondered if the leading article was connected.'

'It might be. At the back is a large advertisement for a meeting and lecture room called Athene's Hall. Can you meet me there?'

'Perhaps.' His voice was less eager than she'd expected. 'Are you a reporter?'

'No. But I'll try to bring the editor of *Athene's Gazette*.'

'How do I know you are legitimate?' This wariness didn't match Margaret's father's description of the young man in the café. 'I'm not a fool.'

'I'm wondering the same about you,' said Margaret. 'But the hall will be full of suffrage supporters who won't hesitate to apprehend anyone involved in what the article describes. So if either of us thinks the other is lying, we can just yell. An offender would be like a pigeon among cats.'

'Don't you mean—'

'Think about it, Mr Parkin. We'll see you in half an hour.'

Margaret ended the call. It seemed unlikely that Mr Parkin was part of the gang. Trying to find out who had seen what in Daffodil Street risked drawing attention to the asker. The gang wouldn't want to do that, but they might be watching for someone who did. Perhaps Mr Parkin had belatedly realised that. She telephoned Fox, who wasn't available, then Inspector Silvermann, who had gone to Frimley.

Finally, she telephoned Maude. 'Can you drive the car by yourself, collect me from the alley behind the house, then drive us to Athene's Hall? This is about Hilda, Evie and finding Violet Brown. Whatever you record, you'll have to promise to share it with Inspector Silvermann.'

'In this instance, yes.'

'Only I'll have to bring the twins.'

'Really?' said Maude. 'Explain on the way. I'll be as quick as I can.'

Margaret put down the receiver and turned to find Freda standing behind her. 'Leave the children with us, ma'am,' she said, her eyes bright with tears. 'And wear your hat with a veil. Find Violet. The last thing you need is a distraction, but I need all the distraction I can get.'

Cecil Parkin was a tall, strong-looking man in his early twenties. He sat at a table with three cups of tea, turning a cigarette case over in his hand. An audience listening to a suffragette in prison uniform speaking about Holloway paid him scant attention. Any doubt Margaret might have had about Cecil faded. He looked exhausted and despondent.

'My name is Dr Demeray,' she said, shaking hands. 'I spoke with you on the telephone earlier. This is Mrs Holbourne, who owns *Athene's Gazette.*'

Cecil raised his eyebrows. 'A doctor?'

'I treated a girl who escaped after being interviewed for a job which seemed too good to be true.'

The despondency was replaced by sudden eagerness. 'By Hector Radden?'

'Why do you think so?'

He appraised them both and seemed to come to a decision. 'It's a long story, but in the simplest terms, I met a man like the girl in your article did. That was his name.'

Margaret peeked at the copy of Radden's list hidden in her notebook. Rosie had been interviewed on the sixth. CP had been invited for the seventh, but had not arrived.

'Were you interviewed too?' asked Maude.

'No,' said Cecil. 'I simply accepted the offer of an interview. I wanted to follow Radden, then confront him.'

'Why?' asked Maude.

'Because I knew something was wrong about the job, but I didn't know if Radden was doing anything wrong himself. I still don't. Was he?'

'Perhaps you should start at the beginning, Mr Parkin,' said Margaret.

Cecil's face fell. He took a cigarette from the case, then re-alised he was surrounded chiefly by women, none of whom were smoking, and put it back. 'A few years after leaving school, I started training in journalism. My half-sister Rachel went into service. A boy had broken her heart in July and she said she wanted to go far away. I thought it would blow over. Then our mother received a postcard from London at the end of August, saying Rachel was about to be interviewed for an office job and not to worry.' He paused and twiddled the case again. 'We did worry, of course, but it seemed all right to start with.'

'Because you received more letters?' said Margaret, thinking of Evie.

'One more in mid-September, saying everyone was very nice and she'd be helping to take important documents abroad. She gave a post-office box address for emergencies, but said she'd be back in a few weeks and would come home for a visit. That was the last we heard, until...' He cleared his throat and took a deep breath. 'Until mid-October. The police came round and told us that German authorities had raided an illegal factory in Berlin and one of the workers was... was...' His voice cracked.

'Rachel?' said Margaret eagerly. At last – a girl they could talk to, who could prove what had happened.

'Yes,' said Cecil. 'But she was dead.'

Thirty-Five

They waited as Cecil composed himself.

'The staff worked with poisonous materials,' he said, at last. 'They lived in the factory, were badly fed and slept crammed together. People died and were replaced. It's amazing anyone remembered Rachel. No one knows where her body is.'

'I'm so sorry, Mr Parkin,' said Margaret.

Maude held out her own cigarette case. 'Smoke. I'm going to.'

'Thank you.'

As they lit up, Margaret glanced at Radden's list again. It started with *R W*, who'd gone to Germany at the end of August. The destination *F* had been crossed through and replaced with an underlined *X*.

'May I ask what Rachel's surname was?' she asked.

'Wade.'

Maude jotted the information down. 'Didn't your stepfather report her missing in September?'

'My stepfather died years ago,' said Cecil. 'I'm the head of the household. Mother wrote to the address we had and received a reply saying Rachel was doing well, but since she was abroad, we should wait another month. By that time we knew she was dead.' He rubbed his forehead. 'We informed the police, but we didn't know which advertisement Rachel had answered and the post-office box led nowhere. They implied Rachel was a gullible girl whose death was her own fault. They said they wouldn't record that she took papers to Germany, as it made her sound like a spy. They hinted that maybe she was.'

'You and your mother deserve an apology,' said Maude.

'It won't bring Rachel back,' said Cecil. 'I discovered the advertisement had been in a local paper – not mine. I gave that information to the police, but they still... Anyway, in late October a similar ad turned up in a different paper.' A fleeting grin. 'They miscalculated. My home is on one side of the county border, the big house where Rachel worked is on the other. I bet those who placed the ads thought we were miles apart. Townies.'

'So you answered it,' said Maude.

Cecil nodded. 'I told them I was seventeen, bright but alone in the world. I accepted an interview with a Mr Radden at the Daffodil Café and was sent a rail warrant. So up to London I came.'

'And?' said Maude.

'A little before the given time, I entered a bookshop opposite the café and watched. A man arrived, waited about half an hour, then came out looking annoyed. He made an irritated sort of gesture then walked off, so I followed until he entered a pub.'

'Weren't you worried he had colleagues there?' said Margaret.

'Nah. He just wanted a pint. He sat by himself, put a note-book labelled "*Interviews*" on the table and started reading *The Strand Magazine*. So I got a pint, sat down with him and asked if there were any good stories in it. He was a bit surprised.'

'You don't do that sort of thing in London,' said Margaret.

'You don't often do it in the country, either,' said Cecil. 'But it meant he thought I was a fool of a bumpkin. I told him I was new to London and wondered if he'd ever met my friend Rachel Wade who'd got a job here. He looked patronising and said no. I pointed at the book and asked if he was a journalist. He said

"I work for important clients. No one you'll know." I said "I see", then settled back with my pint. I thought if he was guilty of anything, he'd leave. But he seemed calm enough, sipping away, reading his magazine. Then I said I was sad because Rachel had been killed in Germany as a spy. That was when he changed.'

'How?' said Margaret.

'He looked horrified and asked when. I said I wasn't sure, but she'd got the job when the papers were reporting all that stuff about stolen gun designs and Dublin riots. I couldn't actually recall if she had: it was just a journalist's hunch. Do you understand, Mrs Holbourne?'

'I do. How did he react?'

'He went very still. I decided to push. I said something like "Nothing changes, does it? There's still trouble in Ireland and talk of spies and gun running." Radden said "I'm sorry about your friend," downed his pint, then left at pace. I followed, keeping where he couldn't see me. He went to the telegraph office, then to a house in Tibberton Street. I watched as long as I could without looking suspicious and went back to my hotel at about five o'clock.'

'And this was on Friday the seventh of November,' said Margaret.

'Yes. I felt...'

'Deflated?' said Maude.

Cecil nodded. 'I had to write a story for my paper in the morning, so I couldn't return until the afternoon. But the fog started early. I got lost.'

'What time was this?' said Margaret, recalling the drive to take Katherine home.

'Around six? I'm not sure. I was completely disoriented. Someone ran past me like wolves were after them. A young girl, I thought, but not a child. I wanted to see if she was all right but I lost her in the fog.'

'And then?' Maude sat, pen poised.

'I ended up in the Edgware Road,' said Cecil. 'I had a drink to calm my nerves and started again, finding Tibberton Street at maybe eight o'clock. There was hardly anyone out. A woman – I think – passed me going the opposite way. Then a man – I think – ran towards the Marylebone Road. I didn't see anyone else, which isn't to say there wasn't anyone.'

'Were there lights on in the house?' said Margaret.

'No. I knocked in case Radden was out back, but there was no answer. I returned to my hotel. I tried again the next morning. Still no answer. I went home to decide what to do next.'

'Is that truthfully all you did?' said Maude. She had lifted the pen from her notebook.

Cecil banged the table with his fist. 'You're wondering if I murdered him, aren't you? Well, I didn't. I wanted to know who he was working for. When I heard he was dead I felt sick, because it was too late. And yes, I should have told the police, but they hadn't cared about Rachel and they'd probably think the same as you.'

'I don't think anything,' said Maude. She waved a hand at the suffragette on stage, who was describing an arrest. 'And I don't like the police much, either. Go on.'

Cecil took another drag, exhaled, then nodded. 'When I read about a murder near Daffodil Street, I came back to investigate some more. And now I want to know if what you wrote in *Athene's Gazette* is the same thing. What do you think happened to the other people Radden interviewed? I'll keep quiet if it means justice being done.'

'One died of cold while seemingly trying to escape,' said Maude. 'Another is missing, presumed dead. We don't know beyond that but...'

Cecil crushed the cigarette stub in his saucer. 'Bastards.'

'We're looking for a girl they recruited very recently,' said Margaret. A thought struck her. 'I know you were disoriented when a girl ran past on the eighth, but do you recall anything about that street?'

'If I saw it again, I might,' said Cecil. 'The fog parted briefly, so I saw its name. Something about it tickled me. I forget what.'

'Shall we go for a little drive to see if you can recognise anything?' said Maude, standing up.

Margaret shook her head. 'Whatever both of you think about them, we must inform the police. And I have to get home unseen.'

'Unseen?' snorted Maude. 'Is that why you were lurking in an alley wearing that ridiculous hat?'

'Yes. If you find the right road, someone might recognise Mr Parkin or me, because we've both been in Daffodil Street.'

'It's drizzling,' said Maude. 'No one can be recognised through a rain-soaked window. Stop arguing, Demeray. You'll never forgive yourself if you don't come too.'

Arriving home at a quarter to four, Margaret was intercepted by the postman, bearing a telegram.

Going south. Friends in park. Give any news to S. Back tomorrow. F.

South? Did he mean the coast – anywhere from Dover to Penzance, including Weymouth? Surely not France: surely no further than that.

Margaret peered out of the front bedroom window. Light was falling, but she was sure she recognised a man pacing the park who had been at the talk where she'd met Mrs Wantage. But she also recognised a man on a bench, hunched under an umbrella with a tall, broad-shouldered woman. He was one of

Fox's men. Perhaps the woman was one of Elinor's fellow clerks. *Friends in park.*

She went downstairs to telephone Inspector Silvermann and explain about Cecil Parkin.

'He thinks the girl ran past him in Meadow Park Road. He thought its name ridiculously rural in the midst of all those houses. It's not far from where Rosie was knocked down. I've no idea if that's any help, but he's waiting with Maude to give you an interview.'

'Thank you,' said the inspector. 'In exchange, you'll be interested to know that Daisy Brown identified the film studio's photograph as Miss Board, or rather Sadie Taylor. Who's gone to ground, of course. And ...'

'Her alleged employers are involved in the enterprise?'

'Nope. I've spent enough on telephone calls and telegrams to get me a carpeting from the super, but what it boils down to is this. The employers are legitimate. *Their* Sadie, seventeen years old, is home with her family, a bun in the oven and a nice pot of cash, to help her mother bring the baby up as hers if they all keep quiet about who its father is. She's categorically *not* the Sadie Taylor who was in Miss Frampton's class.'

Margaret frowned. 'But...'

'Maid Sadie had told her sorry tale to a friend who went to the same afternoon school as actress Sadie. Perhaps the friend told the class and actress Sadie realised she could borrow someone else's life as an alibi, if necessary. It would only have been good for a month or so. The bad news is that we can't prove Mrs Wantage's story. The girls in the house won't say a peep. She has a history of slandering Endsleigh and his staff have alibis. And she herself has a minor criminal record from her youth.'

'But—'

'Look, I believe her, but I can't prove it. So we've moved her to a different hospital till I can. Any trouble at your end?'

'None. I left and returned by the back. It's becoming a habit.'

'Ha.'

She replaced the receiver and turned. Dinah was walking up the hall with a tray of tea and Margaret was surprised to see her turn towards the dining room. 'Why in there?'

'Mr Demeray says the dining room's best because of the books.'

'What books?'

'They came in a box just before you got back. He's showing the children while Nellie has a cuppa with me in the kitchen.'

'What?'

Margaret flung open the dining-room door. Her father was reading aloud from *Around the World in Eighty Days*. He had had the sense to keep Radden's novels out of the children's reach, but was letting them look through Mrs Vidler's books, which had also been delivered.

'Wanna jelly,' said Edie, pointing at a watercolour of salmon in aspic within the well-used copy of Mrs Beeton.

Alec had found a diagram of intestines in the pristine nursing manual. He said 'Wiggly worms!', then leaned over Edie's shoulder. 'Wanna blammomge.'

'Oh, Father!' said Margaret. 'These books weren't for you! And your hands are all over them and none of you are wearing gloves!'

'Book sticky, Mummy,' said Edie.

'Oh no!' Margaret pushed Mrs Beeton out of the children's reach with an elbow, rang for a maid, and checked the twins' hands. They were all perfectly clean.

'*We* not sticky,' said Edie, with a scowl. 'Book sticky.'

'It *is* a recipe book, Meg,' said her father. 'And the note that came said that Mrs V, whoever she is, wanted the whole lot gone. Including Mrs Beeton, as she can't abide cooking.'

The door opened. 'Oh, Nellie, thank goodness. Please take the twins.'

'Yes, ma'am.'

'I thought you'd like the books to breathe,' said her father, as the door closed. 'Why should we wear gloves indoors? Why are you putting yours on?'

'It's far too complicated to explain,' said Margaret.

'It always seems to be.'

Margaret sat down and turned the pages of each novel. 'Did you find anything odd?'

'Unless you count spaceships and time machines, no.'

To her father's horror, she bent each book just enough to be able to see down the gap between spine and cover.

'Whatever are you looking for, Meg?'

'I don't know,' she said. 'A slip of paper, perhaps.'

He looked too. 'Are we being detectives?'

'Yes.'

Margaret picked up Mrs Vidler's books. If the nursing manual had been bought when Mrs Vidler began to train in the 1890s, she hadn't studied it much before marriage. It looked brand new.

Mrs Beeton, on the other hand, opened easily on simpler recipes, some of which showed signs of spatter. Hadn't the inquest into Radden's death said that when Mrs Vidler was away, the maid was sent on leave and Radden shifted for himself? Perhaps he'd made his own simple meals.

Margaret looked through slowly until she came to the section on preserves. Several pages were stuck together so well that she couldn't prise them apart, even with a fingernail.

Her father tutted. 'Whatever are we trying to discover?'

'The people who kidnapped Freda's cousin.'

He gasped. 'Then we must be brave! Here's my penknife. But do be careful, in case Mrs Beeton's innocent.'

'I shall, but I suspect she isn't.'

Margaret was right. Separating the pages revealed a shallow space cut in the middle of six of them, leaving only the edges intact. Within the neat, rectangular space was a thin, coverless notebook of exactly the same shape and depth, fitting so well that it was barely detectable when sealed in by the other pages.

'Whoever would do such a thing?' said her father, as Margaret winkled it from its hiding place with a hairpin then opened it to reveal minuscule, immaculate print.

'Someone who wanted to hide a record in a place where anyone could find it,' said Margaret. 'But where no one would ever think to look.'

Thirty-Six

O n Monday morning, drained from poor sleep, Margaret
went to work as normal.

Pigeon had collected Radden's record and the books the previous evening, to be scrutinised with a better lens. She'd told her father the record was in code and he'd accepted it without quibble, excited to have been a detective.

In fact, the only code appeared to be the names, and an oblique reference to circumnavigating the earth which must relate to *Around the World in Eighty Days*, the book he'd been reading on the evening he died. It would have to be dismantled completely to see what it was hiding. Otherwise, the record expanded on Radden's list by including notes of daytime meetings.

Bloom couldn't be Mr Quill. He'd have to be in the constituency office from eight thirty till six every day. So Quill must be someone else. Endsleigh? Abney?

When she arrived at Dorcas Free, Margaret paused at the desk to collect her post and watched Miss Upton tear November from her desk calendar. Today was the first of December. The postcard Evie had sent to Freda said that Violet would join her on the third. Was it now too late to find her?

Dr Gesner asked Margaret to his office to discuss the day's work, yet when they sat down, remained silent. There was a suppressed fury in his face she'd never seen before. When he finally spoke, his words were low and bitter. 'The boy found near the Kaiser Wilhelm Kanal is coming back to Britain under guard.'

Margaret blinked. She'd seen one or two references to German militarism and mass arrests in newspaper headlines as she'd walked to work, but nothing about the boy. So how did Dr Gesner know?

Before she could think of a response, Dr Gesner slammed a palm on the desk, making his pen tray rattle. 'He can't even remember his own name. *Der Abschaum! Sie haben ihn vernichtet.*'

'Which scum? Who's destroyed him?'

'Radden's colleagues, by selling him on.'

'We don't know—'

'Of course we do.' He sat back, and the anger in his face faded into concern. 'Rosie Levene, Daisy Brown and Mrs Wantage all spoke with you, and they are now hidden. Why are you not in hiding?'

'I want to do something.' Margaret clenched her fists. 'How do you know about the boy?'

Dr Gesner scratched his nose. 'I cannot precisely say, but... I will say that there's a man I've been watching for. He was in London once or twice, but I missed him. Then he went south, before leaving Britain in early November. He was sighted in Ostend a few weeks ago.'

'Ostend?'

'Yes. Now he's in Calais. There is never enough evidence to catch him buying and selling secrets. Never.' He leaned forward again. 'Why was Daisy's name changed from BROWN to BRAUN?'

If Dr Gesner knew so much, it seemed pointless to hide anything more. 'Her sister Violet has been taken by Radden's colleagues. She's due to arrive somewhere on the continent on Wednesday. Maybe she's already gone.'

'Do you feel in your bones that she has?'

Margaret considered. 'No. But that's unscientific.'

'Do we not use instinct all the time in our work? Maybe Violet hasn't gone, but maybe Calais is where she's going. It takes less than seven hours from Charing Cross.'

'I need to—'

'Send a telegram to Fox about Calais?' Dr Gesner smiled. 'I have already done so. So now, having got something off my chest, we must consider someone else's. And use both science and instinct, I think.'

Margaret rubbed her eyes. She was too tired to concentrate. 'A chest patient?'

'In a way.' Dr Gesner opened a file. 'Mrs Vidler.'

'Mrs Vidler? I thought... What happened?'

'She was admitted to the accident ward a few hours after you saw Mrs Wantage. She said that after an assault by a stranger in the street, she fell, banged her head and reopened the chest wound.'

'She told me a week ago that she'd been attacked. I wasn't sure whether to believe her.'

'And you may be right.' Dr Gesner tapped the file. 'Her head bore no sign of any contusion, nor did she seem concussed. The chest wound wasn't quite as expected so they photographed it, re-dressed it, and discharged her, only to find her wandering the corridor shortly afterwards, peering at the side-room doors. And after being politely guided outside, she entered the mortuary wing through the outer door and when stopped, said she intended to wait for you in your office. Her excuse was that she, as a trained nurse, could repay the hospital by helping. She held her head as if to suggest that the blow had rendered her confused.'

'She's not trained.'

'Indeed. Nor was there any reason why she should have been confused,' said Dr Gesner. 'The whole incident was so odd that Dr Innes asked our opinion.'

After the doctors' morning meeting, they compared the photographs of Mrs Vidler's original wound before and after treatment, and as it had been the previous afternoon.

'These stitches have been cut,' said Margaret, peering through a lens.

'Her excuse was that she'd done it herself to check progress. But she denied making that slight incision, which would have created a bleed quite unlike a wound reopened by an assault.'

Margaret peered again. 'Looking at the original wound, what would we have concluded if she'd died?'

Dr Gesner took the lens as she stood straight. 'The angle is odd.'

'Can I experiment on myself?'

'If you are very careful.'

'I shall be.'

The inspector walked in just as Margaret raised a knife above her chest, her thumb down, while Dr Gesner stood by with a notebook. 'What the blue blazes—'

'Oh good,' said Margaret. 'A witness. Ready, Dr Gesner?'

'I think so.'

It was awkward. Every instinct told Margaret to stop. She brought the knife down with just enough force for it to mark the fabric of her white coat, then turned it in her hand so that her thumb pointed upward. She tensed, then brought the knife down again. 'What do you conclude, Dr Gesner?'

'I repeat,' said the inspector, 'what the blue blazes are you doing?'

'We think Mrs Vidler stabbed herself the day Lizzie died,' said Margaret, looking at the marks on her white coat. 'Thumb down, I think. We'd have to prove it in a more scientific way, but it would change everything. If someone else had stabbed Mrs Vidler at that angle, they'd have to stand in an awkward position and she would have to stand still.'

'Unless she was restrained,' said Dr Gesner. 'But there were no signs of that, nor did she claim it. Everyone took her word for what had happened.'

'She may never have finished her nurse's training,' added Margaret, 'but Mrs Vidler knew exactly what she was doing.'

'Hang on.' The inspector flicked through his notebook. 'Here: before marriage, her mother was a cook for the sort of nobs who hunt deer. If Mrs Radden taught her daughter butchery...'

'One doesn't need a deer for that,' said Dr Gesner. 'Any trained cook understands it to some degree.'

'Either way,' said Margaret. 'If Mrs Vidler added that to whatever knowledge of anatomy she learned during her brief nursing training...'

'Then she would know where to stab herself, and where to stab Lizzie to make her death look as if it was caused by that, rather than a bullet.' Dr Gesner folded his arms. 'If Higgins hadn't raised the alarm, maybe she'd have stabbed Lizzie in the back too, obliterating the bullet evidence.'

Margaret nodded. 'Maybe she shot Lizzie first and threw the gun into the alley... Although Higgins saw the foreign-looking man she described.'

'Only Mrs Vidler said he was foreign,' said the inspector. 'I bet it was someone else who did the shooting. Maybe the one who escorted the kids and was seen around the alley so much: no one would spot him.' He made a note in his notebook. 'That means Vidler's guilty of more than ignoring what her brother was up to. She's involved. May I have a word with Dr Demeray alone, Dr Gesner?'

'Certainly.'

For a short while, Margaret had been concentrating so hard on proving a theory that she'd forgotten why it was necessary. In her room, her fear for Violet returned.

The inspector remained standing. 'Late last night, I took Rosie on the same tour you and Mrs Holbourne took Mr Parkin. It was dark, but she'd only been there in the dark, or near-dark. Rosie identified a house by its gate and front door.'

'So Violet—'

'Hold your horses,' said the inspector. 'I can't get a warrant on hearsay. But I've got a watch on that house and men gathering evidence.' He donned his hat. 'Much as it'll kill you to do it, stay away. If they guess we're on to them, who knows what they'll do to Violet. Do your job today as normal, Dr Demeray. As soon as I need your help, I'll ask.'

The day passed in routine duties, under a cloud of dull anxiety, but there was no more news and shortly after five, Dr Gesner sent Margaret home.

She arrived to find that her father had gone to visit a friend earlier in the day and had since telephoned to say he'd be staying overnight. She wished he'd left a note to say who he was with, but at least it was one less person to worry about.

At seven, Fox returned and she told him about the knife experiment. 'If Mrs Vidler hadn't been in Southampton when Radden was murdered, I'd think she was responsible.'

'I suspect she was,' said Fox. 'Acquaintances *think* she attended a busy gathering that evening, but apart from Mrs Warner, all anyone *recalls* is saying goodbye to her at the end. I believe she received her brother's telegram on Friday, returned home on Saturday evening, found him sleeping off his cold, killed him, then returned to Southampton.'

Margaret recalled the details of Radden's death. Her initial pity had long been replaced by disgust. Now, a little returned.

'She must have locked the door, pocketed the key, watched him die and put the postcard on top of him before leaving. How unbelievably callous.'

'Radden was a potential traitor to the group, so he had to be executed,' said Fox. 'But maybe Mrs Vidler didn't watch. She had to burn the letters and the interview book. Taking the extra key was a mistake, so afterwards she had to turn all attention onto Higgins.'

'Do you think she's always been involved in procurement?'

'Not sure,' said Fox. 'But your hint was helpful. Some of her little trips coincide with missing intelligence. A few days before Radden died, for example, torpedo designs were stolen from a south-coast naval base. I think those are what Violet is supposed to smuggle.'

Floorboards creaked, the fire crackled. Two floors above, Nellie sang a lullaby.

'Let's go and say goodnight,' said Fox.

'I want to lock them up safely for ever.'

'Me too.'

The doorbell rang as they were making their way downstairs. Fox held Margaret back and hurried down to answer it, hand inside his inner jacket pocket. But before he got to the bottom step, Freda had opened the door to Pigeon in his motorcycling clothes.

He burst in and grabbed her hands. 'I've got news about Evie!'

'Pigeon?' said Fox.

'She's alive!'

'Er, Pigeon...' said Fox.

'She'd been hiding in the docks, waiting to sneak aboard a boat with a large group. Then she saw her parents. She's safe.'

'Oh, Eric!' Freda flung her arms around him.

'Eric?' Margaret mouthed at Fox.

'Pigeon...' said Fox.

Pigeon detached himself and cleared his throat. 'May I give a report, sir?'

'I think you just have.'

'There's more,' said Pigeon. 'Perhaps someone could make you a cup of tea, Miss Mead. I need to talk to Fox in private.'

'Go on,' said Fox, a moment later.

Pigeon removed his motorcycling goggles and cap. 'I'm sorry, sir, but Miss Mead needed to know.'

'Never mind that now. What's the whole report?'

'An agent sent coded telegrams. A photograph of Monsieur Andreyev was identified by Miss Young and thanks to Dr Gesner, he was arrested in Calais. He said he gave Kay a sleeping draught and put him somewhere safe, but didn't mean for him to die. He gave an address: number fifty-five, Meadow Park Road. It's protected by armed—'

'My God,' said Margaret. 'We have to get Violet now!'

'Wait a moment, Mrs F. Originally she was to have smuggled the papers to Calais on Wednesday, but the plan changed today. A whole crowd of them are leaving Charing Cross at nine a.m. tomorrow.'

'Does the agent believe him?'

'Yes. Andreyev wants to save his skin. He said he found Kay a nuisance and left him sleeping in a boatshed for the night until they sailed the following day. When he discovered Kay dead in the early hours, Andreyev put him in that rowing boat hoping it would drift out to sea. He knows a good deal less about tides than espionage.'

'Poor Kay,' said Margaret.

'Does he give any proper names of the people he was working with?' said Fox.

'Mrs Vidler, Mrs Warner, Miss Taylor,' said Pigeon. 'He won't reveal the others without more assurances. Dark men, fair men, a dark woman – well-to-do people, with reputations to protect and good connections. But he's haunted by Kay and worried for the next kid. He thinks Violet will get no further than Calais.'

'Then...' Margaret headed for the door.

Pigeon reached out to stop her. 'Vidler, Warner and the Pendleberrys haven't been seen since yesterday afternoon.

'The Pendleberrys were cleared.'

'Not entirely, Margaret,' said Fox. 'I'm sorry.'

'What about the Endsleighs?'

'They had a guest arrive today, then left,' said Pigeon.

'Everyone must be in Meadow Park Road!'

'It's been watched front and back all day, Mrs F. Sadie's probably in there, but no one else has entered or left. If we try to rescue Violet now, the armed guard will kill her.'

'They need Violet to do the smuggling,' said Fox, putting his arm round Margaret. 'They don't know what Andreyev has told us. They'll convene at Charing Cross tomorrow morning and the inspector and I will trap them there and rescue Violet. But you need to—'

'Behave normally?' said Margaret, pulling away. 'No! You need a woman, in case the women go into the ladies' waiting room and try to escape from there. Dr Gesner will give me leave.'

'I can use Elinor,' said Fox. 'Or one of the other clerks. I'd rather not involve you.'

'I'm already involved,' said Margaret. 'I promised Rosie and Daisy I'd find Violet. I won't rest until I've done it. Take Elinor, if you want. But I'm coming too.'

Thirty-Seven

At eight a.m., Charing Cross was crowded and noisy, full of the stench of smoke and oil.

Commuters scurried. Porters rushed. A gaggle of sailors jostled each other while catcalling passing women. Ladies in furs and gentlemen in top hats stood in an elegant group, perhaps travelling to Paris. Two suffragettes offering leaflets were being shoved and given sidelong, sneering glances.

Margaret recognised two of Inspector Silvermann's men. She could see Pigeon, dressed in country tweeds, apparently waiting for the destination boards to be changed. Fox waited a little further off. How hard would it be in the melée to spot anyone else and keep them in view?

She wore black, her head covered by a thick Spanish mantilla that rendered her nearly blind. Beside her stood Elinor, also in black and a heavy veil.

A porter approached, blocking their view. 'I hope you aren't after the Necropolis Railway, madam. I'm afraid it's near Waterloo, not Charing Cross. Near, not at. Which waiting area did you want? Anglican? Catholic? One of the others? Tell the cabbie, he'll get you to the right one.'

'We don't want the Necropolis Railway, thank you,' murmured Margaret.

'Which train are you after? I can help.'

'Please don't trouble. We're expecting someone.'

She moved away and Elinor nudged her. 'Is that...?'

Dimly, through the mantilla, Margaret saw a man who looked like Percival check his watch. Then his arm was caught by an elegant woman in a velvet toque, with a motoring veil over her face. Could she be the woman who'd made the taxi turn in Glassmakers Lane? Maybe she wasn't. But even with his face obscured by a low-brimmed hat, Margaret was nearly certain the man was one of the landlords who'd been at the talk so many weeks before.

'I'm sure it's not Percival.'

'Leave it to the men,' whispered Elinor. 'Look.'

Sadie, dressed to the nines, was walking briskly into the ladies' waiting room with a girl who must be Violet.

The ornate lace obscuring Margaret's view was like thick foliage. She feared people would stare as she and Elinor followed to sit as close as they dared. But everyone seemed intent on avoiding eye contact with two women in deep mourning.

Mrs Vidler and Mrs Warner entered and sat by Sadie and Violet. Margaret nudged Elinor, and they moved to sit back-to-back with them.

'Is this Violet?' said Mrs Vidler. Her voice had the practised refinement she'd used when speaking to Maude in the park.

'It is,' said Sadie, equally refined. 'Such a lovely girl. These are Miss Bull and Mrs Stitch, Violet. As you can see, they are very respectable.'

Violet's soft country voice said, 'I'd like to ask Daisy before I go.'

'Is everything all right, dear?' said an unfamiliar female voice. 'Does your mother know where you are? I recently read about a girl who...'

Margaret risked turning. One of the suffragettes she'd seen earlier was addressing Violet. In any other situation, Margaret would join in. Now, she cursed her.

'My big sister is seeing me off, madam,' said Violet. 'She won't let me go if it's not safe.'

'Are you quite sure?'

'Come on, Angela!' called another suffragette, from the doorway. 'Our train's on the board!'

'I'll be all right, madam,' said Violet. 'Thank you. Don't miss your train on my account.'

With evident reluctance, Angela left. Margaret faced forward again before someone noticed her looking.

'What a kind lady, Violet,' said Mrs Vidler. 'Now, go with Mrs Stitch to buy some sweets for the journey.'

'But what about Daisy?'

'She'll come and say goodbye on the train just before we leave. Off you go. Don't forget your valise.'

The seats creaked. 'Good girl.' Mrs Warner sounded encouraging. 'Come along.'

'Where's she going after Calais?' said Sadie, after a brief pause.

'I have a quiet place planned,' said Mrs Vidler. 'Why?'

'I read something about a girl, too. It made me wonder.'

'Never mind. Have you found my brother's interview book?'

'No.'

'Damn. Surely the doctor doesn't have it after all. Her father thought not, although if she'd told him, she'd have told the world. Never mind. He'll be useful once we're in France.'

Horrified, Margaret started to turn again. Elinor's fingers dug into her arm.

'Why's it matter?' Sadie's accent faltered. 'I want to talk about that article. It made me wonder where those kids go.'

Mrs Vidler's voice was amused. 'Are you really that stupid?'

'Quill said they were going to better lives.'

'Quill?' A snort of laughter. 'You should call him "sir", and not believe everything he says. Those lives were valueless. The world needs a better breed.'

'A better breed?' Sadie's voice was sneering. 'What breed do you think *you* are?'

'Someone who doesn't like being crossed.'

'I haven't crossed anyone,' said Sadie. 'I'll have my wages now, please. I'm not coming to France: I'm going back to acting. Quill is staying behind, too. He says his wife is insufferable and only I understand him. He and I will start afresh. We'll forget you, and you can forget us.'

'By all means stay. You'll find out soon enough that he won't want to be disgraced by divorce and saddled with a common girl like you.'

'How—'

'You're every bit as forgettable as the others.' From the sound of her voice, Mrs Vidler had risen. 'No one will notice you've gone.'

Margaret pushed Elinor's hand away and turned. Mrs Vidler was striding to the door, leaving Sadie hunched, sobbing and gasping.

Elinor indicated that she would stay to watch her.

Margaret rushed to the door. They'd already have arrested Mrs Warner, the man who looked like Percival and the woman with him. They would now arrest Mrs Vidler. She needed to find someone and tell them about her father. Where was he? What had they done to him?

The mantilla caught on the door handle and started to rip. She flung it back.

But as she stepped onto the concourse, she knew something had gone wrong. Above every other noise, she could hear shrieking. 'Daisy! Where are you? Daisy! Help me!'

Near the platforms, Pigeon gripped Mrs Warner with one hand and the valise with the other, while one of the inspector's men fought with the suffragettes over Violet, who was trying to pull herself free from all of them.

Midway across the concourse, Mrs Vidler stopped dead. She turned, saw Margaret and her eyes widened.'You!' She recovered herself and reached into her handbag. 'Where's the book?'

'I don't know! What have you done to my father?'

'He...' Mrs Vidler looked beyond Margaret then turned and ran, shoving through the melée, jabbing, making the crowd part before running on, the throng closing in after her.

'Hell!' said Fox. 'She's armed. Stay here, Margaret. Keep out of sight.'

'Father—' But he'd gone.

Inspector Silvermann slowed as he passed. 'Someone needs to reassure Violet. Can you—'

'Margaret!' Elinor rushed up. 'Quickly! Sadie's bleeding and can barely breathe.'

'Right,' said the inspector. 'Let Miss Edwards talk to Violet. You do your job, doctor, and let me and your old man do ours. We've got almost everyone.'

Margaret grabbed his arm before he could run. 'They think I know where the interview book is. They're going to hold my father hostage till I tell them.'

'What? Let me go. Sadie might know something, if it's not too late. We'll find your father, Margaret. I promise.'

He ran on.

'Doctor!' someone shouted. 'Ambulance! Police!'

'I can't...' Margaret couldn't move. Ahead of her, beyond the throng, were Mrs Vidler and Fox. Who knew what the former would do to escape? Who knew what was happening to her father?

'You can,' urged Elinor. 'Go.'

Margaret hurried into the waiting room, reminding herself with every step that she had to put everything else aside to concentrate on her oath to heal.

Sadie lay on the floor. A woman pressed a paisley shawl against her right side, Sadie's blood merging with the swirling pattern.

'I'm Dr Demeray from Dorcas Free,' said Margaret, dropping to her knees.

'Nurse Williams from St Mary's,' said the woman. She half-shook her head.

'I'm sorry,' Sadie whispered. Bloody froth bubbled on her lips. 'I...'

'Where's my father?'

'I don't know. I'm sorry. Those kids ... hurt?'

'I think so.'

'How could he lie?' Tears streamed. 'He wrote that he did. The Friday night before...'

'Who wrote what?'

'Mr Radden said Augustus was lying.'

'Augustus Endsleigh? Not Percival Pendleberry?'

'Perci— No. I'm talking about Augustus.'

'She shouldn't talk,' said Nurse Williams.

'Mr Radden said the world held the proof ... or the earth ... the ... something...' The words were barely audible and the bubbles on Sadie's lips were pinker. Her pupils were dilated and unfocussed. What could she see as they closed? All the young people she'd helped to abduct? Augustus Endsleigh, telling her lies she chose to believe? Radden, hiding the book? 'Why's it going dark?'

Nurse Williams felt Sadie's neck and looked up at Margaret. 'We might save her. I hope they catch the man who did it.'

'It was a woman.' Margaret's heart began to hammer. She looked up as the ambulance men, a constable and a man in a suit entered.

'Dr Jones,' said the man. 'Charing Cross.'

'Dr Demeray,' said Margaret. 'Dorcas Free.'

'What's happened?'

'Sadie Taylor, aged nineteen, stabbed. I believe she has a punctured lung. If only that, she has a chance. I should stay, but... My father...'

'Dr Demeray!' someone called from the doorway. 'You're needed out here.'

'I'll take over,' said Dr Jones. 'Be where you need to be.'

Margaret scrambled to her feet and pushed past the people crowding round.

On the concourse, constables were trying to control passengers as they tried to reach their trains while Mrs Vidler turned slowly, keeping Fox at arm's length with a knife.

Margaret scanned the area frantically as she worked out how to help, then— 'Oh please God, no!'

Coming in the opposite direction was her father, stumbling a little, his cane barely touching the ground as he was marched along by Mr Endsleigh in a way that suggested a concealed gun was being held to his chest.

'Father!' Margaret rushed forward.

Endsleigh had seen Mrs Vidler but kept moving, shaking his head, secure behind his shield: an elderly man with a cane; an irritating, exasperating, beloved man, whom Mr Endsleigh could shoot or push towards Mrs Vidler's knife with the lightest of touches.

Oh, Kitty, thought Margaret as she ran. *What should I do?*

As she neared, Endsleigh stopped. 'I didn't expect you, doctor, but it saves me sending a telegram later.' He moved the gun very slightly. 'Now you can explain what he won't. Where—'

'I don't know about anything you could want me to explain.'

'You must,' Mrs Vidler snapped, backing closer to Mr Endsleigh. 'I found nothing in my brother's books, but after I sold them, they went to your house. Why? What clue did I miss?'

'Neither of us found anything in Hector Radden's books.' Margaret's father sounded weary.

'Let Mr Demeray go, Endsleigh,' said Fox, aiming his own revolver. 'You have nothing to gain from hurting him and everything to lose. Your wife and most of your colleagues have been arrested.'

Mr Endsleigh paled, pulled Margaret's father closer and forced the gun into his side. 'Under what charge?'

'Conspiracy, to begin with.'

'With what evidence?'

'We have witnesses.'

'Anyone the courts would believe? I doubt it. Have my wife brought here and give us safe passage out of the station. Once we know we're no longer followed, I'll release Mr Demeray. Eventually.' He smirked.

'No!' shouted Margaret.

'Such a sweet old man, and so easy to lure with the promise of a first edition to buy as a present for you. So easily fooled.'

'Let him go,' said Fox, circling as Mrs Vidler, back-to-back with Endsleigh, continued to wave the knife. 'He's done you no harm, and he's an old man.'

'I'm not so very—' said her father, then winced as the gun dug deeper.

'Sadie Taylor...'

'She's dead,' said Mrs Vidler.

'She isn't,' said Margaret. 'You picked the wrong side.'

A moment's doubt, then Mrs Vidler tossed her head. 'She soon will be.'

Mr Endsleigh continued smiling. 'Sadie's none of my concern.' His gun still trained on Margaret's father, he glanced at Fox. 'Keep your distance. I have no qualms about shooting, and Mrs Vidler has none about stabbing.'

'Very well,' said Margaret's father, straightening up as much as he could. 'If you both stop threatening people, I'll tell you the whereabouts of what you seek.'

Mr Endsleigh's cold smile faltered. In that moment of hesitation, Margaret's father wrenched his arm away and pushed hard, making Endsleigh stumble and drop the gun. Then he swung his walking stick and whacked Mrs Vidler behind the knees. Her knife flew out of her hand, missing Fox's face by inches. As she collapsed, Fox restrained her.

Endsleigh regained his balance and started for the exit, but Margaret's father tripped him with the handle of his walking stick and Margaret put a foot on his back as he tried to stand.

'I'll take it from here, doctor,' said the inspector, dragging Endsleigh up and away as Fox did the same with Mrs Vidler. 'Augustus Endsleigh, I am arresting you...'

'Isn't this thrilling, Meg?' said her father, as if they'd met unexpectedly in a bookshop. 'I told you I could protect both myself and you. I suspected Mr Endsleigh wasn't a true gentleman, so when he asked me to visit, I didn't hesitate to go and see what I could find out.'

'But Father, you should have—'

'He's slandering Phoebe's brother, did you know? And he meant to do you harm. But I was prepared. I've been learning ju-jitsu in a class for older people.'

'You—'

'I'm afraid I did tell a falsehood, though. I don't know where this book is.'

Margaret hugged him tightly. 'I might. There's a battered globe in Radden's house. I suspect it comes apart at the equator.

There was a reference to the earth in the notebook, and I think he hinted to Sadie, too. I bet that's where it is.'

'Marvellous,' said her father. 'I can't wait till Kitty gets home and I can tell her that you and I are detectives, too.'

'And I can't wait till she takes you back to live with her,' said Margaret, kissing him. 'Keeping you under control is well and truly beyond me.'

Thirty-Eight

In France, Andreyev admitted to exchanging stolen documents. Privately, he offered Fox as much additional information as he had in exchange for mercy.

'Is Abney involved?' whispered Margaret, when Fox told her. They were sitting at a large quiet table in a Hendon restaurant.

'Yes.'

'Oh God.'

'I know.' Fox touched her cheek gently. 'Whoever died in June must have been one of his men. Abney already knew what both Andreyev and Mrs Vidler were doing. Through the latter, he discovered that Endsleigh had employed Radden to manage the administration of his established empire of vice. Bringing it all together was Abney's idea. Endsleigh hasn't explained what the lure was yet. Given how convoluted his efforts to implicate Percival and cover his own tracks were, it's possible he's in deep waters and was being blackmailed himself. Or, of course, it was simply greed. Once we've repaired the damage Vidler and Andreyev have caused by selling military intelligence, I'll get Abney. I'll get him by next Christmas if it kills me.'

'Don't let it kill you.'

'Mmm.'

'Will Andreyev be tried with the others in January?'

Fox shook his head. 'He has to face the wrath of several countries. He's talking to save his skin.'

'Will the interview book make any difference?' asked Margaret.

'Perhaps. It confirms that other than using Kay to get into Whitehead's, and taking documents from cases on the Continent, Andreyev had nothing to do with any of the young people. He visited the house for meetings occasionally, just as he did when Rosie overheard him describe her with a slur, but otherwise preferred not to know the detail.

Was the book simply a record of interviews?'

'No. It held notes which Radden must have thought worth keeping safe. The codenames were based on Happy Families – Mr Quill the solictor's son, Miss Board the actress, Mrs Stitch the seamstress, Miss Bull the butcher.'

'Oh my word.' Margaret swallowed, remembering Mrs Vidler waving the knife at Charing Cross and the wounds she'd inflicted on her brother.

'The man Mrs Endsleigh used to escort the girls to Meadow Park Road was one of the more refined agents Endsleigh employed, who conveniently looked rather like Percival.' Fox paused. 'I'm afraid his notes confirm that the four X's on the first document you found were deaths. Mrs Vidler or Endsleigh witnessed three apparent accidents when people tried to escape. Radden believed his sister, but doubted Endsleigh.'

Margaret felt tears well up, and looked down to compose herself. Of the twelve sets of initials on the list, they had identified Rachel, Hilda, Kay, Evie, Rosie and Cecil. A girl called Petunia Roberts, who had been warned off by Dotty on the fifth of November, had come forward after an appeal. That left five unidentified victims. Perhaps the boy who'd been found wandering in Germany was one of them, but he was still lost in his own mind. It wasn't a personal pain, but surely a human one. How could anyone willingly be involved in such cruelty?

Margaret repeated Dinah's words. 'A handsome face can hide an evil soul.'

Fox held her hand. 'We'll find the missing five whether they're alive or dead, I promise. And we'll make Abney pay. In the meantime, the gang will pay.'

Margaret lifted her head. 'Herb was merely a burglar. Maybe Sadie was little more. Endsleigh was charming.'

'Did he charm you?'

'Hardly. I've met too many charming snakes in my time. Presumably it's worn off for Mrs Endsleigh, too.'

'She allowed houses she'd inherited to be used however he saw fit and she escorted the young people,' said Fox. 'She only agreed to testify against Endsleigh when she discovered what he'd been promising Sadie. She's as much of a snake as he is.'

'At least the rumours about Percival have largely faded, even if he and Etta are maintaining a front for their marriage. I can't believe Bloom has been promoted for uncovering financial anomalies.'

'Isn't it often the way?' said Fox. 'His seniors know what he really did and where he goes of an evening. He knows what'll happen if he steps out of line. Let's forget the whole thing for a few weeks and have a normal Christmas.'

'Can we?'

Fox grinned. 'As normal as we can, considering Christmas will involve your family.' He checked his watch and looked up. 'Ah, here we are.'

Margaret turned to see Inspector Silvermann walking towards them with Rosie and Violet in tow.

Rosie was transformed. Her injured arm was hidden under a fashionable cloak. Soft, shiny hair was tied back in a thick coil under a smart blue hat. Her face was filled out and healthy. There was only a hint of anxiety in her expression.

'I'm so glad to see you!' said Margaret.

'You too, doctor.'

'You look as if life is good.'

Rosie glanced at the inspector, who nodded. 'I'm staying with a clerk's family hereabouts and going to school with their daughter. They're reformed, not orthodox, but my grandparents are coming round and I'm hoping they'll move nearby. I don't want to go back to where I came from. Nor does Violet – do you?'

Violet shook her head. 'Daisy and I have never had much of a home. But now she's in the best place and I've got a job in the hospital office, and lodgings with a kind family. I can see her whenever I want for as long as it takes.' There was a catch in her voice, and Margaret didn't want to ask what she meant.

'You've both been so brave.'

'Pfft,' said Rosie. 'We didn't suffer what the others did.'

'You suffered enough,' said the inspector. 'Including speaking to the police.'

'Can't speak for Violet,' said Rosie. 'But that's true enough for me.' She gave Margaret a rueful grin. 'You won't tell Anna, will yer? She'd never talk to me again if she knew I'd been hobnobbing with bluebottles like they were decent people.'

As promised, Margaret took leave at Christmas. She and Katherine paid for the family to spend it in a house near Lausanne, not far from Gil's sanatorium. It was a major expense, but life was passing too quickly. Their father was eighty-four and Aunt Alice sixty-six. Ed had been accepted into the Air Corps and Lucy, having cut all ties to her natural mother's family and rejected the trust fund, was deciding her future.

'So,' said her father, after they'd exchanged presents on Christmas morning, 'have you reconsidered whether to employ me as a detective, Kitty?'

'I keep telling you, Father,' said Katherine. 'If I need a book expert I will hire you, but I'm not having you use ju-jitsu again. I'll never understand why Meg let you do that class.'

'I didn't know where he was going!' said Margaret.

'Don't blame Meg. I found it through a suffrage magazine in your house after I moved in, Kitty. The teachers were a little startled, but they agreed that older people needed to look after themselves too and started modified training for me and a suffragette of seventy. Now there are six of us learning, and it meant I could save Meg from Endsleigh and Fox from that dreadful woman.'

'Fox was managing perfectly well,' said Margaret. 'What you did meant that Mrs Vidler nearly cut off his ear.'

'Tsk.' Her father turned to the twins. '*You* think Grandpapa's brave, don't you, children?'

Alec and Edie, busy playing with new toys, nodded without looking up.

'Reuben thinks I'm brave, doesn't he, Lucy?' said Margaret's father. 'But he said the moving-picture people prefer young heroes. It's most unfair.'

Ed stiffened slightly at the mention of Reuben, then shrugged. 'You *are* brave, Grandpapa,' he said. 'Perhaps I should teach you to fly next.'

'What an excellent idea! Your mother and aunt would never think of such a thing. Now, when I was adventuring there were only hot-air balloons, but one day in, um, 1883, I think, in the plains of ... somewhere or other, Henry and I... Henry was my assistant, you know—'

'I suppose you wish one of us had been a boy, so we could have followed in your footsteps,' said Katherine. Thirty years before, she had shed bitter tears as she said the same to Margaret. Now, she seemed matter of fact.

Her father stared. 'Goodness me, Kitty! I'm many kinds of fool, but not that kind. Perhaps I should have taken you, but you were so young and Meg needed you. If you like, I could organise an adventurous tour for us now.'

'Goodness me, Father.' Katherine rose and kissed him on the head. 'It would be safer to hire you as a detective. Now, I'll see how lunch is coming on and rescue the cook from Aunt Alice.'

'Talking, talking,' said Edie, and patted her new toy dog on wheels.

'Play throwing outside?' said Alec, waving a ball bigger than his head.

'Good idea, young man,' said Fox. 'Let's see if the Boy Scout's astronomical calculator Mummy bought me works in daylight. Mummy and Grandpapa will remain behind for a while.'

Before Margaret could ask why she needed to stay, Fox and James had swept up the children. With a little grumbling, Ed and Lucy followed.

'I have something for you, Meg,' said her father, reaching over the side of his armchair and retrieving a small square parcel. 'I gave Kitty hers earlier.'

'Oh, thank you.' Margaret took the package and kissed him. 'I thought we'd given out all the presents.'

'These are special,' said her father. 'Kitty wants me to organise my belongings. I fear that by organise she means reduce, which is most unreasonable, but... Anyway, never mind. Open it.'

Inside the parcel was a pencil sketch of Edie, sitting on her grandfather's lap as he read a book. She was sucking her thumb while holding his cravat against her cheek. It must have been drawn at the party in early November, but Margaret couldn't recall anyone sketching. Nor had anyone taken photographs.

But the image was so familiar. She could feel the silk against her cheek, the scent of tobacco on the tweed jacket—

Margaret realised the child wasn't Edie.

The man in the drawing was indeed her father, but as she remembered him from her childhood: in his forties, not his eighties. The little girl was herself. 'Where ... how...'

'Your mother drew it,' he said, softly. 'I thought it was long lost. You inherited adventure from me, but you inherited sketching from her. And this drawing – you and me, lost in a book. It would be worthless to that girl Sadie, wouldn't it? But it means more than all the treasure in the world to me.'

'And to me, Father. And to me.'

A light knock on the bedroom door woke Margaret from a dream which immediately dissolved, leaving her with the sensation of floating in warm, calm waters.

Sunlight coming through the half-open curtains striped the red eiderdown with gold, and outside she could see snow on distant mountains. She slipped out of bed and put on her dressing gown to collect the tea tray, but first she went to the window, opened the curtains and looked out at Lac Léman, where little golden waves rippled towards the shore.

'Come back to bed,' said Fox, half-sitting up. 'It's too cold to stand at windows. Besides...'

'I'm getting the tea.'

'Bother the tea. There are better ways to keep warm.'

Margaret stirred up the smouldering coals in the fireplace to bring them back to life, and straightening, looked at the sketch her father had given her, propped up on the mantlepiece.

'It's lovely,' said Fox.

'Yes. I'd never seen it before. There were always so many more sketches and photographs of Katherine, because she's nine years older. After Mother died, Father either wasn't at home or didn't think to take us for photographs. Then he went missing and we couldn't afford it. Besides, he and Katherine were always closer.'

'Perhaps because they're not as alike as you and he are.'

'Don't be silly,' said Margaret. 'We're not alike at all.'

'If you'd had a mind to go round the world, regardless of anyone else, you'd have done it. Katherine would have been sensible and done her duty.'

Margaret grunted. 'I wouldn't leave the children. Not for more than a few hours, anyway.'

'I leave them. Isn't that the same?'

She stared at him. 'Of course not. You have a job: he had a paying hobby. We'd lost Mother, and we lost him too. It...' *It hurt*, she wanted to say. *Everyone thinks it hurt Katherine most because she was older and more responsible. But it hurt me, too.* 'All these years, I felt angry. But suddenly that anger has gone completely, as if it never existed at all.'

'Forgiveness is more for the forgiver than the forgiven.'

'Good grief. You sound like Nellie.'

'Heaven forbid.'

'I'm getting the tea,' said Margaret. 'The maid's made the effort to make it, even though she doesn't understand why we don't want coffee.'

From outside, she heard whispers. She put her hand on the handle but didn't open the door.

'Do maids argue everywhere?' Fox rolled his eyes and slumped on the pillows. 'One day, we'll go on holiday somewhere too small to bring staff and shift for ourselves.'

'You can do the washing up.'

'I'll be glad to, if I don't have to listen to young women bickering every five minutes.'

'Don't exaggerate.' Margaret waited till the whispers had stopped, opened the door and brought the tray in, then clambered into bed and cuddled up with Fox. 'I'm missing Nellie and Freda, but they both deserve a holiday. Besides, Nellie would have the morbs without Harry and Freda needs time with Evie.'

'She'd have the morbs over Eric, too,' grunted Fox. 'Eric. I had no idea. He's about nine years older than she is. Not that that's unusual in itself, but...'

Margaret grinned. 'She says that hug was a moment of madness brought on by excess emotion, Pigeon is just a good friend, and she still has no intention of getting married. But yes, I suspect you're right.'

'Do you get the morbs over me when I'm away?'

'I'm not eighteen or twenty-three. I enjoy the peace and quiet.' Margaret cuddled closer, pretending she meant it.

'I shall ruin the peace and quiet for several weeks, even after we're home. I have no foreign missions to go on. I'm all yours for ages.'

'Darn,' said Margaret, and kissed him.

Something crossed the sun outside, making the gold on the bed ripple like waves. 'I wish we could stay here for ever.' The words were out before she could stop them. She didn't: not really. But Fox tensed.

'Then let's,' he said, his voice light and happy.

'Not yet. But maybe I'll persuade Father to stay. The air is better for him here.'

'But what if...' Fox fell silent, then pulled her into his arms. 'Yes. The air is better for him and it's safe. We can put it to him later. But for now, we have better things to do.'

Newsletter and Links

To get news about my books and others, as well as the first chance to read Advanced Reader Copies of any new releases, please sign up for my newsletter at

https://BookHip.com/PHNKCAG

For information and links to:

THE MARGARET DEMERAY SERIES

THE MURDER BRITANNICA SERIES

THE CASTER & FLEET SERIES (with Liz Hedgecock)

THE BOOKER & FITCH SERIES (with Liz Hedgecock)

Weird And Peculiar Tales (with Val Portelli)

Plus short story Collections and audiobooks, please visit

https://paulaharmon.com/

I also have short stories in the following anthologies:

DORSET SHORTS

WARTIME CHRISTMAS TALES

Historical Note

Although this is a work of fiction and all the main characters are figments of my imagination, this book is set against a real background. The following events or situations were real:

Senghenydd Colliery Disaster

Britain's worst pit disaster occurred on 14th October 1913 at Senghenydd Colliery. 439 miners and one rescuer died. The rescue/recovery operation took several weeks. Ultimately the manager and company were fined £34 (a sum equivalent nowadays to around £14,000). Newspapers at the time disgustedly calculated that this meant effectively that each life lost was 'worth' one shilling, or nowadays around £7.

Ireland

The Dublin lock-out started on 26th August 1913 and continued until the 18th January 1914. The dispute was grounded in the right to unionise and is viewed as the most significant industrial dispute in Ireland, involving around 200,000 workers and 300 employers. British trade unions provided money and food in support of strikers' families, and a scheme was set up to bring the children to mainland Britain to live with families there, but this was blocked by the Roman Catholic church who supported the employers. The Irish Citizens' Army was set up initially to protect strikers from the police.

On 7th July 1913, the Irish Home Rule Bill was once again passed by the House of Lords. It was rigorously opposed by the Hon. Andrew Bonar-Law, then leader of the Conservative Party and of Ulster descent. He believed that the gap between Ulster Unionism and Irish Nationalism could never be bridged. The rhetoric he used suggested he would not stop "from any action … we think necessary to defeat one of the most ignoble conspiracies … ever formed against the liberties of free-born men.' He spoke at the Theatre Royal in Dublin on 29th November 1913 to put forward his views.

Meanwhile the opposing sides were starting to accumulate arms by whatever means they could.

Preparing for War?

In the wider context in the build up to World War I, although the papers periodically reported the efforts of Britain and Germany to retain peace, and various members of various royal families, including the Archduke Franz-Ferdinand (referred to in the papers as Francis-Ferdinand) making visits, the underlying sabre rattling continued. On 4th November 1913, the papers reported quite publicly that H.M.S. Empress of India 'once the pride of the Navy and costing £900,000 twenty years ago' had been deliberately destroyed to test guns and torpedoes. Her wreck now lies a battered hulk off West Bay, Portland.

There was no hiding what arms were being amassed on either side of the channel. Zeppelins, warships, aeroplanes, the ongoing development of the Kaiser Wilhelm Canal (now the Kiel Canal) was public knowledge. They might have been presented as 'How interesting is this?' articles but the reality is almost certainly that both sides were showing what they were capable of if war was declared.

The Whitehead Torpedo Works did exist in Wyke Regis near Weymouth and a station – Wyke Regis Halt – was built especially for its employees. It has long since been demolished.

However, as far as I know, there were no attempts, successful or otherwise to steal documents/intelligence from there.

Human Trafficking

In 1913, what would now be called modern slavery or human trafficking was known as 'the white slave trade' or 'the traffic in humans'. It was very much in the news. In the UK at least, women fighting for suffrage did not simply want the vote. They also wanted better treatment for women and girls – not just in terms of educational opportunities but also their personal, moral and mental safety. And they weren't afraid to tackle the subject head on.

In the 1880s for example, Josephine Butler, working with journalist W.T. Stead and Bramwell Booth of the Salvation Army, was involved in the infamous Eliza Armstrong case. They proved to a horrified Victorian general public how easy it was to buy a child for immoral purposes, and as a result, in 1885 the government raised the age of consent in Great Britain and Ireland to sixteen.

By the 1910s when 'The Suffragette' was campaigning about 'the traffic in humans', the international White Slave Traffic Act (also called the Mann Act) had come into force, as had the International Agreement for the suppression of the White Slave Traffic (also known as the White Slave convention). Legislation was also introduced in the UK to allow for any procurer to be publically flogged if convicted. There were certainly plenty of procurers, some more sophisticated than others. All the crimes described in Chapter Twenty-Three were reported in papers in the 1910s. Just researching one year in the British Newspaper Archives brought out an appalling number of cases, in some of which mothers were prepared to sell their own child for immoral purposes.

The story Daisy and Margaret had heard about Chinese girls sent by rail in a packing crate was broadly true. In the Illustrated

Police News on Saturday 17 June 1899 with the description: 'Alleged Immoral Traffic in Chinese Girls – they are packed in crates and treated as freight on the railways'. The article says *'An investigation has been ordered into the recent revelations regarding the sale and shipment of Chinese girls, a practice which, it is alleged, has been customary for months. The climax was reached a week ago, when two girls, aged fifteen and sixteen years respectively, were bought at Vancouver. It is asserted they were placed in a crate and shipped as freight over the railway, the train hands giving them food and water. The car containing them was placed on a side track one night, and the girls, being each clad only in a wrapper, caught cold. **The man who purchased one of them demanded damages from the railway company for the injury thus done to his property.** The girls, it is alleged, were sold for immoral purposes.'*

The highlighted sentence is highlighted by me.

Sweated Working

Another interest of the suffrage movement was the welfare of women undertaking sweated work in their own (often inadequate) homes. There was indeed a rally on Wimbledon Common on 16th November 1913 as reported by The Wimbledon News, when a Mrs Davies described the conditions under which such women lived and worked. Houses built for one family often housed four. There was often no kitchen and a woman would be cooking on a bedroom fireplace. It was no wonder, she suggested, that they did not attempt to cook nutritious meals they'd been taught in board school. There was nowhere to cook them.

Suffragettes

Although the references in this book are few and far between, militant suffragettes continued their campaign of violence and destruction during this year. It would continue to escalate into the following year. On the night of the 14th November 1913 suffragettes attempted to blow up the Sefton Park Palm House a few days after damage had been done to a cactus house in Manchester. A keeper at Sefton Park found the bomb surrounded by suffragette literature, a copy of 'The Suffragette' and a postcard with the words 'Stop torturing God's human plants'. The fuses had been lit but had blown out in a gale (which I'm quite glad about, as I've seen the Palm House in Sefton Park and it's lovely).

On a Lighter Note

All the newspaper articles referred to in the book really existed. These include the article about the tango craze in the Sketch in which the female dancer is wearing a skirt just below her knees and very sheer stockings, as well as the article in the Daily Mirror about exercises to counteract the Slinker Slouch in which the young woman exercising also wears a rather frumpier short skirt and much thicker stockings.

In fact there were a lot of articles in a lot of papers condemning the "Slinker Slouch".

It's nice to know that mothers through every age have despaired of their fashion-conscious daughter's posture. I can just imagine the conversation if I tried to show my daughter that article – 'You've got to be kidding Mum. If I have to wear that outfit to do exercises, I'd rather be dead. I'm going to learn the tango instead.'

Best of all, when trying (rather frantically) to find a 'funny' article for discussion at a doomed dinner party, I found the one about the cat holding up the traffic on the tramway at Kennington Gate. No matter what crisis is going on, you can trust a cat to do its own sweet thing.

Acknowledgements

With many thanks to Liz Hedgecock in particular who read and edited more than one draft and deserves a medal for still talking to me. Also to Christine Downes (Mum) and Val Portelli, for their support and eagle-eyes. And also to my husband for putting up with me disappearing to work on this, and bringing me endless cups of tea.

About Paula Harmon and Links

Paula Harmon was born in North London to parents of English, Scottish and Irish descent. Perhaps feeling the need to add a Welsh connection, her father relocated the family every two years from country town to country town moving slowly westwards until they settled in South Wales when Paula was eight. She later graduated from Chichester University before making her home in Gloucestershire and then Dorset where she has lived since 2005.

She is a civil servant, married with two adult children. Paula has several writing projects underway and wonders where the housework fairies are, because the house is a mess and she can't think why.

https:paulaharmon.com

https://viewauthor.at/PHAuthorpage

https://www.facebook.com/pg/paulaharmonwrites

https://www.goodreads.com/paula_harmon

https://instagram.com/paulasharmon

https://threads.net/@paulasharmon

https://youtu.be/7lnov4nPRjE